Famous

For

Nothing

**a novel by
T/James Reagan**

Contact the author:

tjamesreagan@gmail.com

http://tjamesreagan.com

@tjamesreagan

FAMOUS FOR NOTHING

WORTHLESS

HUMAN REPORT:

The Socialite Reference Guide

All of these beautiful socialites are famous because we write about them, and we write about them because you read about them, so if you have a problem with that, stop reading this and break the cycle.

That's what I thought. You're still here, which means you're part of the problem. The difference between you and these socialites (beyond looks) is the fact that you probably have a purpose. I'm sure you read the blogs secretly in your cubical, or in your home office, or by the bedside of someone you care for. You have a way to keep the lights on that doesn't involve turning a night vision camera on when the lights go off.

You've probably said, "How come I can't be famous for nothing like (insert celebrity name here)?" Now more than ever, it's easy to attain fame-just go to the right parties, take pictures with the right people, and fall into the right beds. **Worthless Human Report** is here to provide you with everything you need to know about these social climbing, resource sucking, purpose-free "celebrities." Maybe you can learn a thing or two along the way.

Since none of the people this blog covers have any distinguishing traits that separate them from each other, **Worthless Human Report** strives to provide our readers with clarity, so they know how to make fun of each and every socialite they're forced to discuss on a first date when they realize they have nothing in common with the person sitting across from them.

On the next page, you'll find a quick-guide that you can flip back to whenever you start getting confused about which worthless, self-obsessed socialite you're reading about.

VAULABLE REFERENCE GUIDE OF WORTHLESS HUMANS

LONDON FRANCIS

Why is she famous? Pharmaceutical heiress.
What does she look like? Blonde hair, pointy nose, tall, and skinny.
What's her defect? Most of her close friends are animals. She has the same IQ as most of her friends.
Who is she fucking? The rumor is she has her eyes set on fellow worthless human Tobe Price.

CHLOE WARREN

Why is she famous? Daughter of a real estate mogul, and the once powerful, now missing, Linda Warren.
What does she look like? Blonde, doe eyed, alien looking.
What's her defect? Chloe is dropping weight, fast. She doesn't have a gym membership or a trainer.
Who is she fucking? Surprisingly, she's bagged semi-worthwhile human, Stanley De Vries.

DAKOTA DABNEY

Why is she famous? She's the daughter of a TV producer, and a scumbag.
What does she look like? Brown hair (a redhead in disguise), pale, freckled.
What's her defect? Daddy issues.
Who is she fucking? No one, but refer to the above defect. It won't be long.

KRISTEN PAXTON

Why is she famous? Recently? She got kicked out of her socialite circle.
What does she look like? Blonde hair, boxy face, innocent smile.
What's her defect? She's so unreliable, shady, and difficult that even her socialite friends got fed up with her.
Who's she fucking? Well, the rumor mill has her with Johnny Foster.

SIENNA WOLFE

Why is she famous? You're probably sitting under a billboard featuring the image of her model-mother right now.
What does she look like? High cheek bones, cat eyes, puffed lips.
What's her defect? No one loves Sienna Wolfe like Sienna Wolfe does.
Who's she fucking? Metaphorically? Everyone in her path, so step aside.

celebUtard
"Divorce Party of the Century?"

Remember when we said **Mitchell Haughton** was cheating on **Lindy Porter**?

If you don't, it's because 40 minutes after we broke the story, Lindy's lawyers picked apart the entire article until our headline basically read, "Hypothetically, Mitchell Haughton, a Fictional Character, Might Be Doing Something... Allegedly?"

Apparently, our "source" wasn't reliable enough for Lindy's Lawyers.

That's when we sent him the pictures.

The lawyer claimed copyright on the photos.

That's when we put him in contact with the agency we bought the pictures from.

Then lawyer didn't call us for a while.

That's when we decided to call him directly.

As of yesterday, legal action will no longer be sought against celebUtard.

As of 12 PM PST today, the Haughton/Porter divorce is on!

"Please give my client space during this difficult time," Lindy's PR team requested in a public statement.

"Please join me on a very special night meant to celebrate my return and rebirth," Lindy requested inside the leaked invite to her divorce gala.

Some points we'd like to note:

One- We've received a written apology from Lindy regarding her actions against celebUtard. We framed it.

Two- We weren't invited to the divorce party, despite playing a crucial role in the basic need for the party to exist.

Three- We'd like to remind you, once again, that we were right and Lindy was wrong.

Does this mean that when Lindy Porter said, "celebUtard makes up horrible lies," she wasn't referring to how we accurately chronicled Mitchell snatching up the first beard he could find, only to continue abusing his male PA's?

When Lindy claimed, "The girls who write celebUtard are rumor churning, hateful, nympho-maniacal losers," she must have been making that assessment independent from the fact that we broke the story that Mitchell had kicked Lindy out of the house they shared then, as our source spilled with a confused shiver, "He filled the pool with lube because water chafes?"

If none of this is our fault, I guess that would make it Mitchell's fault.

No one can judge him for choosing Lindy as his wife. It's not often a guy gets to marry a gorgeous, wealthy, 18 year old girl*

* Correction * an *allegedly* 18 year old girl. Maybe if Lindy didn't have so much trouble passing the eighth grade, it would be easier to pinpoint her age.

It's hard to believe that eight long months have passed since the Porter-Haughton marriage/slap to the face of humanity occurred, but the handprint still hasn't faded, so humanity better throw on some extra cover-up tonight because it's time for a gala divorce party!

We took a look at the last minute guest list and we must say, Lindy has impressed us with her over-ambition. We never thought we'd write that sentence. Lindy Porter? Over-ambitious? Her party planner has made sure this divorce gala is the first premier social event of the season. The team who put this all together must also be handling the **California** deficit because it looks like this is going to be a big ticket affair. Maybe *someone* is just trying to even the playing field for all those big ticket affairs Mitchell had with those escorts/that **Republican Senator/** that soccer team from **Paraguay** /you get the picture.

We weren't invited to Lindy's party, but don't worry, we'll find out all the details, then we'll whisper them into your smartphone.

Until next time, stay tardy, celebUverse.

1- Pre-Game Report.

A scream of, "Help!" echoes through the intentionally empty Hollywood Hills, and on the off-chance one of the distant neighbors can hear this yelp, they'll just be appreciative that, for once, it's not an orgasmic cry of sexual ecstasy or the late night male posturing between two brutes who *almost* were the new CK and Michael Lorrie models, but instead are just personal trainers for the models who actually landed those campaigns.

Stanley De Vries, the large-foreheaded, Morrissey-haired, small-eyed man that America grew up watching on a vaguely progressive nighttime teen soap called *Tristan's Landing*, enters the massive, glass-walled living room in a panic. You can tell that Stanley is genuinely concerned because if he was just *acting* concerned he would have attempted this entrance at least three times before he felt like he really "nailed it."

Stanley's frantic gaze scans the room until he locates his girlfriend, Chloe Warren.

Chloe is staring at a blank TV screen and making the same noises a befuddled puppy might make when its ball is just out of reach.

"I can't get the TV to turn on," Chloe whines, her widely spaced eyes looking to Stanley for assistance. Chloe is that type of odd, alien-looking girl that could convince a boy to spend his best years volunteering to turn on her TV or espresso machine every day. The boy would gladly carry her flat screen out to the curb after she cracked it squarely in the center with a cup-turned-projectile during an intensely personal episode of a show where gay men and B-list comedians come together to celebrate their common hatred of socialites. He'd also graciously take her credit card, buy a new TV, then mount it on the wall while she watched, idly drinking an espresso she didn't make herself.

This is circle of commerce in LA; buy thing, smash thing, buy thing again (a better model).

Stanley takes the remote and sighs. Despite acting in numerous poorly received horror movies, it still seems like every question he's asked is TV related. A tiny part of Stanley wants to fling the remote through the screen of the giant television, but then he remembers that he already did that in *Tristan's Landing* (episode 3x05) so he merely gears up for another detailed explanation regarding the finer points of accessing trash television. Stanley always ends up doing the right thing. He's one of the few people in LA that has decided a moral compass isn't just, "-some bullshit I think I have an App for on my phone. Whatever, I barely go hiking anyway. I'm more of a hot yoga type person."

Stanley is willing to help Chloe out because all of her friends have been acquiring full-time maids lately. Despite the trend, Stanley is strongly against the idea of hiring a person to be an underpaid mother to two grown adults. He already has a birth mother and a TV mother. He finally wants to accept responsibility for his life, instead of just transferring his helpless existence from one woman to another. Besides, they already have a laundry guy and he gives Stanley the creeps. Chloe, when pressured to provide a reason why she needed a maid, responded, "Everyone has full-time maids now. Perma-maids are the new smartphone. They're super useful." Stanley doesn't mind doing work around the house. He's humble and easy to work with, mainly because if he was to acquire a diva-like reputation, he'd need two really good auditions with the lead actress to land a part. He's no longer willing to sit around while a gorgeous woman tries to sound out the word "embodiment."

After *Tristan's Landing* ended, Stanley was sent to the post-teen-TV graveyard of shooting every movie in a graveyard. It's a place where B-movie scripts contain vaguely scientific sounding words, which are always clumsily delivered by a scantily clad blonde starlet- the film's "scientist." Notice the prop glasses, she must be smart. They don't hand glasses out to just anyone.

Stanley lowers the remote and shows Chloe, for what could be the third time this week, how to turn on her own entertainment system. "All you do is hit the 'CAT' button, that's it. CAT- cable *and* television," he tells her. Chloe nods to show she understands. Stanley moves his finger to the 'TV' button, "This only turns on one of the components. It turns on the TV, but the rest of the stuff will still be off. You'll be staring at a blank screen if you press this button."

Chloe is a little embarrassed that Stanley has to teach her the most basic of life skills. It reminds her of when her grandmother got Alzheimer's. The Warrens had to label everything in Chloe's grandma's house with a big red "X" if it wasn't edible. Unfortunately, Chloe's grandma interpreted this as "X Marks the Spot" which meant that her treasure map led to a bowl of oatmeal sweetened with Ajax.

Dealing with this particular incident proved difficult for Chloe's mother, Linda Warren. Chloe remembers her mom coming home one day, ranting, "Your grandmother tried to fix herself breakfast today! It's like she totally forgot about the maid. Oh, and she tried to use some sort of floor cleaner as a sweetener, too."

Chloe was pretty sure that if her mother tried to make herself a bowl of oatmeal without help, a similar result would occur so it was hard to gauge how serious the whole ordeal was. The doctor treating Chloe's grandmother kept accusing Linda Warren of a sinister sabotage plot with the end goal of a healthy inheritance. It was all a big scandal. That's the problem with being part of a rich bloodline- every little misunderstanding looks like a cash grab. As if it isn't bad enough that a relative is dying, there's also the pressure of being framed for their death. Luckily, it's not that hard to squirm out of jeopardy here. After all, most of Chloe's prison sentences have been served in hours, not days.

"See this button?" Stanley asks. He points at the keypad on the bottom of the remote, "This button is for the number '7' and won't turn on anything, no matter how many times you press it. 'CAT' will turn on the surround sound, the DVR, the cable; everything."

"I don't like that," London Francis says, suddenly appearing over Stanley's shoulder. London's long skinny nose pokes into the conversation, and her long skinny body separates Stanley and Chloe. London's long skinny arm extends out, and her well-manicured finger touches the remote, then she says in her babytalk voice, "When you press 'CAT' it should play kitty videos... Right? You know? Kitties chasing string, kitties chasing lights on the wall, kitties accidentally falling in fish tanks..."

Both Chloe and Stanley look at London as she nods her head along with her idea. It's almost as if London hopes that they'll see her nodding and just assume she must be right.

Chloe is so confounded by London's suggestion that her anger at the television is momentarily pacified. She hits the "CAT" button, kisses Stanley, then tells him, "Thank you," in a babyish way that only she finds cute. London immediately furrows her perfectly pointed eyebrows. She's offended because Chloe's baby talk coincidentally doubles as an impression of London's voice. London proceeds to somehow blame this offense on Stanley, so she glares at him until he leaves. His importance has started and ended with the television, yet again.

Chloe hits the 7, then the 4 on the remote. She looks at the TV. It does nothing.

"*Please,*" she begs the 80" behemoth of a screen and suddenly the channel changes to the show she was searching for.

"I think I have a poltergeist that controls all of my electronics," Chloe says.

"Ohhh! I want one! Are they reasonable?" London asks, returning to her previous post. She sits on a small set of marble stairs and continues straightening her already straight, long, platinum hair in a mirror she took off the wall.

"You don't pay a poltergeist," Chloe responds.

"I see," London says, then winks, "Like I don't pay my maid on the books?"

"London! No. Illegal aliens and poltergeists are two totally different problems," Chloe huffs.

"So, are poltergeists fluent in English? Do they do hospital corners? I might upgrade from a maid to a poltergeist."

"Just watch," Chloe says, unwilling to explain poltergeists to a girl who's already afraid of carbs, gravity, people with "witch noses," redheads, bathroom spiders, and all of Oakland.

London stands up on the stairs and joins in watching *CTV Online...Offline*, America's favorite TV show-turned-blog-turned-back-into-a-TV show. A dapper man with a receding hairline does his best impression of a gay man as he hosts an extremely cancelable pop culture slush-show. It's almost like he's doing some sort of reverse Mitchell Haughton act. You can tell the guy just wants to be a professional newscaster, but his daughter needs that Michael Lorrie bag that was named after Chloe so he's stuck doing this.

Standing in an all white set and surrounded by a flurry of constantly changing on-screen graphics and tickers, the host comes back from commercial and declares, "Hollywood is on fire tonight, as all of our favorite stars and starlets will be descending upon Lindy Porter's gala divorce party! It's going to be spray tans, designer bags, and exposed privates everywhere! You can see the full guest list on our blog, but let me highlight the people who actually deserve our attention." After taking a deep breath to make sure that his persona isn't wearing thin or turning into more of a screech than it needs to be, the host continues, "The phoenix-girl will be in attendance tonight! Chloe Warren will be arriving sans ashes, and apparently sans Stanley! Trouble in paradise? What she *will* be bringing, is her new body. Let me tell you, I did a triple take when I saw her at Cannes this year! I had more fun watching her than I did the films!"

The host slightly falters, wondering if his cover had been blown with that last line. The footage of Chloe continues to roll, so he proceeds with his pre-prepared script. "This month, Chloe is on the cover of every magazine that means anything, which can't be too many, I mean, who reads magazines?" he inquires with a hard exhale, like he hates himself for the last sentence. This guy just wants to be home in front of the fire with some Dostoyevsky and a good cigar. Chloe watches in quiet appreciation as London stands behind her, mumbling, "Yeah, fuck magazines... well, last week's *People* did have a really great picture of my butt in yoga pants. It was like a double pleasantry because my ass looked incredible, and now I can say lots of lies about my strenuous workout routine."

The host releases a sigh that was probably even more pathetic before it was edited for TV. The same moment that London pops up on the screen, she also pops up and down in short bunny hops while almost burning herself with her straightener. CTV rolls footage of London walking the red carpet at an event she doesn't recall attending. The host continues, "On Chloe's arm tonight will surely be her BFF, London Francis, who's ready to show up in a capacity other than a video bookmark on your favorites list in Firefox."

London brags to Chloe, "They called me the queen of night vision on this show last week. It was awesome. I'm to night vision, what Marilyn Monroe was to daylight film."

Chloe blocks out London's words as she tries to watch the show. She has nothing else to do. She's already dressed for the party in an outfit she planned as a satire on America's fast food culture. Her stylist gave her a white and red striped, extra short, cashmere Alexander Wang turtle-neck dress, and atop her blonde locks is a slouchy, sequined, crocheted Chanel hat. The final piece, bringing the outfit together, is a yellow feather scarf. Chloe will make all worst dressed lists for the week, but the people who "got it" would be the ones that she wanted to talk to. One trip to the worst dressed list meant nothing to Chloe. In LA, you have permission to dress like a bag lady as long as you're rich enough to employ a lady to physically carry your bags. The divorce party will be formal and Chloe's outfit is less than formal, which means people will look, and people will point, and everyone will notice how skinny Chloe is, again. She's wearing what she deems her "Mc-outfit." It's trashy, which is exactly what she's going for. It's a mocking wink. It's a wakeup call to the girls who look up to Chloe.

Fast food restaurants had almost taken Chloe's life earlier this year. Granted, she wasn't robbed of her life in the, "Oh, I think my arteries are constricting from this cheeseburger," way, but instead, much worse, it was the, "Someone should tell her that skinny jeans aren't for *everyone*," way.

Stanley was partly to blame. He acted as an enabler, providing the contraband, night after night. It was fine when Stanley De Vries pulled up at the drive-thru. He's a guy. The paps didn't care he was buying a big, delicious, unhealthy mess of a burger. It was actually super American- an attractive man grabbing a cheeseburger in his luxury automobile.

If Chloe was seen anywhere near that same fast food place, she'd be destroyed by the blogs. It all unraveled when the paparazzi caught Stanley three consecutive weeks in the drive-thru, and at the same time, Chloe started to grow hips. It wasn't difficult to put two and two together, and no one was nice about it. It would've been better for Chloe to have a meth addiction- at least she could go to rehab for meth.

London sits back down on the stairs, totally disinterested with the TV now that her image has left the screen. The host continues, "According to our list, America's 'Bonnie and Bonnie' duo, Dakota Dabney and Sienna Wolfe, will also be arriving tonight. Between those two, CTV has had enough scandalous quotes to fill our Christmas special, and we still have enough left over for the Halloween, Valentine's Day, and Martin Luther King Day specials. If they give such juicy quotes separately, watch out for what we'll hear tonight!" The footage cuts to an all-American looking blonde girl, and Chloe looks away from the screen while the host continues, "One name noticeably absent from the list is Kristen Paxton, proving that a sweet face and a bank account isn't enough for a ticket to this party. If Kristen does show up, I hope they have an ambulance ready on the sidelines like it's the Superbowl."

"I can't believe he just said that," Chloe growls, slapping her bare knee.

London stands up and agrees, "I know! All of us being at the same party is way bigger than the Superbowl. Plus, one ambulance couldn't carry all five of us. Wait. Unless he's saying we're so skinny that all five of us could fit on one gurney! I bet that's what he meant. I love this show!"

2- The Above-Regular Season.

The Porter mansion, tonight's party venue, is the type of architectural wonder that causes you to instinctively touch your clavicle when you walk inside. It's that beautiful.

Lindy Porter, tonight's host, is the type of strawberry blonde, curvy girl that causes you to instinctively feel a tingle in your nether-regions when you meet her. She's that beautiful.

Chloe Warren and London Francis walk into the party, but their eyes don't float to the grand ceiling or the ornate chandelier. Their breath isn't taken away by the spiraling staircase because, to them, it just looks extremely dangerous to walk down when you're drunk and wearing heels.

Both girls greet Lindy with a kiss on the cheek. Their eyes don't fall to Lindy's exposed cleavage because they had visited her when she first got her implants and that same area, now very much on display, was engulfed by a vicious yellow-purple bruise. Their breath isn't taken away by her pre-scandal John Galliano for Christian Dior gown because they'd seen it on Mariana White two years ago, and no one can wear a dress like Mariana

This is what happens when you live your dreams. Reality ruins them.

Behind Chloe and London is the lethal combination of Sienna Wolfe and Dakota Dabney.

Sienna possesses a facial perfection so profound that when people criticize her, the best they can come up with is to say, "Yeah her face is great, but her hands seem sorta weird." High cheek bones meet cat eyes, and puffed lips hover over a pointed (but not pointy) chin. Cosmetic surgery for Sienna would be like trying to trick out London's Bentley. Sometimes things just can't get any more physically perfect. Tonight, Sienna's jet black Liz Taylor hair is gracefully flopped to the right side of her face, almost covering one of her eyes- those arresting eyes that make interviewers ask, "Is your father Asian?" They know Sienna's mother isn't Asian because they grew up with 50 foot billboards of Cassandra Wolfe looming over them everywhere they went. Wolfe isn't exactly an Asian last name, but people have a hard time believing that multiple ethnicities didn't collaborate on the creation of this perfect specimen. Sienna stands slender and enviable in a pink Blumarine dress that shows off both her shiny legs and her pair of Roberto Cavalli, four-inch spike heels.

Dakota Dabney, with her chameleon-like appearance, shows up to the party with the same hair color and facial features she had the last time she was photographed at a major event, which happened to be yesterday at the Anny Moore's exhibit at the MOCA. Her chocolate brown hair lands on her pale shoulders, which are spattered with little freckles, like her hair dye had been dripping. Dakota's freckles are a dead give-away that she's a natural redhead, but her steady rotation of hair styles, colors, and extensions have people speculating that Dakota is some glitzy, real-life, highly customized Barbie that Mattel had accidentally released into the wild. Redheads scare London so the hair dying ritual is part vanity, part altruism on Dakota's part.

Dakota rarely wears black, but none of her friends have died recently, and she had bought this cute black Phillip Lim dress with studded sleeves, so she wore it tonight in memory of Lindy's dead marriage.

The four girls kiss cheeks and feign excited screams as they make their way through the usual lineup of socialites and suits. Everyone mingles in the heart hopping bass of the hipster DJ's speakers, as he cues up another song on his laptop.

Chloe Warren locates the familiar face of Tobe Price and begins drifting over to him. Tobe is here because his father hopped on the dotcom bubble (the third or fourth iteration- Hollywood loves sequels). Mr. Price rode the bubble all the way to the top, then firmly planted a knife in its thin skin and bailed before it burst.

It's not uncommon or even looked down upon for someone to arrive at the party because of a nasty thing their father, or grandfather, or great grandfather did. Everyone has at least one reason they're able to live this life.

The Cliffs Notes version for this group of girls is as follows:

London- Pharmaceutical heiress.

Chloe- Real estate heiress.

Dakota- Entertainment heiress.

Sienna- Commercial Modeling heiress (and whatever her possibly Asian dad does).

This is the type of party where everyone has a story, but all the stories blend together, and the people with the stories would rather make fun of someone's new lopsided boob job than explain what makes them significant. No one here has to work a real job because their grandfather was exceptionally skilled at his. This room is a minefield of trust funds, and Tobe Price has only recently appeared at the party so he hasn't quite mastered navigating the beautiful chaos.

Despite being "new money" Tobe Price has a voice that sounds rich. It's the type of voice that can somehow pronounce Connecticut like it's spelled and not sound affected. He looks like he belongs at this party so no one questions it, even if they don't know who he is. It's possible that Tobe's longish, shocked blond, swept to the side bangs may actually be plastic, as a single follicle has never once protested the pattern it had been styled in, even on last year's windy *Vanity Fair* red carpet. Tobe Price's image is a pillar. As Chloe speaks with him, Tobe's forest green eyes look at her with distrust. He hasn't seen Chloe in person for at least four months and now she looks so different that he has to wonder if he's talking to Chloe's sister. It's common knowledge that Chloe doesn't have a sister, but... maybe she does? Maybe this secret sister is just one of those people who remains hidden, embarrassed about her money and status, until she finds out what all of it can really do for her. Sienna's sister is like that, at least according to a particularly revealing Sienna Wolfe cover story (last February's issue of *NYLON*) that Tobe found to be riveting.

Tobe arches his back to look beyond Chloe, or Chloe's secret sister; it doesn't matter to Tobe which Warren is blocking his view of the new arrivals, it's just imperative that she move to the left about 11 inches.

CTV was playing in Tobe's personal gym this afternoon, and he stopped doing curls when he heard that Sienna Wolfe would be in attendance tonight. Lindy's divorce was a long time coming, but this party was slapped together at the last minute. The invitations were received yesterday. The guest list was leaked today. Sienna Wolfe's name appeared on that list. This made Tobe Price feel nervous- an emotion so foreign to him that he had to have a Manhattan after his workout.

Sienna Wolfe is able to evoke this response in Tobe because of a single issue of *GQ* magazine.

Upon becoming notable at age 19, Tobe had acquired a secret habit of cutting out every article that even so much as casually mentioned him. His ritual has been to carefully X-acto knife out whatever story, picture, or blind item he's a part of, then deposit it in a shoebox. It's a lot of work, but like his mother's knitting or his father's womanizing, it's something he can do at night, after a long day, to center himself. Granted, nightfall approaches mere hours after Tobe wakes to start the day, but those first four to six hours of sunlight can be tremendously stressful.

Two years into this hobby, when Tobe was cutting out a quick one pager he did in *GQ*, he noticed that on the page opposite his article was an exceptional picture of Sienna Wolfe. Opening the *GQ* and seeing Sienna's image mirror his own did something to Tobe. He and this beautiful stranger were pressed against each other, a million times over, all across the country. Tobe had such a strong reaction to this fact that, after he had sliced himself out of the magazine, he also cut out the page that Sienna was on. She went into the shoebox too.

Now, two shoe boxes later, Tobe and Sienna are pressed against each other hundreds of times over, yet they've never shared a single word.

While slicing pictures from an *OK!* earlier tonight, Tobe told himself that Lindy's divorce party would be the perfect time to make his long overdue introduction.

Sienna showed up.

Tobe showed up.

Perfection did not. Yet.

Tobe spots Sienna standing at the edge of the party with Diego Mestizo. Diego is making Sienna do that double cheek kiss thing, and she hates when people do that (according to a recent interview in *Details*), but she goes along with it. Diego is launching his new reality show with a party of his own later in the week, and if Sienna doesn't attend this celebration of an accomplishment that barely could be considered such, she'll sit at home, depressed, with a carton of Häagen-Dazs. Worst case scenario, Sienna will actually watch Diego's train wreck on TV. At least at home there's no risk that Diego will walk up behind her while she's throwing out hateful one-liners about him. On the downside, the coke she'll be doing while watching the show wouldn't have anything on the shit Diego is usually holding.

Diego wins.

Tobe loses.

Sienna remains divisive, desired, disinterested, and deadly. No one overlooks this fact. She wouldn't allow them to.

WORTHLESS HUMAN REPORT:

Diego Mestizo

This week's featured Worthless Human, Diego Mestizo, has reached the pinnacle of worthlessness by landing his own reality show on CTV. We aren't going to tell you when the show premieres because we value our loyal readership and we'd never do anything to harm them.

Diego was able to swing this TV deal because he's the son of a powerful Mexican drug kingpin. It's alleged that CTV is working with the ATF on the show so, thanks to the government funding, the premiere will be presented with limited commercial interruption.

Based on our sources, nothing significantly illegal has occurred during the filming of the show, so far. Unless drinking your own ejaculate is illegal. If it's done by accident, it can't be punishable by jail time, right? The footage of this unsubstantiated act hasn't surfaced, so everyone will just have to wait until the show's third episode. The executives at CTV wanted hold the footage until the eighth episode, but then someone in the boardroom made the good point that if this show makes it to an eighth episode, the event will probably happen on camera at least two more times.

Diego Mestizo's *Fame or Bust* still has five more weeks of filming left, so when historians look back on this decade, it's almost certain that this month will be viewed as the lowest point in human existence.

3- Everyone Who's Anyone.

Dakota begins to feel the claustrophobia of the party. The faces, the names, the bass, the randoms taking sly pictures to sell to websites; it all buzzes around her in a well-lit, bursting hive.

Amidst the commotion is Jake Wesley, whose father, Donald Wesley, is the CEO of a prominent defense contractor named CARDIN. Dakota slides into Jake's field of vision, blushes, then immediately comments in her smoky voice that they have to get together for lunch. This vague date is necessary because during the taping of a British chat show last week, Dakota *might* have joked that CARDIN bought all the copies of Jake's last novel because they'd never seen such a devastating bomb before. Dakota plans to make this same joke to Jake's face during their lunch, then apologize in a fun little way for at least 30 seconds, but for no longer than a minute. This will ensure that when the chat show clip ends up in Jake's inbox as a YouTube link, he'll just think that Dakota was sharing their little joke with the world. Jake has been on a talk show before. He knows how hard it is to fill that awkward eight minutes before you get your plug in.

What was Dakota plugging on that show last week? She's not totally sure. A perfume? Did the chat show just have weird shaped glasses? Dakota is mildly confused about British people. They seem to like her and at least they aren't Australians, so doing promo there is alright, as long as there are people to make fun of like big, dumb Jake Wesley.

London approaches a panicky Dakota and a relaxed Jake. She gives Jake a kiss on the cheek so that she can get close enough to see if he has any nicks from shaving. London has always been very suspicious of Jake Wesley due to his father's profession and the fact he also happens to look like a super soldier. Jake's charcoal pinstripe Dolce & Gabbana suit strains to contain his bicep as his arm bends to put his hand at the small of Dakota's back. His mocha tinted jawline is so strong that there must be a solid inch between its end and his lips. Jake Wesley is uncompromisingly massive. London attempts to wrap her mind around an artificially manufactured human existing in society, but then she sees Lindy's teacup chihuahua and abandons her thought process in favor of chasing the dog. The chihuahua runs away terrified, because of the mass of people with razor sharp heels, because of the loud music pumping into his oversized ears, and now because this giant praying mantis of a girl is chasing him.

Chloe, Dakota, and Sienna continue their greetings, undeterred by London storming away in a flurry of knees and elbows. The girls have adopted a ritual of stopping to speak with their peers to make sure that everyone continues to love them. This is also how they find the bar at any exclusive party. The martini and highball glasses are always clear, so the girls make their way to the people who just got out of rehab, then take note of how full their drinks are. More than half full- they're close to the bar.

After the girls eye Jenny Preston holding a full martini glass, the contents certainly all vodka, they know they're close.

London reappears when they reach the bar and Lindy's dog is mysteriously absent. It's possible that London has the ability to speak to animals, like Aquaman, and she promised to leave the dog alone if he spilled on where the bar was. It's also possible that London has dog-like senses that can sniff out alcohol.

Standing at the bar, London asks, "Could I have a Mojito?" then looks back at the girls, "Four Mojitos?" The server, dressed in a black vest and a white shirt, nods to acknowledge the order. London carefully watches the drink preparation because bartenders have been shortchanging her drinks ever since the blog *ThisSpoiledBitch* ran a story about a $1,700 cleaning bill that the club "Perch" had to pay to get London's vomit off of a white VIP sofa.

"Come on. Don't be a 'Kristen!' Put more rum in," London cheers, leaning her bony elbows on the marble bar-top.

"My name's not Kristen, it's Beth," the server with the bulbous nose and the frizzy hair tells the girls.

"Yeah. We know," Dakota says, trying to get an elbow on the bar so that she can get her drink faster.

"You know my name?" Beth asks, secretly excited that a celebrity noticed her. Maybe Dakota did remember that time, two years ago, when Beth was a bartender at The DarkHouse. She made Dakota drinks, then let her do coke off a menu snatched from one of the servers.

"Oh, I just meant we could have guessed that your name is something basic, like Sarah," Dakota says, then lays on a cute, innocent smile to show that she knows not what she says.

Beth doesn't bother to issue a correction, she just continues pouring the drinks. London pops back into a conversation that seemed to have been resolved by Beth's disinterest and asks, "Sarah, aren't you curious why we use 'Kristen' like that?"

"I have an idea," Beth says, hoping this puts an end to the topic.

London, growing frustrated, says, "Okay and ideas can be wrong, sooo..."

"Why do you use 'Kristen' like that?" Beth asks, but it's only to pacify London. She eyes her fellow server who's moist with sweat from having to pick up her slack. He doesn't seem angry or bitter because he's been in the same situation with London before.

Dakota flirtatiously leans over to Beth and says, "We use 'Kristen' like that because there used to be five of us. Want to guess who we kicked out?"

"Oh. I read about that," Beth murmurs, eyes now averted.

"Yeah," London says, waiting for the Sarah-Beth to use "Kristen" properly in a sentence, like a Spanish teacher who had just taught the class how to modify adjectives. London was spared ever having to actually interact with a real Spanish teacher thanks to a tuition donation she made so that some inner city kid could attend her elite private school. "I don't need to know Spanish anymore," London advised the administration, "I have an on-campus interpreter now. Comprende?" A picture of London ironically dressed in a graduation gown was cut out of a magazine and sent to St. Katherine's so that if anyone tries to research her education, London will be in the yearbook.

Chloe claims the first finished Mojito off the bar. She immediately sips the drink, squints her doe-eyes shut, then proclaims, "Okay, you're sooo not a 'Kristen.' This is good."

Watching Sarah-Beth accidentally over-pour glops of rum into the next Mojito, Chloe hands her drink off to Dakota. A room full of people... celebrating a divorce. How uneasy and unsteady. Chloe needs something stronger to counteract the uncomfortable feeling she has in the pit of her stomach. To ensure her drink is made properly, she reaches over and drops a fifty into the tip glass. Beth appreciatively receives Chloe's generous tip, as well as her look that says, "Sorry about our conduct," peppered with a, "Yeah, it wasn't photoshop. I *am* this skinny again."

After purchasing Sarah-Beth's full attention, Chloe is able to claim the stronger Mojito before Sienna can. Both socialites pause for a moment, a tiny rivalry re-igniting with a lighting fast flicker.

"Your outfit is making me, like, totally crave cheeseburgers, but then London's dress makes me feel guilty about even thinking about eating one," Sienna says, engaging Chloe in conversation because Beth's hands are visibly shaking as she makes the rest of the drinks. Jittery people creep Sienna out. What if Sarah-Beth is nervous because she's poisoning the drinks? If Chloe's grandma can handle an Ajax breakfast, the girls damn sure can handle a turpentine cocktail, but Sienna would prefer not to watch it being made.

Chloe responds vaguely to the cheeseburger comment, while London snatches up the next completed drink. Sienna lets this happen because she's somewhat okay with London drinking poison. Since London *will* puke at some point tonight, a poisoned Mojito is just cutting to the chase.

"I can't believe Stanley didn't come tonight," Sienna says, as though it's beyond her comprehension how someone could willingly deny an invitation to celebrate something as beautiful as a girl divorcing her rich, closeted husband.

Chloe, nodding her head to acknowledge her better half's absence, explains, "Stanley admitted that he dated Lindy so it would be awkward for him to celebrate her divorce. I googled and couldn't find any pictures of them together, just some *Page 6* stuff, so who knows."

"Tell Stanley to stop being gay," London says and this scares the girls. They didn't expect her to stay by the bar after she got her drink. Maybe it was the lack of pregame that kept London tethered for the moment.

Chloe looks back at London and says, "I know, a lot of people have been saying that lately, but I think those pictures are doctored. Something about the tongues doesn't look right."

"Maybe the fact that they're wrapped around each other?" Sienna laughs.

London's eyes go wide and she clarifies, "I didn't mean gay as in Lindy's husband type gay, I'm not homophobic. I love gays. Homophobic people are beyond disgusting for judging others like that. Sometimes I think homophobes are *almost* worse than fat people. I'm positive that Stanley isn't gay, those pictures were faked so that some loser could have a photo as a lead-in for his homo-fanfic," London assures her friend, then mentions, "I was just bringing up the fact that Stanley totally just laughed off my 'CAT' idea like it would be silly to assume that people want to watch cat videos. I mean, hello, has he ever been on YouTube?"

Chloe shakes her head, and responds, "No, not recently. People make a bunch of videos about his romances from the old show. They take *Tristan's Landing* clips and set them to bad early 2000's music. I think he's afraid to look on there because it will collapse his self-image."

"Whatever. I wish that people would edit my night vision videos with sappy songs and upload them," London says.

Chloe shakes her head again and responds, "I think your videos would violate the terms of service."

"Why? Because they'd be so cute that they'd make even people like Stanley go on YouTube?"

"No, it would be because your nipples and labia are featured in almost all of the shots," Chloe points out.

"Yeah, they are," London proudly professes, then puts her drink up to the music and dances away.

Sienna notices the worry in Chloe's eyes so she tries to provide some comfort, "Don't worry about the pictures. People on the internet photoshop all sorts of stuff, it happens to me all the time. I've seen like a hundred pictures of me holding two big black di-"

"-Mrs. Porter! I'm sorry, I didn't notice you *behind Sienna*," Chloe interrupts and alerts all involved to their unexpected company.

Chloe leans in and gives Scarlett Porter a hug. "You look amazing!" the infinitely supportive parent is informed. Imagine attending your own daughter's divorce gala. Imagine having to bankroll it. Despite the circumstances, Scarlett remains glowing. Mrs. Porter's crow's feet seem to get less and less deep by the day. Her forehead seems to get smoother by the week. Her hair is still as blonde as ever, like she's spent the past 20 years at the beach, while her skin looks like it's never felt the cancerous char of natural sunlight.

"Where's Stanley?" Mrs. Porter asks in her ever-so-slight southern accent. Like a true southern belle, she's pretending that she wasn't eavesdropping on their conversation moments ago. By re-asking a question that was already answered, it calms everyone down and gives the girls the illusion that their potentially disturbing words had remained private. Of course, because of the girls' proximity to the blaring speakers, every conversation became an unconsciously loud yell.

"Stanley's under the weather and couldn't make it out," Chloe says, then she immediately tenses up when the ever-present headline machine in her head churns out, "Gay boy Stanley De Vries Battling Mystery Disease." It's so damn good that it even rhymes. Chloe gulps down her drink.

"Something seems to be going around," Scarlett Porter says discreetly. She's been married for 22 years, she knows the routine.

Scarlett wed the 15-years-her-senior, Ron Porter, when she was 19. Lindy was born eight months later- a familiar story. It was fairly obvious that Mrs. Porter was a gold digger, but she remains a fiercely loyal gold digger so she has one of the healthiest marriages on the West Coast. Like a newly ex'd husband who believes he was born to intern with the Paraguay national football team, Scarlett felt that she should have been born a rich girl. Unfortunately, she was born middle class in Atlanta, Georgia. Fortunately, she was born gorgeous, and stayed gorgeous. It's easy to be born gorgeous. Everyone starts baby-cute. It's harder than it looks to *stay* baby-cute. Not having a baby is a good start.

Lindy is an only child.

Chloe grabs a flute of champagne off a server's tray to wash down the tear inducingly strong Mojito, then Mrs. Porter locks arms with her. Together, they make their way through the mass of young bleach blondes trying to get to the bar. It wasn't awkward or unusual for Mrs. Porter to pull Chloe aside at a party. Scarlett is one of the few responsible adults Chloe remembers from her childhood.

Away from the deafening music, inside a sitting room decorated with carefully sculpted statues, weird paintings, and antique rugs, Mrs. Porter sits Chloe down on an unjustifiably expensive white loveseat. Lowering her voice a little, Scarlett says, "I haven't seen your mother at our little dinners lately." It's a statement soaked in equal amounts of worry and discretion.

The "little dinners" Linda is referring to are the biweekly cocktail-fests at Corturi. Linda Warren had Chloe at 40, and Scarlett had Lindy at 20. They were an unlikely pair to become best friends, but Ron Porter and Charlie Warren were college buddies, and there are only so many communal vacations you can take with a person before you start to form a bond.

"Oh. Mom is... Yeah, about that..." Chloe says, uncomfortable that she has to make excuses not only for her boyfriend, but also for her own mother, "...she's been under..." she begins to explain, then stops, realizing that she just used this excuse for Stanley. Chloe does the best she can to swing it, "...a lot of stress with the remodel."

"Linda's remodeling? She never mentioned it to me."

"Mom is, putting up, new, curtains. You-know-how-that-can-be," Chloe says, at first spacey, then rushed.

Mrs. Porter accepts this explanation because, with this group of women, it would be more alarming for Chloe to report that her mother *wasn't* remodeling.

The champagne quickly disappears from Chloe's flute and a man dressed in a black and white uniform identical to the one that Sarah-Beth is wearing provides her with a replacement, then collects the empty stemware. Chloe remains seated for the entire transaction.

"It's never easy," Scarlett says, then suggests, "Maybe I could help her?"

"I'll mention it to her." Chloe remarks, standing up, slightly wavering, but expertly making sure that not so much as a drop of her drink drips on the carpet that Mrs. Porter had flown in from a place that people assume her husband to be from when he says he's in oil.

"Are you alright, dear?" Mrs. Porter asks an unsteady Chloe. It's the first time in a long time someone asked Chloe that question in a tone that only can be described as "concerned parent" and not a panicked, "Are you going to puke in my car?"

"I'm great," Chloe says, wiggling out a smile, then taking a deep breath.

"You look so different from the last time I saw you," Mrs. Porter says, standing up from the loveseat.

Chloe nods, acknowledging that the last time she was face to face with Mrs. Porter, her face was a little chubbier.

"You'll have to tell me your secret," Mrs. Porter says. This request is not made so that Scarlett can learn how to shed some extra pounds.

Letting out a non-laugh laugh, Chloe walks back into the party. Her vision is still a little cloudy, but she'll blame it on someone slipping something in her drink if there's another *incident*. She knows that no one has roofied her drink because she grabbed it straight from Sarah-Beth, then from the trustworthy looking butler guy. These people wouldn't risk their crappy jobs just to roofie a celebrity who has a reputation for being pretty messy without any outside assistance. If they were going to roofie someone, it would be Sienna. Or maybe London? People love/hate Chloe, but they don't love/hate Chloe the way they love/hate those two. There's a special type of fond, fiery anger that London Francis and Sienna Wolfe provoke in the general public.

Chloe quickly realizes that London hasn't been roofied because she's reading off of her phone to a crowd of people in the living room. Unless they've invented roofies that expand your mental capacity? The market for those would be incredibly small though. Tobe Price has never lamented, "Why can't I just find a genius to fuck?" Generally, the further the girl is from a genius, the more Tobe wants to fuck her.

"...that's what *celebUtard* says," London announces to the group. Everyone acts really shocked at the news, or maybe they're really shocked that London can read.

"Wait, that was *celebUtard*? You read *celebUtard*?" Sienna asks.

"Of course," London responds, as though *celebUtard* is a source with prestige on par with *The Wall Street Journal*.

"That site is horrible to us," Dakota says, disgusted that London would spread such a virus of a blog.

London shakes her head in disagreement, "Not to me, they always run my pictures."

"Yeah, but then they write horrible things under them," Dakota points out.

"A picture is worth a thousand words. Do they say a thousand horrible words about me?" London asks.

"Sometimes, yeah," Sienna and Dakota respond in unison.

"Whatever," London brushes the conversation off as she scrolls on her phone, "Okay, here's the picture."

The girls huddle around the phone like cave women around a fire. The rest of the party huddles around the huddle, like horny cave men, around the cave women, around the fire. The wait staff and randoms huddle around the huddle, as though they're predatory animals, huddling around the cavemen, who are huddled around the cave women, who are huddled around the fire.

Everyone at this party thinks they're *so evolved*.

After seeing the picture, all of the girls suck in a deep breath, then exhale hard, as though the predators pushed the cave men's fists into their stomachs. They begin to sweat, as though the crowding from the cavemen left them too close to the fire.

"That's him! That's Johnny Foster kissing Kristen!" London says, displaying the phone to everyone in the vicinity.

"Are you sure?" Sienna asks.

If Kristen Paxton is seducing Johnny Foster, this could only be stopped by enlisting a pre-pubescent blonde to bop into Johnny's back yard wearing a schoolgirl skirt while holding a box of thin mints under each arm. This entire scene would be filmed, for leverage. Right now, Sienna is like a queen whose kingdom has been invaded to the point that she's run out of soldiers fit enough to fight the war so she'll have to resort to arming 16 year olds.

"Banging Johnny Foster is very un-'Kristen,'" Dakota declares, frowning.

Johnny Foster models for pretty much any company that's made trendy jeans for the past ten years. He has a great body and brown longish hair that he pushes back behind his ears. If you make him laugh, or make him mad, or push him onto the sofa in the VIP, then the autumn hair falls down in front of his face, instantly transforming him into a wounded poet. He has a very clear and powerful way of speaking, which makes girls sure not to disappoint him. Johnny's voice, combined with his direct delivery, once issued the most devastating rejection Sienna Wolfe has ever felt. That night, instead of getting revenge after being slighted by Johnny, Sienna sat drearily at a table with the cast of whatever show replaced *Tristan's Landing*, as they all debated what cause they were attending the benefit for. Sienna can't remember the reason why the night was put together, but she thinks it was for some beautiful animal that refused to fuck. It might as well have been a benefit for Johnny Foster.

Sienna downs her entire drink in an effort to forget Kristen, then she grabs Diego and staggers toward the sitting room at the same time Mrs. Porter is walking out for another drink. The rest of the girls are dripping in disbelief that Kristen has recovered from her ousting so fast, so big. The only solution to this bounce-back is to do exactly what Sienna just did and find a security blanket.

The girls don't want to look like a bunch of "Kristens" sulking at the party. Or *do* they?

One blog post can change everything.

4- Nap Time.

Chloe walks toward the bar. Walking is a generous term, stumbling is an accurate term. Three drinks- two flutes of champagne and a Mojito- that's all she's had. The old DWI checkpoint excuse was actually a reality tonight.

Grabbing the edge of the bar, Chloe manages to coo out, "Please refill me."

Beth, bound by the tip she received earlier, immediately attends to Chloe.

The frail socialite's smile flickers and her fingers tense as they grip onto the bar for support. Chloe is immediately deconstructed by the discerning eye of a girl who, for the latter part of her life, has been tending numerous bars, but never tending to her dreams. She's been watching these spoiled socialites live a perfect life, and she's at the party, but there's always that bar separating Beth from the girls she envies and pities at the same time.

Beth grabs a glass and begins to prepare the Mojito, but her eyes never leave the socialite in front of her. It becomes too much. Is she watching someone Monroe right before her eyes?

The last drink. It would bring Beth fame, but it's the type of fame that no one wants. Infamy. There would probably be a two year prison sentence in retribution for the perceived over-serving of America's favorite weight fluctuating, heart pumping, erection inducing, helpless little fawn.

"Are you alright?" Beth asks. After all the time she's spent on the couch, staring at the TV and refreshing the blogs on her laptop, Beth feels like she knows Chloe Warren, and she's able to tell when something is wrong with the fragile girl.

"I'm fine," Chloe says.

Convinced by those doe eyes that she wants to believe, Beth turns away to finish making the drink. She sets her feelings aside and does her job.

When Beth turns back around, Chloe is missing and in her place is a group of concerned individuals in a downward-facing panic.

5- The Sniffing Room.

Sienna tries to force Kristen's happiness out of her mind as she looks around at the gaudy art and creepy statues that surround her in the sitting room.

"I'm using this party as a dry run for my reality show premiere party," Diego says. Sienna doesn't bother responding. "I have my own show now, you know. I will have a party for that show as well. I have a show and a party... exclusive. VIP?" Diego says, trying to assemble any combination of words that will get Sienna's attention.

"A reality show, huh? Niceee..." Sienna responds in a way that makes it immediately clear she doesn't give a shit.

Diego turns away from Sienna, then his eyes settle on a large painting of some old guy. "You think these have alarms on them?" he asks.

"The paintings? How do you put an alarm on a painting? Paint one on the back?" Sienna responds, giggling to herself in her mild drunkenness.

Diego doesn't laugh. "No. You wire the mounting," he says, then he walks up to the wall and places his hands on either side of the frame. "You have the painting rest on the alarm so if someone..." Diego stops, flinches, then makes his move, "... grabs the painting off the wall, an alarm sounds."

Sienna looks up and to the left to see if she can hear an alarm. She can. Quickly, she realizes it's just part of the dubstep song that the DJ is playing on his laptop, so she sits down on the love seat and Diego joins her. The painting is flipped on its face, then balanced between Diego and Sienna's legs. The painted eyes of... whoever, probably Lindy's dead relative, is staring at Sienna's crotch. The Porters have the typical old money relics that memorialize past relatives who actually did something brave and bold to begin the family's wealth. On the outside, hanging these aged portraits makes it look like the family is paying respect to the people that gave them this life. In actuality, they keep the stuff around because if a relative paid ten grand to be immortalized in art, this relative will be staring at you as you bring the piece out to the curb, and the guilt is generally too much to bare.

Diego comments on the flipped work of art, "This is a good painting. It has this big sheet of brown paper covering a solid back."

"I didn't know that's how you value a painting," Sienna marvels, then files this little fact away so that she can look at the back of all of the paintings in her mom's house to see if any of them are worth some cash.

"I didn't mean good painting like it was rare or expensive, I just meant the paper is a nice flat surface to do coke off of. Without this paper and the solid backing, it would've been just wood and canvas, then we'd have to find something else."

Sienna scratches out the mental note. Excited for coke and generally apathetic about art, she says, "I feel like if the artist didn't consider that someone might want to do coke off the back of their work, they weren't a true artist."

Diego doesn't respond because he's pouring out the white contents of a zipperless sandwich bag onto the flipped painting.

Sienna looks up and, for the first time, she realizes there are other people in the room. Some of the guests look at her and smile, others are in an intense conversation about their last vacation.

A woman that Sienna met at either a benefit for a prospective Republican senator, or at a gay rights rally, notices Sienna's wandering gaze and immediately cuts across the room to take advantage of the moment. The woman starts flirting, as Diego steadily chops up the lines. After an awkward minute, Sienna shoos the woman away because Diego is finished with the preparation. The woman, as she leaves, says, "See you soon, us Republican gals have to stick together in a city like this."

Jostled by the entire interaction and almost positive that she can't even legally vote anymore, Sienna waits for the woman to disappear from the sitting room, then she takes Diego's rolled up hundred and sniffs up a giant line. Sienna sniffles, then squeezes her nose. As her cells begin to celebrate and conversation becomes borderline desirable, she turns to Diego and says, "I just think Lindy is disgusting for doing this."

Diego looks at Sienna- then he looks past Sienna- and his eyes go wide. He shoots back in his seat, almost disrupting the lines, and yells, "Ay dios mio!"

Sienna realizes, at this moment, that Diego Mestizo is Mexican. She looks away, trying to process this.

Sienna immediately notices that Lindy is standing in the entryway of the sitting room. She looks pissed.

Looks like *someone* just reclaimed the center of attention. Suck it, Kristen.

6- Shots From a Balcony.

London has escaped the panic. The view from the Porter's balcony provides her with a different perspective. The city looks brighter from this angle; maybe it's the perfect night, maybe it's the perfect boy she's with, or maybe it's the fact she's finished a fourth of the bottle of vodka that she slipped Sarah-Beth a hundred for.

Tobe was the first person to take to the balcony. He retreated outside, losing his tie, gasping for fresh air after watching Sienna slip away with Diego into a sitting room that was expansive enough he could have followed, but too intimate for it not to seem creepy. That's Tobe's main concern with his approach. He doesn't want to come off as the type of guy who has a shoebox full of magazine clippings of Sienna, primarily because he's a guy with a shoebox full of magazine clippings of Sienna. If Tobe is undeniably charming, Sienna could probably overlook his bizarre hobby. Maybe the collection could even be endearing? Following Sienna into the sitting room never would have worked. Tobe couldn't win against Diego, unless he continually asked about Mexico to the point that there's no mistaking that Diego is, in fact, Mexican.

Since Tobe didn't have Sienna, again, the night just melted into another failure born out of being one upped by a dick with a reality show. When Sienna fled, she took all the oxygen in the room with her, and Tobe couldn't catch his breath. He fled to the balcony and as soon as he sealed the door shut, he lit a joint. As he smoked, he began to feel better. He even uncharacteristically smiled.

Every time Tobe sees Sienna in real life, it's like when a kid goes to Disney World and sees Mickey Mouse. There's something incredibly exciting about seeing a person's 3rd dimension when you're used to them being flat.

Tobe is pinned by London tonight merely because when she appeared, bottle in hand, she walked right over and sat on his knee. Since then, Tobe has been stroking London's smooth hair extensions because, in his high mind, the texture of the doll-like strands makes him feel a strange calm. In the same way that London nervously pets the dozens of animals in her house, Tobe is petting her. She always loves when boys touch her hair, and she doesn't mind when they touch her extensions- even if it does shorten the amount of time in her mane rotation.

"Why don't we hang out more?" London asks Tobe in her baby voice.

"I haven't really been in LA very long. I used to live in New York," Tobe croaks out an already known recap.

"Do you love it?" London responds.

"LA?"

London nods.

"I guess it's alright."

"Alright!? LA is amazing. It's always hot, and there are a ton of famous people here!" London celebrates.

Tobe squints for a moment, then asks, "The same thing could be said about Hell though, couldn't it?"

"I don't know. I've never been."

"I guess we'll find out someday," Tobe says.

"Right, and when we end up there, we'll need to get in contact with each other," London suggests, snatching Tobe's phone, quickly typing in her number, then calling her own phone.

"I don't think they have cell phones down there," Tobe says.

"Yuck, that really does sound like hell," London says, then hands Tobe back his phone.

Suddenly, there's a quiet moment that Tobe enjoys and London abhors.

"Do you have a shot glass?" London asks, popping off Tobe's lap, no longer content to swig the bottle alone.

In a high haze, Tobe pats his pockets and mumbles, "No. I don't. I think I left it at home." He instantly feels like less of a gentleman for not being able to offer the lady a shot glass as though it was a match for her cigarette.

London sulks for a moment, then spots a square, blue glass encased candle on the iron end table to her left. Removing the candle, London sloppily pours the vodka- about a shot and a half- into the square glass. Tobe's eyes open wide as he watches London kick back the shot.

This is a girl that lives in a 4.25 million dollar mansion, and she's drinking bad vodka out of a porch candle. London sloppily pours another shot and a half into the glass, then sits back down on Tobe's lap and stares at him until he takes the candle jar.

"Don't worry, alcohol kills germs," London says, noticing Tobe furrowing his brow as he reviews his beverage and all the decisions that have led him to this point in his life. London provides what she thinks is a soothing fact, "When they had to sterilize wounds in Vietnam, they would pour booze on the soldier so the wound wouldn't get infected."

This mental image confuses Tobe, and he asks, "You mean to tell me there was a guy in the war whose entire job was to carry bottles of vodka in his backpack, and he'd pour the vodka on wounded soldiers like they were girls in a rap video?"

London shakes her head in her signature "Please just believe me" way.

Tobe makes a face that often follows a rough shot, then downs the alcohol from the candle jar and recreates the face again, only this time not as severe. He's running with this whole situation because he feels a bit guilty about masturbating to one of London's night vision videos right before the party. He had to get the poison out so his judgment wouldn't be clouded when he spoke with Sienna.

Tobe continues petting the drunk socialite as they both look out at the lights of the city. He's happy that London sat on his lap again because it's tough to look someone in the eyes when you've spent twelve minutes earlier in the day looking them straight in the vagina.

7- Gated Community House of Cards.

Dakota is too drunk to anticipate or notice the impending shitstorm she's about to walk into. She's also too intoxicated to notice the pre-existing shitstorms that her best friends are effortlessly conjuring around her. Anderson Westin, LA's premiere weatherman, has observed most of the shitstorms tonight from afar and would probably classify this unique situation as a, "...high pressure clusterfuck that will move in quickly, then leave just as fast."

Dakota pushes Anderson aside as she tails the server who demanded her presence. Gliding through the party, past the commotion Chloe is causing, toward the front door, Dakota takes a Pall Mall out of her black quilted leather Diane von Fürstenberg clutch. She lights the cigarette herself because she doesn't see any stooges like Jake Wesley who will do it for her. The black and white outfitted help slices through the maze of partygoers, while Dakota stomps along, a trail of smoke hovering in her wake.

Dakota is focused on not letting *him* do this. *He* always does this. Always.

Stupid CTV bought the stupid guest list and the stupid Google Alert with Dakota's name must have gone right to *his* inbox.

The front door is still being manned by two black security guards, and both imposing men are in the midst of receiving such a brutal verbal thrashing from a perspective guest that they were forced to request the assistance of the same girl that they were supposed to be protecting. Dakota is Lindy's friend. That's why she's going to the door

As soon as Dakota lays eyes upon her desperate, red faced, receding hairlined father, she explodes with an inherited temper, "You do not belong here! You do not belong here! You! Do! Not! Belong! Here!" Dakota spits at her mercy pleading father.

Short soundbites of, "I just wanted to see you," and, "I've missed you, you're my daughter," and, "You need help, Dakota," are churned out by Paul Dabney so fast that the "anonymous sources" within earshot can individually claim their own unique quote to sell to various blogs for sad $500 checks.

"He's not my father," Dakota says to the security guards, but they know this man is her father- everyone knows- because of nights like this.

"Dakota, baby, I-" Paul pleads, but he has nothing to jog her memory to remind her he is, in fact, her parent.

There's no, "Remember the pony I got you for your birthday party?"

No, "It was fun when I dressed up like Santa that one Christmas, wasn't it?"

All there is to remind Dakota of the familial ties she shares with this pathetic monster are a couple features on the tired face of a middle aged man at the door of an exclusive divorce party realizing for the umpteenth time that his claims of, "Dakota, I am your father," are less believable than the twist ending of a dorky Sci-Fi film.

Dakota stands at a safe distance as she stares down the one man who has done more to make people hate her than any other human being or blog has.

Paul Dabney can only plead with his eyes, because he's unable to defend his intrusion.

The scales tip, Dakota's power is asserted, and by simply flicking her pointer finger toward the door, a command is given, then carried out. Dakota watches her father kick frantically, like a protesting child in a supermarket, as he's pulled out of the party by security.

Once outside, Paul will probably go through his usual theatrics of punching himself in the face and blaming security. He might call all the pap agencies he knows, then he'll give interviews on the curb as he ices his self-inflicted wound. He'll make a desperate plea to connect to his "little girl that he barely recognizes anymore" then, with the money he makes, he'll pay the mortgage on that empty house he bought himself because, as he stated to his mortgage broker, "The father of Dakota Dabney can't be living in an apartment."

Dakota drops her cigarette on the marble floor, steps on it, then swivels as smoothly as someone in heels can. She faces the crowd that has gathered, each freckle on her body representing a burning star of attention.

Maybe all these people were standing behind her during the fight because they have her back?

When her eyes steady enough to unblur the leering faces, she sees a mob of disapproving, self-satisfied strangers.

"Can't she go anywhere without making a scene?" Dakota hears someone complain, and Paul Dabney succeeds, again.

8- Don't Lose Your Head.

Diego Mestizo flies out of the sitting room, clutching his collarbone like he's been shot. Everyone looks at him, searching for blood. Was this the assassination attempt that the ATF and CTV executives were hoping for? The network will be furious if one of their newest stars has been killed and there's no HD footage of it. Lindy refused to let Diego's cameras in tonight so the producers probably gave him strict instructions to act like a human being, instead of like Diego Mestizo. Seeing all the attention he's garnering Diego wails, "It's like Vietnam in there!"

Inside the room that Diego just left is a group of carefully dressed white people. If this is Vietnam, the Vietnamese are grossly outnumbered. All of the Ho's in this room are named via rude blog posts instead of birth certificates. If this truly was a war and the guest list for this party was wiped out, *OK! Magazine* would have no choice but to run blank covers for the rest of the year.

Lindy Porter is freaking out.

People are pouring out of the room, running toward the bar to get at least two more drinks before they drive home.

"He was looking at me weird!" Sienna screams. Her perfect skin is glowing like she's pregnant, and depending on which blog you read, she might be. If it's true, she's not showing, plus the guests would definitely hear the fetus in her belly yammering away from all the coke Sienna has ingested in the past 72 hours.

Lindy yells back, "He was not looking at you!"

"Was to," Sienna protests. "I don't need to take that from him, I'm Sienna fucking Wolfe."

"You really think he was looking at you, are you that insane?"

"He's super creepy- like twins level creepy. Will anyone agree with me here?" Sienna asks the crowd, then she gasps when she spots the Mannheim twins near the fireplace.

"*It* was a sculpted bust of my great grandfather," Lindy points out.

"Ohhh yeahhh. He's sooo greattt. Just because he's dead and probably haunted doesn't give him the right," Sienna says, then she's grabbed by two men in black suits.

The carnage began when Lindy walked into the sitting room and saw that her father's priceless Crabner was being used as a coke plate.

After calling upon God for intervention, Diego looked down at the painting covered in coke and mumbled, "What is this?" and Lindy responded angrily, "Coke," then Diego, out of habit, asked, "Are you offering me more?

We already have some... maybe this isn't enough, you might be right. Good Point."

Sienna, insulted that she couldn't even quietly do coke off a painting of a dead person in a private residence, started ranting. Ranting turned into rage, and the rage turned into, *Okay, now that I've got everyone looking at me, stop looking at me because I'm not sure this is the right type of attention.*

Sienna is carried out of the party by security due to this disturbance.

Chloe is carried out of the party by Jake because she's white as a sheet after fainting.

London is carried out of the party by Tobe since he's pretty sure she can't possibly have anything left in her stomach to puke out.

Dakota is carrying a bottle of wine out of the party, swinging her hips with a confident swagger because she's leaving on her own accord, not being kicked out.

Once outside, Dakota directs the security guys to put Sienna out on the front lawn. She directs Jake to put Chloe on the front lawn. She directs Tobe to put London on the front lawn. They just need a breather before they'll drive away. That was the excuse. This is a disaster for everyone involved, besides the girl who left the party as the last one standing. These new lawn ornaments are Dakota's next move in the battle against her father. Paul Dabney will be treated like the flea that he is now that these hot little kitties have come out to play in front of the paps.

At the end of the night, the perfect girls end up on the Porter's perfectly manicured lawn, in perfect view of the telephoto lenses; the ultimate sign of an imperfect night.

Tonight will be an issue tomorrow.

An issue you can purchase at your local drug store or supermarket.

An issue with some pictures tinged in blue and red lights.

9- Band of Sisters.

Maybe Diego Mestizo was right?

Maybe last night *was* Vietnam.

If that's the case, things need to change.

Vietnam was an unpopular war.

What's the best way to escape an unpopular war? It's a question that's troubled JFK, and LBJ, and Nixon, and Obama. London isn't totally sure if we're still in Iraq, nor does she know anything about the Vietnam War, other than one imaginary, medicinal-vodka related fact. When the girls find themselves in a situation like this, when they're trapped in a corner regarding an issue they neither know, nor care about, they employ the ultimate deterrent.

They switch the topic.

Chloe, Dakota, and London sit around a circular table outside their usual hangover hangout, "Candrol," which may also coincidentally be the name of one of the mood stabilizers Dakota has been prescribed. This meeting wasn't organized by rumbling stomachs or lonely post-party depression. These three girls arrived at this table because their PR agents called them at 11 AM this morning and told them that they had to show up bright and early, together, to prove that last night couldn't have been as bad as it actually was.

All three girls applied their makeup carefully, "accidentally" forgot their bras, then met up for some greasy food.

The girls have pushed their untouched plates to the side so they can scroll through the new posts on their phone.

It becomes clear that London must have hired a tutor because she's reading aloud again, and she's sounding out most of the words correctly.

She scrolls down the page on *FameDiet*, then sighs.

FAMEDIET
London's Shadowy Enabler.

Last night, during **Lindy Porter**'s gala divorce party, **London Francis** was spotted on **Scarlett Porter**'s balcony with a mystery man, taking shots of vodka. After a few rounds, London was pouring out more than shots and her heart, as she unloaded an **Exorcist** worthy spew of vomit on the defenseless, yet totally used to it, **Hollywood Hills**.

The photographs are a little dark, and we don't have the luxury of London's usual night vision, but who does the mystery man on the balcony look like to you? I'm not sure what you're seeing, but I see two people, and only one of them has their hair blowing in the wind.

9.5- Reviewing Reviews of a Night They Did Not Wish To Review.

"Wow, they haven't even confirmed Tobe carrying you out yet?" Dakota asks, looking up from her phone.

Chloe warns the girls, "Don't go celebrating yet, *ThisSpoiledBitch* just posted pictures of London in Tobe's arms."

London smiles at Chloe's description of the situation. It sounded so romantic.

"Stop reading *ThisSpoiledBitch*!" Dakota says, reaching for Chloe's phone.

Blocking Dakota's attempted grab with a leaning defensive move, Chloe scrolls down to the next story. "Chloe Warren..." she reads aloud, her voice already showing signs of panic, "...lets her diet secret *slip*."

The hungover girls fall silent. A conversation that should arrive waits patiently to be invited to the table.

Chloe slaps her phone down next to her untouched plate, then she fixes her sunglasses with shaky hands. She puts her thumb between her well glossed lips and begins sucking on it.

The girls nervously look off toward the other diners, it's easier than looking at each other. Chloe makes eye contact with the group of paparazzi near a line of bushes that's supposed to act as a fence. A tall man with a spiderweb tattoo on his neck, a squat middle aged man with a businessman haircut, a guy in a Yankees cap- normal, normal, normal people. In the same way that the cops have surveillance on Diego's father, the paps have surveillance on the girls.

"What are we gonna to do?" Chloe's little voice asks. She begins chewing her red nail polish off and spitting the flakes on the ground next to the table.

"They're already photographing us together so..." Dakota trails off.

Chloe drops her thumb from her mouth, almost as though the lead in her nail polish brought great ideas along with its potential to cause birth defects. Dakota had used the girls' misfortune last night to teach her father a lesson, and Chloe became an unlikely student. With so many stories driving an insane amount of curious traffic, there's a subsequent lack of interest in an abusive man doing what he always does. A bad situation was given a bit of a silver lining by manipulating what those villainous cameras showed the world.

"You think they'll break the story for us... three girls instead of four at lunch?" Chloe asks, putting the scheming on the weak shoulders of a fat middle aged pap in a black t-shirt.

There's a silence as the girls realize that the key to their prison resides in the flat stomach of one of their own. This presents two options- destroy the girl and grab the key- or rot in a jail where the food is terrible, but getting a good table is simple if you're pretty and have a shitload of Pall Malls.

The girls have already bailed Sienna out of hundreds of messy situations, what more do they owe her? If last night could be painted as a Sienna issue, then they'll be golden. It will create an escape route to bigger and better parties. Parties where the girls will behave more responsibly.

"Who knows what they'll leak. I can't figure out what the paps will do. Every time I think that they're releasing something nice about me, I turn on my laptop and see a picture of my vagina," London says.

"Well, I think you have a very photogenic vagina," Dakota comments, trying to lighten the mood of the meal, yet simultaneously ruining everyone's appetite in the process.

"Aw. Thanks. It's just the surprise of it all. I'll do something really good and then all they care about is my pussy," London pouts.

"Someone's going to have to provide an anonymous quote," Chloe decides, redirecting the attempted tangent.

"I'll call my agent," Dakota says, then she grabs Chloe's phone to make sure that her call isn't ignored.

"And he'll call it in?" Chloe asks, suspicious of Rod.

Rod Tobin is Dakota's agent. He seems to be the most practical of the bunch and scheming has never been a strength of his. He's more traditional, responsible, and realistic. Chloe wants London's agent, Joel Harper to call it in. Joel knows a thing or two about making girls cry, then apologizing with a "fuck off."

"Rod won't call it in, but his secretary will," Dakota says, copying his office number from her phone to Chloe's.

"Do you really trust his secretary?" London asks. She sort of just wants Joel to call it in too.

"Yeah. She was the anonymous tipster who told The Sun that I was getting my implants done in the UK," Dakota tells Chloe.

"Oh. The Sun did a good job covering that. You got the whole front page, with your boobs in little side by side comparison boxes," London says, remembering how proud she was of Dakota.

"Yeah, that was Courtney's doing."

"And she'll be okay with this?" Chloe asks.

"Who gives a shit, it's her job," Dakota says as she puts the phone to her ear.

"You're really going to do this?" London squeaks. She's shocked that Dakota would be so willing to pull the trigger on her own best friend.

Like so many of their daily conversations, before the important decisions are weighed, they're made.

Dakota, turning away from the paparazzi lenses, whispers into the phone, "Hi. Rod? Go with the plan we talked about earlier this morning. Yes, I'm sure... I'm sure."

The girls pause and consider this statement... the plan we talked about *earlier this morning?*

10- Casualties of War-ren.

The girls are led to a rectangular glass table in Sienna's newly renovated kitchen. Sienna is still debating on if the kitchen was actually renovated, or if some Mexican looking guys just put plastic over everything, then removed the plastic a month later and left her with a bill. She's pretty sure that she has the same kitchen as when they started, but she can only truly verify that they didn't replace her fridge.

"Don't do this," Sienna says, sitting down in a high backed black chair. When she looks across the table, she sees her three friends sitting in a row. No one chose to take Sienna's side.

The girls look put together. Sienna feels washed out and tired. Her face is puffy and shiny.

It has suddenly, yet not completely unexpectedly, become Sienna on one side, her friends on the other. She's never had a desk job, but Sienna imagines this is what it's like to be laid off. No wonder people seem so bummed about the economy.

As Sienna's eyes begin to get that fresh gloss that always precedes a cry, Dakota squirms in her chair. It's much easier to argue with just a voice. They should've done this over speakerphone, instead of coordinating an awkward judges-table-on-a-reality-show moment.

"We have to distance ourselves from what happened. This is the only way," Chloe says.

"Such bullshit, I can't even explain myself?" Sienna snaps, "You won't even give me the common courtesy-"

"-there's nothing that needs explaining. We all know what happened," Chloe tells her directly.

"She's right, it's not fair," London blurts out. Chloe and Dakota both turn to London, dumbfounded.

London Francis does not care about fair- ever. When she sees those commercials for African children, she says that their starvation is "self-imposed" because "they could just go to a McDonald's" since "literally all countries have McDonald's. The UN sanctioned it or something."

Somehow, today of all days, with great fanfare, "fair" has made an entrance during the one situation that demanded nothing more than London's signature unwavering apathy.

London scrambles because she realizes she just power drilled a hole in the bottom of their boat. "Think about how many times a day we read stories about us that aren't true. Like Chloe, your story toda-"

"-fine!" Chloe says loudly, then gives Sienna a chance to explain. "What happened last night, Sienna? Do you even remember?"

Sienna tries to run her fingers through her matted hair. She can't. She tries to piece together everything that happened last night. She can't. She tries to defend herself. She hopes she can. "Yes, I know what happened. Okay. I wasn't that bad. The only picture I've seen from last night was from the end of the night and everyone looks shitty in end of the night pictures. Show me a picture of me being *that* bad."

"You were that bad," Chloe says.

"Why are there no pictures of me being evil?"

London, realizing what she's done, makes the necessary move. She brings a picture up on her phone, then shows it to Sienna.

"Shit," Sienna says as she sees herself. She needs to think of an excuse. "That's not me... it's that Dani girl they always get me confused with," she tells them, then nervously laughs.

"Dani was in Saint-Tropez last night," Dakota says.

Chloe sighs and looks at Sienna, "It's a microscope world we live in, you can't-"

"-I can't have a night out with my friends, Chloe? Remember that creepy director's Oscars party? Remember Cory Beck's soccer- football- whatever, remember that party with the guys in jerseys? Rem-"

"-stop," London demands.

"One day! I messed up one day!" Sienna shouts, hitting the table, then visoring her eyes with her right hand.

Chloe leans closer, even though she's still far away from Sienna, and she explains, "It's the 21st century. One picture, one e-mail, one sound bite can destroy you. One day is pretty big now."

"This. Sucks," Sienna spits out, her eyes shielded like she was caught makeupless at LAX.

"It does suck," London agrees.

Sienna wipes her face, then looks at a numb Dakota. "I thought that we were-"

"-we were," Dakota confirms, her smoky voice cracking.

"Then-"

"-why? Because it's not just me and you in this world," Dakota says, finally looking at Sienna.

"I wish it was sometimes," Sienna tells her.

When Sienna looks at her friends, she has to blink back her tears. If her eyes move down to the table, she catches her reflection and she immediately has to look away.

The girls don't say anything as they watch Sienna fight everything the world is showing her.

"Don't-" Sienna huffs, then she looks around the stupid kitchen she got ripped off on. She takes a breath, then completes her plea, "-don't let this happen."

"It's not my decision," Dakota says.

"It is your decision. It's totally your decision!" Sienna sobs, her cool predictably cracking.

"Did you happen to read the fucking blogs today, Sienna?" Chloe snips, unwilling to feel guilt over self-preservation. Last night, the fainting wouldn't have been that big of a deal if it didn't coincide with a screaming dust up. Any other night, Chloe could've dusted herself off, blamed the heels, then held a martini glass full of water for the rest of the night.

Sienna manages to say, "You're my only friends."

"You know that's not true," Chloe responds, but a contorted cry-face on Sienna's part proves that she's not so sure.

"This conversation is over," Chloe says, standing up, then the two other girls mimic this action.

"So that's it?" Sienna asks, still sitting.

"That's it."

"Well... goodbye then," Sienna says sharply, her mood changing from apologetic to bitter.

Chloe and London each force out a husky, "Goodbye," then walk toward the front door. Dakota stays behind for a moment. She can't move, she can't say goodbye to her Bonnie. This meeting had to happen to keep the girls' image stable, but nothing seems stable in Dakota's watery eyes as she looks at her friend and searches for the right words.

One fact remains amid the rubble. It was only a matter of time before Sienna beheaded another famous family's grandfather and, next time, artistic restoration may not be an option.

OXYGEN WASTER
The Feckless Four Strike again!

All of the details are in on **Lindy Porter**'s divorce party and it lived up to the reputation of her marriage! We thought Lindy had some serious problems before, but now it looks like she needs to get rid of more than just her cheating hubby. As soon as **The Feckless Four** made their entrance last night, all in attendance knew that they needed to have fun while they could, because by the time this band of bimbos made it to the bar, the party would turn into a disaster.

And a disaster it was!

A horrifyingly skinny **Chloe Warren** entered the party last night looking like the lovechild of a Halloween skeleton and **Ronald McDonald**. She's shed at least 30 pounds in the past three months, which equals ten pounds a month. I guess it wouldn't be hard to lose that weight if you had no job to go, no children to take care of, and not a single important life responsibility, right? It seems that Ms. Warren utilized a special vodka-only diet to slim down, and it finally caught up with her, when she caught up with the floor for a center of attention "nap."

Not to be outdone, Chloe's BFF, **London Francis**, showed up looking like her pimp gave her the night off. As the party progressed it appeared that she did not, in fact, have the night off, as she was seen on the balcony in the lap of none other than **Tobe Price**. Lucky for Tobe, he didn't have to suffer London's presence for the entire night because she was photographed vomiting vodka, stomach bile, and probably three different types of semen off of Lindy's balcony. Like a true gentleman, Tobe held London's bad extensions back as she unloaded his baby makers faster than she drained them.

Since everything is a competition with these girls, **Dakota Dabney** and **Sienna Wolfe**- the "Bonnie & Bonnie" duo as they've been dubbed- showed up to destroy, destroy, destroy. Parties, reputations, nights- these girls ruin it all. Never say that they're untalented, it takes skill to be such harbingers of absolute debauchery and disaster. It's a full time job to ruin so many good things in LA, and these two seem fully dedicated.

Dakota Dabney, in her typical rebellious teenager ways (Dakota is 22), had her own father, **Paul Dabney**, thrown out of the party. She was making such a big fuss that the bouncers seemed to get a little rough with Paul, as evidenced by the shiner he was nursing when we caught up with him outside the gate. I don't know which would be worse, getting hit in the face and ending up with a black eye, or fathering one.

Last, but certainly not least, **Sienna Wolfe** made such an mess of herself last night that if anyone asks her for an autograph today, it won't be because of Sienna's pointless fame, but instead because she may be the most worthless human being on the entire West Coast.

Sienna quickly found recovering drug addict and reality TV star, **Diego Mestizo,** then latched onto his hot hips for the night. In an obvious ploy to get a starring role on Diego's new show, Sienna fed him drinks (she herself had twice as many), then Ms. Shameless pulled Diego into a very full room and began to act as though they were the only people at the party. After grabbing a priceless **Crabner** self-portrait off the wall, Sienna placed the art on her lap and poured out a bag full of coke. Diego has been battling his own drug demons and last night he had a bigger devil- Sienna Wolfe- to deal with. Everyone knows that he needs help right now and Sienna chose to "help" Diego by forcing him to do the coke.

When the woman of the night, Lindy Porter, confronted Sienna about her drug use, and the painting, and Sienna's disaster of a life in general... Wolfe flipped out. By night's end, a bust of Lindy's grandfather was broken, Diego's sobriety was broken, and the girls found themselves thrown out on the front lawn of the Porter complex.

Everyone says that Lindy is spoiled, but last night she stepped up and finally took out the trash.

Let's hope the police were wearing gloves when they arrested Sienna because they had to pick her off Lindy's lawn like a steaming pile of excrement.

Check out the mugshot <u>below</u> if you're curious what such a pile looks like.

11- Rock Bottom.

"What the fuck was that?" Chloe asks, looking back toward London as they walk to Dakota's black Benz parked just outside the gate.

The same paps from earlier in the day take even more pictures, and the camera flashes cause the fight to be postponed until the girls get inside the car. The weak link has been removed so now the girls must form a strong chain. It's all about changing the subject. If there are bombs being launched, get a very public blowjob so people won't notice the bodies piling up. The girls realize they'll have to come up with a real plan this time. Enough of the blowjob sleight of hand. If they're going to make this bad buzz disappear, they'll have to control their good buzzes and act responsibly.

"She needed a chance to explain herself," London says, sliding in the front passenger seat of the Benz.

"Explain herself? What could she possibly say? That she was reprimanding a statue for loitering in her drug den?" Chloe asks, settling into the back seat. Dakota slams her door, turns the car on, then immediately guns the engine, not to evade the paparazzi, but because Sienna's car hasn't appeared in the rear view mirror yet, so now is their chance to escape. Some of the photographers give chase as the girls leave Sienna for good. Others seem disinterested because the girls weren't inside Sienna's house long enough to drink a DUI-worthy amount of vodka.

"I don't approve of sacrificial lambs," London says, checking herself out in the visor mirror. She flips it back up, happy with what she sees, despite what she just did.

"Listen. You have to do some things that aren't nice to stay interesting, you know what I mean? No one wants a book with no plot," Chloe says.

London shakes her head in disagreement and says, "I think all books are equally undesirable, plus, like, to stay relevant you can still be nice, you just have to build a jet pack so people can fly to work. That would definitely get a lot of interest. People would be like, 'Oh, there goes kindhearted London Francis, creator of the jet pack,' then they would fly away using their jet pack."

This statement makes Dakota smile at a time when she thought those muscles in her face were paralyzed. She looks in the rear view mirror and Chloe is holding in a laugh.

As the Benz curves down the winding road, a silent chase announces itself. London turns on the radio to break the silence. Chloe checks her phone to see if even one person is sympathetic toward her. There are too many articles. The Google Alerts are a mile long. If someone was to cull all this content and write a definitive summary of the judgments, points, and opinions contained therein, it would be as follows- famous for being famous girls are as pathetic as they are vapid.

Chloe pries her eyes away from *ThisSpoiledBitch* and looks back to see the line of cars following them.

"It's not enough," she says.

London looks back, "Yeah, I think some of them didn't even bother to follow us."

Chloe shakes her head, "No, what we just did is not enough. They want more."

Dakota sees an opportunity headed straight for her and she takes it. The Benz eases to a stop on an emergency shoulder that's big enough for only a single car. The girls check their mirrors to see how the paps will react. There's no way that the photogs could block traffic on this twisting, narrow road so there's only one choice for them- to continue on.

Each car full of cameras passes slowly, while the girls look the other way.

London turns to Dakota at the exact moment the last car, a big black van, slows and the fat paparazzi with the businessman haircut leans across the front seat of the van. He gives London a crooked toothed smile instead of flashing his camera at her one last time. London felt like it was an oddly nice, human gesture for an inhuman pap shitbag. As the van passes, London stays in the moment. The little fat man seemed vaguely proud of what the girls had done. This is not good, London knows this from experience. Anything that makes the men with the cameras smile is something that can be sold. How would London end up with money for betraying her friend? She doesn't want that check.

Dakota turns off the car, then gets out quickly, leaving the keys in the ignition. Chloe and London both watch Dakota as she approaches the left passenger door, then pops it open and rejoins her friends inside the car. London doesn't want to be left out, so she squeezes between the seats, then sits in the back seat of the Benz, a girl on either side of her.

"Alright," Chloe says, taking the lead, "It's just the three of us in here and we have as much time as we need so let's figure this out. Things are bad. Worse than I thought."

"Don't even tell me what you read while I was driving," Dakota says.

"Fair enough, let's just suffice it to say that for us to continue on in the position we're in, for us to keep getting invites, for us to still be enjoyable to hate- instead of making people feel that angry hate- we're going to need to change," Chloe says.

"We did change. We got rid of Sienna," Dakota responds with a hint of bitterness.

"That was the first step, it wasn't the entire journey."

"Ew," London reacts to Chloe's statement.

"You're right. Uncalled for," Chloe says, acknowledging that no one in the car needs trite quotes to motor on; they could just find a reflective surface if they needed a reminder life is beautiful.

"The point is, we need to do something," Chloe announces.

"We *are* doing something, I mean how many other times have we camped out in the back of a parked car, without making out with a cute boy?" Dakota points out.

"No. You're not understanding me. We need to *do something*. No one will ever respect us if we're just living this blissful, responsibility-free existence," Chloe tells the girls.

London suddenly gets it and says, "Right now we're like one of those species of pretty looking animals that could become extinct, and if that happens, it doesn't impact stuff too much because they weren't contributing to the ecosystem!" London has been learning about endangered species because various protection agencies keep taking pets away from her after she purchases them.

"Right, London," Chloe says warmly.

"So, if we find something that we're good at, then we won't just be famous for being famous."

"Exactly," Chloe encourages Dakota, "Now we just need to decide what our something is going to be."

"We could work for an animal charity!" London suggests.

"I'm not throwing out my furs," Dakota immediately responds.

"Or another charity, I guess."

"No charities," Chloe says, "Any rich person can head up a charity. You just give money and show up to events. We already do that and no one gives a shit."

"You're right," Dakota agrees. She takes out her phone and begins a list. "Our something," she says aloud as she types, then under the heading, she puts a "1."

"Name things that we can do to become worthwhile members of society so people will stop being mean to us," Dakota demands.

"It needs to be a talent that people can see," London says, and Dakota notes this.

"It needs to be something that takes a really long time to finish so we can develop our talent."

"It needs to impress people."

"It needs to make money."

"It can't include a giant penis being inserted into a mouth."

"It needs to be different."

"It needs to be awesome enough that people will go, 'Sure, that devastating fire was her fault, but we'll forget about it because she has that amazing talent.' Of course that's... just, you know... a hypothetical situation," London mumbles.

All of these points are typed out, then Dakota places the phone on London's lap like it was a Crabner on Sienna.

"What could we do that fits all these requirements?" London asks.

After digging through her purse and retrieving a Pall Mall, Dakota puts the cigarette in her mouth, but before she flicks her lighter, a spark ignites inside her. Everything melts together perfectly. Dakota lunges into the driver's seat, lights her Pall Mall, exhales, then looks back and announces, "We're forming a band."

celebUtard
"Outwolfed."

We just got word from a source, of a source, of a blog, of a source, of a sister to someone in the know, that walking skeleton, **Chloe Warren**, was joined by walking hurricane, **Dakota Dabney,** and stumbling bimbo, **London Francis**, when she paid a visit to **Sienna Wolfe**'s house this morning. Our 45th hand source tells us that the meeting essentially dissolved the axis of evil the girls had with Ms. Wolfe. The <u>pics after the jump</u> show the girls leaving Sienna's house, looking like they cut off a toxic limb before it killed their entire tree.

Apparently, the girls had given Sienna a warning that if she got in one more mess (this week), she'd be cut loose, and since all Sienna knows is how to destroy lives/houses/brain cells, she was unable to control herself.

Here's where it gets extra juicy. Dakota's agent, **Rod Tobin**, has pumped out a rambling press release that announces that there will be a reveal by the girls regarding their "new project" next week. Don't you need an "old project" before you can announce that your "new project" is coming out? Regardless, in about an hour we expect to receive a press release about the press release, which announces that there will be an announcement on a secret website. Life was better when you had to buy a shitload of stamps to get the word out.

We can only assume that the girls' new project will consist of the following- macaroni/paper plates/gold spray paint.

Maybe they can recreate Sienna's mugshot in gold pasta as their first "project."

Until next time, stay tardy, celebUverse.

12- It's Cali. Learn to Ride The Wave.

The press release went viral.

The story broke.

The plan is in place.

Now, it's time for the leak. This is necessary so that people will feel like they've acquired information they weren't meant to receive.

"The people who follow us are secret vampires," Chloe explains to London as they sit with Dakota inside a red-themed restaurant that has an "excessively French-sounding" name. This is the second day in a row that they are very much in public, all together, looking great, without Sienna.

"We know secret vampires?" London asks, bug eyed. She reaches up and cups her neck, and her eyes turn to slits as she peers at the other diners. She attempts to deconstruct which people are rich from the entertainment industry and which people are rich because they've been alive for seven lifetimes as a secret vampire. Ultimately, making this distinction proves to be too difficult, and it's abandoned.

"She doesn't mean they're *secret vampires*," Dakota says, touching London's bent arm.

"Don't sugar coat this for me. She said, 'secret vampires.' I'm not a child I can handle the truth."

"Dakota's right. I meant to say that they suck secrets out of people. It's what keeps them alive."

"That clarification might have made things worse," London says, scared like a child. This is new information that London will have to lock away so it doesn't haunt her. There are a lot of secrets and repressed memories under that mess of extensions. London is no stranger to concealing information about a secret sucking.

Chloe and Dakota look across the table at each other. They know that if they don't fix this now, they'll get call tonight from a very drunk London as she sobs about how the secret vampires are plotting something outside in the gazebo behind her house.

"Know what I'm gonna to do?" Chloe asks, looking at London, "I'll let you spill a secret so the secret vampires won't bother you."

Finally taking her hands off her neck, London wiggles her butt excitedly back and forth on her chair, then asks, "What do I get to say?"

"You get to tell the guys outside with the cameras about our band," Chloe says.

"Those guys who follow us everywhere are the secret vampires?" London asks to confirm their identity.

"Yup, and they won't do anything bad to you as long as you 'accidentally' tell them about the band," Dakota informs her.

"Oh! Okay. Yay for secrets!" London celebrates, like *Secrets* was the name of a basketball team that just beat *The Lakers*. Chloe and Dakota smile at each other, while London smiles at her menu. She happily browses her options, looking for a dessert to celebrate the fact that she's protected herself from the secret vampires without having to order anything with smelly garlic or carry around a gaudy wooden stake to make it happen. She does have this one clutch that's the perfect size for a stake though so she won't rule out accessorizing to defend herself.

London's smile suddenly fades. "Peaches Sorbet has a dessert named after her here! This is criminal," she says, frisbeeing her menu across the restaurant.

Dakota opens her menu, "Um, you pronounce that sore-bay. And Peaches' last name is Sebert," she snarkily informs London.

"Oh," London says, looking over at some poor bastard of a waiter who fetches the menu, then returns it to her like he's one of her puppies.

"Okay, then I'll have one of those and maybe they'll name it after me!" London decides. She looks at the fetch-it waiter and asks, "Can I have the peaches sore-bayyy?"

"Could you bring an extra spoon, too?" Dakota asks.

The waiter stares at London as she shakes her head, and mouths, "No," at him. He admires London's make-up, both in the Maybelline way and the pedigree way.

"Okay, I'll have the peach sorbet too," Dakota decides.

"She means the cheesecake," London clarifies.

"Is the cheesecake okay, Ms. Dabney?" the waiter asks.

"I'm not hungry," Dakota says, then shoots the waiter a fake smile, dismissing him.

As soon as the waiter turns around, Dakota pinches London's upper arm and informs her, "You're a bitch."

"Dakota. Stop. They'll never name a dessert after me if we both order it. We aren't on a date or in a Ponderosa, so I'm not sharing with you."

"It's gross that you even know what goes on in a Ponderosa," Dakota says, as her phone vibrates for longer than a text message. She looks down and sees an unhappy, messy Sienna Wolfe looking back up at her. Dakota saved Sienna's most recent mugshot on her phone and now it pops up when her ex-best friend calls.

The mugshot shows a defiant Sienna who didn't care if her actions got her arrested. It also shows that she didn't listen to Dakota. Sienna looks miserable and high in her mugshot. Her hair looks damaged; her makeup, smudged.

After Kristen got arrested earlier in the year, Dakota explained to the girls that they should always smile when their mugshot is taken because it's a known fact that it's hard to totally hate someone if they look like they're having the time of their life. If a person is singing in the rain, other people will point and laugh because of how douchey it looks, but no one is going to push the singer in a puddle. An angry passer-by wouldn't want to destroy whatever the tapshoed asshole had found in the world that produced such happiness.

The waiter returns with the peach sorbet and places it down on the table. Now is London's chance. She has to make sure that everyone will forever associate her with the mediocre desert. Before any of this can happen, Dakota licks her finger and stabs it into the center the peachy mush. London feels the table shake from Dakota's forceful claiming of the sorbet and, thinking fast, she grabs the peach dipped hand, then aggressively licks the sorbet off Dakota's finger. The performance is capped off with a *i-D* magazine inspired wink to the waiter. London is doing everything she can to get this dessert renamed the "London Francis Sorbet," but the restaurant would never think of giving it that name for fear of all of the, "Does that come with a side of Valtrex?" jokes.

"Get off my finger, vampire," Dakota whines, pushing London away. The rough shove is part of the territory as far as London is concerned. No one has ever gotten their name on a menu without getting a couple of bruises too. Except Shirley Temple. Well, hopefully.

Chloe looks at her two best friends as they fight like sisters, then she pulls the sorbet over with her spoon. She wants to eat it. She wants to eat it more than London wants the dessert to be her namesake. The mush melts as the girls fight. Eventually relenting, Chloe puts her spoon down and watches the delicious fingerfucked food go to waste. Another meal that had everything to do with status and nothing to do with sustenance. Chloe has to push the dessert back to London. London pushes it to Dakota.

"Oh, now I can have it?"

"Yeah, all I wanted was a taste," London says.

Deserting dessert, the girls start to look around for the waiter. They find him toward the back of the restaurant, aiming his phone directly at the table. The waiter stares into the little screen and when he sees that all three girls are looking back at him, he quickly snaps a picture, then starts waving his cell phone around in the air. "I can't get reception," he mumbles loudly.

"Annie Leibo-ditz, when you finish your shoot, can we get the check?" Dakota yells over to him, frisbeeing her words across the restaurant like they were a menu.

Chloe tosses a napkin over the "London Francis Sorbet."

The waiter brings over the little black book and Chloe slides her credit card inside before the book leaves his hand. He leaves quickly with the card, then all three girls check their faces in the reflection of their cell phone screens. They like what they see. When the waiter/puppy/amateur-photographer returns, they'll give him a good tip because that picture on his phone will be sent to whatever blog he reads. This starts the wheels turning in Dakota's mind. More than likely, the offer the waiter will receive for the photo will be less than the tip that Chloe will leave. Does the tip buy them security? Does the waiter send the picture anyway? Dakota wonders what the price of a man's integrity might be, mainly so she'll know how much money it will take to finally be free of her father.

The meal is over, the sorbet is mush, and it's time to send London Francis, stupid London Francis, the character "London Francis," out to those secret vampires so they can bleed her dry of her poisonous blood.

This afternoon, three girls will begin their quest for fame with merit.

"Ready?" London asks, her lanky frame towering over the sitting girls.

"Are you ready?" Chloe asks, remaining seated with Dakota.

"I have to face the vampires alone?" London whines, a little scared.

"That's the only way it'll work. If Chloe and I go with you, the paps know we'd shut you up. If you're on your own, then they'll pump you for secrets because they think you're an easy target."

"I'm not an easy target," London says, scrunching up her face.

"Today, you will be," Dakota tells her.

London checks her reflection in her phone again, then heads out to Transylvania, CA.

"London! London! Over here, London!" the vampires chant as the door opens and photo-fresh socialite appears. London responds to her name like one of her animals would, scooting along with a little tail wag of a walk. The paps' cameras flash, and the group moves with London as she makes her way to her car.

"London! Is it true you banned Sienna from your life?" the pap in the Yankees cap asks.

"I just had a delicious brunch with Chloe and Dakota," London says, smiling. She lights up even more when she realizes her opportunity, "I had the sor-bayyy," she tells them. The bushy haired pap asks the question they all want the answer to, "Any hints on the announcement you'll be making?"

"Nope," London says, unwilling to be an easy target.

The chubby businessman haired pap asks, "Just a little hint, London. Please?"

London makes eye contact with the man for a moment, and she remembers him from yesterday, when he drove by her and waved. He's keeping a respectful distance as he snaps photos. London is charmed by this pap, like he was a big, slick haired baby.

"Okay," poor, stupid, easily fooled London Francis says, "But you have to promise to not put this on the internet until we make the announcement."

The secret vampires nod their head, and London declares, "We're starting a band!"

"What kind?" the businessman haired paparazzi asks quickly.

London is tripped up. She didn't expect this question. She's tries to think of the kinds of bands there are, but only comes up with "Britney Spears" and she's pretty sure a computer sings the songs, then they push Britney out on the stage to dance for an hour and twenty minutes. London assembles a group of vague words that come to her, "We're a... new... wave of rock band," she blurts out.

"You're starting a New Wave band?" the slicked haired man asks, as the bushy haired pap drops to his knees to try to film up London's skirt. London keeps her eyes on the kind chubster as she responds with vitriol, "That's what I said, isn't it?"

The chubby lowers his camera and stops walking. London looks back at him as the group continues to move toward her car. She sees him writing down what she just said. Maybe the little guy will be the first to break the story. She feels sort of sorry for the fat pap- he isn't a monster like the rest of the secret vampires. His only crime seems to be that he's fat, which is a felony crime in London's mind, but she's been convicted of felonies in the past and she doesn't consider herself a bad person.

"This whole thing seems a little weird," the bald pap says.

"What? We can't record music because we're girls? Your sexism is gross. Britney is a lady and people like her music," London says, giving them what they need.

"What's the name of your band?" the bald pap asks.

"Don't be a nosy little 'Kristen.' I don't like you anymore," London scolds the man. "We're holding auditions for the name right now," she adds, because naming a band seems hard and some virgin person on the internet would probably be really good at it. The blogs give the girls new nicknames all the time.

"You're auditioning names? What does that mean? Can people suggest names and you'll pick the most popular one?"

"Sure. Bye bye, bald man. This is my car with the parking ticket on it." London grabs the door handle on her Bentley.

"London, what about the ticket?" a paparazzi in a black track suit asks.

"It's okay I don't have to pay them," London says.

"I'm pretty sure you do," he responds.

"Okay. I'll look into it," London lies, then she gets into her Bentley. Immediately noticing the birds have pelted her windshield in her absence, London actives the wipers and they begin squeaking back and forth, sloshing blue liquid and bird shit across the secret vampires. The chubby paparazzi with the businessman haircut reappears, only to get hit by London's soggy parking ticket. He picks the ticket up while London is mashing on the window button to keep the toxic mixture from ricocheting onto her. The fat pap has only a brief moment to slide the ticket through the crack in the window so he makes his move. The window shuts with most of the ticket on the pap's side.

London reverses the car in a wild whip, and like the wishbone at Thanksgiving, the pap is left holding the big end of the soggy, torn ticket. A small sliver of the citation remains wedged in the window. The pap puts the piece of ticket in his pocket as he watches London get away. He hopes to see London again soon and he knows, no matter what, he will.

Later, sitting in traffic on the 405, London decides to put the window down so she can talk to the dog in the passenger seat of the car to her left. As the driver's side window slides down, a tiny slice of ticket falls in her lap. She picks up the piece of ticket and balls it up, then tosses it out the window. London notices that a business card had fallen into her lap as well. She picks it up and reviews it:

Martin Turner
Photographer
XV3 Photo Agency
323-555-7939

She looks at the back of the card, and in hurried script is the message, "I know that you don't know what New Wave music is."

London doesn't ball up the business card. She tenses up.

Martin Turner is a secret vampire and he can read London's mind.

OXYGEN WASTER
~~The Feckless Four~~ The Three AmigHo's Making Waves?

Oxygen Waster photographer, **Jimmy Pixx**, was on scene as **The Three AmigHos- Chloe Warren**, **Dakota Dabney**, and **London Francis**- were caught at a Wolfe-less brunch this morning.

When London made her way out of the restaurant, she was oddly solo and looking nervous, like she was being photographed for the first time. Jimmy acted fast and pumped London for all the secrets he could. Of course, she made the mistake of letting slip what this week's big announcement would be about! Jimmy outsmarted London Francis. What an accomplishment...

London makes for a bad human being, but she'd be an even worse spy given that after only a couple questions she admitted that The Three AmigHos are starting their own band.

These girls can't sing, nor can they play instruments, so how do they expect this to work?

Here's what has **OW** tingling about the whole situation though... London told our guy that they would be making New Wave music!? That's... sort of... awesome? Everyone seems a little nostalgic for 80's **LA**, minus the race riots, panic filled AIDS breakouts, and that unfashionable crack epidemic. Who better to bring back a decade of ridiculous style and self-absorbed excess than these three girls?

Like everything else that sounds vaguely promising in their lives, the girls will probably forget about this idea in a week, but the question now arises, what happens if they don't? What happens if they *do* learn how to play instruments and write songs? What if they're so good that they get on stage and perform in front of sold out crowds? What if it all doesn't suck?

Luckily, these thoughts won't ever have to be confronted, as they only exist in the stable safe category of "What if?"

But... what if we're wrong?

13- Life is About New.

London's maid, Alonja, rushes to the door before the doorbell finishes ringing. Ever since she was presented with the threat of being replaced by a poltergeist, Alonja has displayed extra effort to please Ms. Francis. It's not like being London's maid is a dream job, but most job postings don't start with, "Seeking an overweight illegal alien with a drinking problem." At least Alonja has the language barrier as an excuse for believing that a maid and a poltergeist are interchangeable.

As soon as Alonja cracks the huge wooden front door open, Chloe and Dakota burst inside. Chloe steadies the overweight El Salvadoran, then asks, "Where is she?"

"Upstairs, Ms. Warren."

"Thank you," Chloe says, then storms across the huge entryway, Dakota in tow.

Alonja follows the girls as they all sprint up the curved staircase in a race to reach London first. Chloe is motivated by anger. Alonja is motivated by fear. Dakota is motivated by the fact that she doesn't have anywhere to go tonight and she's hoping that London knows of a good party.

"Ms. Warren is here!" Alonja yells, bursting into London's room. The three dogs, two cats, and one bird on London's pink canopy bed all look to the door.

London is buried under a pile of pillows. She doesn't move in response to Alonja's screech.

Chloe walks into the room and looks at all the animals, each species appearing in a different number, like London was a retarded Noah.

Dakota appears next to Chloe, and they look at each other, then exchange a smile. Their brains are nearly synchronized, like their periods, so both girls know what must be done to wake up the sleeping stick-monster. Dakota flanks right, while Chloe opts for the left.

3-2-1... Both girls take off into the air and land squarely on either side of London. A muss of tangled extensions pops up from under the pink comforter and London lets out a battle cry of, "Whaaa-stoppp-ittt."

Both Dakota and Chloe get under the pillows, then burrow under the covers and pull London up by her armpits.

Groggy, makeup-less, and naked, London looks at the girls, then immediately tries to fall asleep sitting up. She almost succeeds. London possesses a rare ability that all her pets also have; she can fall in and out of consciousness in a matter of seconds. Sometimes she can even do it without the aid of prescription substances.

"Care to explain what a New Wave band is?" Dakota asks spitefully.

This is a sobering, eye opening question, and London is now totally awake, "You guys don't know?"

"No, London. Enlighten us," Chloe says.

"It's...uh..." London stalls, then yells, "Alonja!"

The maid hurriedly enters the room again.

"Bring me my laptop," London orders, then receives a dagger of a look that makes her add, "Please."

Alonja walks to the foot of the big bed, picks up a custom pink MacBook, then places it in London's lap.

"Please tell me you know what a New Wave band is," Dakota whines, "Please tell me that this is a real thing and not something you created in your little squirrel sized brain."

"Squirrels can grow to be up to 2 feet long," London says.

"I meant their brain size, not their body size," Dakota clarifies, but London shrugs it off with a pouty mention that, "The SPCA took away my squirrel."

"Right. So... New Wave?" Chloe asks, unmoved by London's perceived tragedy. London stares at her blankly, so Chloe grabs the computer, "Okay. Fine. I'll do your homework."

"New Wave" is searched.

The Wikipedia entry pops up, and Chloe silently digests the first paragraph, then paraphrases, "New Wave is an old genre of music from the 80's."

"No way! I thought I just totally made that shit up on the spot!" London says, slapping her long fingers together with a loud smack. The gesture sends thundering sound waves through the room. All the animals on the bed wake up, consider fleeing, then fall back asleep again.

Dakota sighs, then says, "80's music," with a disappointed tone. She tries to think about a song from the 80's. Unsure of how devastating their fate is, Dakota suggests, "London, call your mom, she was alive in the 80's."

"The math doesn't work out on that," London points out.

"I don't mean your stepmom, I mean your birth mother," Dakota tells her.

London shakes her head and whispers, "I found out my stepmom is a witch."

Through her giggles, Dakota asks, "So what's a New Wave band do?"

"It says here they mix punk rock, electronic music, and mod subculture," Chloe says.

"What's mod subculture?" Dakota asks.

"I think it's a typo. They mean modern subculture," London says.

"If you had to describe what modern subculture is..." Chloe trails off.

"I'd probably just give a round-about answer, then hug the next person that walked through the doorway like they were a friend I had been waiting all night for," London says.

"I sooo do that, too!" Dakota spurts out with a little bounce on the super soft mattress.

"I think I learned it from you," London tells Dakota with a nod.

"Aw. Wait. Okay. Google 'Modern Subculture,'" Dakota instructs Chloe.

Chloe types "Mod Subculture" into the search, then clicks on the first link, "Ohh! It's British!"

"Like Kate Moss?" Dakota and London both ask.

"Yeah, looks like it," Chloe says, closing the little window instead of reading the information that might disprove their assessment. Any music with a tinge of Kate Moss in it must be amazing. Just ask The Libertines. Or The Kills.

"It's perfect," Dakota says, grabbing her phone, then navigating to the notes she had made about the plan. "Alright, I'm making a 'To-Do' list. We need electronics, big hair, punk rock stuff, and we need to generally just act British."

"I don't know. Acting British didn't work well for Madonna," Chloe says.

"Alrighty, we'll just dress like New Wave British people then," Dakota says, then she modifies her entry.

"How do they dress?"

"I don't know, let's look at it later, I'm too tired from all this work we've been doing on the band," Dakota says, then the girls drift off to sleep in London's bed.

14- Predatory Pricing.

Tobe Price sits at the foot of his bed and uses his phone to photograph his freshly dyed roots. He wants to make sure the blond is uniform before the hairdresser he sleeps with on a monthly basis is kicked out of his penthouse. Once satisfied with his hair, Tobe takes out one of the shoe boxes from under his bed. After popping its top, he begins to flip through the loose, carefully extracted pages that are stacked four inches high. The articles about him just feel like clutter now. What he's looking for are the pictures of Sienna- that delicate, misunderstood little girl. She hides behind jokes, like the kid that was picked on all through high school because she was different.

Sienna *was* different in school, but she was on the other side of it all. She was the queen. Having money and no awkward phase is a lethal combination when you're a teen. In Sienna's case, she had to be funny because otherwise people would've thought she was stuck-up. If she couldn't laugh, and make people laugh, then everyone would say she's fake and egotistical. Sienna is only one of those things.

Tobe knows about Sienna's high school days because of all of the interviews in his boxes. He's taken the time to cull through everything, and he's paid attention to every word, back-checking it against all the information he's been able to compile previously. His conclusion is that at the bottom of this monument of physical perfection is a sensitive little girl.

As the hairdresser announces that breakfast is served, Tobe hides the shoebox and grabs his phone.

Sitting out on his balcony, Tobe uses his bookmarks to track the most recent developments in his Wolfe hunt. He mulls over his lost opportunity to realize his dream at Lindy's party. Tobe did everything right, Sienna did everything wrong, and they both wish things had turned out differently that night. Tobe was nice to Sienna's friend, London, at the divorce gala. He sat out there on that stupid balcony with her. He spent his night drinking her bad vodka out of a fucking candle jar just to keep her smiling. He held her smoke and vomit smelling extensions back as she unloaded the contents of her stomach onto the ground below, as well as onto his Gucci patent leather oxfords. Tobe didn't even send London a bill for the shoes. They were really nice shoes.

The divorce gala, and its aftermath, bothered Tobe. The thought that someone as essential as Sienna Wolfe could be thrown to the curb, both physically (Lindy's party), and mentally (the girls exiling her), was a shining example of why a New York boy like Tobe despises Los Angeles.

He hates the traffic, and the bums, and the gangs, and the tourists, and, most of all, the girls.

As Tobe reads ugly words about pretty people, it occurs to him how to make an undeniable first impression on Sienna.

Tobe Price will not only right the universe, but he'll also have Sienna Wolfe calling him after he's finished. She'll ask if he wants to meet up for a cocktail, and he'll pat the top of his perfect hair, he'll smirk with pride at his genius, then he'll tell Sienna that they have reservations for 9 PM at CARGO.

It's a good thing that London programmed her number into Tobe's phone.

London had ruined something of Tobe's, now it's time for Tobe to even the score.

15- When A Semi-Stranger Calls.

The vibration of a phone wakes Dakota up. She sleepily looks to the foot of the bed just to make sure the rhythmic hum isn't one of the animals about to barf. Most of the ark attendants are still asleep, so Dakota begins searching through the sheets for the trembling phone. Finally locating the pink encased cell, Dakota looks at the screen and sees that it's Tobe Price calling.

This kind East Coast boy is extending an olive branch when the girls need it the most.

"Shit," Dakota says, then pushes London into Chloe.

"London. London. London!" Dakota chants successively louder.

London's vibrating cell is placed in her hand, causing her to sit up quickly. A vibrating phone is a girl's Prince Charming; it will always wake the sleeping beauty.

"It's Tobe Price!" London says, instantly peppy when she sees the name on the screen.

"Answer it!" Dakota commands. She likes Tobe Price because he seems like one of those guys who's wild in bed, and he'd know how to do the *hot choking* and not the, "Ow, fuck, please stop," choking. Dakota had spoken with him at length during one of London's perfume launches in New York. Some party planning genius had filled a fountain with London Francis brand perfume and everyone's eyes were bloodshot from the rolling vapors. The tabloids had a field day with the pictures, and they were able to put about ten different people in "off the wagon" features. At the party, even though Tobe probably *was* high, in addition to just *looking* high, he would laugh at things Dakota said- when he was supposed to and sometimes when he wasn't. He was fun enough to allow himself to be photographed in the middle of a less than flattering laugh at an event where everyone was trying to prove they weren't faded. It was a momentary crack in his Teflon coating and it won Dakota over. If Tobe could stop being an apathetic statue for a moment so that a mutual friend's haircut could be brutally ridiculed, it proved that he could hang with the girls.

"You will be ignored," London says, putting the phone on the bed, not sending the call directly to voicemail, but not answering it either.

"Are you insane?" Dakota asks.

"No. I can't answer it right now. I'll call him back."

"Don't do this high school 'I need to wait three days before calling back' shit."

London's hooded eyes look to Dakota, and she explains, "I'm not talking to him now because I just woke up from a nap, which means I have man-voice."

"Oh. Okay. At least that makes sense. You do have man-voice," Dakota responds.

The phone buzzes again, this time with a text. Dakota glances at the screen, "Hope U ignored me b/c u girls r2 busy gettin beautiful for Diego's premiere party tonight."

"He wants to see me again!" London says.

"This is the perfect rebranding night for us, there's that dumb reality show party tonight," Dakota says.

This is a party that they aren't formally invited to. Yet. The girls dropped Sienna, so it's time for Diego to drop his issues with the girls. Lindy's party was old news and the only people who read old news are old losers who purchase newspapers. Dakota is young and she has something to do tonight. It's time to make today's news.

"Tobe picked *me* out of all the cool slutty girls he knows to join him at a party!" London realizes aloud. She feels very excited to have a new slice of perfection to be photographed alongside.

"This is the first day of our non-loathworthy lives," Dakota says, getting out of the bed.

"Wakey, wakey, it's time for a party," London whispers into Chloe's ear.

"We must skip it," Chloe tiredly declares.

"Nope!" London responds, then hops out of bed, still naked. She quickly snatches the comforter from Chloe, and the animals scatter off the end of the bed in a scene that looks like a vaguely disastrous magic trick.

"Come on, you can wear one of my dresses," London says.

This raises Chloe from her slumber. It's true, Chloe *could* fit into one of London Francis' designer masterpieces. A couple months ago, this would be unfathomable.

Instantly energized, London puts on a bra and underwear, then starts laying options out on the bed for the girls. All of the dresses seem pretty slutty, but that's only because London is a giant, so she's chosen the super short pieces for the other girls. If she took out one of her flowy dresses, the girls would look like five year olds playing dress up with their mother's clothes.

The thought of being London's daughter horrifies the girls. They noticed that her perpetually stressed out cat, James Dean, was mysteriously missing from the bed today.

London gets another text and she doesn't even read it. She knows that it's from Tobe.

"Wouldn't miss it 4 the world. We're picking up the outfits we had made," London texts blindly, while Dakota tosses away a bunch of dresses London has already been photographed wearing. Dakota looks for pieces still in the plastic garment bag or with a tag.

"Let's get each other ready tonight. None of our makeup girls, none of our stylists. Let's pretend it's eighth grade again," Chloe suggests.

"Why?" London asks.

Chloe quietly responds, "Because we didn't know Sienna in eighth grade."

15.5- Reality Tell.

Dakota changes in London's shoe closet so she can have a moment of privacy. She's chosen a strapless white Balmain mini dress that laces up in the back. As the laces hang loose, she tries to pretend that she's getting ready for an eighth grade dance. No one ever writes mean shit about you after a school dance. On the off chance something awful is written, it's usually only in a diary that isn't even read by the author.

Dakota drifts out of the makeshift changing room. Her arms hug her big boobs so the dress doesn't fall, like it did that one time on the red carpet for that River White movie about some sort of sad supernatural creature.

London's room is spacious and oddly dark. A giant TV faces the bed and soundlessly plays an animal show- this one is about wolverines. To the left of the bed is a wall that London's heavily coached interior designer has lined with pictures of various editorials and ad campaigns that London was able to book. On the right side of the bed is an ornate vanity that Dakota recalls seeing in Kristen's house before. It's difficult to ascertain whether London purchased an identical vanity (not likely), or if she hired Mexicans to move the furniture out of the Paxton mansion after Kristen was exiled from the girls' circle (likely).

London looks Dakota over, then purrs, "Cuteee," obviously approving of the dress. She grabs a pink straightener off the possibly stolen vanity, then informs Dakota, "We're doing your hair down tonight."

"If that's a London Francis brand straightener, you do not have permission to use that on me. I hear burning to death is, like, in the top five for shittiest deaths," Dakota says, then she cautiously sits down in front of the large mirror. She lays her phone close by so she can monitor it for texts about better parties than Diego's.

"I'd never keep something as dangerous as a London Francis straightener in my house," London responds, then begins to work on Dakota's chocolate locks.

Chloe walks next to London so that she can lace Dakota's dress up, then she grabs onto the straps, and says, "Tell me when you can't breathe anymore."

Before Dakota can be tied off, her phone jitters on the vanity, so Chloe puts one of the dress straps in her mouth, and uses her free hand to grab the phone. Dakota can't lean over to answer the call or the lacing would go slack, so with the strap still clenched in her teeth, Chloe puffs out the name on the caller ID, "Tindery Carter."

Dakota grabs the phone because she doesn't know any Carters, but she would like to.

"Hello?" Dakota squeaks, answering the phone at precisely the same time Chloe pulls her dress straps extra hard.

"Hi. I know it's totally insane to call you right after I texted London..." Lindy Porter begins, "...but I wanted to let you know that I'm going to be at Diego's tonight too. I think, maybe, it will be better to get all the weirdness out of the way beforehand, over the phone."

"Oh, don't worry about what happened the other night, we don't blame you," Dakota says with a laugh.

"Righttt. Okay. Good," Lindy's responds to a statement she definitely wasn't expecting.

"It's Sienna's fault, I think we can all agree about that," Dakota says.

"Oh!" Lindy gasps, perking up after hearing the exact name she was worried about, "I read on *FameDi-*"

"-yeah, all true. She won't be coming tonight."

"I'm sorry to hear that," Lindy says. She's not sorry to hear it, but she acknowledges that Sienna was Dakota's best friend up until the divorce party disaster. Lindy knows it's not easy to lose your best friend. At least Dakota didn't have to catch Sienna in the middle of a gay sex act in Paris. Delightful pre-divorce memories.

As Chloe finishes with the lacing on the dress, Dakota finishes the call.

London and Chloe disappear into London's shoe closet to find the perfect shoes to complete the outfit, but Dakota remains seated at the vanity. She studies her reflection, silently acknowledging that this is the first dress she won't be sending Sienna a picture of before the party. She wonders if Sienna would hate what she's wearing. The tightly tied straps will be the only thing holding Dakota together tonight.

16- Showing Howard Hues.

Chloe returns home, as Stanley, unaware of her presence, sits on the white sofa in the living room and hammers keys on his laptop. Chloe sneaks up behind him, drops her garment bag, then wraps her arms around Stanley's broad shoulders. This would startle a normal person, but Stanley was a teen heartthrob so girls randomly hopping onto his back had become part of sitting, or walking down the street, or weighing a bag of produce at the supermarket. Stanley rubs his two day stubble on Chloe's arm, making her giggle, but she pulls away because she doesn't want her tan skin to show an irritated discoloration in the pictures.

"Look... at this!" Chloe says, grabbing the garment bag, then flopping it on the sofa.

"Great, a body-bag. Like I don't see enough of those at work," Stanley says, briefly glancing over, then going back to his laptop screen.

Chloe walks around the sofa, then quickly slides off the garment bag and exposes the dress London gave her. "Ta da!"

Stanley takes his eyes away from the screen in the way that a parent being beckoned by their child would review a shitty drawing of the family cat surrounded by disproportionately large balloons.

Chloe holds the short, gold sequin Emporio Armani bandeau dress up in front of her forced-thin body.

"Mmm," Stanley responds, interested, "You should wear that tonight," he says, raising an eyebrow.

"I am! It's going to be so fun. I mean sure we might have to be subjected to some of Diego's show, but if we just face the screen when we have conversations, we'll be fine."

"Wait. What? That's an outside of the bedroom dress?" Stanley asks, the smile falling from his face.

"Tonight is Diego Mestizo's premiere party for his new show."

Stanley closes his eyes, almost as if to mentally prepare himself for the fight that's about to commence.

"No. No. No," Chloe repeats, dropping the dress on the floor.

Eyes shut, fingers on the keyboard, Stanley tells her, "I'm making progress. Please don't make me go. It will interrupt my flow."

"Interrupt your flow? Did you just say that? Did you really just say that?" This comes out as a yell because Stanley can't see Chloe so she has to be extra loud to accurately convey her dissatisfaction.

"I'm making progress," Stanley says, his fingers tensing on the keyboard.

"So you're just going to sit in front of your computer? Again? Instead of acting like a normal human being, you're going to stay home and do nothing?" Chloe continues her tirade.

Stanley finally opens his eyes, then turns to Chloe and in a quiet, intense, metered voice, he says, "I knew you thought that. I saw that you didn't believe me about Lindy, and now you don't believe that I have a purpose beyond moping around in some silly teen drama or hatcheting off a monster's arm. I have experiences, Chloe. And I have a personal life that I've kept personal. Just because you didn't read about me every day in the blogs doesn't mean I was the kid next door. I'm not some fucking loser."

Chloe's demeanor softens a bit when she realizes her needling got too sharp and cut Stanley pretty bad, "Aw. I know you're-"

"-no. Don't aw. Don't aw that. Come on, Chloe."

"Stanley, you're taking this in a totally different direction."

"What direction did you plan on this conversation going?" Stanley asks.

"I don't know. The direction of the door, so we can leave," Chloe mumbles.

"I'm not going."

"People are going to talk."

"They'll talk no matter what."

Put off by Stanley's passive attitude in the wake of some of Chloe's most aggressive and manipulative defenses, she explodes, "Awesome, Stanley. Make sure you put this in your mystery project so you can clear everything up for people years after the fact. That's going to help. I'll just let everyone know that it may appear awkward that my boyfriend refuses to be seen with me at an event that has any photographic devices beyond a gas station security camera, but two years from now, it will all make sense."

"Oh please. Look at the blogs. There are pictures of us from last week."

"Paparazzi pictures of us entering and leaving a bunch of stores."

"Yes. Public places."

"Thank God for the paps because without them, we wouldn't have any pictures of us together," Chloe says.

After scooping her dress off the ground, Chloe storms away, buttoning the conversation with a slamming of the front door. She walks out. She leaves the house. She could never walk out-walk out. She could never leave-leave. She knows this. Stanley does too. This is why the girls mean so much to Chloe. They could leave, and that's scary.

17- Being Kristen is No Longer "Kristen."

Chloe made sure that Brent was her driver tonight.

A salt and pepper haired black man with a quiet demeanor, Brent is the driver of choice for the girls when they have to do something private. Brent is aware of *the history* these girls carry. He chose to dump whatever B-list zero he was driving tonight and pick up Chloe on short notice because he knows that when he's called, he's needed.

In the back of the town car, Chloe catches up with Brent and types the names of his kids into her phone for reference the next time she uses him.

"Could you get off there?" Chloe asks, her arm pointing toward the windshield, gesturing to the right.

"Of course," Brent says, taking the exit. He doesn't make a comment. He knows where they're going.

"We'll make a quick stop off at Kristen's house," Chloe says. It feels redundant, but the driver needs his destination. Chloe doesn't want to get Brent involved in the situation so she doesn't elaborate further. Brent doesn't say anything, his eyes remain on the road.

Chloe looks out the tinted window at the dulled sunset, and she reminds Brent, "LA is a Pet Semetery."

A small silence begins to balloon in the car, then Brent asks, "How's Ms. Francis?"

This is a tool he's fashioned over the years. He's keeping his distance from whatever story could be unfolding in the back of his car. An experienced career driver, Brent is painfully aware that the less he knows, the less likely it is he'll give into temptation and exchange his trust for a quick check. He's really trying to do the right thing by knowing as little about everything as he possibly can. He's sort of like Stanley in a way.

"London is really good," Chloe says, believing it. "She'll be there tonight. She's going with Tobe Price."

"That's an interesting couple," Brent says, but not until he's safely stopped at a red light. He's learned to make sure the car isn't moving when discussing London's boys. Sometimes a small fact about London's personal life will be followed up with an unfathomable story that mutes everything else going on. For a while, the same thing could be said about Kristen, but Brent wasn't the one saying it. He considers himself neither the judge, nor the jury- he's only worried about getting his client to court early.

As they begin moving again, Chloe looks down at her phone. She wonders if she should be texting the other girls to let them know what she's doing. She types out the text, then deletes it.

Chloe hugs her dress tight as they approach the gate of Kristen's house. Brent speaks quickly and efficiently into Kristen's intercom, then he's promptly let inside the gates by a familiar voice. Brent didn't mention Chloe's name and, at first, the omission seemed like the most deceitful thing Brent had ever done.

As they slowly move up the driveway, Chloe realizes that Brent did the right thing. By announcing Chloe's presence, he would've become the messenger. Brent is not the messenger, he's just the driver; it's up to Chloe to make her presence known.

Brent's miles are badges of experience that allow him to continue successfully at his profession.

As the car comes to a stop, Chloe leans up toward the front seat. "I'll be no more than a half hour," she promises, then she quickly pops the door open before Brent even unbuckles his seat belt. She doesn't want him to get out for a pointless moment. It's going to be a toss up if Chloe will even be allowed inside the Paxton mansion.

The dress that Stanley loved, then hated, remains in Chloe's arms. She *will* wear it tonight, with Kristen as an accessory, and the two reunited friends *will* effortlessly walk into The Pit. They won't force their way in; they'll practically be pushed inside. Chloe's sure of this, but she's not sure why she's so confident about an imagined fact. She clings to this fantasy because it's guided her to Kristen's doorstep and it hasn't failed her yet.

With a deep breath, Chloe raises her arm and knocks on the large wooden door.

Nothing.

Another set of knocks.

Nothing.

She tries the handle.

The door is unlocked, and Chloe views this as an invitation. Kristen has always locked her doors in the past. Pushing the door open, Chloe peeks inside, and except for a couple of wall sconces that illuminate the cranberry fabric wall cover in the entrance way, it's completely dark in the Paxton mansion. Chloe walks inside and shuts the door behind her, then waits for Kristen to appear. The faint sound of a piano is the soundtrack to this breaking and entering... this entering and re-assembly?

Chloe tries to remember if Kristen owns a piano. Maybe she traded London her dresser for it? If a piano *is* in this house, it would just be something to rest a wine glass on. Chloe sets her dress on the back of an armchair, then makes a decision to continue with her plan.

Using her memory of Kristen's carefully planned house, Chloe navigates through a series of dark, well lived-in rooms, until she reaches the library. Her heels go quiet on the carpet as she walks into a high ceilinged space filled with so many books that if Kristen was bedridden for the rest of her life, she wouldn't even get through half of them. Unlike most socialites, Kristen would probably get pretty close to the halfway point on these shelves because she actually completed high school in the old fashion style of class attendance and testing- how painfully last decade.

At the far end of the library, Kristen sits alone, playing the piano. Chloe's sure Kristen couldn't play the piano before she was "Kristen," but now that Kristen is "Kristen," Kristen can. The girls told the blogs that Kristen had changed, but this isn't what they meant. It's hard to hold a talent like this over someone's head. No marriage has ever ended in a giant fight when one partner exclaims, "You finger those keys more than you finger me!"

The sweeping waves of Kristen's imperfect practicing manage to calm Chloe as she walks slowly and silently toward the black piano. Atop the piano is a bottle of wine. Chloe was half right, but it feels weird being only half right about someone she knows everything about.

Hair in a high blonde bun, eyes on the sheet music, Kristen says, "I told you that I don't use Brent anymore. I gave him to the girls."

"How about sharing him tonight?" Chloe asks, and Kristen swings around with a look of horror on her face. "Holy shit," Kristen yelps, "You scared me... I thought you were... someone else."

"I didn't know it was possible to scare the Phantom of the Opera," Chloe jokes.

Kristen lets out a little laugh, "The Phantom of the Opera played the organ."

Chloe furrows her brow, "No way! I mean, my Aunt Agnes played the organ and she was a saint."

"The same aunt who left you the oil painting of Tom Selleck in her will?" Kristen asks.

"Oh yeah, I forgot about that. I guess she was pretty creepy," Chloe says, then she immediately senses that Kristen is weighing a decision. There are two paths that Kristen can take. She could look back on this memory with nostalgia, thus returning to a time when she and Chloe were inseparable, or she could turn off the little projector playing back the moment, then show the audience out of the theater. Chloe needs Kristen to stay with her, otherwise she'll have to walk out of the house knowing that her friend is gone for good, and Aunt Agnes killed herself because the people who were supposed to care about her, didn't.

"Remind me again, what did you do with that painting?" Kristen asks, staying seated, her lips holding in a smile.

Chloe puts on a fake annoyance, "Ugh. Kristen. Okay. I might have, possibly, given the painting to a homeless person in Redondo Beach."

"An oil painting of Tom Selleck is the worst gift ever. The only way to make it even more terrible is to give it to a person who doesn't have any walls," Kristen says, then she lets a laugh burst out. Chloe giggles and reaches for the bottle of wine on the piano, then takes a sip.

"I remember all the-" Kristen says, but then can't control her growing laughter. Taking breaks to get through the sentence, she recalls, "I remember... they... the paps, asked the bum where he was going to hang... hang the painting... and he set Tom up above his pile of shit... like a picture... like a picture of Jesus watching over him," Kristen says, gasping for air, while Chloe has to put the bottle back because she's afraid she'll spit wine while laughing.

This is how things turned out for the girls. There was the PR nightmare of giving a homeless person home furnishings, but as soon as the story was buried by new posts on the blogs, it was just a happy, funny memory they have of their time together. Every moment of their friendship has been captured by strangers, so even if their recollection is fuzzy, the internet can remind them in an instant search.

Kristen allows this moment to happen, and she instantly feels like she made the right choice. It's funny how quickly the two girls could drop back into being the best of friends.

Kristen wipes the tears of laughter out of her eyes and, now wearing camouflage, she remembers that the world is more than two girls, "They're going to hate you for this."

"No, they aren't," Chloe says, as though she's the general of this socialite army. If Chloe's going to call the war off, her troops should just be happy that they can go back to their old life, with their old friends.

"They won't forgive me... I don't blame them," Kristen says, wiping away a final, ambiguous tear.

Chloe had considered this, but recent events have led her to believe that there's nowhere to hide in this city, and every issue will have to be confronted eventually. "We realized that pushing you away was the wrong way to handle your situation," Chloe softballs.

"You were right to push me away. I fucked up."

"We all fuck up. It's what we do," Chloe responds with an edge.

"We fuck up in the opinion of other people. I fucked up in your opinion," Kristen says, her shoulders retreating into her body.

"Yeah, well."

"I'm better now," Kristen tells herself, her form returning back to a recognizable human figure.

"I know."

"He's helping," Kristen whispers, aware that the entire world knows who *he* is, but she's still not comfortable with talking about him at a regular volume.

"Johnny seems like a good guy," Chloe says.

"You've met him?"

"Not extensively, but I've read stuff."

"Oh, and that's how you get to know someone, right?" Kristen says, a little defensive.

"If the blogs can't find shit on him, you know he must be saintly."

"Or they haven't found it yet."

"Have you?"

"No."

"Then, what's the problem?"

"No problem," Kristen says, shaking her head.

"Was he coming over tonight?"

"I thought you were him."

"I could be him tonight," Chloe responds.

Kristen lets out a steam-release of a laugh.

"Come with me to Diego's party tonight," Chloe asks her friend, getting down on her knees so she's below the still seated Kristen.

"For his reality show? Ugh, no."

"So you're still reading the rags?"

"Old habits..." Kristen says.

Chloe looks at the wine bottle. Kristen looks at Chloe's tummy.

"Truce," they say, simultaneously, as their demons push them together, toward peace.

18- Living Assisted Reality.

The cameras are rolling at The Pit tonight. Vague waivers have been initialed by everyone in attendance just so they could get inside the cold concrete walls. The agents and managers had worked out prices with CTV beforehand, and the girls are blissfully unaware that everything in this room is the result of careful orchestration and a lofty appearance fee.

Appearance fees, a guest spot on a show that will be canceled by midnight, bringing sand to the beach; none of it matters. Tonight is about reinvention, not repetition.

Dakota and London assume that Tobe's +1, and his bonus +1 for just being Tobe, are what got them into the party, so they stay close to him.

Tobe's blond hair is flopped in reliable perfection as he makes his way through the crowd with a girl on each arm. This steadying force makes London feel safe at an event filled with potential ways to get into trouble. Tobe's securing gesture allows her to feel permanent at a celebration for a temporary show. By first reaching out a hand, then locking a toned arm with Dakota, Tobe has provided some much needed relief during a nervous time. As a girl who's always worried about the plumplife of her lip injections, a little permanence for Dakota is nice once and a while. Tobe Price has always been considered cold and uncaring so the fact that he doubled back for three girls everyone else was anxious to abandon made a statement to the crowd at The Pit tonight.

As Tobe excuses himself from the chain to get the girls some drinks, he calls over Lindy Porter to take his place. Lindy is showing off her big fake boobs in a severe necklined Zac Posen dress and her hair is pulled back tight against her skull so she looks very surprised by everything. "So they're filming a reality show at the premiere of the same reality show?" Lindy asks Dakota, while the cameras swoop in and circle the girls like curious vultures.

"I know, I feel like we're about fall into a black hole," Dakota responds.

"This show is going to be sooo 'Sienna,'" London says, then she spots Mr. Porter. London knows that it's very important to show that the girls are at the party, but they're not the "party girls" everyone once knew. She wants to make it clear that they're still great room fillers, but they're no longer room destroyers. Ron Porter greets the lanky socialite with a wide smile on his cheery, bloated, red-under-the-tan face that most men in this city acquire when they hit 60. Immediately addressing her embarrassing past, London says, quietly, "I had Joel cover the power washing bill your secretary sent over."

"She sent you a bill?" Mr. Porter asks, taken aback. "That woman. Well, you know how *they* can be," Mr. Porter remarks about his secretary Kat Greenberg.

"Oh, I know, secretaries act like they have a mind of their own sometimes," London responds.

Mr. Porter eyes the HD camera as it finds London again, then he smiles a big smile to keep up his public image. He's also smiling because he got away with his anti-Semitic remark. Even if it makes the show, London's obliviousness will outshine his comment's offensiveness.

Cutting in front of London, Dakota hesitantly approaches Mr. Porter. He immediately breaks up the awkwardness by telling Dakota, "I'm sorry to hear about what happened with your father," then he follows it up by giving her a hug. Scarlett keeps Mr. Porter abreast of all the goings on at his house so that he can combat any potential lawsuits or pap questions that might pop up.

"I'm sorry about..." Dakota says, trailing off, holding the embrace a moment too long.

Mr. Porter senses something's wrong so he steps back and holds Dakota by her waist. He looks the off-kilter socialite in the eyes with a searching review. Dakota's dark eyeshadow makes her eyes look like glass marbles sitting on a city street, and Mr. Porter is reminded what it's be like to be a confused, excited, bored kid.

"I feel like my pit bull attacked your family," Dakota says, moving away from Mr. Porter hands. She fears he noticed just how wobbly she is without her best friend's inconsistency keeping her on her toes. Immediately locking hands with Lindy to show Mr. Porter that everything is okay now, Dakota takes another shot at being *okay* tonight. She usually doesn't search for *okay*, but at this party it's an ambitious goal.

Mr. Porter looks fondly upon his baby girl, Lindy. She's *his* girl again. He had finally reclaimed her from a man who had a bigger fortune than Mr. Porter himself. Nothing makes a white man's face redder than fortune envy... besides alcoholism. Maybe Mr. Porter can blame his coloring on residual jealousy, then they'll stop calling him a booze hound.

Fixated on Dakota's dog bite statement, London scolds her friend, "You do realize that not all pitbulls are aggressive and the actions of few get placed on the entire lot?"

"Yeah," Mr. Porter clears his throat, "I've heard that defense used before, although it wasn't about dogs and it had to do with the theft of my SLS."

Lindy sighs, then leans back and asks London, "Where's Chloe?"

Mr. Porter takes this time to split away from the camera and head to the bar. If he wasn't scolded for making overtly inappropriate remarks yet, he clearly could finish off a couple more Manhattans to no detriment.

"Chloe's convincing Stanley to come," Dakota says.

"Stanley's not coming. He's not a socialite, he's an actor," Lindy responds dismissively.

"Well... then he should be able to *act* like a socialite," London decides. She takes a test sip of a mystery drink that may or may not have been provided to her by a staff member at The Pit, then things start to feel easier.

"Is it because of me? Is he avoiding me?" Lindy asks, making it all about her, as she tends to do. It's a blogtality that so many of London's friends now possess. The poison pens of these bloggers are able to make *anything* look like it's a celebrity's fault, and since the girls all read these posts, they can't help but sop up this way of thinking.

"It's not about you or whatever naughtiness you two did. If I had to avoid every person I've banged, I'd have to move to Canada," London declares, then takes a large gulp of a drink she can't name, but can verify will "get the job done."

No one reacts to London's comment so she tacks on, "Well, I'd still have to avoid Vancouver and Toronto, but the Yukon and Alaska are on the table."

"Alaska is part of America," Lindy says.

"Still?" London asks, like Alaska continued living with her parents even after she turned 18 and got the bank code to her trust fund.

Dakota smiles wide, not at London's comment, but because Lindy verbally confirmed the *Page 6* rumor about her fling with Stanley. Lindy is worried that Stanley is avoiding her. She seems to almost miss him. Maybe Stanley misses Lindy a bit too? Maybe it hurts him to see what a mess she got herself into? Suddenly feeling for Chloe's boy, her honest boy, Dakota says, "He's Stanley. He's America's sweetheart. It's different with him."

London makes a disgusted face after downing the rest of her drink, then warns Dakota, "He'd kill you if he heard you saying that."

"No, he wouldn't. He genuinely *is* a really big sweetheart," Lindy says. Her tone is that of a woman who escaped a relationship without a bruise on her face, wrist, or ego.

"Obviously, but he'd think really hard about killing you and maybe sketch a picture of it in his journal," Dakota says, then she sports a sly smile.

London giggles, realizing that she's already beginning to feel a buzz from the drink. This sensation reminds her of the Porter's balcony so she eyes the crowd until she finds where Tobe ran off to. He's standing in the corner doing an awkward interview. He looks even blonder than before, but London assumes it's from the bright lights shining above him as he addresses the camera like he's recording a video guest book at a stranger's wedding.

Lindy and London walk toward the corner because Tobe's perfect indifference is like a magnet.

Dakota finds herself suddenly alone, but before she can feel abandoned, a pair of large arms snake around her. Unlike every girl in a music video that this happens to, she doesn't relax into the grasp, instead she pops away from it.

"Dakota. It's me. I didn't mean to scare you," Jake Wesley apologizes. He raises his hands, but it's more of a cease-fire than a surrender. He's dressed in a half formal, half rocker outfit and only half of it works. There aren't very many frontman/lineman combinations in the world for a reason. The rock look only works on boys that look like girls, not boys who are men.

"Your giant superhuman arms almost squished me, how could I not be scared?" Dakota's smoky voice meters up to an eventual squeak. She's mean, yet flirtatious, as she bats her glued on eyelashes at a man who wants to continue this conversation, no matter the topic.

"Are you scared enough that lunch is canceled tomorrow?" Jake's deep voice asks her. He takes a drink from one of the servers, and Dakota realizes that she hasn't had a drink the entire time she's been at the party. She also realizes she'd forgotten about the lunch date she made at Lindy's party. At least Jake hasn't seen the clip yet. Dakota keeps replaying the hug she just got, and each time it ends with her eyeballs popping out of their sockets from Jake's anaconda-like grip, so she enthusiastically accepts the invitation. "Can't wait for our lunch! Would it be okay if I brought the girls, though?" She asks, seeing a promo opportunity.

"You can bring as many girls as you want," Jake says, arching his eyebrows.

"You're gross," Dakota counters, then grabs the drink out of his giant paw.

"I'm just trying to catch up with your number of female conquests," Jake says, acting like a cat playfully prodding a bunny.

The bunny, possibly due to the friendly pussy reminding her how long it's been since she's found some friendly pussy, bites back at her physically imposing taunter, hissing, "Don't be mad that I've had more female partners than you have female readers."

"Ohhh," Jake moans, as he grasps his chest like the words bore directly into his heart. He stumbles around in a circle, holding the dramatic pose. Conversations stop as everyone's attention begins to focus on the scene. Dakota's face goes red- as red as Mr. Porter's face under that faux tan. Jake holds his giant man peck until his circular stumble reaches back to Dakota, then, smiling at the confused socialite, he straightens his posture and fixes the collar of the Just Cavalli leather jacket that he's wearing over a white Brioni dress shirt. By the time the cameramen can reach this situation, it's no longer an attention grabbing outburst.

Jake slowly raises his hand up to Dakota's cheek. Her entire body starts buzzing. Everyone in the room holds their breath as they anticipate the kiss- a connection between two absolutely stalkable people.

Jake leans in close, then moves past Dakota's waiting lips, and whispers in her ear, "Tag. You're it."

After pulling away, and straightening his red Brooks Brothers tie, Jake flashes a smile at the camera, then drifts into the crowd. Dakota looks around, at all of the eyes not following Jake. Not only did that asshole make her look ridiculous, but he also made her fall in love with him.

There's only one other person that can make a big, terrible scene in a goodhearted way like that, and she's no longer in Dakota's life.

19- The Prodigal Moon.

Arm in arm, Kristen Paxton and Chloe Warren make their flash filled way to The Pit. Before they reach security, Diego bursts through a line of nobodies, then pauses a moment so the guy hoisting a boom mic can get out of the cameraman's shot. Both girls pause their strut, then direct smiles to the camera as they try to interpret Diego's manic coke-stare.

Kristen is happy that she's being greeted at the door.

Chloe feels like this is where her night ends.

All Diego cares about is if his producers have the definitive footage of this blockbuster story.

"You're back!" Diego announces, arms wide open as he approaches the girls. He traps them in a double hug that won't be broken until the paps snap a couple hundred photos. Diego continues the hug while sidestepping to the right so that the entire extended moment will be framed in front of a giant poster advertising his new show.

Diego is impressed with Kristen Paxton. The *new* Kristen.

She has the same blonde hair, same boxy face with the same deceptively innocent smile, same bony body that seems to float with an invisible mist of *softness*, yet the wild look in her eyes is tempered, under control, restrained.

Kristen is familiar, yet new.

Diego leads his old/new friend inside, and Kristen yanks Chloe with her. Part of Kristen refuses to let go of the scary suspicion that this might be a set up, but that part isn't as big as this second chance is.

"Will your band do a song for my show?" Diego begs Chloe.

"No, probably not," Chloe answers back flatly.

"I respect that, but I'm still going to tell people you're scoring the second half of the season," Diego says.

"Knock yourself out."

"I love you girls! Not so much Sienna, but it seems that you've euthanized that problem," Diego affirms, as London appears by his side.

"You shouldn't euthanize a problem," London says, as thoughts of puppies in ovens dance through her head. She had approached this situation to ask Chloe what the fuck she was doing, but embracing classic avoidance tactics, another conversation option arrived and she hopped on it. As the group moves toward the center of The Pit, they *become* the center of The Pit.

"Don't worry. I'm not judging, I get it," Diego whispers to Chloe, then he smartly makes his exit before Vietnam II happens. The cameras continue to follow the group of socialites so the girls weave through the party, attempting to lose their tail like a cat caught in a closing storm door.

"Oh my. Vanessa Thach is here," Kristen says, as they pass a table stacked with nearly shirtless men.

"She's banged every guy sitting at that table," Chloe notes, then tags on, "And it's not even a totally accurate representation of the big picture. There are only so many chairs you can put around a table."

Kristen looks away from gross Vanessa and, suddenly, the moment she feared presents itself without warning. Kristen isn't sure what to do, so she simply greets the moment with a friendly, "Hi."

Dakota turns quickly, a familiar voice commanding her attention. She gasps, then melts her shock into a smile. "Hi," Dakota responds, caught completely off guard, yet experienced enough with handling people popping up unannounced that she doesn't flinch. Immediately noticing that Chloe and Kristen are bonded together, Dakota politely asks, "Could we borrow Chloe for a minute, Kristen?"

Kristen looks at the ground and swallows hard as her arm unhooks from Chloe's. Chloe whispers something into Kristen's ear, then she follows London and Dakota back into the mess of people.

Lindy happily stands by to keep Kristen company. Now that Kristen is in a committed relationship and Lindy no longer has to hold onto that anger of what happened during her rocky marriage, the friction between these girls transforms into glue. Kristen has returned to the party, literally, with Chloe. This type of healing is exactly what a freshly divorced Lindy needs. Without looking at each other, Lindy and Kristen lock hands.

They're okay, together.

At the edge of the party, Dakota and London push Chloe toward the bathroom because there's nowhere else this discussion can take place without all of it being filmed.

Inside an overly graffitied stall, the three girls stand around a toilet covered in band stickers and, finally, Dakota explodes, "What the fuck are you doing?"

"Investing in our future," Chloe says sternly.

"By digging up corpses?" Dakota asks.

"Corpses who can be in our band," Chloe reveals.

"We're going to have corpses in our band?" London asks, horrified.

"Kristen is fucking Johnny Foster. Do you think Johnny Foster would fuck a corpse? He wouldn't even fuck Sienna and everyone wants to fuck Sienna."

"Johnny Foster is a corpse fucker?" London asks, panicking.

"No. Johnny Foster is a Kristen fucker and that's not going to change so if we want to be friends with a Johnny Foster fucker, I suggest we bring her back," Chloe says.

"I've heard some bad rumors about Johnny Foster," London says, her confusion compounding, "Do we really want to be friends with him?"

"Yes. We want to be friends with Johnny and we want to forgive Kristen."

"This is not Mod subculture," London says definitively.

"Do you think Kristen knows how to play an instrument?" Dakota asks.

"As long as she can hold one, we're fine," Chloe says, shrugging.

"What happens if we take her back?" London asks, confused about the protocol of re-friending.

"We regain someone who cares for us. We find someone who actually knows something about the music. And we complete our band," Chloe raises a different finger to punctuate each benefit.

"Isn't our band already complete?" London asks.

"There's only the three of us," Chloe says.

"Aren't there only three people in most bands?" Dakota asks, wrinkling her freckled nose.

"No. There are four or five, just because you're only willing to fuck the three main members doesn't mean the others don't exist."

Dakota agreeably nods at this, then asks, "What happens if we pick someone else? Someone new? Lindy maybe?"

"If we pick someone besides Kristen, we risk not getting along with them, being embarrassed by them, and having all our personal secrets exposed... but, on the other hand, we'll get to keep our 'That's so Kristen' catchphrase."

"Hmm. Shit. You're right. This *is* a tough decision," Dakota says.

London thinks about it for a moment, then asks, "What if we just start calling things that are 'Kristen,' 'Sienna?'" She can't remember if she was using this replacement out loud or if it was only during conversations in her head, but she already feels like Diego's show is very "Sienna," and not very "Kristen."

Kristen looks pretty in her white, ruffled, one shoulder, Gucci cocktail dress tonight. Seeing both Chloe and Kristen walking into the party together confused London, but it also felt like a beautiful redemption. The thought of a sanitized beginning, while standing in a bathroom stall at The Pit, seems incredibly attractive.

Dakota originally wanted to make fun of Kristen's dress for looking like a tampon, but she wants this band more, so she declares, "You're a genius, London. 'Sienna' the new 'ew' and Kristen is the only thing that's Kristen... besides other girls named Kristen."

"Yay! I can't wait to tell Gregory that Mommy's a genius!" London celebrates.

"Who the fuck is Gregory?" Dakota asks.

"Um, hello. My bird, Gregory Peck," London says, angry that Dakota could forget Gregory, even after being formally introduced.

"You're going to tell your bird that you're a genius," Chloe asks, then smiles worriedly.

"Yes, of course," London says, "Gregory totally gets me. Honestly, a lot of the things that come out of his mouth, I can imagine myself saying."

"Okay, I take the genius thing back," Dakota states.

"Fair enough," London concedes, then gets back on track, "So we're going to do this?"

"Yup, because, guess what? Kristen can play the piano," Chloe announces, then arches an eyebrow.

London rolls her eyes, "Okay, awesome, but we're a New Wave band. We don't need a piano."

"But we do need a synthesizer," Chloe reminds them.

London throws her arms up in the tiny stall, "It's all poltergeists and synthesizers with you!"

"Okay, who here knows what a synthesizer is? Show of hands," Chloe says.

London puts her hand down. Dakota doesn't raise hers. London wipes her hand on Dakota because she's afraid she accidentally touched the stall wall.

"Exactly," Chloe says, "A synthesizer is like an electronic piano and guess who can play it?"

London keeps her eyes on the ground and meekly says, "David Bowie?"

"Ugh. Probably, but he can't be in our band," Chloe responds, annoyed.

"You asked him?" Dakota inquires, not believing he'd turn down such an opportunity.

"No. I didn't, but he doesn't want to be in the band."

"Don't speak for Bowie," Dakota warns.

"David Bowie is dead," Chloe breaks it to the girls.

"In that case we can't have him around because we need to keep his corpse away from Johnny," London points out.

"Girls. Focus. We need to recruit a fourth member," Chloe says, directing her bandmates.

Dakota looks around the stall, and agrees, "I think you're right, Chloe. I mean, we're three girls. That's a terrible New Wave group. There's a four person minimum for a band, like when they add the gratuity automatically to a check. If you're a New Wave band, there's a gratuity automatically added into your lineup to ensure appropriate cuteness levels."

The girls agree to bring Kristen back into the fold. Then they take turns hovering over the gross toilet to pee. Then they check their makeup in the bathroom mirror. Then they go back out to Diego's party, camera ready.

As they push through the crowd, the girls spot Kristen across the dance floor. She hasn't moved. As soon as Kristen sees Dakota smiling, she knows that she didn't make a mistake coming here. Chloe has fixed things because she trusts that Kristen has fixed herself. The work Kristen has been doing finally feels like *enough*. Not *enough* in the way it's usually used when referring to the girls. It's not the *enough* that someone yells at them when they cross a line. Finally, Kristen feels *good enough*. She never thought she'd get to this destination with careful footsteps and daily lessons. *Good enough* always seemed to be promised in invitations, yet it only arrived when her options dried up.

People keep obstructing their view, but when the girls get glimpses of Kristen, she's looking back at them with an expression of gratitude that wasn't expected, but was appreciated. It's a hopeful story, for once. If Kristen can be accepted back, then Dakota thought, maybe, possibly, one day she would get her best friend back too. Since there are cameras everywhere, Dakota takes the lead, making it clear that the path to forgiveness is always on offer, but it has to be earned.

Finally reaching her long lost friend, Dakota says, "Okay. So are you ready for the audition?"

"I just want things to be back to normal," Kristen says, to the girls, not the cameras that are now circling. "I'm sorry for everything I did, and I'm being good. You read the blogs. I'm bettering myself. I made sure to be better, for all of you. I've missed you."

This clip, after the girls' agents sign off on it, will be better promotion for the band than a million windshield fliers could ever be.

"So you're ready to audition then?" Dakota asks.

"I just poured my heart out to you," Kristen says, stomping her heel.

"Right, but merely having a heart doesn't make you part of the band," London tells her. After messing things up by going off script with Sienna, London needs to go back to the basics for Kristen's trial by fire.

Dakota points out, "You aren't auditioning to be the lion in the Wizard of Oz so finding your heart isn't your motivation."

Kristen laughs a single "Ha," then says, "The lion had a heart. His weakness was that he was a coward. That's why they called him the Cowardly Lion."

London puts a hand up, "Whoa there. You aren't going to get into the band by slandering others. Like Dakota said, we didn't audition the lion. He's not your competition so you're coming off a little petty. A lion would never speak like that about you, they're too majestic for that."

"Um. Okay. So what do you want me to do?" Kristen asks.

"Play the bass," Chloe says.

"That's a guitar?" Kristen asks.

"Yup. You're in," London says quickly, impressed.

Kristen looks at the girls, not the cameras, then reluctantly admits, "I'm not sure I could play bass at the level of an actual musician."

"Of course you can't *yet*, you just joined the band. You'll need to practice," Dakota says, putting a hand on Kristen's shoulder.

"So I'm in the band?"

"Absolutely, you're back and Sienna is the new 'Kristen,'" London says to the camera.

"Hey!" Kristen protests, smacking her heel on the floor again.

London puts her bony fingers on Kristen's other shoulder, "No, you're not 'Kristen,' Kristen. Sienna is the new, 'Kristen,' and you're now Kristen Paxton again."

"No! I'm the new Kristen!" she tells them, trying to prove that she's the same, but different.

"Right, as long as you aren't being 'Sienna' you can be Kristen," London reassures her.

FAMEDIET
The Reunion.

Last night, during the premiere party for **Diego Mestizo**'s new reality show, *Fame or Bust*, there was a reunion of epic proportions. You can be sure that not a single person was watching the flat screens playing Diego's show when **Chloe Warren** marched into **The Pit** with none other than **Kristen Paxton**.

This was the first time that Chloe and Kristen have been seen together in 40 blog years, and even **London Francis** and **Dakota Dabney** seemed unsure if things were going as planned. They immediately pulled Chloe into the bathroom to discuss why Kristen was back, and a source who was changing her tampon in a nearby stall tells us that the girls were debating about letting Kristen into their yet-to-be-named band. You know, the band that's just been announced by London's power-agent **Joel Harper**... right after London accidentally leaked the information... right before Chloe's agent, **Rod Tobin**, was going to make a press statement. Ugh. Fuck it. Know what? Don't ask us. Do you know how many times we edited that sentence while attempting to make sense of the leaks, and the secrets, and the hearsay, and the stories from girls on their heavy-flow period?

CTV tells us there's exclusive footage of the big reunion going down, and, of course, they'll be airing everything later in the *Fame or Bust* season. Finally, a reason to look forward to that awful reality show.

20- Dawn of a New Wave.

Kristen joins London on Diego's balcony which overlooks the purple morning. London's long stick arms are triangled on the railing as she looks out toward a new beginning. The sky looks bruised, like Lindy's boobs did after the operation. London doesn't look back at Kristen, but she always knows when someone's watching her; she's had experience with being spied upon. Maybe her extrasensory perception isn't limited to just designer animals.

"Thank you," Kristen says, walking toward the railing.

London doesn't respond. She doesn't move.

Kristen is scared to stand in London's vomit radius, so she stays a foot back, and says, "And I'm sorry if I hurt you before."

"Was it really that hard to just stay put when we helped you get there?" London asks, disappointment clouding her little girl voice.

"Yeah. It was."

"Well, that sucks for us because we weren't doing all that shit for us, we were doing it for you," London reminds Kristen.

"I know that, and it was amazing that you all cared so much, but I felt like I'd go insane if I stayed there the whole time."

"Did it even help?"

Kristen points back to the living room where Diego, the rest of the girls, and some Michael Lorrie models are hoovering up lines. "I'm not in there, am I?"

"You were in there before you came out here," London says, eyes still fixed on the sunrise.

"I promise you, I didn't have a drink tonight, last night... this morning?" Kristen scrambles because she's not purposely trying to confuse London, it's just too easy to do. That wine bottle on the piano was for Johnny. Kristen was able to put the bottle there and not reach for it. This fact soothes her and she refreshes her attempt at explaining things to London, "I appreciate this second chance, so much."

"Rehab was your second chance. This is your third chance," London reminds Kristen.

"Fine, three strikes rule, I totally understand. This band is going to help me stay stable. It's perfect."

London watches as the bruise in the sky slowly heals, and she asks, "What if we fail?" This is the part of London's personality that makes her a particularly crushing friend. Since she's mentally fourteen years old, she's dumb, but she's also naive... sensitive... worried. She sees the world from a very uncomplicated vantage point. Sometimes, this leads to very complicated questions.

When London was failing Spanish, she hired a Hispanic person to deal with it. Now she's failing as a productive member of society, and she's already hired one Spanish speaking productive member of society, but it hasn't fixed anything besides the mold problem in the guest bedroom.

"We can do this," Kristen says, as she finally stands parallel with London at the edge of the balcony.

"Can we? What if we can only do that?" London asks, her long arm pointing back to the group inside.

Kristen turns briefly to see everyone still in the living room; Tobe inhales a line, then Diego laughs with pure maniacal happiness. The cameras aren't filming, but this is the interesting shit. This is what the fat housewife and the unfuckable college student want to see- Kristen knows this, and she asks, "So what if that's all we can do? Being a sexual dynamo, or a picture of perfection, or the ultimate catch is infinitely more impressive than someone who can unclog a toilet, or change your oil. Why are those people worth more than us just because they have one little skill?"

"What if we're just party favors?"

"What do you want, London?" Kristen asks.

"I don't know. I'm 20," London says.

This is one of those odd realities of the remedial, yet accelerated world these girls live in. At 20, most people are waiting tables, or serving coffee, or going to class. No one knows what they want to be, they're just living life. When the weekend comes, when their day off arrives, they get dressed up, and they go out, and they hook up with someone after knowing them for only three hours.

Your average 20 year old counts down the moments until the weekend hits, then they can finally act like a spoiled little socialite.

celebUtard
"Exiled from the Cool Kids Table."

It's a miracle her divorce is official because it's clear **Lindy Porter** has trouble giving up bad habits. This afternoon, Ms. Porter was caught dining with the party wrecking/criminal record holding/friendless phenom, **Sienna Wolfe**. The last time these two were seen together in public, Lindy had Sienna arrested. This time, she had Sienna join her for some pasta and wine.

We don't have any sources to tell us what happened during the meal so we're going to make up a conversation. (Let us stress that this conversation is a work of fiction. The names/ likenesses/ medical conditions contained herein are not indicative of anyone living or dead.)

Sienna: It's good, or whatever, that you got over me trashing your family heirlooms.
Lindy: Actually, the only reason I invited you out today was so I could murder you for ruining my party, but then I realized I was wearing white and I didn't want your cheap blood to ruin my outfit.
Sienna: I totally understand. I've thrown out so many pairs of white yoga pants for that reason.
Lindy: That must have been very difficult for you. Luckily, you seem like someone who buys sweatpants in bulk.
Sienna: So True. I own more elastic waistbands than a pregnant woman.
Lindy: You mean you aren't pregnant?
Sienna: As of 11:17 AM PST, no.
Lindy: That was an hour and ten minutes ago.
Sienna: Well they don't have anything for me to piss on here to tell me if I'm pregnant, now do they?

From the looks of the pictures, the lunch went smoothly, but **Chloe Warren** by day, Sienna by night- Lindy is getting wrapped up in something worse than her last marriage.

Always remember the first rule of war- Don't stand in the crossfire.
Until next time, stay tardy, celebUverse.

21- Reddy for a Challenge.

"I'm surprised you remembered the date," Jake says, as Dakota sits down under the vine covered pergola in the outside dining area of CARGO.

"Oh, the date..." Dakota says, checking the calendar on her phone to see what holiday today might be. "I never forget... uh... Martin Luther King Day... he was... like, my favorite member of the royal family," she mumbles.

"What?" Jake asks, confused.

Dakota shakes her head, also confused.

Piecing it together, Dakota realizes that Jake called *today* a *date*. Now everything requires additional scrutiny. Jake is wearing a tight distressed gray Dolce & Gabbana Marlon Brando T-shirt that wordlessly says, "Yeah, I spent over a hundred dollars on a t-shirt," while also saying, "I'm wearing a T-shirt, why did you show up wearing a black Elie Tahari mini skirt and a cream Stella McCartney blouse?"

Jake has secured reservations at CARGO, a middle of the road place. Celebs don't flock there, but it's not some common person restaurant with ketchup on the table. It's the right balance of expensive enough that middle class people would balk at the menu, and popular enough that both Jake and Dakota know how to pronounce the name of the restaurant, unlike that French place.

"Is this a date?" Dakota asks, eyes wide.

"Only if we fuck at the end of it," Jake responds with an arched black eyebrow.

"Okay, I guess it is a date then," Dakota jokes. Was that a joke? She isn't sure.

"Someone sent me an interesting YouTube link this morning," Jake says, then he opens his menu.

Dakota shoots him a glance, puts her chocolate brown hair behind her ears, then shrugs her freckled shoulders. Shit. She's been caught. She'll definitely have to bang him now.

Playing dumb, Dakota asks, "Was it... a Martin Luther King tribute video... to celebrate today?"

"It was you making fun of me," Jake says, quickly closing his menu.

Dakota sinks in her chair. This is officially the worst Martin Luther King Day of her life, and Dakota has had some pretty rough MLK days.

Jake, not mad, asks, "Do you think your agent could call my agent and help get me get booked overseas? He must have the connections if you scored an interview to promote... vodka?"

Dakota looks at Jake and tries to fight her worried expression. On the outside, Jake appears to be a guy that can put up with her shit, but could he also actually recognize the humor in it all?

"I'll ask my agent," Dakota promises, nervous. Ohhh, nervous at lunch. This is a new feeling. This is what Chloe must feel like, but not.

"I think it would be fun. I'll go on, and you know what I'm going to say?" Jake asks. He's planned all of this. He thought about this meeting. This date? Maybe he was even excited to see Dakota? Maybe he didn't care how or why today happened, just that it happened?

Dakota flatly issues what she thinks he'll say, "That Dakota Dabney is a real cu-"

"-Iraq will be rebuilt before Dakota Dabney's album drops," Jake delivers the punchline he was working on his entire commute to CARGO.

"That's the best you can do?" Dakota asks, unimpressed, "Is Iraq still even around? Don't we own it, like Puerto Rico, but it's a terrorism destination instead of a tourism place?"

"Well, there was another one I was going to say, which was, 'Yeah, I heard Dakota has a new album coming out. Apparently, it comes in a box set. You get the album and some tampons.'"

Dakota scrunches her nose and doesn't laugh.

"Get it, because only girls are going to buy it so... it would... cut down on their shopping..." Jake says, trailing off. Dakota feels like the power is slowly returning to her side of the table.

"We can't do a tampon box set because girls use different types of tampons depending on how bloody their vaginas get during their periods. Some girls leak like an old faucet, others, not so bad... so whatcha hungry for?" Dakota asks, flipping Jake's joke back on him.

Dakota's phone vibrates and she turns it off. She's too interested in Jake to be on her phone. This is some sort of milestone. She's found someone more interesting than texting. She grabs her menu and flips it over, then notes, "Ohhh, they have Bloody Mary's here!"

The waiter comes up to the table, and Dakota warmly smiles at him. It's a smile that says, *Don't mention the fact that I'm back, Jake doesn't know that Kim Nueman took me here earlier this month.*

"Hi, my name is Freddy Pashman and I'll be your waiter," the man in the black shirt and black pants says. This is how waiters in LA introduce themselves- full names- as though Jake would be shooting his spread for *GQ* and when the need arose for a male model, he'd be like, "We should call Freddy Pashman, you know, the waiter at CARGO."

"I think we'll just start out with drinks, Freddy," Dakota says happily, "I'd like a Bloody Mary... extra bloody."

"Make that two," Jake says, holding up a peace sign.

Dakota feels herself begin to sweat like she was the one in all black, instead of Freddy. Why can't she shake Jake? Was she going to have to get the pasta and spread the sauce all over her face just to get him to gag at her period jokes? How could it come down to Operation: Period-face? As tempting as a lunch consisting of a Bloody Mary, tomato soup, spaghetti, and cherry pie is, Dakota can't go through with it because she's actually enjoying herself. A lunch that originally was just to kiss Jake's ass and get on his good side, has now had its objective shortened to "Kiss Jake."

No. Don't kiss Jake.

"I got a ticket for parking in a handicapped spot the other day," Dakota mentions in an effort to repulse him.

"They must not have seen you get out of the car," Jake responds back instantly.

Dakota smiles, then buttons the smile and says, "I'm thinking about being the drug addict of the band."

"You can't pick that. It's not like a drummer. A band has room for more than one drug addict."

Dakota can't believe it. She must forge ahead, "So you're saying that another one of the girls would be better at doing drugs than me?"

"I think it depends on the drug. Each of you have different attributes that give you advantages and disadvantages for particular drugs," Jake says.

"Oh, so how would you divvy up the supply?" Dakota asks.

"Obviously coke for Chloe, painkillers for London, booze and ecstasy for Kristen, then, for you, heroin," Jake says. The way his voice got soft when he gave Dakota heroin boarded on romantic.

"How did you do that so quick, have you thought about this before or something?" Dakota asked, scared, mostly because of how fair and appropriate his distribution seems.

"Not in depth, I don't have a spreadsheet on it or anything," Jake says, shrugging casually.

"Why am I heroin?" Dakota asks, sort of not wanting to hear the reason, while simultaneously desperate to find the inspiration behind his choice.

"Because the most talented one is always the heroin addict. Kurt, John Frusciante, you know..."

"So you're saying that I'd be addicted to heroin because I'm the star of the band?"

"No, not the star, the most talented."

"That's really sweet," Dakota says, butterflies ruffling up. No one had ever called her the heroin addict to her face before. It felt good. Better than heroin. Being called talented also felt nice.

"Plus you have the reliability of a heroin addict," Jake adds.

"Hey. I made our date today," Dakota says. Now she's the one getting offended.

"Yeah, but you're missing your first band meeting."

Dakota leans back in her chair. She completely fears this man sitting across from her. Does he have some sort of super soldier-like ability to read her mind? London was right- Jake *was* made by the government. Dakota needs some downers- maybe some heroin. This is all too much.

"Chloe just texted me," Jake says, deconstructing Dakota's look of horror, "She wants to know why you're ignoring her. She says twenty minutes from now, you have to meet them at Rod's office. That doesn't even give us enough time to have a Bloody Mary."

What the fuck was Jake doing checking his phone while she was ignoring her texts out of respect? She was supposed to be ignoring *him* while he missed texts. Everything is all confused.

"Oh... I guess this isn't a date," Dakota says, making direct eye contact with Jake, daring him.

"I guess you'll just have to ask me out on one then," he responds, daring her back.

Dakota stands up, and she waits for Jake to stand up, but his giant frame doesn't rise to give her a kiss goodbye.

Thinking fast, Dakota lifts up her phone and takes a picture of Jake.

"What was that for?" he asks.

"Ask me again tomorrow and I'll let you know," Dakota responds, then she deletes the picture and walks away, smiling.

22- 80's, Not Eighty.

"Ew. Look at that floppy he has on," London says, glaring at an old man who's wearing a droopy hat that almost covers his tired eyes.

"The only thing that should be inside that hat is a steaming pile of excrement," Dakota says.

"I agree... Huh?" London reacts, realizing halfway through her confirmation that she didn't know what she's co-signing.

Dakota shows off a recent addition to her vocabulary, "Excrement means shit."

"Gross," London says, looking at the man.

Dakota shakes her head in agreement, "I know- it gets the point across, but it doesn't give you that mental picture of me squatting."

"Still. Gross," London says, scrunching her pointy nose.

"Grosser than the hat?" Dakota asks.

"Um. Okay," The guy in the floppy hat says to the group of girls standing two feet away from him, "Your agent brought me here to teach you about New Wave."

"When is he bringing you back to the home?" London asks.

Dakota begins typing into her phone to see if it was her agent who caused this disaster.

Chloe figures it out, "Girls. It's obviously Rod who set this up, I mean, hello? Dakota asked her agent to send over a New Wave legend."

"And they sent over his Dad?" Kristen asks.

"You are aware that New Wave was popular in the 80's, right?" the man in the hat asks.

London sighs, "Ugh, yes, I know. We Wikipedia'd it."

The New Wave legend takes a deep breath. A couple of decades ago, these girls would be going wild for him; now they're not even happy with the fact that he's in the same room as them.

"Dakota's agent called me because I'm Robin LaManche," the old man in the hat announces.

Blank stares.

"I was in a little band called, Robot Tapes."

The girls look at each other. When they've silently confirmed that they have no idea who this man is, Dakota says, "Neat, Sir. We're a big band so I'm not sure your little band can help us."

With an eye roll and an in-place stagger, Robin says, "I was joking when I said little band."

"Wasn't a very funny joke then, was it?" London asks him point blank.

"Alright, listen. I can go, I'm being paid one way or another," the old man with the bad hat and the little band says.

"Awesome," Kristen agrees to this plan. The rest of the girls just stare at Robin until he gets the point. The old man grabs a notebook full of pictures and walks out of the white room.

"I'm going to call Rod," Dakota says to the girls, as she gets on her phone. "I bet he set this up. Think about it, we're standing in his office."

The girls mentally agree Dakota has cracked the case and they start getting bored.

Kristen decides to google the old man's band on her phone.

Chloe checks Sienna's location by reviewing the blogs.

London watches a video on her phone of a kitty running around on a sheet of ice trying to catch the fish under it.

"He didn't pick up," Dakota says, frustrated with this whole situation.

As the girls grab their purses so they can leave, Rod Tobin and his secretary, Courtney, enter the office, each holding a tray of various Perrier bottles, glasses of non-Perrier water, coffees, and teas. Rod is a fat, bearded Jewish guy in his late 50's. Courtney is around 20, black, tall, and unfashionable.

"Please don't spill on the carpet," Rod pleads, as his short little arms carefully balance the tray. He places the drink selection down on a glass table, then looks around the room and asks, "Where the fuck is Robin?"

"He left," Chloe says, pointing to the door, "You probably passed him in the hallway. He can't get places fast because he's almost dead."

"What did you do, girls? Do you know what I had to do to get him in here?" Rod asks, knowing it's their fault.

"I thought the surprise you had for us was going to be something funner," London admits.

"Funner?" Rod asks, angry.

"Yeah. Me too. He sucks," Kristen says.

"Kristen Paxton? What's Kristen Paxton doing in here?" Rod asks. He hadn't had a chance to read the blogs. He was too busy calling in favors to get Robin.

"She's our keyboardist," Chloe says, putting her arm around Kristen.

"I thought I was the bassist?" Kristen asks.

"Shit. Dakota. Why don't you tell me these things?" Rod grumbles, walking over to his desk, then tiredly plopping in his chair.

"Why didn't you tell me that the New Wave specialist you found was going to be your dad?" Dakota counters.

"Robin LaManche is not my father," Rod says, swiveling slowly in his chair while looking at the ceiling.

"Good because he's gross. I wanted to say something earlier, but I was being polite," Kristen says.

"Just thirty seconds ago you said he sucks," Rod points out.

"Was I wrong?" Kristen asks, raising an eyebrow.

"Yes, you were, he's a legend!" Rod says.

"Yeah, so is, like, Bloody Mary, but you wouldn't invite her to teach us New Wave," Dakota says.

London immediately looks worried. Chloe puts a consoling hand on London's bony shoulder, "Don't worry, Bloody Mary isn't coming," she says.

"We just said her name twice. One more time and she'll be here," London squeaks out, then shivers.

"Speaking of, are any of these drinks a Bloody Mary?" Dakota asks, nostalgic for her date.

"That's three times. We're doomed," London warns.

"I had a Bloody Mary date today, but you ruined it with that gross saggy bag of man," Dakota says.

Rod looks at her. "That's what happens when you age. You get saggy," he teaches the girls.

"Exactly. I'm glad you see it my way," Dakota says, pleased that it was acknowledged she's right, but sad that her Bloody Mary is sitting untouched at CARGO right now. Some Mexican busboy probably drank Dakota's special MLK period-joke date drink.

"No, I meant he's not gross, he's just old," Rod says.

Dakota picks up an elephant tusk off the only non-white item in the office, a black bookshelf, and she says, "You said, 'just old,' like it's not that bad."

"Dear, of course he's old. He's famous for his New Wave band. Remember, you're making music that was popular a couple of decades ago."

"It's going to be popular again," Kristen declares, then Dakota pokes her in the butt with the elephant tusk.

"Not if you don't have anyone to play the music!" Rod moans. "And don't put that in Kristen's butt."

Dakota pulls the tusk away, "Don't judge."

Kristen shrugs. Rod looks at the girls and offers some free advice, "Each of you have to be more careful about what you allow in your butt."

"Likewise- remember Ric Scaro?" Dakota asks Rod.

"That wasn't me! I'm not gay!" Rod says, pointing at Dakota.

"She's right it wasn't him. The Ric thing was with my agent's butt," Kristen admits.

"Oh! Sorry," Dakota apologizes. She's told that story with Rod as a main player at least fifteen times since the new year.

The tired agent takes a deep breath, while the girls grab their drinks. They're finally ready to have a band meeting.

"Alright, the point is, you girls need a band to play your music. We need someone to create the tracks," Rod says.

Chloe realizes he doesn't get it, and it's time to shut this meeting down, gracefully. The old man in the hat stormed out of the office and it was ugly and babyish, so keeping this in mind, Chloe stays put. She relaxes, she blows on her still steaming black coffee, then she asks, "Why are you pushing us? We have time. That's the whole point of picking the music business."

"The point is, you could actually stand to make a lot of money off this," Rod informs them.

"I'm already rich," London says, tonguing the plastic top on her paper coffee cup. She's synced with Chloe on the game plan. Joel will manage this band, Rod will make sure the t's are crossed and the lowercase j's are dotted.

"You don't have enough money to sustain your lifestyle until you die. Not at the rate you consume," Rod warns all of the girls.

"I know, but other people will die along the way and give us more money," London says casually.

"That's a toxic way to live life," Rod warns the girls.

Dakota shrugs, then says, "We live in LA, everything is toxic. That's why there are so many health food stores, to trick people into thinking that their life isn't just a DNA helix of toxins that they climb every day."

Kristen processes this, then abandons her glass of water on the table.

23- Welcome to Petsville, LA.

To decompress, London immediately drives home from the meeting, then walks down the street to her favorite relaxation hangout, "Petsville, LA." She'd never buy an animal from there- the population mostly consists of half retarded products of puppy and kitty mills- but this fact is also the reason why London spends so much time in the store. All of these imperfect little puffballs need London's love because their time in front of the general public might be cut short soon. Something about the fact that people will form quick opinions on these perspective pets by watching them for a slice of their day, behind a distancing pane of glass, makes London feel bonded to the little baby animals.

Petsville, LA is filled with animals that were bred with the sole purpose of being easily purchased and given to a middle class girl. London knows how that goes. She's allowed her name to be put on a couple of perfumes and a hair straighter- things that could be easily purchased and given to a middle class girl. Like the puppy mill animals, the products with London's name plastered on them are somewhat defective. London is dressed like a mermaid on one of the perfume bottles. The hair straighter was built based on numerous London Francis trademarked ideas, and it might have caused an apartment complex in Compton to burn down. The case hasn't gone to trial yet, or it has and the insurance company just settled it; either way, London hasn't had to pick out a "taking the stand" outfit, which was kind of a bummer because she already has some credible looking and courtroom ready looks all picked out.

London peacefully walks into Petsville, LA, alone. There aren't even paps taking pictures through the big picture window at the front of the store. The cameras had followed Kristen post-meeting and this doesn't bother London like it would have in the past. It felt nice to have a little freedom.

London greets Marky, a bored employee of Petsville, LA, and she patiently listens to a story about how his car broke down on the way to work. Once Marky is finished recapping how much his life sucks, the only obstacle standing between London and those jailed puppies would be the customers in the store. Generally, seeing kittens and London in the same blink of the eye is such cute overload for a customer's brain that they end up hiding behind the gerbil cages, quietly taking pictures with their phone.

London drifts to the "nursery," where a large plexiglass pane provides a full view of the animals in little cubes. This baby animal jail used to make London sad, but Stanley once mentioned that most Americans spend their day in little cubes too and this changed London's perspective.

London waves at the kitties and smiles at the puppies.

After she talks to the bunnies in a black wire cage in the center of the store, London feels level once again so she leaves Petsville, LA.

Instantly joined by the fat little paparazzi with the businessman haircut, London gets snapped in four quick photographs as she crosses the street. The fat pap breathlessly catches back up to her, and London provides a worried, "Hi." The last time London saw this man, he dropped a card into her car with the revelation that he was onto the scam London is running.

So far, London hasn't seen anything on the blogs about her band being a sham. To date, her Google Alert has been filled with confused musings and oddly excited speculation about this new project. Maybe music is so boring now people are dying for something to shock them? That, or the blogs are just trying to build a wall of hype for the event so that it will be a sure-fire letdown once the songs hit iTunes.

Given that this fat pap has an interest in London, she wants to make sure that he stays at least somewhat neutral. She feels it's better to confront the issue so that it can be discussed, overweight man to perfect woman, instead of rudely argued about on a blog that's filled with commenter observations like, "London's small tits suck my dick."

"Nice card," London says, toying with a moment that made her nervous. She had to acknowledge that she received his message, then she had to pretend like she didn't give a shit. The fat little pap continues to take photographs as London walks, so she keeps talking to get him out of work mode, "I forgot your name- I'm sorry, remind me?"

"Martin Turner," he says, clicking a couple more pictures as they walk up the block toward London's house. Proximity to a pet store was one of the big selling points of the house for London. That, the stripper pole, and the 1:79th scale replica of the house in the back yard that she uses as an elaborate dog house.

"Right. Martin. You're interested in our band, huh?"

"I'm just curious how exactly you're going to pull it off," Martin admits, rushing ahead, then backing up in front of London, snapping photos, all the while expertly avoiding the oncoming pedestrians that London gives little, deceptively shy waves to.

"We're going to be the craziest, most kick ass, out of control New Wave band," London promises as she shakes her extensions and Martin captures this.

"Aren't you afraid that'll be a self-fulfilling prophecy?" he asks.

"Aren't *you* afraid of that, little fat man?"

"No," Martin staggers back, totally caught off balance that London knows what a self-fulfilling prophecy is.

"Because if we OD or commit suicide, you'll lose something amazing," London says to him in a playful way that makes her words all the more sinister.

Suddenly it occurs to Martin that maybe London *is* right. Maybe he *is* like the rest of America and, as profitable as the pictures would be of a knock-down drag out fight between these girls, it would really disappoint him if they flew apart.

Martin has photographed it all; he's seen how happy the girls make each other.

Reminding himself of what he does for a profession, Martin lies, "Not really, your inevitable crackup won't affect me at all."

He's at work. Martin is at his job, doing work. It's a tough position to hold because when he's at Walgreens, buying a candy bar, trying to get on with his life, he has to stare at a magazine filled with his work. His snap is always buried under an irresponsible headline. Only on occasion is the headline true.

"You aren't afraid?" London asks, trying to get closer, but Martin backs away like a panting animal being hunted. In the same way he, the photographer, pretends London, the socialite, is just another a job, she tries to pretend he's just a fly. London wants to convince herself that Martin is a pest no different than the others, but the truth is, she's seen him so often that he's become a part of her life. She can even tell when something is wrong with him. Today, something is wrong.

"I am little afraid- mostly about what this band will sound like," Martin continues with his intimate distance.

"Afraid for your mind because we might blow it? Don't worry, I'll call Joel and he'll get you tickets, way in the back- so we don't get too close to your mind," London says with a giggle.

"I don't want tickets from your agent. I'll get front row tickets if my agency sends me, and if they don't? I'm all the better for it. I'm not curious," Martin Turner says, putting his pug nose in the air.

London stops walking and looks through the camera to Martin, "So you've never rubbernecked while driving by a car crash?"

Martin stands still, his finger on the shoulder of his camera, but he doesn't snap a photo. He doesn't follow London as she starts walking again and moves out of frame.

The gorgeous socialite passes the non-photographing photographer who can't take his eyes off her.

London turns around, then backs away, staring down the camera, posing like this shoot was commissioned. She begins wordlessly begging Martin to photograph her.

Martin remains frozen in place. A shock shoots through him when he realizes that, all this time, he was photographing lies, even when he was praised for getting "the scoop." Martin reviews the box score so far. The girl who's been portrayed as a functionally retarded socialite is somehow winning. Does she have America completely fooled? Looking beyond the lens, Martin puts together fractions of facts and they start to form a picture of London Francis. This picture feels more genuine than the photographs Martin has sold. It's becoming increasingly obvious that those angry commenters have become pawns in London's game. *They're* the dumb ones.

When a quarter of the internet wrote angry emails after London described herself as being "politically retarded," it looked bad for the careless socialite, but now that Martin has insight into the women, he suspects London might have used the term intentionally. They had called her a retard a million times in their heads, and on their blogs, but when she agreed with them, they attacked her for using their own word. They created an uproar about their own opinion. When it's time for a new blog or comment, they'll have to think twice before firing a big boldface **RETARD** at London. Maybe they'll think of a different headline next time, hopefully something a little softer.

Being one-on-one with London today has changed Martin. He'll still sell pictures of her after this, but when he's loading them onto his computer, he'll feel like he's at work. He isn't a photographer, at least not in the way he used to view himself on these assignments. He's not capturing "real moments." He might as well just photoshop the entire mess. Martin tells himself that he's no more a journalist than those guys who paste celebrity heads on porn star bodies to live out their sexual fantasies involving people they are too starstruck to talk to, much less have sex with.

Martin always assumed that London would never look at him as a person, then she did. Martin always assumed that London wasn't capable of having a tense argument that didn't begin with a pre-interview, then she got the last word in. Martin always thought that London Francis had no business pretending she was in a band, then she invited him to her concert. London Francis is a person. An interesting person.

This was like finding out that Santa doesn't climb down the chimney. This was Martin watching his mother put the fun sized snickers in yellow plastic eggs for the Easter egg hunt. This was an e-mail account left open, its contents clearly confirming a relationship is over. The shock of this entire moment makes Martin want to go back to school and become a dentist. He closes his eyes tight and, in the back of his mind, a paralyzing question is asked, *Has photography become 'Sienna?'*

Martin holds up his camera and snaps one last picture of London as she walks away. Even if photography has become "Sienna," Martin knows that it won't take much for "Sienna" to become a good thing again.

celebUtard
"It's Not Called 'Old Wave.'"

Kristen Paxton is back! She's so back that we've taken "Kristen" out of the "synonyms for un-chic" column.

Only hours after **Robot Tapes** frontman, **Robin LaManche**, was spotted storming out of the office of super-agent, **Rod Tobin**, Kristen had already given the statement that Robin was dismissed because, "It's not called 'Old Wave.' We have a vision for this band and it can be a little complex for some people, I suppose."

The cameras caught Robin on his way out, and we asked him what caused the blowup. He simply said, "These girls are not the future of New Wave. They're not the future of anything."

We look at this as a pitch perfect endorsement of **London Francis'** band considering Robin, in the 80's, viewed the future as keytars/ robots/ swooping hair/ fog.

If Robin is still just as bad at predicting what's coming up next, then it's all but written in stone these girls are going to be the new-New Wave.

Chloe Warren was even briefer with her statement upon leaving Tobin's office, saying, "We've never been much for yesterday's news."

Kristen Paxton has seemingly escaped exile with an ultra-hyped band and a hot BF, while **Sienna Wolfe** has become trapped as "Sienna."

No longer just a name or color, "Sienna" is now also an insult.

Until next time, stay tardy, celebUverse.

24- A Friendly Wave.

"Hi," Dakota says into her phone, her voice almost cracking under the pressure of the two letters. She grinds the toe of her red Saint Laurent pump into the edge of a cracked brick paver in her back garden, then makes a mental note to tell the gardener, whatever his name is, that the pavers need to be re-laid in this area. She makes a second mental note to bring him to the problem area, then she'll make a horizontal smoothing motion with her hand because the last time she verbally told the gardener to do something, he somehow interpreted it as, "Please cut all the bushes in my yard to look like circumcised penises."

"I know why you're calling," Lindy says, her nerves obvious even over the phone.

"I'm not mad," Dakota assures her.

"Of course you are."

"No. I'm not. Lindy, can you keep a secret for me?" Dakota asks, the toe of her red shoe grinding harder against the fractured paver.

Lindy wavers for a moment. Her track record with secrets isn't stellar. After her failed marriage, Lindy despises secrets. "I don't want to know anything," she tells Dakota.

"Oh," Dakota says, her eyelashes fluttering.

"I'm just trying to keep things neutral. You have to understand, Mitchell got custody of a huge chunk of my friends. I can't afford to write people off, no matter what they've done to my grandpa's head in the past."

"I miss Sienna," Dakota yelps out, then she touches her mouth. A silence on the other end of the phone crackles just loud enough that it's clear the call wasn't dropped. "Does she miss me too?" Dakota asks.

"Of course," Lindy says, answering honestly.

"I wanna talk to her," Dakota admits, biting her lip after the words hop out.

"I know you do, but have you been reading the blogs lately? The last bad story they ran about you dates back to when Sienna was still a part of your little... cult? Are you sure you want to undo everything that you've done so far?" Lindy asks, acknowledging that Dakota is better off without Sienna. As much as Lindy wants to stay neutral, she still has the responsibility to advise her friend against making a potentially devastating decision.

"I just want to talk to her, I'm not letting her back in."

"That's not a good idea," Lindy says.

"I have to."

After a short pause, Lindy responds, "Then that's a selfish idea."

"We brought Kristen back. Maybe we'll look back on this and-"

"-Kristen cared enough to get help."

"She didn't care enough to stay."

"Well, based on my conversation with Sienna, she doesn't even care enough to go on the website and look at the place," Lindy admits.

"Did you mention it to her?" Dakota asks. She never talked about stuff like that with Sienna.

"Obviously. We're famous. Rehab is the answer to everything."

"I'm going to call her," Dakota verbally decides.

"Please don't put me in the middle of this. I want to be friends with everyone," Lindy pleads, lifting her feet so that it would be impossible to step on anyone's toes.

"I know. I won't. Do you want to go to dinner with us tonight?"

Dakota had organized a dinner, and Lindy needed to be there, whether she wanted to go or not. Dakota wants her friends to re-meet Jake. They've met him at parties, but since he looks so big and stupid, the girls probably have an opinion of him that's strikingly similar to what Dakota first thought as well. Now, Dakota can't stop thinking about Jake. She kicked that man with the shitty hat out of her agent's office, just because she thought if she hurried back to CARGO, maybe she'd catch Jake five Bloody Marys deep, drowning his sorrows about her premature evacuation.

She drove all the way back to the restaurant, but Jake was gone by the time she arrived.

Possessed like a madwomen, Dakota decides that she needs her meal with Jake, and she says, "I want you to come tonight- out to eat with us. I think that the band should have a dinner together, you know, to center everything at the start, and I need you there, to help me. Will you do that for me?"

"Really? Dinner? That sounds nice. I've noticed that if I have to eat alone, I forget to eat," Lindy admits.

"At least when you do go to dinner, you eat what you order," Dakota hints at an entirely different issue that she immediately regrets bringing up. Lindy hops on the slipped statement immediately, "Oh no, is she bad again?"

"I'm making sure that Stanley comes tonight."

25- A Hard Fact to Swallow.

"I'm literally barfing," Lindy says to London with a gleeful laugh. The rest of the girls at the big, long table- Chloe, Kristen, and Dakota- match Lindy's happy horror. Tobe, Stanley, Jake, and London all shrug.

The restaurant of the night is "Detore." No one at the table is totally sure if the name is pronounced "Detour," or "Deter" as in "prevent," or "Dieter" which might be the name of the very talented German head chef. The ambiance is dark except for a series of 10 watt light bulbs hanging above the table. The decorating theme of the restaurant is "natural" wood glossed with about thirty coats of polyurethane. A collection of wine bottles flank either side of the rectangular table; Kristen is placed in the center, next to a choking Johnny Foster.

Johnny Foster has a rock look, with a stone public persona. He's exciting and safe, rebellious and courteous, your best friend and the crush you've never spoken to.

"Why should *I* be ashamed? *He* was the one calling me 'Auntie,' I was just the one spanking him with the TV remote!" London responds, giggling, then proving the boys' point, she turns to Kristen and asks, "Remember that time a guy asked you to take a 'Sienna' on his chest?"

Without a hint of embarrassment- these stories had all ended up in print and electronic ink already- Kristen giggles, "No one ever asked me that! There was only the guy who liked a chick's excrement to fall onto a glass table, while he laid under it."

Kristen was paying attention this time, she was picking up on every look, every word.

"Did you do it?" Jake asks, then takes a giant bite of his mashed potatoes. Maybe coming from a military background, he can deal with period jokes and soiled coffee tables because his dad showed him footage of what a roadside bomb can do to someone.

"No way," Kristen protests, "I was too pissed at him. I mean, when he mentioned it I had just finished chopping up some coke on his glass coffee table."

Stanley, in mid chew of Chloe's sturgeon, almost spits it across the table, but he manages to get the fish down.

Kristen asks, "Why else would he have a glass table, except to do coke off of?"

"Did you do the coke?" Jake asks.

"It was already chopped up on the table. I didn't want to waste it. There are socialites in Africa with no coke."

"I don't think that they have socialites there," Johnny theorizes, redirecting the conversation. London wonders why a corpse fucker like Johnny Foster is being so modest about their dinner stories.

"If there are socialites in Africa, they're missing a lot more than some coke," Stanley says. It's a joke that's fired over the entire table's head, except for Johnny's.

Johnny quietly laughs, while Dakota pouts, complaining, "I don't get it."

A slow smile slides across Jake's face as he realizes what young women in Africa might be missing. He leans to his left and whispers into Dakota's ear. Dakota's response is pure terror, "No! No way. No. Wow. Cut it off? What? I mean. What? Okay. Cross 'African safari' off the list of things to do before I die."

There's a small lull in the conversation as everyone retreats to their pair. Except for Lindy. She just watches. She's okay with this, maybe.

Jake touches Dakota's bare thigh under the table as he orders a Bloody Mary and they both share a quiet, personal laugh.

Dakota is happy that everyone can get together and laugh about the past. It's easy to laugh in the present, it's hard to smile at the things that people leaked to the media to hurt them. Luckily, these ugly stories somehow became the best dinner conversation. Old mistakes found a humorous hue when they were baked in the glow of nostalgia, then left to cool for the perfect amount of time. While this fact makes it all but certain that Sienna will be invited back to the table, Dakota still can't help but shake the thought these laughs are only possible because of Sienna's absence. Unwilling to dwell on her missing friend, Dakota begins a wandering toast to the vague idea that the girls have a band and, as everyone raises a glass, their eyes relocate to Kristen to see what she's holding up. The tall cylinder of water in Kristen's hand sends a clear message. The band was the reason that this meal came together, but as far as Kristen is concerned this get-together was about everyone leaving the past on the blogs, then agreeing to a new life, together. Glasses clink, a pact is sealed.

Post-toast, Johnny attempts to get to know the girls' new venture better. "So, what's the name of your band?" he asks, only because there's a pretty good chance this line of conversation won't end in a story about sex or coffee table desecration.

The girls exchange glances and no one says anything. Kristen, being the girlfriend, has to explain, "We actually haven't decided on one yet... we're... holding an online poll."

"You're letting the general public decide your name?" Johnny asks, his perfect face contorting into a now familiar look of horror.

"Yeah, they can type in what they think our name should be, then the one that gets the most votes will be our band name," Kristen says, winging it. It worked for London before so...

Johnny doesn't say anything, he just bugs out his eyes, then reaches for his wine glass.

Kristen takes out her phone, then e-mails her webmaster requesting he add a poll on her website and on her *PaxtonTraxon* App. "What should we name our band?" will be the name of the poll. Kristen either doesn't know, or doesn't care, about the type of jokes she's setting up.

A name isn't Dakota's concern right now. Chloe has cut everything on her plate into a tiny mush, and she occasionally feeds a clump of it to Stanley. Unable to hold back anymore, Dakota says, "Chloe, try this red snapper. I might take my grand momma here and snapper is her favorite. I don't really have the palate for it so I need to know if it's any good."

Stanley is sure that Dakota's grandmother is dead. His eyebrows raise at the comment, but he doesn't say anything.

Dakota picks up her plate and begins passing it down to Chloe at the end of the table. An uncomfortable silence follows the red snapper as it swims downstream.

Chloe takes the plate and pushes her own out of the way. She picks up her fork and knife without shaking. Never looking at the quiet crowd around her, Chloe cuts off a piece of the snapper, brings it up, sniffs it, then puts it in her mouth. She chews. She swallows. She looks down the table with a "fuck you" smirk on her face, then says, "It's Hong Kong style, so you'll have to ask grand momma Dabney how she likes it prepared."

Almost on cue, a waiter comes by and takes away Chloe's abandoned plate of mush.

The girls all decide that Chloe will be the lead singer of their yet to be named band.

No one can fuck with her.

26- Cars.

London walks out of the restaurant with Tobe on her arm. Tobe is okay with this because he actually had a really good time at dinner tonight. He's hopeful that Sienna will return and he won't have to ruin London's life in an act of brutal vengeance. When the girls used Sienna's name as a derogatory term during dinner, Tobe's heart raced. He made sure to engage everyone at the table in conversation so they could later be referenced as mutual friends he shares with Sienna.

The paps are currently concerned with Kristen and Johnny, who are still in the restaurant, so London and Tobe have a relatively relaxing wait as their car is being brought around.

"I paid your parking tickets, you know," is the statement that breaks the calm. London looks over her right shoulder, searching for the source of the familiar voice, and she sees the fat businessman haired pap, Martin. He's not snapping pictures, he's just standing there in a black t-shirt and dad-jeans, his camera around his neck, his hands in his pockets. Happy to see him, but unwilling to admit this, London responds, "I don't understand most things you say to me, Martin."

"You know this guy?" Tobe asks protectively. He feels like this fatso looks familiar, but can't place where he knows him from.

"Yeah. That's Martin. Martin, this is Tobe," London says.

Martin reaches out to shake hands. Tobe has no reason to shake this stranger's hand, so he dryly says, "Hi, Martin," then goes back to impatiently waiting for the car. Martin's hand gravitates toward the lens of his camera so that he doesn't look like a fool, then he continues to ramble, "It cost me like two grand to pay all of your tickets."

"That's a waste of money, I don't have to pay tickets here," London explains with a smile.

"Here, as in this lot?" Martin asks. Considering that the parking is valet, she's probably right.

"Ha. No. Here like LA, you know, the city we're standing in?"

Martin explains in a soft tone, as though he's talking to a child, "Actually, no, you do. Those little tickets on your car, you have to pay them."

"Do not," London says.

Tobe doesn't tell Martin to leave because he fears being alone with London. One on one, Tobe runs the risk of learning that London's actually a person and that might cause him to pull punches later on. He would prefer to have ignorant conversations fill every moment he spends with London.

"You have to pay tickets, it's how the legal system works. They said they send you letters biweekly," Martin says, feeling fatherly.

"If they don't include return postage, I never sign the head shots. Most of it is a business anyway. eBay, stuff like that. Not real fans," London informs him, totally distanced from something as regular as parking issues.

"They're sending you letters about the tickets, they aren't fans," Martin persists.

"Liar. Of course they're fans."

"Ohh, trust me, they aren't," Martin says with a jokey honesty that London resents and appreciates at the same time. She arches her long body and looks down the street for her Bentley, but she doesn't see it so curiosity gets the better of her, and she asks, "Why did you pay my tickets?"

"Because I find this project interesting," Martin says.

"No, that's not it," London says confidently. "It's just because I didn't answer your questions. Don't worry, you'll get over it."

"Alright, good. At least you remember our conversation."

"Actually, I don't. I'm just assuming that I didn't answer your questions," London says. She has to plead temporary amnesia because, if she's forgotten that scary message, Martin would be left alone with his suspicions.

"How could you not remember? You referred to me as a 'little fat man' while I was taking pictures of you on your way home."

London nods, "Okay, I believe you. This whole time, in my head, I've been marveling at what a little fat man you are, and I wasn't sure if it was because I call you that as a nickname or if it was just because you're a little fat man"

London doesn't want Martin to bring up the message he scrawled on his business card so she's entertaining herself by entertaining Martin's conversation. Maybe part of Martin's good guy act is grounded in a legitimate belief in London's band, but she suspects the prime motivator here is guilt. Martin paid those tickets with money he made from selling violating images of London.

"I owe you a favor now, do you want an autograph?" London asks the lingering paparazzi.

Martin, too eager, says, "Actually, I was wondering if I could help you with your music. I used to be in a New Wave band."

"Nope. Sorry," London says immediately, "We already kicked out one old man, we don't need another, so you get an autograph."

London takes a Sharpie and a folded head shot out of her purse, then demands, "Tobe, lean over, I need to make out an autograph for Martin."

"Who the fuck is Martin?" Tobe asks, with a snarl.

"The little fat man standing next to me," London says, then points to her left.

Tobe looks up in the air, as though he's begging the carcinogenic LA smog to enter his body and quickly seal his lungs, and before he can look back down, London is pressing on his back, writing in Sharpie on a head shot. She finishes signing the black and white picture of her face, then hands it to Martin. The paparazzi takes the gift, depressed that his chance to help London has disappeared.

London's Bentley pulls up and it seems to put a period at the end of this sentence.

Tobe tips the valet, then leaves with London.

Martin, with an empty memory card in his camera, looks down at the black and white picture of London's pointy face. This is the only picture he got tonight and he didn't even take it.

Next to London's smirk, he sees the personalized autograph, "Dear Martin, Tomorrow. 3 PM. Joel Harper's office. <3 London."

27- Don't Judge a Book by its Author.

In the glow of the floodlights beaming down the driveway, Dakota's eyes reflect a worried tenderness, as she asks, "Were you horrified?"

Jake puts his back to his Range Rover that's parked inside Dakota's gate. "Horrified? No. It was weird though," he says, then smiles.

"What type of weird? Was it the Kristen thing?"

Jake laughs, "You do realize that I read the blogs, don't you?"

"What was weird then?" Dakota asks, like a sensitive teenage girl.

"Tristan was there."

Dakota giggles, "His name is Stanley."

"Not to me," Jake says, bursting with nostalgia.

"Thank you for not mentioning it at dinner, he's a little... sensitive, about *Tristan's Landing*," Dakota says with the experience of numerous failed jokes related to the show.

"We all are, I mean, when his dad died, it almost killed me," Jake says, sincere.

"That wasn't his real dad. That was a character."

"Either way, it was heartbreaking," Jake sighs.

Dakota feels relieved to be focused on fiction. It's the same feeling she has when they print an untrue story about her. She doesn't have a problem discussing secrets that never existed.

"This was the first time I was able to really talk to him. He never really comes around. Chloe's always solo," Jake says.

"She's not solo. She has us," Dakota reacts defensively.

"It felt almost wrong seeing him with Chloe. I was in love with him being in love with Jenny," Jake admits, unsolicited.

"Kim Neuman?"

"Jenny," Jake repeats with conviction, then shoots Dakota a sly smile.

Kim Neuman played Jenny, Tristan's soul mate on *Tristan's Landing*. It was a sick love triangle between these fictional characters and their viewers. Tristan and Jenny were soul mates, but the female fans felt like Tristan was their soul mate, and the gay fans felt like Tristan was their closeted homosexual soul mate, and the jocks who secretly watched felt like Jenny was *their* soul mate. Everyone was in love with everyone else and maybe that's why it turned out to be such good TV.

"Aw. That's cute you watched the show," Dakota says to a man willing to admit that he not only watched *Tristan's Landing*, but that he was also part of the love triangle too.

"It's not cute. I was 21 when I was in love with Jenny. She was 16."

"Wait, you were 21 when *Tristan's Landing* was airing?"

"We're straying from the point," Jake says, exhibiting another distinctly female trait.

"That's not that bad," Dakota says, going along with it, but also making a mental note to Wikipedia Jake Wesley's age when she gets inside.

Jake begins to shake his head about the way things work. Still a little slurry from the wine, he says, "It's not fair, guys should mature faster than girls. How come a 16 year old girl can look 25, but a 16 year old guy looks seven years old? If it was the other way around, it would fix a lot of stuff and the American prison system wouldn't be over-capacity."

Dakota begins to grind the toe of her pump into the driveway. These flaws and gaps in logic have always worked for her.

Prison overcrowding is the reason that Dakota has only served ten cumulative hours in jail.

The fact that she matured early provided her with all the essential tools to get famous around the same time that she got pubic hair. Dakota got into clubs as a teen because she matured faster; she got boys because she matured faster.

Still not invited into Dakota's house, Jake prolongs the moment, "I think it's an Adam and Eve type thing."

"Teenage girls give you the compulsion to go fruit shopping?" Dakota asks.

"Not particularly. Unless they work at the grocery store. I just mean that there's that temptation factor, and if you give into that temptation, then you're going to be punished."

Dakota looks up the driveway, to her house, and she considers if she's going to be the old Dakota or if she'll try something new. What would happen if she didn't sleep with her crush tonight?

Before Dakota can decide which Dakota she is, Jake leans in and kisses her on the lips, then thanks her for a great night, and gets in his Range Rover. All of this happens in a split second. Dakota has been caught off guard for the thousandth time.

For a while there, Dakota forgot that *good* surprises exist too.

celebUtard
"Worst Idea In The History of the Internet."

A reader sent us a link to **Kristen Paxton**'s website and, as of yesterday, a poll has popped up. The poll allows anonymous people on the internet to choose the name of Kristen's band.

Is Kristen the lead singer? Who's officially in this band? What are we a fan of?

Okay. Full disclosure. No one sent us the link. We were actually googling Kristen Paxton because she's become the queen of redemption, and we wanted to copy down some pointers so we can get our parents to speak to us again.

The way the name selection poll is set up on the site, you can vote on previously entered names... or you can type in anything you want. Yup. You read that right. A celebrity who was such a mess that her own messy friends sent her to rehab felt it was a good idea to freely allow anyone who registers for her mailing list to type whatever they want her band to be named.

The name that gets typed in the most, wins.

Is Kristen really this confident with her rebooted fame that she thinks people will forget the past decade of underage hookups/DWIs/car crashes/weekends at rehab? We have to admit, our suggested name was mild compared to what it would've been earlier this year. Either we're getting soft, or we're afraid of naming the band something terrible, only to find out that they put out our favorite album of the year.

It's hard to get your friends to listen to the new RetardWhoreMachine album.

Until next time, stay tardy, celebUverse.

28- Focusing on Not Paying Attention.

Stanley averts his eyes from the barely nibbled waffle in front of Chloe. He briefly considers confronting the orphaned brunch, but swallows his improv and reads his boring lines, "So, do you have a name yet?"

"For the band?" Chloe asks.

"Yeah. What else would I be asking about? You aren't pregnant are you?"

"No. No!" Chloe says, hugging herself. She hasn't gotten her period in months. "I don't look disgusting like a pregnant woman, do I?"

"Of course not, you look... beautiful," Stanley says, then there's a silent beat he can't stomach, so he pushes the conversation back into Chloe's lap, asking, "When's band practice? What are the rock rules about practicing without a name?"

"Oh," Chloe says, mentally coming back to the table, "We're having an internet poll on what the name should be. You know this, you were at dinner last night."

"I thought that was a joke!" Stanley says, as the waitress brings back the little black book with Chloe's credit card inside. "What Kristen said last night, she was serious?" he asks.

"Yup! It's on Kristen's website. You should vote."

"I don't want to see what they're writing on there."

"Oh, I know. I want to be surprised about what the top five are. The webmaster is going to let us know in a day or two, then we'll get together and pick one."

"What are you going to play in the band?" Stanley asks, trying to be positive about the whole thing because the more time Chloe practices, the more time he can spend on his laptop, uninterrupted.

"Hm," Chloe hums. "I hadn't thought about it. Kristen is going to play the keyboard and... London- Dakota and I, will, perform music..." Chloe trails off, then picks up the little black book and takes her credit card back. It's time to go.

"I like your singing voice. You should sing," Stanley decides, reaching over and grabbing Chloe's cold left hand.

"Really?"

"Yeah. I hear you in the shower. It's nice, I'll lay in bed and listen."

"Really?" Chloe squeaks, embarrassed, but also flattered.

Stanley should have said that Chloe's future is on the drums, that way she'd be practicing all the time, away from Stanley, giving him hours on end to work, but her voice is interesting and almost tortured sounding. He doesn't want her to waste her talent, and he doesn't want her to rule out this release. Stanley couldn't make this about himself. This band is a very good thing for

Chloe and it has the best chance of being a success with the mic in her hands.
Out of a sea of faces, Stanley picked Chloe for all the same reasons she'll be
the perfect frontwoman.

This is one of the million things Chloe loves about Stanley. She knows that
he could never be America's favorite man-boy without all those episodes
coming from a pure place. That's why none of the horror movies he's starred
in ever hit the mark. The thin plots, small budgets, un-scary monsters, and big
titted illiterate leads might have contributed to the failure, so maybe it wasn't
all his fault.

"I'll try singing," Chloe says, more to herself than to Stanley.

Stanley smiles, then his eyes move past Chloe. "Mrs. Porter!" he exclaims,
popping up out of his chair, then moving around the table.

Scarlett Porter's toned arms extend out of a dark green Donna Karan
sleeveless draped top, and she accepts Stanley's big hug- the type of embrace
saved for a mother figure. Chloe begins to realize that Stanley and Lindy did
happen... and it was not insignificant. Uninvited, but obligated, Chloe stands
up and joins two individuals who are very aware of Chloe's full plate.

"Chloe! Are you meeting your mother here?" Mrs. Porter asks hopefully.

Chloe shakes her head. It's a wordless confirmation of what Mrs. Porter
already knew.

Putting the pieces of this moment together, Chloe realizes that today is
the day of the week all her mother's friends meet and spend their husband's
money. It's hard enough remembering her own schedule, Chloe doesn't want
to babysit her mother too. She's fine being responsible for her boyfriend-
Stanley's schedule isn't very hard to remember- but apparently, Chloe's
mother's schedule *is* that hard to remember.

Scarlett, in a quick move, clutches Chloe's cold wrist and whispers, "I still
haven't seen your mother. She hasn't called. Now she doesn't show up today?
Is she okay?"

"She's just going through a lot right now," Chloe whispers. Her eyes dart
around the restaurant to see where the rest of the old ladies are.

"I'd really like to see her. These lunches have become unbearable and they
make me feel like a crazy person," Mrs. Porter whispers, then finally lets go of
Chloe's wrist.

"I'll tell her," Chloe says, then she grabs Stanley and makes a direct exit
before the rest of her mother's friends descend upon the table to make
backhanded compliments about Chloe's reshaped frame.

Walking to the car, Stanley asks, "Was she whispering about your Mom?"

"Yup."

"What did you say?"

"Nothing. I have no news to tell."

"Do you want to go visit her?"

"What's the point? Plus, I have something at three."

Stanley inwardly applauds himself. He got a bunch of good-boyfriend points for the lunch and asking if Chloe wanted to see her mom, yet he also gets to work on his laptop for the rest of the day. This is how Stanley manages to stay sane without hiding in Chloe's beauty sanctuary and silently weeping because his agent hasn't sent him a script in four months. He's less likely to check the mail seven times a day or wait out in the driveway for the FedEx guy if he's inside on his computer.

His laptop is just a diversion.

A diversion from everything.

Some days, Stanley wants to climb inside that screen, like a scene out of a bad horror movie.

29- Like Ripping Off a Band-Aid.

London casually leans on the secretary's desk in the glass lobby of Harper LLC. She's early and for some reason this makes her feel oddly guilty and a little vulnerable. To pass time, she reads the blogs on her phone, until she starts to see flashes and the rest of her band appears on the other side of the glass.

Kerry Kay, Joel's secretary, gets up and opens the door for the girls. The band without a name arrives at their meeting, on time, and it's a good start. After exchanging various hello's and hugs, London leads the girls back to Joel's office.

As soon as the door is opened and the girls walk in, Kristen locks eyes with a man sitting at Joel's conference table. She stamps her foot down in anger, "You didn't, London! Please tell me you didn't. You have to learn to drive *around* the shitty scumbags. Ugh, look at the poor bastard, his face is already swelling!"

London's normally confused look becomes even more confounded as she shakes her head, then says, "Everyone, this is Martin Turner. He's here to help us."

"So, you didn't assault him?" Kristen asks.

"Nope," London says, proud of herself, "He's just fat, that's why his face is like that."

"Oh. Sorry, Mark." Kristen apologizes.

"M-Martin," he responds meekly, then no one says anything so he continues, "It's okay, people have always told me I have the type of face you'd want behind the camera instead of in front of it."

The girls don't laugh. Joel Harper, the ex-rocker turned agent, directs the band toward the conference table, and they all sit down like schoolchildren.

Joel's looks have held up well considering the hell he's put his body through. He's in his early 40's and still has a full, floppy muss of black hair. His five o'clock shadow doesn't have any gray in it.

Joel was the lead singer of "Launa" in the early 2000's. Launa was a vaguely successful band that cranked out a few songs that a certain segment of the population may regard as hits. Joel is the most qualified of all of the agents to manage the band, considering that the rest of the agents are fat Jewish men who love Sinatra.

Joel is aware of what happened with Robin LaManche and now it's up to him to make sure it doesn't happen again, when, one by one, the girls realize, yes, the fat little man sitting at the end of the table *is* a paparazzi who photographs them on a daily basis.

"Yeah...um. So what's this guy going to help us with?" Chloe asks, a little impatient that this was the big surprise London had planned. She was hoping that Joel had some dumb reality show the girls could sign on for, then the band thing could be dropped. Now that Chloe has picked herself to be the lead singer, it was becoming too real. If she sucks, she'll be taking the whole band down with her, and when Sienna almost took everyone down, she was cut loose. Chloe can't handle that type of rejection. It would confirm too many of her worst fears.

Before the girls arrived, Martin was told by Joel that he should give a short introduction, then he could get into the major details. Joel said that there are three rules he lives by when he speaks to these girls:

1. Be brief.
2. Be complimentary.
3. Be brief.

When Martin pointed out that 1 and 3 are the same rule, Joel responded, "In that case, you better not forget it."

Martin clears his throat, then begins his introduction, "I know you think I'm just a guy that follows you around and takes your picture, and that's true, but the more I get to know you girls, the more I find myself liking you- all four of you. It's been a pleasant surprise to find out you aren't a bunch of dilettantes."

London smiles at Martin and tells him, "Yeah, we aren't. We're all super liberal."

"Right," Martin says, almost regretting the mini-monologue he just gave. "After I expertly extracted the information from London that you girls are starting a New Wave band, I went back to my apartment and dusted off my old Bright Feathers stuff," Martin says, then he looks up quickly to see if the girls have any reaction to the name. None of them display any acknowledgment beyond an annoyed smile. Martin nods at this familiar response to his former band. He manages to clarify, through his shame, "That was the name of a New Wave group I was in-"

"-sorry Martin, we've already kicked out one old dude and this is getting repetitive," Dakota says as she stands up.

"Who? The lead singer of Robot Tapes? Please, that band was 'Sienna' even when New Wave was popular."

"What did you say?" Dakota asks, getting up, then approaching the wannabe music producer.

Martin is nervous to see a celebrity walking toward him- they're usually walking away from him, as fast as possible. Martin doesn't have his safety blanket of a camera, so he mumbles, "I was just saying... Robin LaManche... he's so 'Sienna'..."

"I love this little fat person!" Dakota says, bending down and throwing her arms around Martin. Suddenly the words *little fat person* seem like a warm apple pie of a compliment. Dakota has that amazing ability to flip a switch and change a situation in a moment. Instead of coming off as offensive, outspoken, and mean, Dakota can become your best friend- your best crush- your best fantasy. It's crude, yet flawless manipulation. It makes people want to inhale her exhale, like she was blowing pot smoke into their lungs.

Dakota is glad that people are using "Sienna" as they once used "Kristen" because Kristen is now making future plans with the girls as though she never left.

Even if Sienna doesn't get any jail time for her actions at Lindy's, she'll still be in jail; she'll need to look for a way to get paroled. Hopefully, she'll go about it in the right way, and won't take hostages during an attempted breakout.

Joel asks, as delicately as possible, "Dakota, would you take your seat? I took an interest in Mr. Turner's work, and I think he can help us with this band project."

"Of course," Dakota says, then she goes back to her chair and tries to shake off the fact that she hugged a fat person.

Martin now feels flush, dizzy, comforted, and excited. He briefly considers that he may be having a minor heart attack, but ultimately decides it's just an anxiety he hasn't felt since oral report day in 11th grade.

"Do you have my folder, Mr. Harper?" Martin asks, ready to begin his presentation. Joel grabs the folder off his desk, then hands it to Martin. The cautious agent delivers a glance that silently demands the shaking paparazzi compose himself. The pictures will only sell if they're taken with a steady hand. Martin realizes, yes, it's time for pictures.

"Check this out," Martin says opening the folder, removing a glossy photo, then sliding it to the center of the table.

Kristen takes the photo, "Ohhh, are these the boys that will be writing our music?"

Dakota leans over, "Wow, the one of the left is cute."

Martin smiles a wide smile, "He is, isn't he? Real good-looking guy. Probably had a pretty wild love life."

"I'm sure he still does," Chloe says, looking at the boy's razor sharp cheekbones and almost too small, too turned up nose.

"I assure you, he doesn't," Martin says, taking the picture back. "That is the only existing photograph of Bright Feathers," he announces.

Kristen arches an eyebrow, "But I thought that- oh, no!"

Chloe catches on, "Gah. I'm literally barfing! I had a sexy thought about Martin. Ew. Ew. Ew."

Dakota isn't that worried about it. She's happy that Martin used to be attractive because it made her feel better about hugging him. She wasn't hugging a fat person, she was hugging the hot person inside him.

"Alright. Okay. You gals really know how to make a guy feel special," Martin says, smoothing out his slick, dyed black hair.

Chloe considers what's being presented by Martin at this table. He does seem like a genuinely good guy. He also seems able to tolerate the horrible, insensitive remarks that he's been receiving, tidal wave after tidal wave. Despite this, he's a paparazzi and paparazzi are fucking scumbags. "How do we know that you're not setting us up?" Chloe asks. She doesn't want to run Martin out of the office, she just wants to ruffle his bright feathers.

"I understand why you girls are starting this band," Martin says, "You're tired of people writing mean things about you. You're tired of being made to look like villains just because the four of you live extraordinary lives."

Kristen looks at Martin. She looks deeply into his eyes, and she believes him, but she also doesn't want to lose what she just got back, so she demands, "Empty your pockets, then take off your shirt and pants."

"Oh, come on. I want to help you with your band, not bust you for cocaine distribution," Martin protests in a high pitched voice.

"Pants off," Kristen demands with a finger pointing to the floor. Her tone makes it clear that *this is revenge*. In the past, Martin has degraded the girls with his camera, so the table of socialites decides to put him on the other side, that way he can see how it feels. It's only fair. Martin has photographed all of their most embarrassing moments- this will even things out. This is payback, like the ticket situation.

Martin stands up and takes his cell phone and keys out of his pocket, then places them on the table.

"Look at his phone!" Dakota says, laughing. She picks up the early 2000's era flip phone and puts it to her ear, "Hello? Benjamin Franklin? This is Martin. Yes! I'm loving the phone you sent over to me, it works great. Tell Betsy Washington I love what she did with the flag."

The girls erupt in laughter, basking in a joyous little celebration of being young, rich, lovely, and free.

When the giggling dies down, the attention falls back on Martin. He's disrobed to his boxers, and he's holding his arms out to prove he's not hiding a wire in his fat folds. All four girls lift up their phones and photograph the embarrassed man. Once their point is made and their phones are lowered, Kristen yells, "For fuck sake, Martin. Put your clothes back on, you creep."

Martin looks at the girls, then flexes his right arm as he points to the chair he draped his pants on. "Could you hand me those, love?" Martin asks. Chloe picks the pants up between her thumb and forefinger and flings them toward the nearly naked Martin. They land a foot away. Martin walks over and begins to lean down to pick up the pants, but Chloe springs up and grabs the pants, then puts them in Martin's hands before he makes that horrifying full bend. The girls breathe a collective sigh of relief that the sight of Martin squatting down in boxers was averted.

Once fully clothed and secret recording device-free, Martin sits down at the table again. He smooths out his shirt, then asks, "Where were we?"

"London was going to tell you about how this all came about," Joel says, then shoots Martin a glance that says, "I won't tell if you don't."

"Okay, you know how I accidentally made us a New Wave band?" London addresses the table.

"Yeah," the girls say, still not sure if this was a stroke of happy genius or if it will be the eventual iceberg that sinks their DiCaprio-less Titanic.

"Well, Martin's band, Bright Feathers, you know, the one in the picture, they recorded a bunch of songs that no labels wanted. I listened to the tape earlier and..." London says, then she pauses to build suspense, "...the songs are really awesome!"

"Um, you said tape," Dakota balks, cutting down London's moment.

Martin takes out a cassette from his folder. "This-" he says, holding the little black rectangle by its edges, "-contains all nine songs that Bright Feathers recorded."

The girls look at the tape in his hands. It seems mysterious and retro, but only vaguely British.

"How does it work?" Chloe asks, excited by this relic.

"You have to go out to my van to listen to it. Joel doesn't have a tape player," Martin says, without enthusiasm. He has enough trouble getting a normal woman in the van, so he has zero optimism regarding convincing a bunch of girl-millionaires to check out his pap-mobile.

"Okay, then... let's go," Chloe says simply, and the girls stand up, ready for this adventure.

Joel looks at them with suspicion. He thought he was going to have to force Kerry Kay drive the van though the glass lobby just so the girls didn't have to go outside and get in... God forbid... a van. Maybe the next time Joel has to beg London to go to the launch of some club willing to pay her 20 grand just for showing up, he'll proceed to strip down to his undies, then fill a party bus with Flock of Seagulls tapes.

Walking over to his desk, then picking up his phone, Joel says, "Hi, K.Kay, yeah... yeah... okay, is that camera that Mario accidentally left when he had his 'Wednesday' still here? Okay, perfect, could you bring it in? Thanks, dear."

Joel has been extremely nice to his secretary ever since an NYU student put together a documentary on Luana titled *Harper is Bizarre*. The film's two hour and twenty nine minute runtime is just a parade of women alleging that they were sexually assaulted on the Luana tour bus. Joel has no recollection if he carried out these acts. Maybe the women were lying, but if Joel had to bet on it, they weren't. Most of their tears seemed genuine.

Kerry Kay walks into the office and hands a Nikon to Martin. "Don't break it," she requests.

Martin puts his tape in his pocket and holds the camera in his hands. Now it's time for him to get kicked out of the office by K.Kay so he can go back to photographing the girls.

It's important that the paps don't find out about Martin's duel identity, and it's also important that Sienna doesn't find out about the tape. Beyond that, it's even more important that the girls pack into Martin's van so they can find out if New Wave can be resuscitated or if it's deader than that walking corpse Robin LaManche.

30- If the Van's a New Wave Rockin'...

Joel had planned this entire day perfectly, with the help of London. It was a dual effort that would not have been successful without complete synchronization and revoked text messaging privileges. Joel was the first man of influence to see that London isn't the girl that's portrayed in the bold headlines. That's why he hunted her down and that's why he's given her so much say in this project. Joel wants London to surprise the world like she managed to surprise him. His life is better because of London Francis and not just because his cut of her appearance fees have paid off his alleged victims' mortgages. Joel feels like this project can fix things. Sure, it will rake in a boatload of cash, but it will also bring more opportunities, which will yield even more cash, but he primarily sees this project as a way to get close to music again. Joel didn't like what being a frontman did to him. It made him act like Sienna Wolfe. Maybe this opportunity will have the reverse effect on the girls. Don't dance on the table, dance on the stage. Don't scream at your friends in the middle of a fancy restaurant, scream into the mic. Now there are roadies, and handlers, and agents. Now there are dates, and times, and lyrics to remember. It could be structure for the structure-less. It could be a home base for girls who live in the public eye.

Each band member walks out of Harper LLC as a girl with a purpose, yet they leave the same way they always do, annoyed by the questions and the personal-space violations that compound as they navigate to their parking ticket covered cars.

In an effort to distract the paps, Jake Wesley has been called in as a decoy. His attention getter? A little shirtless running. Keep in mind who's buying all these magazines that the pap agencies sell to- women... and Mitchell Haughton. London called Jake before they left Harper HQ and she advised, "Dakota has a boner for running, and we'll be driving by your gym on the way home today." This was enough to get Jake to tear off his shirt, then circle the block in a fast- but slow enough that the candid pictures didn't blur- jog around the block until the caravan appeared.

Martin isn't among the men snapping pictures of Jake today. He's waiting in his van, while the girls lose their tails. He'll have to return the camera to Joel tomorrow, but that's fine, they have a business meeting anyway. When Joel told Martin about today's plan, he also leaned in and said, "If I don't continue to see the pictures you take on every single blog on the ghetto that is the celebrity obsessed internet, this whole deal is off."

Martin fully understands that he can't be seen with the girls working on music. Ever since a certain temporarily insane pop star had an affair with a foreign looking paparazzi, agents have set up giant roadblocks to make sure that it never happens again.

Well, they've made sure that it never happens *in public*.

Martin slides the van door open as the girls arrive at a meeting spot Joel had programmed into their cell phones before they left.

Without a tail and with ear to ear smiles, these master manipulators pack inside the same vehicle that has stalked them so annoyingly for the past few years. Martin sits in the driver's seat, London sits in the passenger seat. Chloe, Kristen, and Dakota cram into back.

Before pushing in the volume knob to turn the stereo on, Martin rotates in his seat, the pleather farting from the shift of his weight. "Now these are demos of songs I did. They're very old, but they're still good. They stand up to this day," he says, then swallows heavy as memories of playing this tape for his music business connections come rushing back. Martin's music had been disrespected and forgotten by everyone except himself, and he's chosen to re-premiere it in front of an audience of some of the most apathetic girls on the west coast. The whole situation has the logic of Lindy Porter's wedding.

Martin turns back to face the stereo, remembering that Joel and London have already said they like his songs. The moment becomes as scary as it is thrilling. Martin feels as though he's going to split in two when his instinct to flee matches his need to share his songs with his new friends.

The car stereo is turned on.

The tape clicks and begins playing.

The girls, for once in their lives, actually listen.

"I want you to know that when you girls perform these songs, you'll fix them and it'll be great. It'll be great," Martin repeats to the girls, as well as to himself during a crushingly surreal and beyond exiting moment for the entire van.

"This one is called 'I Should Have Lost,'" Martin says, then he braces for the joke that this song is about his tummy. The girls are silently tuning into the first little taste of piano on the track. The electronic keys are delicately played until the guitar and drum machine join in. Martin, despite his flop sweat, can't help but smile as he listens to the music he recorded when he was the girls' age.

A minute into the song, Martin's Bowie-esque vocals croon, "We wear our shirts with fiction ties."

"This is New Wave music?" London asks.

"This is New Wave music?" Chloe yelps.

The chorus hits and a young, skinny Martin sings a tune that will cycle through the girls' heads all afternoon, in the same way it's cycled through Martin's head for the past 30 years.

"This is New Wave music!" Dakota declares, and the girls let out excited screams that drown out the song.

Danceable, yet atmospheric. So old, it's new.

London has picked the perfect genre, lush with wide appeal and campy anthems.

Martin has the perfect songs, finally. His heart swells with the music while he averts his eyes to hide just how happy these girls have made him today.

And, like that, the four "pointless humans" in Martin's van fill his life with meaning.

OXYGEN WASTER
The Best Idea in The History of Music?

Joel Harper, super-agent to the stars and ex "**Luana**" frontman, issued a press release this morning announcing that he'll be managing the yet-to-be-named **Feckless Four** band. Maybe they could just name themselves "The Feckless Four" and **OXYGEN WASTER** could get some of the residuals for our contribution. This band looks like fun and we want in, but the truth is that our only shot at being involved in this whole exciting mess is if we break an exclusive about the overdose death of **London Francis**, followed closely by the deadly DWI crash of **Kristen Paxton**, the heart attack of **Chloe Warren**, then rounding things out for symmetry, the suicide/patricide of **Dakota Dabney** and her piece of shit dad.

Hopefully all of that happens *after* they finish their first album.

According to the press release that Harper has issued, the yet-to-be-named group has signed on a producer already. Simply referred to as, "**B. Feathers**," the man (woman?) is a total unknown.

OW contacted **Robin LaManche** to see if he knew of a B. Feathers, and his comment was, "It's probably just another name for **Lucifer**. No rational human being would be able to tolerate producing a record for those demons." It's almost as though the whole Robin thing was a setup because he described a perfect storm of outrage, intrigue, societal incorrectness, and rock 'n fucking roll.

After the jump are pictures of the girls leaving **Harper LLC** HQ. This is the best we've seen these buzzy socialites look in a very long time. We might be witnessing the biggest natural disaster rehab since that hurricane that messed up that foreign place we didn't want to visit anyway.

We promise you, our search isn't over for B. Feathers. OW *will* find this person-guy, girl, robot, mythical beast, biblical super-villain, or London Francis pseudonym.

31- Ticking Like a Watch... Back When People Used Watches to Tell Time.

It's a pure, hot, sunny morning; the type of wake-up that LA leaves on your doorstep like a newspaper... back when people read newspapers.

Martin takes the stairs down from his second floor apartment, avoiding the large jagged crack in the center of the second to last stair. Martin is the only resident of the building who isn't a waifish cocktail waitress, so if anyone caused this crack, it was his fat ass. He maintains that this rift in the stairs was the work of a rogue earthquake. Martin's so positive that a magnitude 7 quake was the cause of the crack, he donates $14, twice a year, to the Los Angeles Earthquake Relief Fund. Martin believes in their work, assuming their work is verifying various cracks in the LA sidewalks and private residential staircases are, in fact, the result of evil tectonic plates that had refused to sit still.

Martin moves across the parking lot, his camera bopping around his neck. The fresh air feels good passing through his lungs which had grown accustomed to the pollution of dirty laundry and sour dish odors stewing in his apartment.

Martin pops next door to an oddly popular coffee shop. He doesn't know the name of the coffee shop, despite being a frequent visitor, despite being a neighbor, despite capturing hundreds of LA's brightest walking inside for a hangover cure. As far as Martin's concerned, the coffee shop might as well be called, "Not Starbucks" because that's why people go there. Celebrities are told by their PR people that they'll seem more like a "regular Joe" if they go to a coffee shop that isn't associated with out of control pop stars and corporate expansion excess. None of this matters to Martin, he's a customer there because it provides him with a really simple commute to make easy money photographing tired, sometime makeupless stars. The coffee shop is so close to Martin's apartment that he practically has famous people banging on his front door like the zombies they essentially are.

Martin orders his usual- a large black coffee. "One Green Mile, please," he jokes with a wide smile. The problem is, he's made this joke every morning for the past two years. It's reached the point where it's a joke that isn't a joke, but because Martin reliably says it every day, the joke becomes Martin. Regardless, the humor is hinged upon Martin's words so he gets all he really wants, which is the laugh. Everyone ends up happy. Martin's coffee is quickly dispensed because he always tips a dollar. He likes to think that he's the guy that gives the employees a laugh and a buck every morning. He imagines that this place is his "Cheers." They don't know his name, but he's working on a way to slip it in, and he's sure that they'll remember it on the first go-around.

Martin is blissfully unaware that he already has a name at the coffee shop, and it's Coffee John. The fact that he has a nickname there might make him even happier though. What's Cheersier than a nickname?

Making his contented exit, Martin pops the lid off his steaming coffee, then drops the plastic top in the trashcan next to the door.

As he surveys the road, Martin squints his eyes- everyone else is wearing sunglasses, but not him. He's of the opinion that if he was to wear a pair of sun glasses, he'd see the world slightly skewed. Lighting is an essential part of photography, and Martin doesn't want to have the perfect picture go unsnapped because it was bathed in the muted colors that everyone else lives behind.

Sitting on a bench in front of a kosher deli, Martin sips his coffee and surveys the streets for reality TV stars he can photograph or film so his agency will get off his back.

A black Mercedes double parks a block away from Martin and this sends him to his feet. Whoever pulled this asshole move is, at worst- a CEO, and at best- River White. No, River White wouldn't double park. River White wouldn't operate his own automobile.

The door of the Mercedes opens and out steps Sienna Wolfe.

She doesn't look good.

She looks like she feels.

No one else gets out of the car.

No one snaps a picture on their phone.

An exclusive.

Martin doesn't raise his camera. He looks away.

Sienna moves down the sidewalk with the single focus of getting a cup of coffee. She won't sit and drink the coffee in a booth or on a bench because she has no one to sit with. She doesn't care about her appearance, not only because she has no one to meet today, but because she figures that mistakes heal. She's right, except for when it comes to pictures.

In a photograph, a bruise is a scar.

Martin knows this.

Sienna approaches the standing paparazzi, not to speak with him, but because he's in her path. She knows who Martin is. She knows what Martin does. He's taken thousands of pictures of her, yet this time, he doesn't reach for his camera.

Take a picture, take a picture, take a fucking picture so I feel like someone important, screams though Sienna's mind as she walks by Martin.

Don't touch the camera, don't take the picture, do not do that to this girl, singes though Martin's skull as Sienna passes. If she was able to shake the other paps, totally undetected, then it's meant to be that her image will go uncaptured.

Martin is with the girls now; Sienna is not. There's some sort of code of honor where the ex has to be respected because, if there wasn't something special about her, she never would've had the opportunity to be the ex. It's possible that this photograph could be very advantageous to the girls, but if it's never taken, it won't exist and there will be no dilemma.

Martin sits back down and stares into his coffee, reading the swirls in the cup like tea leaves. When no message appears, the black liquid returns to just being a beverage.

A couple of sips later, Martin sees Sienna walk out of the coffee shop. It's clear by the speed of her transaction that she cut to the front of the line. It's clear by the speed of her transaction that the other customers let her walk all over them. It's unclear if she was able to do this because she's Sienna Wolfe or because she *really* looks like she needs a hot coffee to make it through the day.

Martin pretends to be deep in thought, as Sienna walks by him, but really he's a blank slate. He couldn't argue with himself any longer, so he decided to merely exist in the moment. Ever since he listened to his songs with the girls, he's felt light.

Sienna makes it back into her car. She doesn't find a ticket on the windshield, nor is there a citation stuffed in the crack of her driver's side door. Sienna's behavior was unpunished, yet noticed, as she got her beverage.

How many people had read about Sienna being thrown out by her friends, then instead of posting something awful about her on the internet, contributed a pillow to soften her fall? This is a new perspective that Martin gained the day he stripped down in front of those beautiful women.

Sienna relaxes in the driver's seat of her car. The breath she'd been holding in since she saw Martin is released with a gasp. Her flat stomach expands a teeny tiny bit, but it feels like a mile to her. Sienna can't stop looking at pudgy little man. Her eyes peer through her sunglasses, to the driver's side mirror, and she begins holding her breath again as Martin quickly looks away.

Instinct brings Martin's hands to his camera. He's already resisted the moment when the warrior could destroy his enemy. He didn't deal that deathblow because, deep down, he feels oddly akin to his defeated adversary. The time has passed. Her time has passed. Martin sits and finishes his coffee; Sienna speeds away.

A minute in LA, where walking a block consumes a girl completely.

Just another 60 seconds in LA, where even something as simple as getting a coffee turns into a battle.

32- A Mixed Tape.

"Joel let me take the tape!" London announces. Reyna, Kristen's maid, trails the tall socialite as she walks out of Kristen's mansion into the sunny backyard.

The girls pop up from their lounges and rush over to look at the dirty box of plastic that contains their future.

"Be careful," London says, as she lets Dakota hold the tape. In Sharpie marker, "Bright Feathers Demo" is scrawled on a yellowed, curling label.

"Let's play it," Chloe says, as she grabs the tape from Dakota. When she does this, London sees Chloe in a bikini for the first time in weeks, and she's met with a skeletal, veiny vision. Confusing repulsion for jealousy, London says nothing. She figures the only way Chloe could be gross is if she was fat, and she's certainly not fat.

The girls all run inside the house to listen to the tape, but as Kristen goes sliding across her cold kitchen floor, she realizes, "I don't have anything to play this thing on."

"Maybe we could take it to one of those places that turns tapes into CD's," Chloe suggests.

"I want it on my phone," Kristen says, stamping her sandals on the floor, sending little drops of sweat rolling down her petite body.

"Well you can get the music off the CD, then put it on your phone," Chloe reasons.

"Right. Okay, then maybe that after she could build a jet pack," London says, rolling her eyes.

"Well, I don't know how else we're going to listen to it," Chloe says.

"Call Martin and tell him to drive up here so we can listen to our future," Kristen demands.

London gets on her phone and the girls wait.

"No answer. Ugh. He's probably meeting with Joel," London says, revealing that she knows more than the rest of the band about what's going on behind the scenes.

The girls stare at London, then their eyes move to the window above the sink and they see Reyna walking outside toward the pool house to grab more towels.

The girls pour out of the back door, then across the wet brick pavers toward the focused maid.

As soon as Reyna notices the swarm, her eyes fill with fear. It's the type of terror a small animal would experience when spotting multiple hungry eagles descending down aggressively with their claws open. Kristen reaches Reyna first and begs, "I need your keys," her words colliding with the maid's mumbled prayer.

Chloe pops in front of Kristen, "Yo nessisito...um...la coche..."

"Chloe, she's a maid, she doesn't have anything Coach. Don't be insensitive," London scolds. Thinking of a way to explain what they need, London rummages through her purse, then dangles her Bentley keys in front of Reyna in the same way one might attempt to please a crying baby. London did not learn this technique from her high school interpreter.

Reyna, understanding what's being asked repeats, "Okay, okay, okay," then makes a hand motion for the girls to follow her as she walks inside the house.

None of the girls return inside, instead they walk over to where their purses are. They take out their phones and google themselves until Reyna comes back with her car keys. With a pained look on her face, Reyna gives her keys to Kristen.

"Thanks Reyna! You're the best," the girls all echo, then they scamper away like teenagers with the keys to the family station wagon.

Their enthusiasm waivers when they see that Reyna drives an old red VW Gulf. "How did I not notice this car ever?" Kristen asks no one particular. She looks down at the keys and marvels, "There isn't even an unlock button." She shows the girls the keys and says, "We're going to have to open the car doors like we're keying into a house."

The girls desperately want to get in the car to listen to the tape so Kristen unlocks her door, then she climbs across the rest of the seats to manually pop the other locks.

Dakota and London slide in the back seat, Chloe takes the front next to Kristen.

"That was exhausting," Kristen says, sinking into the seat.

The girls sit sealed in a VW Gulf for the first and almost certainly the last time in their lives.

Kristen pops the tape in the car stereo, not wanting to prolong the experience. The tape clicks and the first song crackles on.

"This car sucks," Dakota says looking around, "It's pretty much just a big smelly tape player."

Slicing through the negativity, the already familiar piano keys play over the tinny speakers, and the girls freak out.

"This is us! This is us!" Chloe repeats.

"I love song three," Dakota says.

"Yeah, go to song three after this," London agrees.

Kristen looks at the buttons on the stereo, then shakes her head, "You can't do that with a tape, you just have to listen, there are no tracks, it's just on one big piece that you have to get through... like life."

"That tape is rolling out our new life in front of us," London says, then compliments herself by saying, "Profound."

The girls listen to the music for a while and try to ignore London's last statement.

As second song begins, Chloe peps up, "Isn't it exciting to hear this? I mean, we were just going to pretend we were in a band, but now here we are with songs, and a producer, and..."

"...no name," Kristen interrupts. She clicks on her phone and opens her *PaxtonTraxon* App, a $1.99 fan App which had recently been launched by Kristen's "creative team." This team is comprised of people that Kristen rarely meets with because she's creeped out by the fact they seem "weirdly obsessed" with her.

"Let's find out what our name is," Kristen decides, sitting indian style in the driver's seat.

The girls wait, listening to their music, humming along.

Kristen scrolls to the poll tallies, then announces, "Here are the top results. The first one is... Vagflash Whores."

The entire car is silent except for skinny Martin's voice and a drum machine.

London decides to break the silence, "That one is catchy. I vote that one!" she says optimistically.

"No!" the rest of the girls eek in unison.

With her pointy nose in the air, London says, "Fine. I'll save Vagflash Whores for my solo project."

"What solo project?" Dakota asks, offended that she wasn't asked to guest on it.

"I'm just toying with some ideas right now," London responds.

"When were you going to tell us?" Chloe asks, her interest peaking.

"Later on, you know, when one of us gets killed by a crazed fan, another loses their passion for music, maybe one of us becomes a Hindu..." London says, cutely.

"Oh, that's way far away," Dakota scoffs, looking at her phone as if it was counting down to that moment.

"Okay. We're in agreement that London gets Vagflash Whores for her solo project?" Dakota asks.

The band gives approving nods.

Moving on, Kristen says, "The next one... is... Lipstink Jokeband," her voice losing excitement with each letter of the band name.

"Next?" Chloe asks, not even considering the idea.

"Third is Talent Vacuum," Kristen reads.

"I think that one is good! We're like a vacuum that our maid is using to suck up all the talent," Dakota says optimistically. The girls uniformly feel confused. Dakota reconsiders her statement, "But none of us would know how to work the talent vacuum. I mean, have you ever vacuumed your house?"

"I cleaned a wine stain out a tablecloth once," Kristen perks up.

"With a vacuum?" Chloe asks.

"No, with an Armani cardigan," she admits, as her shoulders lower in defeat.

Chloe asks the girls, "Do we like Talent Vacuum?"

The girls shake their heads in unenthusiastic disagreement.

"Too many sucking jokes," Dakota says, permanently staking the idea.

"Fine. What's last one?" London asks.

"Socialheavy."

"Socialheavy?" Dakota repeats as a question.

"You don't think we're heavy do you?" Chloe asks nervously.

"No," all of the girls echo.

"I like it, but..." Kristen trails off.

"But what?" Chloe asks.

"I don't know. Doesn't it feel like it's missing something?"

"Such as?" London asks.

"Like, such as..."

The girls are all silent for a moment as they try to figure out what the name is missing. This is what they're good at. They aren't able to answer a question about Iraq. They aren't even sure where it is, beyond, "I think it's on the right side of the map." What they can do, however, is pick out what is keeping something from being truly special.

"None of it should be capitalized," Kristen says.

"Capitalization is capitalist bullshit," London agrees, then picks up the phone and retypes the name in the submission box.

Before she places the phone back down, she presses on the word, then makes one additional change.

The phone is set in the center of a circle of craning necks.

They read what London has finalized.

social!heavy

"That's actually not bad," Chloe says over the music.

Kristen squints, then asks, confused, "What's it mean if there's an exclamation point in the middle of the name?"

"Exactly," London says.

Dakota nods her head, "I like it. It's sort of like a WHAM! sandwich."

"Anyone have a problem with social!heavy?" Kristen asks.

"How could they?" Dakota quickly responds.

"Okay. social!heavy it is," Chloe declares, like a child was just named.

"I'm texting the webmaster so he can fix the name and percentages," Kristen says.

"I'll text Joel to have him issue a press release stating that with 94% of the vote 'social!heavy' won the contest," London reports.

Dakota reflects on the situation, then asks, "Did those assholes on the internet actually just help us for once?"

FAMEDIET

When You Corner a Wolfe.
~-~Exclusive~-~

Yesterday, unexpectedly, **FameDiet** was able to score an interview with the controversial socialite, **Sienna Wolfe**. Throughout the interview, there's the usual amount of, "Feel sorry for me/I'm not sorry for what I did/Sorry I'm hot and the rest of America isn't," but our staff felt like there was a large chunk of Sienna Wolfe missing the entire time we sat down with her. Whether it was her un-assured glances trained on anyone who walked by, or the lack of her usual flirty humor, it felt like we were interviewing a post-lobotomy Wolfe.

To be fair, Sienna has always had post-lobotomy intelligence, but the fact that she can't even throw in a good joke about one of her fellow socialites is almost alarming.

Check out the full interview **here** or read the socialite (abridged) version, below.

FameDiet: Hi Sienna! How are you feeling?

Sienna Wolfe: Like a c*nt.

FD: Do you usually feel like that?

SW: Yeah, I suppose I do.

FD: We saw that you and Lindy had lunch recently, how'd that go?

SW: Good. She dropped the charges or whatever.

FD: So you won't be facing anymore jail time?

SW: No, I will. Probation sh*t.

FD: Why do you think so many of our young men and women in Hollywood are going to jail?

SW: Because they get caught doing illegal things.

FD: Why are they doing those illegal things, though?

SW: I don't know. What do you want me to say? I can't speak for all of young Hollywood.

FD: You have in the past. I have a quote here, "I'm Sienna Wolfe, and I'm the mayor of Young Hollywood. I decree that-"

SW: -I get it, lady. Wow, good detective work.

....

FD: So have you spoken with any of the girls you used to hang around with?

SW: You mean my friends?

FD: Yeah, Chloe, London, D-

SW: -I've spoken with Dakota.

FD: Dakota Dabney?

SW: No, North Dakota. The entire state. It was exhausting.

FD: How did your conversation with Dakota go? Are you two still best friends?

SW: Ask me again next week.

FD: What's next week?

SW: A better time to ask me that question.

....

SW: You mentioned Chloe Warren, earlier.

FD: Right. You said you didn't talk with her.

SW: Yup.

FD: Sooo is there anything you'd like to say about her?

SW: Ask me next week.

FD: Why do all these questions deal with next week?

SW: Because a lot is going to happen this week.

FD: Sienna, are you alright?

SW: I'm going through it... I'm just. I'm going through it...

Apparently, Sienna Wolfe has dealt with her legal troubles by becoming either a super villain or a secret agent. One thing's for sure, it's no secret that she's not the super star she once was.

Stay tuned for more... next week.

33- History is the Language of Old Fat Men.

Peering out the vista window of Tobe's penthouse, London waits her turn to be acknowledged.

Tobe is on the phone, badmouthing a recent cut of a 3D movie about a Roman warrior who rides a giant snake to Africa and kills Cleopatra for being a big skank. Since London wasn't invited to see the movie with Tobe, she can't even bring herself to eavesdrop on the conversation. Searching for purpose, she realizes that she hasn't told Martin the name of the band. Sure, he might have read the press release, but it's more fun to get a call about it. London dials up Martin and walks out of Tobe's radius.

"Hello?" Martin answers, trying to act like he isn't excited that London Francis was calling him unsolicited.

"Hi, Martin? It's London. Are you bus- what am I saying, of course you're not. Okay, well, we chose a name!"

"I wasn't invited to the meeting?" Martin asks, a little hurt.

"Oh, you were there, but you were just too busy singing."

London makes Martin's emotions turn a fast 180, just as Dakota had done during that first meeting in Joel's office. They were listening to his music. These beautiful girls were listening to his band. The songs that no one else would give a chance found an audience with America's tastemakers.

"We picked... ready?" London baits Martin.

An anticipatory silence crackles over the line, and stretches until Martin wonders if his turn of the century cell phone dropped the call. He asks the dead air, "Hello?" then instantly receives a response.

"Hi. You have to say, 'Ready,' then I'll tell you," London instructs him.

"Okay... um. Ready," Martin says, almost as a question.

"'social!heavy' with a silent exclamation point in the middle."

"social!heavy," Martin repeats, to hear how it sounds on his tongue.

"Yeah... do you like it?" London asks, worried, suddenly feeling a bit of remorse that hot Martin was invited to the name selection, but fat Martin was excluded. Although, fat Martin never would have fit in the Gulf, so it's not their fault. Blame VW and McDonald's.

"I think it's a fantastic name for a New Wave band," Martin admits.

"Really?" London asks, excited that she made another right decision for the band. The line is silent for a moment, because Martin feels himself getting choked up. London still isn't sure why Martin has helped her with all of this, why he's being so supportive, why he's chosen to have his songs put on display, only to be, in all probability, ridiculed, and his music deemed "even shittier than I thought possible" by millions of people on the internet. London carefully asks, "Do you still love New Wave music, Martin?"

"Yes, but it's a 'Tainted Love,'" Martin says, then giggles.

"Oh, because you didn't get a record deal?" London responds, worried that the giggle was because Martin still hasn't dealt with his past rejections and might become unhinged while discussing it.

"Well, those things are 'Once in a Lifetime,'" Martin tells her, while smiling and shaking his head.

"Yeah, I guess. Joel says there are four labels bidding for our album," London tells him, now sure that Martin has come to terms with his history of rejection. Of course he has, look at him, it's not like his last rejection happened back in the 80's.

"Well 'One Way or Another' you're going to end up signed so that's good," Martin says, putting his left hand in his pocket, his smile getting even bigger as he paces the dining area of the McDonald's he's in. He's sporting the type of smile that you can hear in someone's voice during a phone conversation.

London, creeped out, tries to forge ahead, "Yeah, I just want to make the right choice, ya know?"

"I know, it would be quite a 'Blue Monday' to wake up and find out you made the wrong decision," Martin says. His smile can't get any wider.

London finally cracks, "Okay, Martin, whatever you are doing on the other side of this line, you can't do it anymore. My friends can be either weird, *or* fat; they can't be both. You can't have your cake and sob uncontrollably about your impending death too."

Martin's smile slowly fades, "You didn't see what I was doing there?"

"Oh, no, I saw, and you're lucky to have a friend like me to make sure you know better than to let others see."

"Don't You Want Me, Bab-"

"-I want you to not do whatever it is you're doing right now. Review what you're doing now, then do the opposite," London says, training Martin like he was one of her pets.

"Okay," Martin says, defeated.

"I'm going to text the girls and let them know you like the name," London tells Martin, then she switches gears, "Did you have a good conversation with Joel?"

"Yup," Martin says. "Joel 'Just Can't Get Enough' of me," he mumbles.

London sits down in a chair, in front of the computer that Tobe uses for his stock shit. She presses the little track-pad on the computer and the screen lights up.

The glowing laptop presents London with a brand new Sienna Wolfe interview.

34- Cyber-Abstinence.

Stanley sits in bed with his laptop, either feverishly working or just hitting random keys to look busy because he doesn't feel like having sex. Chloe can't see his screen so she's just hoping he's accomplishing something. Laying on the other side of the bed with her tablet, Chloe is okay with not having sex because she doesn't have the strength to do anything. She simply lacks the energy required to be on top.

Chloe reads a post on *ThisSpoiledBitch* about the press release that Joel sent out, then she sends the post to Stanley thinking that maybe he'll get bored and check his e-mail. A little part of her hopes this band will prove that she has talent- not only to the world, but also to Stanley. Stanley is this great actor, who often makes *something* out of a nothing role. Even if he only gets shitty monster movies for the rest of career, there will still be a certain segment of the population that will associate a significant chunk of their teen years with Stanley's specific talent. Stanley will always be loved, even if Chloe isn't there anymore. He's the strong one, the talented one. Maybe Chloe would be able to stay home with him if she started believing that she didn't need to keep her buzz alive every night. Changes are needed. The girls *will* perform these songs and they'll do it by stepping away from the spotlight. This way, the next time they're in that light, they'll feel finally like they deserve it. Chloe considers this to be social!heavy learning their lines.

Right now, the only good thing people associate with Chloe is that when she gained some weight, she made a bunch of chicks realize that celebrities are people too. Then, when she lost it all, remarkably fast, she reminded those girls that they're fat, and lazy, and they have no dedication to weight loss so they'll most likely die meaty and bloated, with bodies that look like they've been fished out of a reservoir when, in actuality, they just died from complications of being a fat fuck. People's feelings about Chloe are complicated.

In the end, it comes down to the fact that Chloe is living the life that every girl wants.

She was born into money.

She didn't really have to deal with the pressures of school.

She's always been pretty, even during the acne years.

She's easygoing around boys.

She got a Mercedes Benz for her 15th birthday, even though she couldn't legally drive.

She's dated the same celebrities that other girls her age had posters of on their walls.

She's met actors, and athletes, and directors, and photographers, and politicians.

She bought a giant, perfect house.

She spends her nights with the boy America spent their nights with, for six seasons, 22 episodes a season, and she doesn't even have to sit through commercials.

The girl with the amazing life has to remind herself of all of this before she checks the link that all four girls had sent to her.

That's right, all *four* girls- Dakota, London, Kristen *and Sienna.*

The *FameDiet* page loads, then Chloe begins reading.

When she finishes skimming the blog post, one thing becomes clear.

Sienna is now part of social!heavy.

35- The "Mission Accomplished" Banner.

"Good Morning," Sienna says, answering her own door. She's dressed casually in a vintage Mötley Crüe t-shirt, but her makeup is perfect and her hair is too straight for this unusually early hour of 11 in the morning.

"You win," Dakota says, pushing inside Sienna's house, then immediately strutting toward the kitchen. Sienna follows close behind, happy to have her Bonnie back.

In the rip-off that is Sienna's kitchen, Dakota yanks open the fridge and takes out a bottle of Moët. She pops it open with minimal struggle and obvious experience. Sienna is quick enough that she dodges the recklessly aimed cork, then she casually asks, "A little early for Moët isn't it?"

"No. Let's celebrate your victory, Sienna," Dakota says sarcastically.

Sienna smiles acceptingly at this suggestion and begins fetching some champagne flutes.

Dakota follows close behind, her smoky voice becoming a growl, "Let's celebrate your victory. I know what you did. You don't even have to tell me. I called you because I missed you and as soon as I read the intervie-"

"-oh, you read the interview?" Sienna asks, putting two flutes down on the counter in front of Dakota.

"Of course I read the interview. We read everything. Don't play dumb, you haven't been forgotten for that long."

"Who says I'm forgotten? I got $5,000 for that interview. I love that *FameDiet* is owned by a big shitty corporation with money to burn. They don't offer that much money to forgotten people. Imagine if I had something like audio of a phone call..."

"Awesome, whore," Dakota says, briefly considering cracking the Moët bottle over her ex-best friend's head.

Sienna looks down at the empty flutes and demands, "Pour, retard."

"You're the poor retard," Dakota retorts back childishly, on Sienna's level.

"No, I'm not. I happened to have graduated from high school," Sienna says, grabbing the Moët bottle, then pouring her own glass.

"Retards can graduate from high school. They don't just keep them locked in the school for their entire lives," Dakota says, grabbing the full champagne flute from Sienna.

"I fully support retards' rights to graduate high school. If you don't, then shame on you," Sienna says, pouring another flute of champagne.

"So this is how you're getting back in? Like this?" Dakota asks, disgusted.

Sienna puts the bottle down and takes a sip of her champagne, "Doesn't winning taste good?"

"You're going to be a part of this, but everyone is going to hate you," Dakota tells her ex-best friend.

"Everyone hates *all* of us," Sienna says, clarifying things.

"They have a reason to hate you."

"They do? Or *you* do? Or Chloe does?"

"What was that part about Chloe?" Dakota asks, trying to play off her curiosity as a protective big sister line of questioning.

"You'll find out... if I don't get back in."

"Fuck. Sienna, you're back in."

"That's not your decision alone. Call the other girls. Have them meet us for lunch."

"It's 11 in the fucking morning, they aren't awake yet."

"Then text them. They'll wake up to answer it," Sienna says, leaning against her counter, downing her victory drink.

After grabbing the bottle and filling up her flute again, Sienna says, "I'll have Brent take us so we can finish this bottle... we wouldn't want to match Kristen's impressive DWI record."

Powerless, Dakota agrees to follow Sienna's plan.

Sienna had recorded Dakota's ill-advised phone call. If she releases the file, social!heavy will be boobs deep in so much gossip bullshit, that they'll be destroyed before they even hit the stage.

36- On Your Mind, Like Extensions.

Chloe wakes up to the vibration of her phone on the nightstand. After "accidentally" kicking Stanley's laptop off the corner of the bed, she leans over to check the text. Looking at the phone, Chloe sees it's not a text, but instead a call. It has to be bad news. People only use their phones to make calls when something devastating is happening.

"Hello?" Chloe answers the phone, moving into the bathroom to have the conversation so Stanley can get his mandatory 11 hours of beauty sleep. Or depression sleep. Chloe hopes he's sleeping that long to preserve his looks, not to avoid reviewing hers.

"You didn't respond to Dakota's text," Sienna's voice accuses Chloe.

"What do you want?"

"I just want to make sure you'll be meeting us for lunch at The Ivy," Sienna says, her voice rich with a happiness that worries Chloe.

"Us as in?"

"Me, you, Dakota, London... Kristen."

Chloe grits her teeth, "If you-"

"-whoa, whoa, whoa. I'm here with Dakota and you're on speakerphone. Be careful what you say, everyone can hear, and you don't want to do that to Mommy, do you?

"Dakota?" Chloe asks with morning manvoice.

"Hi, Chlo. I'm sorry."

"I am too."

Sienna takes the phone off speaker, disgusted, "I'm not killing you bitches, we're just going to be friends again! Way to make a girl feel special."

"I'll be there Sienna, but what's this going to solve? Are you going to hold this over our heads for the rest of our lives?"

There's a pause on the line as Sienna considers the last question, then she says, "Yeah. Probably."

37- Tannedmail.

Chloe had no choice but to agree.

Dakota had no choice but to agree.

Kristen and London didn't know what they were walking into, they simply received a text from Dakota to meet them at The Ivy. Arriving at the restaurant, the unsuspecting socialite duo gets within eyeshot of the table, then they both stop, realizing that they've strutted into a trap.

"Oh good, you're here," Sienna says, grinning at the frozen girls.

London and Kristen look to Chloe for cues. Chloe tries to smile, but it comes off looking crooked and inauthentic.

The girls reluctantly take their seats at the table and Sienna looks around at everyone, then gloats, "One big happy family."

"We're not a family," London says, putting a napkin in her lap.

"We are now," Sienna snarls at London. "And this is family dinner," she says, with a big smile as she bats her fake eyelashes at the girls.

"But it's lunchtime," London says innocently.

"Well, imagine we're old people and we're having our family dinner at lunch," Sienna tells her.

"Gross, no. You're lucky we're even here, don't make us pretend we're old. You're pushing it," Kristen says to Sienna.

"Chloe and Dakota invited me today, so if you have a problem..."

None of the girls say anything. They all read the interview. They all know why Sienna was "invited" to lunch, or at least they sort of know why.

"Well. This is fucking awesome," Kristen says sarcastically.

"Don't be a jealous 'Kristen,' Kristen."

"Oh. I wasn't. But I suppose I was being a little 'Sienna,' Sienna."

"No, you weren't being awesome," Sienna says.

"Guess that makes two of us," Kristen snips.

"So, Sienna," Dakota interrupts to stop the infighting. "What did you do while you were... away?"

"Oh, you know, the usual."

"So coke?" Kristen asks, unwilling to give up this fight so soon.

"Sure did. Are you thirsty, Kristen?"

"Nope, but you must have been. You smell like Moët."

"That's... a new perfume," Sienna says.

"It's not new. I wore that scent for a while too," Kristen responds, rolling her eyes.

"Why are you speaking in past tense?" Sienna asks.

"Okay," Chloe exhales, "This is how it's gonna to be. Sienna is back and she can be in the band as long as she knows how to play an instrument. I know you all hate this idea, but I'm sorry... I'm sorry."

The table is silent.

"That waitress is pretty," London notices aloud, looking fondly at the young blonde probably-struggling-actress from across the restaurant. It was the first positive thing London could think of to say. It's *her* responsibility to change direction of this meal. London *needs* this band. The members are both important and unimportant to her. It's time to build, no matter the blocks.

"Another failed model, like the rest," Sienna says, dismissing the waitress. She had already made her assessment in a split second, she didn't need to waste another.

"So what?" Kristen asks.

"You guys are still-"

"-still what?" Dakota interrupts Sienna.

"Doing this. This weird thing where you try to humanize yourself by saying like, 'Oh, look at that white trash lady, I bet she's a good bowling... playing... person.' It's transparent," Sienna says, attempting to establish some sort of authority.

Chloe reaches toward her knife, but Kristen grabs it first, then explains, "Don't you get it Sienna? Waitresses are us without money."

Chloe looks over at the woman and says, "I think it takes a great strength to be around food all day and not turn into a fatty-ass."

"Is that why you fired your cook? Because he looked like he was skimming off the top?" London asks, hoping this was the reason.

Chloe shakes her head, "No, I fired Marcos because he was stealing my underwear. Stanley caught him."

"Holy shit! Is this why Stanley hates the maid trend? What did he do to the guy?" Dakota asks with excitement.

"Nothing, Stanley can't tell Marcos apart from Ricardo, my laundry guy. I walked in the room and Stanley was talking with Marcos, which was odd, then it got even odder when I saw Marcos had one of my thongs in his back pocket."

"Did you freak? How have I never heard this story?" Kristen asks, feeling like her last exile lasted for years.

Chloe shrugs and says, "After Stanley left the room, I let Marcos go."

"Oh, wow," Kristen says, impressed that Chloe had the self-control to not force Stanley to beat the guy up.

"Yeah, I let him keep the thong so he still brings food by every now and then," Chloe says with a smile.

London cocks her head, "Aw, that's sweet... for such a disgusting pervert."

"It's nice because if he ever threatens to write some tell-all book about my... issues, I can just send him a package of my unmentionables and my secrets will remain unmentionable. Stanley can't figure out why the laundry guy keeps bringing scalloped potatoes, but they're so yummy, he doesn't sweat it."

"I don't really have to play an instrument, do I?" Sienna asks, dismissing this story as a lie because it ends with Chloe eating a starch. "I mean, you aren't really doing this band thing, are you?"

Chloe looks to Dakota and she feels a thought beamed into her head. Using techniques she sponged from Stanley, Chloe lets out a huff, puts her elbows on the table, then says, "We'll be faking it. If we tell people we're making an album, then they'll start saying 'popstar' Chloe Warren, instead of 'socialite' Chloe Warren. We never have to actually release anything for this to work. The band thing is a red herring."

"Oh my gosh, we're adopting a red herring. So cute!" London celebrates.

"We might as well tell her, Chlo," Dakota says.

"Oh no, did the SPCA take away our red herring?" London asks, now pouting.

"We're fabricating this band to pretend we have talent," Chloe says.

"Looking hot is a talent," Sienna says, not understanding.

"Some people look at it as a gift, not a talent," Chloe says.

"We are gifted, aren't we?" Sienna reflects warmly.

No matter how gifted Sienna is, she's the type of person that would be re-gifted at a moment's notice.

"Chloe's right," Kristen says, "It's fake."

"Of course it is. But this band will exist. And I will be in it," Sienna tells the table. They aren't going to trick her out of her spot.

"It's just an illusion," Chloe says, looking down at her silverware.

"It's an idea that seems to be able to generate a lot of cash, ergo, the band exists. And I'm in it. Right, Chloe?"

"Right, Sienna," Chloe says, under such duress that this contract would not be valid in a court of law.

celebUtard
"Wolfe Knows."

Hey! Look at that! A picture of **Sienna Wolfe** with all her old friends, and it was taken yesterday. Hmm. That's super weird. I mean, Sienna was totally exiled after her 84th arrest the other week, yet now she's back like nothing happened. Sienna was originally removed so that the girls could turn over a new leaf, right? By turn over a new leaf, we mean that they chose to not get as shitty in public, and they decided to start an odd, electric band.

Despite this history, here they are, all together, eating lunch. Hmm. It seems like the only way that this could happen is if Sienna went to a large news outlet and started airing out dirty laundry. It's almost like **Chloe Warren** and **Dakota Dabney** read an interview from a huge corporation's desperate attempt at securing a portion of the celebrity blogosphere, then the girls realized that Sienna was going to drop bombs next week.

We love being right. And we're always right, even if we stole our rightness from another source that has actual reporters, instead of a staff of failed models who are bitter about their lot in life so they have to rebel against all archetypes of beauty to feel better about their own crappy meaningless existence.

We had to admit that because we were afraid that Sienna Wolfe would find out about it and blackmail our blog. That is one cold bitch we don't want beef with.

We escaped the lawsuits from Lindy, but we're still worried about the Wolfe's teeth.

Until next time, stay tardy, celebUverse.

38- In The Warm Embrace of the Enemy.

"I had a bad day," London says, her arms raised like Frankenstein's monster as she walks into Tobe's kitchen.

Tobe holds in a smile when he sees his sad, drowning, pawn of a girlfriend. "Aw, come here," he says, not because he wants her to, but because the sooner he has his arms wrapped around London, the sooner he can sport a joker smile.

London shuffles over, then wraps her long arms around Tobe's rock hard middle.

Tobe mentally compliments himself for being so firm, and he concludes that his ab exercises, while possibly bastardizing his posture, might actually be working. He tries to decide if his core definition is worth losing another quarter inch of height. He makes a mental note to google what type of shoes Tom Cruise wore during the Kidman/Holmes eras. He hopes they were Gucci, but he'll settle for the signature Saint Laurent blake zip cropped 45 boots that he saw River White wear during the *Vanity Fair* Oscar party. Still trapped in the grip of London Francis, Tobe decides to make the best out of the situation and feed off his girlfriend's misery, "Why are you sad?" he asks.

"Sienna's back."

The words hit Tobe's ear and those little sound waves smash him so hard that he almost falls back onto the active burners of the stove. If he didn't have London grounding him, Tobe might have suffered a fame ending burn.

"What's the matter?" London asks, feeling Tobe's entire body shake.

"Sienna Wolfe?" he gasps, wobbly, reaching up past London's pointy shoulder blades to wipe away the sweat evacuating out of his pores.

"Do we know another Sienna?" London asks, trying to lean back, but Tobe's embrace has turned into a bear hug.

"I've never met her," Tobe says, finally letting London go.

"You definitely have. Sienna was always at the parties we both went to."

"I've never been introduced," Tobe says, casually, going back to the crackling eggs on the stove.

"Good," London snarls, her trademark smile fleeting for a moment.

"Babe, if we're going to do this, I'm going to need to be introduced to your friends."

"I agree, but Sienna isn't a friend," London declares, negating the reinstatement that occurred earlier today.

"I thought she was back?" Tobe asks, a little too fast. He looks to the eggs, then immediately turns off the burners because the kitchen feels unbearably hot.

"Um, yeah... she's back, for now. She has shit on the other girls so we have to bring her back... until we figure it out," London laments with a pout.

"What does 'figure it out' mean, London?" Tobe asks, moving back to his girlfriend, fast.

"Until we find out what she knows, then either leak it before she can or..."

"Or what?"

"She stays part of the group and holds us hostage."

Tobe has just been handed an instruction manual for keeping Sienna around. Knowing that this queen has beaten back the rioting villagers and regained her throne is almost too much for Tobe to handle. He's completely and totally apathetic about London, but she's going to get him close to Sienna and, for that, she's become Tobe's best friend. For that– he gives her a kiss.

Sweeping London off her feet, Tobe carries his lanky girlfriend out of the kitchen, through the living room, then down the hall to the bedroom.

Tobe wants to make sure that London keeps him around as long as she keeps Sienna in social!heavy.

39- Courtside.

Joel arranged for the girls to meet at a studio his brother owns in Burbank.

The once frontman- Joel Harper- gives the failed frontman- Martin Turner- strict instructions on what must be done when the "band" arrives at the location, "You'll snap as many pictures as you possibly can at the front entrance. Rolls and rolls of pictures. Even after the girls leave, take pictures of palm trees and passing cars. After the band is inside, I'll have Chloe pop out of the back door of the studio. As soon as you hear the commotion and the paps catch her scent, I'm going to need you to slide inside the front door. I've done this million times during my career and the plan works."

Martin notices a little sparkle in the retired rocker's eye as he talks about how he'd sneak random girls into various hotel rooms so that he could cheat on his wife. "It wasn't about the sex, it was about the creative process," Joel tells Martin, who shoots back a quick, inauthentic wink. For most paps, it *is* all about the sex- the nipple slips and the upskirts- so perhaps it wasn't that odd that Martin moved on from music to invasive photography.

On speakerphone, Martin and Joel call Chloe and inform her of the plan. They request that she put on something simple-cute and maybe get some acting tips from Stanley.

Chloe agrees to everything, then ends the call. Today, Chloe is important. Today, she has a task. Today, she needs to look good because these pictures will be everywhere.

Walking down the hall to one of her closets, Chloe texts the girls the details.

At Lindy's divorce party, Chloe dressed to get attention. Today, it doesn't matter what she wears, the hype will put a spotlight on her regardless. With this knowledge, she chooses a sky blue long sleeve stand collar Chloé shirt, then puts a tight white unbuttoned Paul Smith button-down over it. Since layers might be too hot, she slides on some patchwork Ralph Lauren short shorts. She doesn't wear a bra because none of her bras fit anymore. They're all too big.

For ten full minutes, Chloe adjusts mirrors and contorts herself to see if there's any way someone could snap a mid-stride, cellulite exposing photo of her. Despite being content with the content of her thighs, Chloe continues to stare at her body. She feels fat and she knows she's not fat, but she reviews every angle, waiting for the truth to be revealed. There's a fundamental gap between what Chloe sees reflected back at her and how her brain interprets this image. She can't explain what's going on in her head because she's still trying to figure it out herself. She knows that if she can see her ribs, she's skinny. Chloe moves her body. At certain angels, her ribs disappear under a layer of fat. Or maybe it's muscle? No, how could there be any muscle left? Her body has been dining on her muscle to stay alive. Despite hating the way she looks, Chloe still wants to be photographed today. She wants it, she needs it, and she doesn't have any more time left to stare at herself because she has to appear in front of a group of judgmental eyes and their lenses. If they tell her she looks skinny, she'll feel nothing because the one photograph where she looks otherwise will be the one that gets sold. Chloe throws her phone into her Chanel 2.55 classic flap bag, then heads to the work, leaving Stanley with his laptop for yet another afternoon.

Chloe decides to take her electric car to Burbank today. She wants to make simple statements. She wants to rebel against waste. She wants to reject common thinking and embrace the future.

The quiet car pulls up in front of the studio and brings immediate chaos. None of the paps expected Chloe to arrive early- they didn't even expect her to arrive on time- yet here she is, a full half hour before the time that K.Kay leaked to the pap agencies this morning. Chloe instantly charms every last one of the scrambling secret vampires. They each need their shots and Chloe makes sure they're happy with their coverage. She also makes sure everyone gets a good look at what she's wearing so when they spot her again, they'll immediately swarm her. It was up to the paparazzi to make a scene later, and because of this scene, they'll miss the real story.

Chloe gets her picture taken a couple hundred times, then disappears inside the studio to read the blogs on her phone.

Whenever Chloe visits Stanley on the set of his monster movies, she sees taped "X" marks on the ground. The actors use these X's to make sure they're in frame. Chloe is picturing little X's everywhere today. It's all about staying in the frame. It's all about getting the shots that people will pay to see. It's all about creating a fictional story that will entertain.

Eventually, the rest of the girls arrive, and Chloe puts her phone away, hiding it from any Wolfes.

Grabbing a half empty can of Diet Coke out of Dakota's hand, Chloe makes her way to her next mark. Normally, a can of Diet Coke isn't a good attention-getter, but when there are only four pictures of Chloe ingesting *anything* in the past month, suddenly it becomes the ultimate prop. Plus it doesn't have that many calories.

The back door of the studio flies open, and like a bunny hopping into a hyena den, Chloe is spotted and surrounded.

"Chloe! Chloe! Chloe!" chant the paps.

Meeting the lenses again, the solo-socialite hits her mark, then she looks around. Joel neglected to mention that the back door leads out to a grassy undeveloped lot and some cracked basketball courts. What was Chloe going to say that she went out there for? A quick pickup game?

"Chloe! Chloe!"

The paps have their vans parked in the lot and it's almost like they can't believe their luck. "You look pretty, Chloe!" is followed by, "Did you get kicked out of the band, Chloe?"

Those instantly recognizable doe eyes look to the man who yelled a hearsay headline. It's oh-so-simple to these sheep. They assume that anyone leaving the studio solo was ousted from the group in some epic, headline bursting manner. Or at least they hope that's the case. Or maybe they don't hope that? Chloe could never tell, until the story broke.

"I just stepped outside for some air, guys," Chloe says.

"Back off guys, give her some air, give her some air," the pap with the bushy hair says.

"Chloe, is Sienna in the band only because she threatened to give up secrets about you and Dakota?" a pap in cargo shorts and an absolutely filthy t-shirt asks.

Chloe takes in one big breath of fresh air, acts like she's about to answer the question, then turns around and heads back into the studio.

39.5- Who Will I Be?

Chloe drops the half full Diet Coke can in the trash, then follows the sound of an argument until she reaches a studio lounge. At first, the room seems unnecessary, but then she realizes it's probably a place for rappers to smoke pot with their entourage while they're working on their album.

Martin is safely inside and he's leaning ridiculously against a pool table. Already in deep conversation with Sienna, he didn't waste any time addressing the Wolfe in the room. The girls "forgot" to tell Sienna about this meeting, but Sienna's agent, Max Corby, anxiously made a call last night to Joel about the business end of this matter. After Joel confirmed with London that Sienna is back, he informed Max of the studio plans.

Sienna remembered Martin as soon as she saw him. He's the pap who didn't take her picture. She waited and waited, and he just sat there with his stupid coffee. Sienna felt like Martin had power over her when he chose to let her go uncaptured. His inaction spoke volumes. She wasn't going to acknowledge that the moment occurred, and maybe, hopefully, he wouldn't either. It was humiliating enough having to share the sidewalk with Martin, she didn't need to relive it amongst a bunch of girls who absolutely would have been photographed in the same situation.

Instead of leaving a window for Martin to pull the *You looked a little shitty the other day* card, Sienna made her presence felt and initiated an argument.

Of course, Martin jumped right into the disagreement- all it took was Sienna's offhand mention of a recent purchase and the subsequent trouble PETA was giving her for it.

"It's about evolution, fat man," Sienna says as she lounges in a cranberry armchair.

"Martin," he responds in a quiet voice.

"Okay. It's about evolution, Martin," Sienna amends her point, annoyed that this little pap had the audacity to actually have a name.

Chloe leans next to Martin on the pool table, and begins paying attention. It seems that even although Sienna hasn't discussed this band with the girls in detail, she's already up to speed about what they're aiming for. Evolution is the perfect word. Maybe this *will* work out with Sienna in the group?

"Evolution has nothing to do with it," Martin says, shaking his head.

"Does so. If Mother Nature didn't want us clubbing those seals, she would have given them a shell."

"Evolution happens over a period of millions of years," Martin says to Sienna, not sure if she's really serious with her seal defense.

"Right, they've had all this time to prepare and they didn't, so don't blame humans for these lazy ass seals."

Martin blinks his eyes quickly like he's staring into the sun, then he turns to Chloe, "Oh good, you're back, we were just..."

Obviously not talking about music like Chloe had assumed. She should've known better than to think Sienna understood their vision.

"Sienna was talking shit," Kristen says, "Absolute shit."

"I had a point," Sienna defends herself, with a snarl.

"No, you didn't," Kristen dismisses her, "But then again, if you needed a point, evolution would have provided you with one, right?"

Martin giggles like a schoolgirl until he catches multiple burning glances, then he immediately regains composure and begins his presentation. "Thank you all for coming," he says, grabbing a folder off the pool table, "I wanted to start by giving you copies of the lyrics that London wrote."

"What? How come London gets to be the lyricist?" Sienna whines. Sienna's not sure if the lyricist sings the songs too, but it still seems like a power position that she was passed over for.

Martin counts out five packets of lyrics, then hands the first one to Sienna and says, "London is the lyricist... because she wrote the lyrics."

Sienna leafs through the stapled together pile of songs, "These are-"

"-like Bowie in the 80's? Remarkable isn't it?" Martin finishes Sienna's sentence before she can verbally destroy one of his proudest accomplishments.

Stretching to give London the last packet, Martin winks at her and she smiles. London Francis begins to read her masterwork for the first time.

Sienna doesn't know the lyrics are actually just K.Kay's transcription of what the girls heard on the tape. No one has let it slip to Sienna that the cassette of demos exists, so Chloe does a little acting, and says, "These lyrics look like they'll make great songs."

Martin giddily interjects, "Arguably some of the finest songs of the genre."

Chloe shoots Martin a warning glance, and he contorts his face into a near-frown. "Next," Martin says, taking out five different sheets of paper, "I've printed out the instruments that you're going to need to order."

The girls wait with such an anticipation on their perfect faces that Martin nearly begins second guessing his selections, so he gets right down to it.

"Kristen," Martin addresses the beautiful piece of American pie sitting in the center of the sofa, "This is the keyboard you're going to need." Kristen takes the piece of paper and looks at it. She nods in agreement, accepting the challenge.

"Sienna," Martin says to the outcast of the group, "You're going to want to buy this synthesizer." Sienna doesn't get out of the chair so Martin has to walk over and hand her the sheet. Looking at the paper, Sienna says, "I got the synthesizer," then frowns, like it was the 'Old Maid' card. Martin remembers Joel's rules, and he tells Sienna, "You shouldn't be disappointed with that, it's the centerpiece of the band. The synthesizer is what makes you a New Wave band. Plus, you and Kristen can help each other learn. The synthesizer is like a keyboard with a ton more knobs. It's like a super-keyboard. And it's all yours."

This synthesizer is huge, too big for a twig-armed girl to move. This means Sienna doesn't have to leave the house to practice, which means she can lie about practicing and just hang out in her house with her cat, The Box. If she finds a cute instructor, he'd have to come over to her house for the lessons. This crappy box of knobs is an instrument that two people could sit behind, very close to each other, and play. Maybe Kristen would have to come over to Sienna's house to help her learn. During all that practice time with her bandmate, Sienna could surely find some dirt that she could use to get Kristen kicked out of social!heavy. Sienna accepts her instrument and plans on converting it into an instrument of destruction.

"Dakota, this was made for you," Martin says, presenting the next piece of paper to the nervous girl with the jittering freckled legs.

"It's the guitar!" Dakota squeals. She wanted to be the guitarist because it was bad ass enough that a big brute like Jake would respect her for it, and it also wasn't the shitty ass synthesizer. Plus, it could easily be painted pink to look cute. "Thank you, Martin. I love it!" Dakota says, embracing her new identity. She pauses for a moment and asks, "Wait, do bands have two guitarists? Am I playing second fiddle?"

London cranes her long neck so she can see Dakota's paper, then she comments, "That's definitely a guitar. No worries."

Martin looks at London with one of those looks that seems to indicate he's rethinking the feasibility of the entire band. He stifles the expression and says, "London," then he passes her the piece of paper with her future on it.

London looks at what Martin selected her to play, then, almost worried, she says, "Drums and a drum machine?"

"You're going to need both."

"You think I can handle both?" London asks, with hesitation.

"I do. Once you learn drums on a kit, programming them isn't that far off. You just need to get the beat and you'll be fine."

London looks at the sheet of paper with trepidation. Slowly, little by little, a feeling of glee overtakes her. She wasn't given just one instrument like the other girls, she has two- double the responsibility. She also "wrote" the band's songs. Kinda. Sorta. That little white lie was required so that Sienna didn't have the key to sink them.

The dialog in Sienna's sabotage movie is already written:

```
                    SIENNA
          An old fat man wrote the
          songs. The girls can't
          play their instruments.
          They lip-sync their
          live shows. That's if
          they make it to the stage.
          Their look-alikes are
          pretty believable though.
          This band is not a passion.
          It's a transaction.
```

It is essential that the girls keep re-writing this script until Sienna can't remember her lines.

Holding out the final piece of paper, Martin announces, "Chloe. This is yours."

Chloe looks down at the white sheet, then up at the girls, and says, "It's blank."

Panic.

"Take it," Martin says, still holding the paper out.

"Are you asking me to not be in this band?" Chloe squeaks, accepting the empty assignment.

"You aren't going to play an instrument. You're the lead singer. Joel gave me a list of some good voice people he trusts," Martin says casually.

"Martin! You think I need a voice coach?" Chloe yelps. There's too much mixing inside of her, and she can't figure out if she's pointless when it comes to the band.

"Even Britney has a voice coach," Martin says.

"But she doesn't even si-"

"-exactly," Martin interrupts, and this pacifies Chloe enough that she presses the piece of paper against her bony chest, then responds, "You can't make this decision, Martin. Girls?"

The girls don't even have to look at each other, "We've already decided, together," Dakota says, remembering how Chloe totally shut her down at dinner.

"We all agreed that you're the obvious choice," London confirms.

Sienna's foot bobs in the air, her right leg balancing on her left, which could be sort of like an agreeing nod.

Chloe blushes and the tears build up in the corners of her big eyes. "Thank you," she says. Earlier today, Chloe wanted to tear her fat face off. Now, that same face has been selected to appear at center stage for the most important adventure these girls have ever attempted.

Martin takes in this moment. He's made these un-pleasable girls happy and that's something to be proud of. He got five socialites to smile without having to yell, "How about a smile! Please! Look over here!" like he normally does, out on the street. Sienna was standoffish, but she seemed to eventually accept her role. She placed the piece of paper in her purse, instead of balling it up like it was a parking ticket.

Chloe wipes her eyes, then giggles, "You were talking about this while I was gone? No wonder I walked in to such a ridiculous conversation, you were covering up your real discussion! I'm so relieved that it was all an act, I thought she was serious," Chloe says, pointing at Sienna.

"Ohhh," Martin coos, "That wasn't a fake conversation, she really does think that."

Chloe nervously looks at Sienna.

"What?" Sienna springs up, "I was just saying that baby seal fur coats shouldn't be illegal. Baby seal coats and kid touchers aren't in the same league."

No one can argue the second part of this point and the first part was already argued, so the girls happily leave the studio with their new identities.

Left alone in the studio, Martin begins work on replaying all his tracks with the equipment Joel's brother provided. This will only be a guide- the girls will still need to play these songs. A group of socialites, living the simple life, have been presented with a real challenge, and the results will either crown them "just another pretty face" or "the new face of rock music in the twenty-first century."

Martin has identified each of their strengths, now it's up to them to do the heavy lifting.

40- Drumming Off-beat.

"Tobbb-" London eeks out as she walks through the hall of Tobe's penthouse. Popping into his room, she lets out the rest, "-beeeeeee."

Tobe takes his eyes away from the TV and looks at his stretched Barbie of a girlfriend.

"Guess what I am!" London caws, as she launches her long frame onto Tobe's bed.

"Please don't tempt me," Tobe requests, his eyes moving back to the TV screen.

Since she wasn't looking for an answer, London pays no attention to Tobe's comment, and proudly holds out her piece of paper that displays the drum set and drum machine she's been assigned.

"I'm going to be a drummer," London announces.

"A drummer," Tobe repeats, almost as a question.

"Yes, look," she demands.

Tobe takes the piece of paper and glances at it, then immediately hands it back, opting to hold the channel changer because it provided a more promising future. The channels click by fast as Tobe mumbles, "Oh. Congrats. I'm sure you'll be a famous drummer like..."

London lays on the bed, deep in thought, trying to think of a drummer's name. She can't.

"Hm, now that I think about it, I don't know any famous drummers," Tobe says, then lets London lay in this fact.

"That's why it's perfect!" London realizes, "If I'm only even half good, I'll still be the most famous drummer in the world."

"Don't you want to be..." Tobe swings the channel changer in the air as he looks for the right word, then finds it, "...the *star*, not the drummer."

"I'm going to be the star-drummer."

"You do know that they put the drummer at the back of the stage, right?"

London shrugs, "I know, that's fine, you can't have the drums at the front of the stage. It would look shitty."

"As long as you're happy with it, that's all that matters," Tobe says, his eyes moving back to the images on the TV.

"I was happy until I came here," London says in her baby voice, then she pouts for sympathy.

Tobe turns the TV off and realizes that if he's going to find out about Sienna's instrument, he's going to have to play along with London.

"Let's go order your drums," he says, getting up with a sigh.

"Yay!" London celebrates, shooting off the bed, then running out to Tobe's laptop in the living room.

"What website do you use to order this stuff?" London asks, sitting on the sofa, then resting her talons on the keyboard of Tobe's laptop.

"I'll do it. How about you tell me what everyone else is playing while I order," Tobe says, wandering into the room in just his tight white underwear.

"Okay," London agrees, moving over a tiny bit so that Tobe can wedge his ass between her and the edge of the sofa. Tobe sits down, then puts his laptop on his legs so when London mentions Sienna, she won't notice how hard he gets.

"Chloe is the singer…" London says, excited for her best friend.

"Chloe?" Tobe asks, quickly bringing up a random window so London doesn't spot his Sienna Wolfe background (December- two years ago- *Vanity Fair*- eating an apple).

"Yeah, Chloe is the only one of us that can sing."

"I guess I've just never seen anything going into her mouth, so I can't imagine lyrics coming out," Tobe dryly responds.

London breezes over the comment as if it was never said, "Kristen got the keyboard, obviously."

"Why's that obvious?"

"Because she plays the piano."

"No," Tobe gasps, unable to fathom this.

"Yeah, that dude they said she was dating before Johnny was actually her piano teacher. Plus a piano is pretty much like a big coffee table so it's super easy to do drugs off of."

"What's Sienna going to be playing?" Tobe asks. He impatiently plugs in the numbers that he has memorized off his credit card so he can buy $1,989.76 worth of drum related paraphernalia. He isn't even going to ask London for her card. This is a gift. A big, noisy, immovable gift. It's something that will keep London occupied, at her house, and out of Tobe's penthouse. It's like paying two grand to a nanny so she'll watch his 5'9" child.

"Sienna got the synthesizer," London says, her interest minimal.

Tobe quickly types in London's address as the delivery location, orders the items, then goes back to the page and begins to order himself a synthesizer.

"Did Sienna happen to mention what the model number on her synthesizer is?" Tobe asks, trying to sound casual.

"What?" London asks.

"Er. You know. How'd she feel about that instrument, it's sort of, I don't know, a shitty choice."

"Is there no satisfying you, Tobe Price?" London giggles, "She was mad, but that's Sienna. Plus Martin said that it was the centerpiece of the band."

"She believed that horse shit?" Tobe asks, looking over at London as he hits "Enter" and completes his synthesizer order.

London shrugs, "I don't think Sienna believes anything we say. I think she only believes what those nasty blogs write about her. And that's a little shitty."

"Who the fuck is Martin?" Tobe asks, returning to the casual mention of a mystery man. Is this Martin guy Sienna's boyfriend? Sienna can't have a boyfriend. Sienna *can't* have a boyfriend. Sienna *cannot have a boyfriend.*

"Oh," London says, then, with an odd crimp in her heart, she lies. "He's, like, Sienna's agent."

It wasn't that bad of a lie, London tells herself. Tobe has met Martin. He knows who Martin is. If Tobe isn't paying attention, it's his fault.

London was sure she was becoming a *new* girl, but this new girl is still acting like the *old* girl. She had to lie, right? It was required to hide the truth so that she doesn't lose her once in a lifetime chance, right?

Lies, lies, lies, yeah.

"Oh," Tobe says, mimicking London.

Sienna Wolfe's agent is Max Corby. Anyone stalking her would have this information.

Tobe quickly googles, "Is Max short for Martin?"

Google agrees it's not.

41- Wrong Size.

"Keep them closed!"

"They're closed! I can't close them any tighter or I'll start getting crow's feet," Kristen says, while Johnny makes sure his slow moving girlfriend doesn't fall in the pool as a result of her mandated blindness. Johnny's hand and the cool night breeze both guide Kristen across her yard. When she's ten feet away from the house, Johnny says, "Okay, open 'em!"

Kristen's eyelids lift to reveal a huge gift wrapped box leaning up against her back door. She immediately looks back at Johnny. "Go ahead," he says, then his oft photographed smile starts overtaking his defined bone structure. This is the first present Johnny has purchased for Kristen since they started seeing each other, and he hopes this will cement their relationship.

Johnny is so taken by Kristen because she looks very innocent on the outside, but she's gossiped about as a girl never possessing innocence. Kristen doesn't give pieces of herself away, but the sections that Johnny has stolen have been magnificent.

The entire- bright blonde, perfect teeth, mathematically improbable dipping nose- appearance is just a front. The presentation provides a complete story and never requests anyone to delve deep in order to feel like they truly know Kristen Paxton. This is how the real Kristen Paxton hides, behind an avatar so pretty that people use it as their avatar on message boards and comment threads.

Kristen bends down and unwraps the big box, tearing the paper away to reveal... a synthesizer.

Johnny bought her a synthesizer.

It was the most misguidedly sweet present she'd ever received.

"Johnny," Kristen says, backing away from the box, slowly trying to figure out how to react. "They actually made me the keyboardist, and Sienna got the synthesizer."

"I know," Johnny says, his smile not fading.

"Holy shit, are you sleeping with Sienna?" the confused socialite asks, backing toward the pool. This was Kristen's worst fear. She knew Sienna was going to get even with her, but this betrayal seems particularly brutal, even for Ms. Wolfe. Maybe it was karma for what Kristen did to Lindy?

"No, no, no," Johnny says, rushing to put his arm behind his girlfriend so she doesn't fall backwards, "I spoke with Martin."

Reacting fast, Johnny scrapes a metal chair across the concrete and Kristen sits down in it, her body rigid. Johnny crouches on one knee in front of the chair. It's a gesture that looks cute because he's attractive, but if he wasn't, would look horrifyingly cheesy.

"You- you aren't supposed to know about Martin," Kristen says, her thoughts spinning.

"There are things... going on... behind the scenes," Johnny tries to explain carefully.

"Oh no. Are you not really here for me? Is this something that my agent put you up to? Is he paying you?" Kristen asks, her body folding.

"No. Okay..." Johnny says, collecting his thoughts. This is the first time that he's witnessed a visible crack in Kristen. He now feels like he's talking to the fragile little girl that has been kept isolated.

Figuring out how to discuss this situation without making it seem like a sinister plot, Johnny huffs out a breath, then begins, "I called your agent because I wanted to know when your birthday was. Wikipedia said it was the 5th of March, your IMDB said August 17th, your website just said 'Julyish' and it linked to your Amazon wishlist, which declared that your birthday to be 'everyday' so there was some confusion. I wanted to make sure I didn't miss that important day, no matter when it was, and the only person that I could trust to know the real day was your agent. With no greater agenda, I called him, and he told me the right day. We filled the rest of the call with a little casual conversation, and I was telling him how happy I am. He took down my number, then clearly informed me if I messed this up, he'd 'destroy me.'" After Johnny says this, his smile punctuates the retelling.

"He actually said he'd destroy you?"

"Yeah. And he didn't even do the tension-release laugh."

Kristen giggles through her nervousness.

"Yeah, that's it, right there," Johnny says.

On a scale of disastrous presents, this has gone from honeymoon voyage on the Titanic, to receiving a Blu-ray of "Titanic" despite already owning a copy.

"Anyway," Johnny continues, and it feels good that he can to do this. It was nice to share information with someone about their personal life without having to reference details from a blog post. "I guess he gave my number to Martin, who in turn, called me."

"Why did Martin call you?"

"Are we being totally honest here?"

"I'd hope so," Kristen responds, nervous to be totally honest with someone she likes this much.

"Alright. He called me to make sure that you're serious about this, the band thing. And... he was calling to see if you were drinking again."

"I'm not drinking ag-"

"-I know and I told him that," Johnny says, putting his hands up to block her outrage.

"He needs to back off. He's not some musical genius. His songs failed. He's just a fucking photographer," Kristen hisses, her emotions rollercoastering.

Johnny finally pulls a chair close and sits down next to Kristen. "Maybe he's just a photographer, but he's the one photographer that gives a shit about you as a person, and that's pretty rare."

"He's trying to be something he's not."

"Is that uncommon here?"

"No. And that's the problem. Martin is fucking common," Kristen spits, confused about exactly why she's feeling angry and scared.

"You're afraid of him," Johnny says, quietly marveling.

"You're out of your mind," Kristen says, leaning over, her elbows on her thighs.

Johnny's voice gets a little louder, "The rest of the story is that Martin believes in you, and he doesn't believe in Sienna. He wanted to make sure that you have a synthesizer... so you can take over for Sienna when it all falls apart for her."

Kristen's mind spins as she tries to process all of this transparent planning. She's worked for a new beginning, but her old insecurities still threaten to turn her back into the mess she once was. Her producer, a guy who's about ten minutes removed from being a scumbag pap, is discussing things with the one boy that she actually likes. Even though she wanted to let Johnny in, he chose to climb through a half open window to get to her. A couple of minutes ago, Kristen almost backed into the pool because she thought she was being destroyed by Sienna- now she's fearful that Martin is becoming too involved in all of this. Is this band serving as some sad attempt for a failed man to compensate for the way his own shitty life turned out? Martin knows how to make a good song; he doesn't know how to be a socialite. Despite this, Johnny defends Martin as though he's the influence that will solidify this project.

Ignoring Martin's shortcomings, he's put his faith in Kristen, and he did so based on a conversation with the boy she likes. He was writing Sienna off at the same time he was asking Johnny to make sure a synthesizer ended up in Kristen's possession. In this case, Kristen had become the fail-safe, not the liability. This is all very *new*.

"Martin wants me to play the keyboard and synthesizer?" Kristen asks a question she already knows the answer to because she believes the expected response will clarify things for her.

"What he said to me was, 'When they show up at their first gig, I want someone I trust on the synth'... whatever that means," Johnny says, ignorant and in-the-know at the same time.

Kristen wasn't able to unlock the combination of how to stay in rehab, but these new keys might make up for everything. She stands up and reaches her hand out. Johnny locks his fingers between hers.

Kristen whispers, "Thank You," so quietly that Johnny briefly considers it may have just been the wind.

OXYGEN WASTER
It's House Arrest (Again) For The Feckless Four.

When your band consists of a bunch of ex-convicts like **Dakota Dabney**, **London Francis**, **Chloe Warren**, **Kristen Paxton**, and **Sienna Wolfe**, you have to know that there's a good chance that you're going to arrive at your first gig without one (or more) of your bandmates. The band's manager, **Joel Harper**, knows this better than anyone. Remember those **Luana** concerts you saw on YouTube? Remember how, at every concert, a least one of the members looked unfamiliar? That's the fault of both Joel Harper's ego and the fact that these men had the freedom to do whatever they wanted, on and off the stage. Joel's agency tells us this is exactly why he's put the girls on house arrest. How about that? When even Joel "King of Ruining Gigs" Harper is worried about you missing gigs, you have to know that you're one of the top five most unreliable human beings alive. Assuming you make it to the stage, look to the left, then the right, to figure out who rounds out the top five.

For five long days:

- We haven't seen Chloe sneaking out of the gym in those ultra-tight workout pants.
- We haven't seen London at the **Petsville, LA** located by her mansion. Oops- trade secret, if you need a picture of London then Petsville, LA is where to go.
- We haven't seen Kristen sneaking out of that old church basement after **AA** (which says more about her booze addiction than it does about her musical dedication).
- We haven't even seen Sienna Wolfe out committing hate crimes, so we're starting to think that this whole house arrest thing might be legit.

The girls are used to being arrested, but usually their jail time is measured in hours, not in days. Like all prison movies, someone is going to grab a spoon (in this case a silver one), and they're going to start digging their way out of their cell.

Follow Oxygen Waster for the up-to-the-minute details on who escapes first!

FAMEDIET

Paul Dabney: "The Media Is Slowly Killing My Daughter!"

Today, the **FameDiet** office was visited by **Paul Dabney**. We had a full meeting (with a working lunch) about whether Paul Dabney would even be given the security clearance to come up to our floor of the **Tertin Werner** building.

Editor's Note: FameDiet is owned by subsidiary Tertin Werner.

Things have been rocky when dealing with Paul Dabney after that nasty incident where he threatened to "F**k-in" the head, of Tertin Werner CEO, **Jack McDempsey**. Since then, Mr. Dabney has been banned from the building.

The whole issue started because a TW station chose to broadcast video footage of Paul attempting to sell a sex tape of himself and then-wife, TV Producer, **Lynne Dabney**. Paul wanted TW to air the tape in a late night slot after a semi-popular hidden camera show. "It can be the first sex tape to premiere on cable!" Paul told Mr. McDempsey. "This is why you're losing to the internet, you aren't giving the people what they want... kinda famous people screwing in poorly lit videos," Paul informed the CEO of an incredibly successful company.

It turns out Mr. McDempsey appreciated *part* of this idea, and after Paul left, Mr. McDempsey requested the security footage that was filmed via the camera in the corner of his office. Ironically, this footage was aired on the same semi-popular hidden camera show that Paul wanted for his lead-in.

Despite this history, Paul was given the clearance to come up to our office, because, well, his daughter has been laying low lately and we need to know why.

Speaking exclusively to FameDiet, Paul Dabney said that his "little princess" (**Dakota Dabney**) hasn't been seen for the past week because the media is crumbling her fragile mind-state.

Throughout the 40 minute speech Paul Dabney gave, he mentioned the following:

•Because of the media, Dakota's bone density has been found to be that of a menopausal woman.

•Because of the media, Dakota now requires **Ambien** to fall asleep at night.

•Because of the media, Paul Dabney has shortness of breath.

•Because of the media, Paul Dabney no longer participates in activities he once enjoyed.

•Because of the media, Dakota has acquired an astigmatism from the constant, bright, unmerciful flashes bursting from the cameras that "...might also be robbing Dakota of her precious life essence."

So there you have it, from Paul Dabney himself. Dakota's life has been ruined by the media, so Paul did what any concerned father would do... he sold the story to a media outlet with worldwide reach. Makes sense.

celebUtard
"When The Girls Are Away, The Wolfe Will Play"

With the rest of her **social!heavy** band-mates on a **Joel Harper** imposed exile, we're forced to talk to **Sienna Wolfe**. It's not that we don't like talking to Sienna- we love it- she's one of the most honest voices in LA today, but we can't ignore the fact that she'll probably destroy one of the most intriguing bands of the past five years. We even started a Music section here at celebUtard so that we could cover each and every track that leaks from this super-group of girls who have no musical background.

It's been two weeks since we've seen the girls so we had to do our own hunting. A little bird gave us a tip that Sienna was ending her media blackout so we put on that outfit that makes guys try to touch our ass, then we went Wolfe sniping.

It only took 43 seconds for Sienna to give us a quotable after we approached her in front of **Halogen** (don't judge us, we have to get out of the office too, you know). That timestamp is not an exaggeration, watch the phone footage we shot, after the jump.

Here's a transcript if you're at work and can't watch the video:

Our Girl: So where's your band tonight?

Sienna Wolfe: I don't know, why don't you ask them?

OG: Because I'm asking a geography question. I don't know where they are so I can't ask them.

SW: They all got the kissing disease, at the same time.

OG: Mono?

SW: What?

OG: They got mono?

SW: Listen, this music stuff is their bag, fashion is my bag.

OG: Um. Okay. What are you wearing tonight?

SW: Clothes and a necklace.

OG: That's all you're going to give me? I thought you really like fashion?

SW: I do. I said I like fashion, not nosy d-bags.

OG: Meaning me?

SW: Don't be so hard on yourself.

OG: Oh okay, you meant the paps.

SW: No, I meant you, but you could at least argue the point. Have some fucking self-esteem.

After that, we awkwardly walked away. Then we drank three vodka sours. Then we think we got roofied, or the spring roll we ate from the celebUtard fridge earlier was expired. Then we puked in a cab. Then we ate some Ben and Jerry's and went to sleep.

Sienna Wolfe has a way of getting under your skin, like a disease.

Until next time, stay tardy, celebUverse.

OXYGEN WASTER

Paul Dabney: "Cocaine is Slowly Killing My Daughter!"

Multiple recent attempts by **OXYGEN WASTER** to get any new information regarding **The Feckless Four** have been unsuccessful. **Chloe Warren, Dakota Dabney, London Francis,** and **Kristen Paxton** are still locked up in their houses, and their agents still claim that the talentless socialites are working on music for the forthcoming **social!heavy** project. The only people we've seen visiting the girls, besides their boyfriends, are their "coaches" who are helping them learn their instruments. We researched these mentors and everyone who's teaching social!heavy how to play has previously been somehow tied to Joel's band **Luana**. If they were able to keep the secrets about what Joel did to *those girls* in the studio, they will definitely keep the secrets about *these girls* in the studio.

Sienna Wolfe, a card carrying member of social!heavy, has been seen all over LA which seems to contradict numerous pages of the Harper LLC Guidebook To Selling a Boatload of Mediocre Novelty Songs. It doesn't make sense; Sienna is a social butterfly while the rest of the girls are trapped in their cocoons.

So what's going on? What has gripped these girls like a never ending sale at **Fred Segal**? One man has an answer to that question. According to Dakota Dabney's father, **Paul Dabney**, Dakota has spent the last few weeks locked in the house, doing cocaine. That's right, Kristen Paxton, a well-known ~~coke-head~~ ex-coke-head has re-introduced all of the social!heavy girls to cocaine- well, that's if you believe Paul Dabney. Paul tells OW that his daughter has been doing "Scarface levels" of coke. Paul has already "witnessed" the devastating side effects. "The coke is traveling through Dakota's sinus passages and melting her brain to the point that she can't remember even the most basic of facts, like that she's my daughter," Paul told us, then he wiped his running nose on his sleeve.

After the jump is a plea that Paul Dabney made us film. It's him addressing the camera, profusely sweating, grinding his teeth, and rambling for 22 minutes. Paul begs, "Dakota, I need you to get off the junk before that white devil takes away my only baby girl." Better have an eight ball handy if you have intentions of sitting through the entire Paul Dabney show.

celebUtard

"Kristen And Johnny Sitting in a Tree.

No. Literally. We aren't being witty here, <u>after the jump</u> you can visually see **Kristen Paxton** and **Johnny Foster** sitting in a tree. Like physically their asses are on the branches of a large shade tree.

THERE IS NO K-I-S-S-I-N-G. OR F-U-C- Okay, You get the point. It's two people in a tree, and one of those people has been turning her life around in quite the about-face.

Doesn't it seem like only a couple months ago that Kristen had a massive drinking problem and was coming off yet another failed attempt at rehab? It also seems like only a couple months ago that even Kristen's stalkers were worried about her mental health.

Oh, that's right, it *was* only a couple months ago. That's why we're keeping such a close eye.

The story with these two lovebirds in the tree is that the paps were camped out in front of Kristen's house when, much to their satisfaction, they heard cries.

Cries of worry and fear.

No, Kristen wasn't DWI backing out of her driveway into a school bus of kids.

What actually happened was London Francis' ex-cat, **James Dean**, had climbed up in a tree on Kristen's property and found himself stuck 30 feet off the ground.

Thank God this story includes a cat because we're struggling to make this exciting, but y'all love cats so no matter what, we'll get hits.

Why was the cat climbing the tree? It's possible that James Dean was attempting to get over the fence to reach Johnny's **Porsche**.

Editor's note: the above is speculation, the cat, James Dean, has made no such verbal declarations and did not respond when reached for comment.

Eventually, Kristen ended up sitting in the tree, with a can of kitty food, doing a, "Here kitty, kitty," screech while hitting the side of the can with a fork. Johnny, in a two seasons old **Michael Lorrie** jacket, climbed to the rescue, like a good boyfriend.

Holy shit this story is boring. This is the most boring thing ever.

Why are we typing this? Why does this exist?

Someday, around 11 years from now, aliens will take over the planet earth and they'll accidentally read this blog post on their super-smartphones. This is how they'll learn about the human race and, because of our words, the aliens will feel no remorse when destroying anything walking on two legs.

Do you want that girls? The complete annihilation of the human race? If you don't want that... then leave the house!

Anyway... back to this bullshit fluff piece about a fluffy piece of London Francis refuse. It appears that Johnny was able to get James Dean out of the tree with no injuries to himself or the cat. The Michael Lorrie jacket looked a little torn up, but Johnny's look is a little rock and roll, so don't be surprised if we see the jacket again.

Above all else, this tree scaling is not being viewed as a suicide attempt. If James Dean was ever going to kill himself, he would have done it when London *allegedly* traded him to Kristen for a dresser.

This is what it's come to. Dressers and kittens.

Until next time, stay tardy, celebUverse.

OXYGEN WASTER
Paul Dabney: "My Daughter is Slowly Killing Me!"

After being escorted off of **Dakota Dabney**'s lawn by law enforcement, and, later in the day, after being asked to leave by security at the corporate headquarters of a rival blog (let's just call them **LameRiot**), **Paul Dabney** returned to the **OXYGEN WASTER** offices to add self-proclaimed "bombshell details" to the story that he told us weeks ago about Dakota doing a mountain of cocaine. We also think that he had nowhere else to go and outside there was a miracle of a downpour happening so he needed somewhere dry and warm to stay until the storm blew over.

According to Mr. Dabney, Dakota's mental issues have forced her into an isolated "cocaine cocoon" which happens to be "one of the most expensive types of cocoons a person can end up in." Dakota's metaphorical cocoon has made Paul Dabney acquire a "near death condition." When pressured for specifics regarding the name of his condition, Mr. Dabney went on a rant about how his daughter can't leave the house because of her new-found racism toward Mexican people, which is a direct result of the fact **Diego Mestizo** is allegedly selling really stepped on cocaine to **Jake Wesley**, which Jake in turn allegedly mules to Dakota's residence.

When questioned about how Dakota was killing him, Paul Dabney stated that a doctor, whose name he can't remember, saw him at a doctor's office which Paul can't locate, and the doctor diagnosed Mr. Dabney with, (exact quote), "...a broken heart. Heard of one of those before? You don't think it's real? Oh yeah? Tell that to **Jackie O**. She died from the same thing after **JFK** was shot."

It was immediately pointed out to Mr. Dabney that Jackie Onassis lived for 30 years after JFK was assassinated and, when she did die, it was because of lymphoma. In response, Mr. Dabney had this to say, "The lymphoma grew in the cracks of her broken heart, smart guy." When our editor responded that the lymphoma was likely linked to a smoking habit Ms. Onassis had, Paul Dabney stormed out of the room claiming that, "OXYGEN WASTER is staffed with a bunch of shitbag socialite apologists." For the record Oxygen Waster is not staffed with socialite apologists.

social!heavy apologists on the other hand? That's debatable.

Maribell's Blog Of Fashions And Much Famous.

Hello. My name is Maribell. I am from Sao Paulo, Brazil. socialheavys come to Sao Paulo. Brazil loves you.

I must start my blog for my favorite band, the socialheavys (sorry, I do not know how you makings exclamation mark).

London Francis is much beautiful woman who is nice and I met once (or I met a lady taller than my pop-pop). London did a band that provide much enjoyment and successful.

Where have they gone? Many days of not new pictures have gone passing.

Is that you, Chloe? Hello? Are you hearing my blog? We are not hide and seeking. Please visit the restaurants in nice shoes again soon.

Yes, message me if you are of the socialheavys group club of admirers. We are the best of the fans from all over the globe.

Socialheavys, when will you arrive for Brazil? Brazil loves you. If you follow my blog, I will die. (Not real death. End violence. Pray for Sao Paulo.)

Sorry of my misspellings, English is not my first language, but is good. socialheavys come to Brazil. Brazil loves you.

~Lovings, Maribell.

celebUtard
"Jake Wesley- Delivery Boy?"

Dakota Dabney has turned into **Howard Hughes**- minus the obsessive compulsive tics, the urine jarring, and the whole multifaceted genius deal.

While on lockdown, Dakota has been getting a daily visit from **Jake Wesley,** who brings over a big bag of goodies. By goodies we mean vodka and eight balls. We haven't seen inside the bags, but we don't need X-ray vision to know what they contain. Likely taking cues from her fellow band-mate, **Chloe Warren**, Dakota has her significant other significantly whipped. Yes, we can confirm **JAKOTA** are a full-on item. This isn't just a charity case for Jake. Unless he goes balls deep in all his charity cases. For the sake of the **Children's Hospital of Los Angeles**, we hope this isn't the case. That is, unless the girls or gaybies have **Make-A-Wish** style requests for such fill-anthropy.

Stop us! Stop us! Stop us!

We have no exciting Chloe, Dakota, **London Francis**, or **Kristen Paxton** news to write about, so we've sunk to the point of dealing in squalid humor.

Tune in tomorrow so we can report on one of Dakota's gutters looking slightly askew, then we'll make some dick jokes!

Until next time, stay tardy, celebUverse.

HOT BLONDE GIRLS WITH HEAVY EYE MAKEUP

HBGWHEM 100.0:
I Destroyed social!heavy.

The girls are gone.

It's my fault.

Is anyone surprised?

Tom loves a girl and the girl leaves.

Tom loves five younger girls and they make him register in a database, then notify his neighbors when he moves into a new apartment building.

My love is toxic and I'm sorry.

Toxic. First it was Britney, then it spread.

I don't think I like being in love. I think it scares me. I think I will always suspect that there's someone else. How could it just be me? How could I be enough? If a girl has the choice of everyone out there and she chooses me, she must be very, very damaged. As soon as she makes that error in judgment and becomes my girlfriend, I start to... I don't know. I sort of, I guess, psychically poison her?

I'm convinced that's what's happened with social!heavy. I have an extensive history with all five girls in the band, despite never meeting any of them. The only time social!heavy ends up in Newark is to catch a flight, and those TSA agents are really really mean to you if you loiter at the gate waiting for female celebrities to magically arrive. They usually will say things like, "You can't do this," then they will follow it up with something like, "And this isn't even a security issue, it's a mental health issue. Tom, you're acting scary." They don't understand. I have a relationship with these strangers.

~-~DAKOTA~-~

I remember the first time I really noticed Dakota. I was sitting in a girl's dorm, drinking. The girl had red hair and she was pretty in the way that a girl who sort of looks like a bird could be pretty. Her roommate was short and had big boobs. The roommate had boyfriend that dressed like he lived below the poverty line. He wasn't there that night because he probably did live below the poverty line so his parents weren't paying his tuition. I was drinking Olde

English. I think the selection was made with the following equation: being cheap + irony + hoping that I would remind the girl with the big boobs of her poor ass boyfriend. That night, on the university provided cable, CTV was airing *C-leb Sixty*, a documentary style program where a baritone voiced narrator would go through all the shitty parts of an excessively famous person's life. We found this show to be comforting because it made our college-age alcoholism seem 'enviable' instead of 'a warning sign' of a problem. The *Sixty* playing on this particular Thursday was about Dakota Dabney. I knew of Dakota before this point, but this show promised to reveal the "real Dakota" so I figured maybe it would show me that I was wrong in my casual assessment of her. Since it was college, of course we turned Dakota Dabney's life into a drinking game. I think Dakota played along. I made out with the redhead, but I didn't fuck her. I used Dakota's problems to get with a girl. A selfish man used Dakota as a pawn to get what he wanted, while he watched a show that detailed how a selfish man used Dakota as a pawn to get what he wanted. Meta enough for you yet?

~-~CHLOE~-~

I remember the first time I really noticed Chloe Warren. The feeling I got looking at her image on that magazine page reminded me of seeing a beautiful painting. Not one of those bullshit paintings with the boxes where you're sitting in art class, and you're pointing at it like, "FUCK. I didn't know drawing boxes was an option! I had to do a still life, with charcoal. I'm not van Gogh. I'm fifteen. You really think that someday I'm going to be sitting in front of the HR manager at job interview, and she'll say, 'I'm impressed you graduated Seton Hall with honors, but I have strong doubts about your ability to draw this shitty old boot with these ashes I have here in a bowl.'" When I saw Chloe Warren, she reminded me of those churches I saw in Italy. God made the man that painted the paintings, and the paintings came from the brain that God programmed with the diagram for these masterpieces. How's it any different with Chloe? Is she less than a ceiling painting because you don't have to crane your neck to see her? Maybe that's all it is. Different modes of distribution. Chloe should ask everyone to mount their flat screens to the ceiling, then people would finally view her as the masterpiece she truly is. That unrealistic masterpiece praise directed toward Chloe Warren ended up destroying her. The wilting was slow. It was that pack-a-day habit that had some pleasure tied to it, but in the end, it was mostly just damage. Those "actress pretty, yet model skinny" statements treated Chloe's doe eyes and long limbs like they were a permanent reality. That pretty shell is living and breathing and it's being crammed into this box of being iconic. They have to repaint those ceilings, you know. That's not the original coat of paint up there. If it was, it wouldn't be immaculate. It would be pretty boring. Despite never knowing I exist, I feel as though Chloe is being crushed the pressure I applied (and continue to apply) by demanding she remain "Chloe." It was too much; it still is. Chloe revolted against our demands for impossible stasis by doing her best to look revolting. Another casualty.

~-~KRISTEN~-

I remember the first time I really noticed Kristen Paxton. What a disaster. I'd trade links with a couple of friends like they were baseball cards. It was a constant dialog of texts and e-mails- *Did you hear about the methadone? Read this. No, dude, look at this post. She's literally an escort at this point. Are these really her tits or is this someone else's body with Kristen's head shopped on? Yeah, it's a really good fake, if it is fake. I thought he was married, why is she kissing him? I thought he was gay, why is she kissing him? I thought she was straight why is she kissing her? Shit, did you see her crying in the airport- I mean, yeah, I've wanted to cry in the airport too, but, ya know, at least I did it in a stall in the bathroom. Oh no, she's in jail. Made bail. She's out. Damn it, she's back in. She's out. She's back in. Damn it. Damn it. Okay, she's back out. She's better now.* Wait, no, Tom still loves her. She's doomed. Another girl, gone.

~-~LONDON~-~

I remember the first time I really noticed London. She started appearing in pictures. A lot of pictures. Anyone even vaguely famous was suddenly next to London Francis. I wondered who this tall, HBGWHEM was, so I started researching. During my research, I wasn't disappointed. When I got tired of researching London Francis, I would put on one of her sex tapes, jerk off, then I'd get my second wind and I'd go back to researching. London made me smile during the filler inter-cuts of her sex tapes when she would film average Americans, then provide her unique commentary on their lives. If CTV produced a weekly documentary series called *London Francis' America*, I would turn HBGWHEM into a fully dedicated fan site with .gifs and vaguely disconcerting fanfiction related to the show. I like the filler scenes that much. Over footage of a group of skating mallgoths, London narrated, "Skateboards seem like a good way to get around once those lawyers defending the people of the California take away your driver's license. Which is bullshit, by the way.

I've spoken with people in California- they confirmed they weren't bothered by my first few DWIs. They were like, 'Well, did you kill anyone?' and I was like, 'I don't know. I was shitfaced. Get off my back, narc.' The people of California were chill though, they deny even hiring the lawyers." When London filmed a mega-store parking lot, she had the revelation, "These people are transporting so many children, and that's why they buy minivans. Without the minivan, they'd have to leave some of their family at the grocery store." It was fascinating being a fly on the wall as London realized that not everyone could use a sports car with room for three as their primary mode of transportation. That part of London will forever entertain me. Then there's that other part of London- the quietly sad part. I remember logging onto the XV3 site and I saw numerous user comments, posted minutes apart, that said things like, "Trent and London look so happy, I wonder if they will get engaged soon!!!!" and, "Trent's wedding to London would be like a fairy tale! Real love DOES exist!!!!" and, "Ya know, sometimes I honestly DO believe London is part mermaid!!!!" I knew London was posting these comments, and they were the only nice comments on the page. She must have read the other comments and I can't imagine how they made her feel. London has always been overly concerned about what people think, but only at a distance. She he made me laugh a guilty laugh when I read a very thinly veiled blind item a year ago where a person that sounded an awful lot like London was caught making out with Jake Wesley, then, directly after, in the bathroom, she was informed that Jake is Native American, and this person in the blind item was anonymously quoted as saying, "Ew," then immediately leaving the party, telling her friend she'd "disgraced America, and not for the usual reasons this time." The London-like subject of the piece reportedly vowed to fix things by, "...writing to the president to let him know I'm not aligned with the Indians. I don't want to regift New York to anyone. I'm fine with the Jews keeping it. I'm not a spy." London Francis' persona has always been part character, and I can't help but feel like we've arrived at the season finale where the body count is always high and no one is safe.

~-~SIENNA~-~

I remember the first time I really noticed Sienna Wolfe. I had just gotten out of work after a long day at that big, shitty, corporate behemoth, and I went to Walgreen's, not because I needed anything, just because I didn't want to go home. I felt suffocated, and I had to have time on my own, even if that time was spent in a drug store run by another big, shitty, corporate behemoth. As I held my basket full of Ramen noodle six-packs, I glanced over at the magazine covers in a nearby rack. Sienna Wolfe was on the cover of a *GQ*, in a bikini. Normally, I'm like, oh great, a girl in a bikini on the cover of a men's magazine, that's the lowest rung of model before you hit those Sunday newspaper department store bra ads that I used to jack off to when I was 14. With Sienna, it was different though. Sienna's personality is so big that it spills out into every dimension. Her personality is like a disease, but one of those good diseases- like a vaccination, where you get the disease by choice, to save you from becoming a victim later on. Sienna covered that magazine better than anyone I had ever seen. I put my basket down and picked up the *GQ*. When I flipped to her interview, her words matched the picture. The picture was beautiful and her words were beautiful too- in that aggressive, funny, witty, head cheerleader who's only interested in the quarterback because she's pretty sure he's gay, and she wants to out him during the next home game in a carefully planned and smile-filled cheer type way. Sienna was everything that I feared my girlfriend at home would be, but when I went home, I hated my girlfriend because she wasn't anything like Sienna. There are only so many times you can cheer dark secrets before someone muzzles you. Sienna is too quick and if you put your hand over her mouth, she'll bite your fingers off, then toss you a bottle of Neosporin so you can tend to your wounds. When your stumps don't catch the bottle, she'll laugh. Sienna Wolfe remains my last love standing and history tells me she's going to end up worse off than any of the other girls.

To the girls gone, I'm sorry.
To the girls still here, stay away and you'll be fine.

celebUtard
"Drag The River."

Four weeks! **Chloe Warren, Dakota Dabney, Kristen Paxton,** and **London Francis** have not been seen for four whole weeks. That's a **Salinger**-esque absence for these girls. We're afraid to leave the house because we think that this might have something to do with the **Apocalypse**. Has the government relocated these girls so that we can raise a race of physically perfect models when we have to start re-populating the desolate earth?

Sienna Wolfe has soaked up every ounce of flash in her friends' absence, and we're wondering how much longer it'll be before someone has to secure a warrant to check her basement. Sienna *is* hiding bodies, it's just a matter of finding out if they're metaphorical or physical. $20 on it being a combo of both.

We would accept that these girls are working on their music, but, according to the **American Musical Society**, learning an instrument takes, "Patience, hand-eye coordination, dedication to the craft, and above all else, respect for the music."

Considering that London Francis once flew a purse first class on **Delta Airlines** because the international shipping was going to take more than three days, it's safe to assume that these girls do not have patience.

According to **Mothers Against Drunk Driving**, alcohol greatly affects your hand-eye coordination, leaving reactions "delayed, lethargic, imprecise, and potentially deadly" so the idea that these girls would still have hand eye coordination any time after 5 PM would be naive.

Dedication to anything besides decadence, hard living, and vampire hours has never been displayed by a single member of social!heavy so we're wondering how that part will shake out.

Finally, last but not least, a respect for the music is necessary. The girls have a respect for the music right? I mean, it's not like they kicked the most famous New Wave singer of the 80's out onto the street.

Oh, and the girls are all reclusive whores. Did you read that Chloe?

Whores. You are a whore, Ms. Dabney.

Whore whorey whorebag, Kristen Paxton.

London Francis = Smelly WHORE.

Why are we doing this? Are we really that pathetic that we've stooped to name calling just to get a reaction?

We tried to be supportive, and we tried to give them time, but enough's enough. If we have to write one more story about someone on the bottom of the "who gives a shit" chain, or worse, a **Broadway** actress, we're gonna start cutting our pretty little wrists. Don't doom us to a life of scar covering accessories, **social!heavy**.

We miss your unclothed vaginas' popping out of luxury cars.

We're tired of the same tired pictures of the never tired Sienna Wolfe.

Maybe if we ask nicely, things will go back to normal.

Come out, come out, where ever you are?

Until next time, stay tardy, celebUverse.

42- The Unshakable T.H.C.

Chloe feels as though a tiny sliver of talent has inhabited her frail frame during these weeks of hard practice. Confident in her progress, she decides to take a little break from this musical boot camp. Rationalizing her actions, Chloe reaches across her dining room table and picks up her phone. The girls all agreed not read the blogs for their little practice period, but Chloe can't help it. "Drag the River" showed up as one of the items in her Google Alert and she *must* click on it. It was a scary title to find in her inbox.

With most celebrities, there's a line that's eventually crossed when a mysterious disappearance becomes permanent invisibility. It's like when a little girl is kidnapped. At first, a large group of people will immediately band together and search intensely with dogs, and helicopters, and ad hoc groups of locals. There's media coverage, and social networking blasts, and a hotline is provided for any details on the disappearance. After a little while, the helicopters start looking for someone else who comes up missing, or maybe for a fugitive on the run. The hotline starts taking calls for other people, and the operators are busy collecting information on someone who might still be able to be saved. Eventually, the dogs lose the scent, and the reporters do segments about new playground equipment that gets very hot during the summer. Four weeks Hollywood-time is like a year of stolen-kid-time. If people don't read about a socialite for four weeks, they'll find someone new to envy. There are *always* new girls and they'll be even more hate-able than the previous crop. At the end of the day, the blogs have to write about something to keep the ad revenue rolling in, and, "Chloe Warren didn't leave her house again today," isn't news. The paps don't even spend the entire day outside of the girls' houses anymore. There are too many mistresses talking, mistresses blowing, mistresses getting in fights with other mistresses; all while their meal tickets smoothly sneak off with new mistresses. It's a full time job keeping tabs on who's getting physically fucked, who's getting chemically fucked, and who's getting metaphorically fucked.

As Chloe reads the post on *celebUtard*, her phone vibrates. Instantly sure that she's been caught, she turns her phone off, sets it on the table, then begins working on a good excuse. She tells herself that she has to go back and practice even more, but moments later, in a whirlwind of guilt, curiosity, and boredom, she picks up her lifeline again. Since it's her only way to communicate with the outside world, she turns her phone back on and decides to look at the text. She feels relief when she sees that it's from Martin, then that relief is washed away when she sees the text is only two words long, "Coming over."

Chloe wonders why they don't just Skype at 7 PM, like usual.

"Bringing presents?" Chloe texts back, and Martin responds with the cryptic message, "No. An angry mob."

If this was an emergency, Martin would've come right out and said what's going on, and since he didn't, Chloe merely goes upstairs, changes into a cute yellow Marc by Marc Jacobs mimi silk dress, then gets to work on a summer sunshine makeup look.

While she sits in front of the mirror, braiding her hair, she's struck by something evil. The sadistic scent of an omelet begins to creep out of the kitchen, down the hall, then up the spiraling steel staircase to Chloe's little beauty sanctuary. The previous owners of the house grew pot illegally in this room. Pot makes you hungry. After Chloe bought the house, she had the room professionally cleaned.

With the room sterilized, Chloe decided she would create a sunny corner of the universe where she could be alone, and where she could perform all those tricks she'd learned to make her cheekbones pop, to dim the freckles on her nose, to get her lips cherry red and not flat-red. She created her own makeup room, far away from Stanley, because it allowed her to perpetuate an image of being effortlessly put together. Chloe likes to look perfect, and she follows routines to realize her vision of how she should look. The mirror is a lie, but Chloe does everything she can to make its reflection as true as possible. The small room's glass ceiling provides the perfect authentic, natural light needed for a socialite makeup routine. Chloe recently found that she couldn't rely on the fake lights above the makeup mirror in the bathroom. A lot of the time, when Chloe's photographed, she's in direct sunlight. About 80 percent of the day-to-day pictures of Chloe are of her going from her car, into a restaurant, then back out. When she'd use a tanner or concealer, it would look totally different under the bathroom lights compared to the natural light. She learned this after *OXYGEN WASTER* posted, "Is that Calamine Lotion on Chloe's Tits?" and when *People* printed a picture of her with a pale face, on the way to Lindy's birthday party, and captioned it, "Lindy even ordered a clown for her party."

Suddenly, Chloe's sanctuary is invaded by Stanley's cooking. As the heat from the stove rises, the food smell drifts along with it, quickly overpowering the little room. Maybe it's not just the smell of food, but also the THC saturated walls from the previous owner's botany project that has Chloe's stomach knotting with a high hunger.

Chloe makes sure that she never asks Stanley to stop cooking the bacon and eggs she so desperately craves. It's an unwritten rule in the house; if she doesn't bring up food, neither does Stanley. He keeps his food downstairs, and Chloe keeps her skinny little self upstairs, in her beauty sanctuary, with a window cracked for fresh air.

43- The Ol' Reverse Grounding.

Martin's text to Chloe was short on details due to the reaction he got from London after he sent her the warning, "Following Sienna n she's headed 2 ur house right now." This text resulted in London initiating a panicked phone call, similar to those recorded 911 calls that were released after Kristen's second DWI crash.

Despite the dust-up, Sienna was able to get London in the car without conflict. Martin assumes Sienna tricked London into thinking that she wanted to go look at puppies at Petsville, LA.

London is easy.

Chloe is not.

Sienna pulls up to Chloe's gate and she's immediately let inside. The paps photograph until the car is out of sight- among these secret vampires feeding off the girls' is Martin.

Almost as quickly as she arrived, Sienna is back at the gate honking at everyone so they'll move. The photographers make enough of a void that the car can pull out, but not enough that it can move once it's beyond the gate.

Sienna waits.

Apparently, there was no argument before Chloe got in the car. The paps don't need an argument today- a picture of all these girls together, even if it's through the vehicle's tinted windows, is valuable in this social!heavy starved climate. Martin hopes that Chloe didn't think it was going to be him driving and she blindly got inside the car.

A bubble builds in Martin's protruding belly when he thinks about what information Sienna must have on Chloe that she just gave up and joined Sienna.

Retreating to his van to snap more photos, Martin remains subservient to the Harper-mandated requirement that his dual identity is concealed at all times. He's even broken one of his rules, and started wearing an awful pair of black boxy sunglasses. He saw them at a gas station and hoped that they would be like a cloak of invisibility, but they only make him look even more ridiculous than usual. At one point he caught his reflection in another pap's lens and he began feeling legitimately sorry for himself. Martin still doesn't want to mute what he's photographing, but he has to continue to look like he's a paparazzi and the sunglasses somehow help.

The paps finally part so Sienna can get by. They realize that if Sienna stays idling for much longer, she's going to run out of gas, then one of them is going to have to use Chloe's garden hose to siphon gas out of their own van into Sienna's car so she can get back on the road.

No one wants to be left behind; everyone wants to see how this ends.

Driving off a ravine?

Five girl ultimate battle to the death?

A surprise concert?

An orgy in Mitchell Haughton's lube pool?

The socialites and paparazzi once again take to the streets in a caravan.

When they arrive at Dakota's house, the chocolate haired girl struts up to the gate, then she stares at Sienna with vitriol. Dakota's gate, unlike the others, is made of iron bars. The rest of the girls have big metal doors, most likely because they have no desire to be behind bars again. Even when Dakota Dabney locks people out of her life, she always lets them peek inside. She provides a gap that, as long as the person is skinny enough, they can snake through and sneak back into her personal life. It's never a total blackout. Today, Dakota uses this weakness to her advantage. To prove that she's in control, Dakota poses behind her gate for the paps. After her impromptu, smile-filled shoot, she opens the door to the gate, just enough that she can slide out, then she slams it behind her. Her home base is now secure and neither the secret vampires, nor Sienna can get inside. Dakota will make Sienna pick someone else to host this pity party.

Entering the car without a fight, forewarned by Martin's text, and two more texts from the hoodie covered captives in the back of Sienna's car, Dakota feels prepared for whatever's about to happen today. She's been practicing her chords, and she's been making careful decisions so, for the foreseeable future, Dakota will be turning kidnappings into band promo, and infighting into an honest dialog.

Sienna drives fast and the girls stay silent. At the final stop, Kristen's house, a waiting game begins. When a girl reads that her arch enemy has taken London Francis hostage, it can be sort of jarring. Kristen briefly considers attempting an escape by car, but she assumes she'll be obstructed by Sienna, then Sienna will be blocked in by the paps. A standoff is always much more dramatic than a kidnapping- there's more to photograph and film. Knowing this, Kristen stays inside, and she leaves the door unlocked because things worked out so well last time she unbolted that door.

Kristen remaining inside was supposed to throw Sienna off, but that's a lofty goal set by an unskilled manipulator.

Sienna drives right up to Kristen's house, then pops the locks on the car. The girls, unsure of what's about to happen, open the doors and file out. Sienna gets out as well, but in a way, she never leaves the driver's seat.

Martin stays in his van, outside the gate. A minute. An hour. A sunset.

Whatever Sienna is up to, it ends at Kristen's house.

Or maybe this is just the beginning.

44- Siren Song.

Sienna storms into Kristen's library, hostages in tow, and she lays down the new rules:

- *You have to leave your house at least once a day.*
- *You have to give interviews to a couple rags to prove you haven't gone insane.*
- *You have to get your boyfriend to bring his friends around so Sienna can meet someone cute.*
- *You have to help Sienna get a modeling contract, like her mother's, but bigger than her mother's, so you're going to have your work cut out for you.*

With her rules are laid out, Sienna sits calmly on Kristen's piano bench, and looks at her hostages. Words slurring from the alcohol the girls fed her between demands, Sienna turns and places her fingers on the piano keys, then says, "I've been practicing too, but I've also found time to not be super fucking lame. Shall I play you something?" She places her fingers on the keys.

The girls sit, worried. What if Sienna actually *can* play a synthesizer? The plan was always that Sienna wouldn't learn her instrument, then she'd quit the band or they'd kick her out. If she can actually play, there will be band practices, and tour buses, and interviews where Sienna will bring her sulfuric personality to this good thing. If Sienna has been practicing all this time and she still managed to live a buzzworthy life, it would be more than discouraging.

Straightening her back, Sienna plays a plink-plonky disaster of a song, singing;

> *Hey! You! Remember us?*
> *We used to be awesome,*
> *And now we suck.*
> *You used to admire us,*
> *And want our life.*
> *Now we are boring,*
> *Just like your wife.*
> *We attend no premieres.*
> *Host no parties.*
> *We're Suzy homemaker,*
> *Sienna's Barbie!"*

Sienna stops playing her impromptu song, then turns back to her silent hostages. It's a relief that Sienna's piano skills don't exist, but it was also kind of startling that she could put together a halfway decent song so fast. The girls didn't appreciate the subject matter, but it was nice to know that when Martin has his inevitable heart attack, Sienna may actually be able to pen their second album- all they'd have to do is tell her to write songs about herself.

London, trying to help Sienna, comments, "You need more practice."

"Why? There's no reason to learn the instruments. Since you whores have been sitting inside... not being whores... I haven't had anything to do, so I cruised by that studio in Burbank, and guess who I've seen visiting there?"

No one ventures a guess.

"Our fat pap producer! Now why would our producer keep showing up at the studio?" Sienna asks, leading her hostages toward the conclusion she wants them to reach.

The girls again treat Sienna's line of questioning as rhetorical.

Sienna proudly recaps what she's deduced is happening, "Maybeee, even the one guy who 'believes' in us doesn't think that we're talented enough to figure out which way you hold a guitar. Turns out, while you were inside practicing your little instruments, he was recording our songs."

"They'd have pictures of that. One of the blogs would've picked up on it," Chloe says.

Sienna smiles as everything unfolds perfectly, and she says, "That's the beauty of the whole situation! Since he's a pap, the guys never find it weird to see his van parked there while he's in the studio."

Picking up her phone off the piano, Sienna makes a couple quick swipes, then shows the girls a picture of Martin, in sunglasses, walking into the studio in broad daylight. Martin wouldn't take a picture of Sienna, so she took a picture of him. Martin has sold a lot of pictures of Sienna. Sienna has kept this picture of him. The image can do more damage to the girls if they see it, if they know it exists, and if they know Sienna has it. "Oh, and if you're wondering, I'm the only one with this information," Sienna says, then she puts her phone on top of the piano, and her fingers sloppily tumble over the keys, churning out another hit;

"Naive little girl,
Practice away your life.
Then when you get good,
You'll go under the knife.
Cuz you'll have gotten old,
Your celebrity will mold.
Sienna will be laughing.
While you're doing what you're told."

Sienna pauses her playing for a moment. She takes a deep breath, then begins hammering out a disastrous, vaguely ragtimey tune while singing loudly;

> *"Beeeeeeecauseeeee...*
> *No one loves old whores,*
> *They love young ones.*
> *No one fucks boring girls,*
> *They fuck fun ones.*
> *Don't like skilled girls,*
> *They like dumb ones.*
> *So if you don't give up,*
> *Your fame's done, hon."*

Sienna turns to the girls and smiles. "Looks like Martin and I are the only ones with anything to show for this career path!" she caws, then gets up and walks over to the corner of the room. Picking up her purse, Sienna scoops out a handful of phones from her bag, then each girl is given her respective device like it was the piece of paper Martin gave them with their future written on it.

Still buzzed, Sienna walks to the window and smiles at her own reflection. It's dark outside. The paparazzis' headlights in front of the house were providing a spotlight for the production that Sienna will now pull the curtain open on.

The Wolfe turns and tells her captive sheep, "Fatboy Pap hasn't quit his day job, so he's probably out front. Well, that is, if he isn't in the studio, recording our music."

45- Fresh-Facing the Music.

Martin's phone buzzes him back to reality. He holds onto the cell as it wriggles like a fish in his hand. When the fish is about to stop moving, Martin takes it off the hook with a shaky, "Hello?"

"Martin?"

"Speaking."

"There's a spot in the rose bushes on the right side of the house that you can fit through. Probably. Maybe. Anyway, go through there and meet me in the backyard," Kristen instructs him, then ends the call.

Martin hoists himself out of the van, crosses the street, then casually makes his way along the side of the house. The rose bushes- tall, overgrown, intertwined- have been planted exclusively and excessively to keep people out. Martin forces his way into the thorny faux wall, holding his camera above his head. He practically uproots the bushes that grapple onto him, but he presses on. It's too dark to see where the long, barbed branches extend to so by the time he's standing at the edge of the carefully curated yard, Martin feels shabby in his newly-torn black t-shirt. Not totally sure where he ended up, he lifts his camera and takes a picture. The flash provides a momentary preview of what's in front of him. On the glowing screen of the camera, Martin sees the alien world of Kristen's backyard, and he's hit by a wave of nostalgia from the retro teal colors and tacky flamingo theme. Photographs of Martin's youth cascade through his mind as the worried pap takes a moment for himself.

Gradually, a slice of light cuts through the darkness. Martin looks to the source of the light, and Kristen is standing at the back door of her home. She looks like the same slice of Americana that he remembers from last time they were together. With a photographer's eye, Martin admires Kristen's image- the harsh light meshing with her soft glow. He quickly turns off his flash and takes a single, beautiful, personal picture. This time, he doesn't look down at the screen. This time, he's sure what he captured.

First captured by Sienna, then by Martin; the caged bird waits at the door between her captors.

Approaching the house, Martin says, "I'm sort of hurt that Sienna didn't stop by my place during the kidnapping."

Kristen doesn't respond, and after a massive gaze at her visitor, Kristen moves back, making room for the paparazzi's entrance into her home. Martin walks inside the giant house that suddenly feels like a courtroom, and Kristen shuts the door, then leads her guest back to the library.

When they enter the book lined room, Martin wants to diffuse the awkward situation so he looks at Sienna, and says, "What are you doing in here? Don't you feel like Superman in a room full of kryptonite?" Martin looks at the books, then at Sienna, then at the rest of the girls, then at books, then at the girls again. He smiles wide, waiting for someone to laugh or at least look like they're holding in a laugh.

"Sit down, Martin," Chloe says, pointing to the only open seat- a 50 percent share of the piano bench. Martin slowly approaches the bench and Sienna scoots her ass all the way to the far edge of the wood. Kristen easily could have had the maid bring in a chair for Martin, but she wanted to thwart any attempt by Sienna to turn the conversation into an insulting musical halfway through, so she decided to utilize Martin as a human shield.

"You look like ass. I've seen pieces of Balmain with less holes in it," Sienna says, eyeing Martin's shirt.

"Did you make a deal with Joel?" London asks Martin directly, with an unexpected edge. This gets Martin's attention.

"Yeah. Of course I did. Don't you remember, I took my pants off?" Martin says innocently. He tries a laugh, but it doesn't come out.

London shakes her head, "What deal did you make with him?"

"That I would produce your album," Martin says, his voice high.

"In exchange for what?"

"So he'll let me make more music with you."

"Are you recording our songs, Martin?" Chloe asks directly.

Sienna crosses her legs and smirks at the girls, knowing that she's no longer public enemy number one.

Martin sucks in his chubby cheeks and looks down at the carpet. He shakes his head in a silent acknowledgment of his sonic betrayal.

"Yes?" Chloe asks.

"Yes," Martin says.

London gets up and leaves the room.

"London," Martin says, standing up.

"Sit down," Sienna barks, and Martin complies.

"I can't believe you were doing this to us behind our backs," Kristen says.

"Joel was making me-"

"-you're a grown man, Martin. Joel can't make you do anything," Dakota growls.

"I thought you got it, but you don't understand at all," Chloe says.

"Listen, I'm not trying to be part of your band, I'm just doing what's best for you, according to Joel. By the time the tracks were recorded, you would've learned your instruments and you'd be ready to perform the songs," Martin says, his eyes weary with guilt.

"We'd be performing your songs, Martin."

"They're London's songs, I'm just working on the instrumentation," Martin says.

"Not anymore," London responds, walking back into the room, her makeup without a single smudge, "I spoke with Joel. I told him we quit if Martin records anything else."

"What'd he say?" Kristen asks.

"I don't know, I hung up," London responds, sitting back down.

"I'm so sorry," Martin says, genuinely.

This is when the screaming should have started. This is when the insults would arrive. This is when Martin would be reminded that he is nothing, then he'd be fired off the project and sent home. Martin knows what's about to happen, then... it doesn't. The girls quietly weigh their options as Sienna's eyes nervously dart around the room.

"We know you're sorry," Dakota says, breaking the silence, "And we should have known better than to leave you with Joel. He can't keep a distance from the music. Both of you got too excited and became impatient." Dakota is conscious of the fact that Martin isn't famous, he isn't a star, he's just a short fat man trying to make these aliens happy so they don't destroy his world.

Martin realizes, in a room full of girls that America considers to be the dumbest people in the country, *he* is the biggest fool present.

"Do you believe in us?" London asks.

"Are you just using us?" Kristen asks.

"What else were you doing behind our backs?" Dakota asks.

"What are you still doing here?" Sienna asks.

"I can leave," Martin says, standing up.

"No," Dakota says, "Stay."

45.5- How to Cater a Kidnapping.

There's an obvious lesson here. In a world where it's easy to be Kristen, and it's hard to be "Kristen," sometimes you're "Kristen" until someone else becomes "Sienna" and takes your place. It's important to remember how awful it felt when you were "Kristen" and how a couple bad nights plus a change in enunciation can put you right back there.

The girls realize that they have to address this Martin situation with class and intelligence. For once, they don't change the subject- they choose to have this difficult conversation because it will make things easier in the long run. social!heavy is about the girls being viewed differently from their ditsy, apathetic, rude ghosts of the parties past. It's time to live up to their band's promise. They've been stretching a rubber band of tension all day, and instead of triggering the snap, each girl takes a deep breath, then forgives Martin. Sienna does not forgive Martin; she forces him to explain exactly what was going through his fat skull. And he does. Carefully, and with the consideration of a friend that carried out an act of dishonesty, Martin answers each and every question that's asked of him. The socialites interview the paparazzi and they're disappointed with what they find.

In that little library, surrounded by stories, Martin tells his, and the girls accept it. They display a kindness that would not be extended to them if the roles were reversed. They take a chance; they trust Martin again. He isn't trying to trick them. He doesn't have some secret plan to take over the band. As Martin gets to know the girls better, he's finding out just how smart they are. As the girls get to know Martin better, they realize just how naive he can be. Martin doesn't need to take care of these socialites, they need to take care of him. The girls try to think of how they can begin to help this short fat man who desperately, and perhaps misguidedly, wanted to help them. The answer becomes clear- order him dinner

A vote is taken, a call is made, the meals are ordered, a night is saved.

When the delivery arrives, Martin walks with Kristen's maid, Reyna, to the front door so he can help her with the bags. He can't step outside because he'll be photographed, and Martin is desperate to hold onto his second chance, so he vows to never appear in front of the camera. Never in front, always behind.

Reyna leaves, Martin stays. There's a chance he sent the maid out alone because he was afraid the girls wouldn't let him back in if he left. Conspiracies swirl in Martin's head, and he begins to wonder if Reyna was instructed to walk him out to the street, then leave him there, because that's where he belongs.

Peering out a window, Martin sees Reyna walking back with the Jackyl branded bag, and he becomes confident that he'll be allowed to sit at the table with his new family tonight. When she went out to pick up the food, she didn't take any money. Martin had seen this before when he was working. The bag that the food came in is a giant advertisement that will appear on thousands of blogs by 8 AM PST. All five members of social!heavy reuniting to eat your restaurant's food more than offsets the $900 bill.

Martin takes the bag from Reyna, then returns to the dining room. When he places the bag on the table, he casually remarks, "Who knew that you could order steak from Jackyl for delivery?"

"You can't," Sienna says, then takes her place at the head of the table. "Where's the rest of the booze?" she asks eying her empty glass.

"We don't need booze," Chloe says, considering Kristen.

"It's fine, Johnny left a couple bottles here," Kristen admits, walking back to her wine closet. Johnny trusts Kristen. He left the bottles with her, knowing she wouldn't slip back into old-Kristen habits.

"So, did I kidnap you bitches for nothing?" Sienna asks. The girls get comfortable in their seats and they don't respond. "We're eating in, instead of going out and celebrating. Even worse, we're eating with that little fat man," Sienna points out with equal amounts of disappointment and disgust.

"We need him. Don't speak like he isn't here," London says quietly, then arranges her silverware so it's perfectly straight.

"Even though he lied to you? Even though he was doing all this shit behind our back?" Sienna asks.

Before Martin can defend himself again, Kristen brandishes two bottles of wine, and says, "Everyone here has had a second chance, Martin hadn't used his yet. Now he has."

This shuts Sienna up. As much as she wanted Martin to be ousted, if she was too successful with that goal, it meant that *her* next chance could be revoked too. In an act of self-preservation, Sienna abandons her attack, and waits for Martin to pass her a plastic container of chicken and chanterelle mushrooms.

Martin notes this, and reminds himself that he's returned to an alternate universe that he hasn't inhabited for a month. He had been watching this planet from his monitor; everything is different when his feet are planted inside the perfumed atmosphere of social!heavy.

The meal begins, and Sienna's container is passed down to the head of the table, then she waits for someone to open it for her. No one does.

Martin reaches into the bag for the next meal and takes out a slim plastic container. "Great," he says, annoyed, "They only sent us an appetizer size of the salmon."

Chloe leans over and grabs the container, "It's fine. Their salmon is amazing, but it doesn't come as a main course."

"Sort of like it's not available for delivery?" Dakota asks, knowing all they'd have to do is make the request and it would exist for them.

"Who the fuck would order salmon as an appetizer?" London asks.

The entire table is quiet.

Martin rushes for the next container, "Okayyy. Duck with pear?"

Kristen raises her hand, and Martin walks over, then places the container in front of her. As he's opening the lid for Kristen, London reaches into the bag and takes out her meal.

Martin returns to the big bag, then says, "Alright, next we have roast beef."

None of the girls speak up.

"No takers on the roast beef?" Martin asks.

London leans over and looks in the container, she stands up and, cupping her hand around Martin's ear, she whispers something. With a red face, Martin puts the container back in the bag. "Okay," he says as he pulls the container out again, "Next we have a loin of venison."

Dakota raises her hand while sporting a knowing smile. Martin brings the container over, opens it, then walks back to claim his steak.

"Take a picture, Martin!" Kristen squeals, happy with the results of leaving the door unlocked again.

"It's alright, my agency isn't expecting anything more than a couple of pictures of today's kidnapping," Martin responds, then he inhales the scent from the most expensive piece of meat he's ever sat in front of.

"I meant take a picture for us," Kristen says.

Martin immediately springs up from his chair. It never occurred to him that they'd want pictures of tonight. The day started out as a kidnapping and ended as a full-on trial. It was *12 Angry Men*, with five angry socialites, which means it was even scarier. Everyone fears being judged by the popular girls.

Martin grabs his camera from the library, then walks back into the dining room and stands at the opposite end of the table from Sienna. He snaps three quick pictures, then looks down at the screen. The last picture is beautiful. Martin wishes that he could send this picture back in time to himself 30 years ago, when no one would even listen to his demo. He wants to go back 20 years, when he was working in that awful cubicle, still writing music on his days off, and assure his younger self that all of his songs will be loved one day. He wants to tell the Martin from five years ago- the man parked in a van outside a teenage celebrity's opulent mansion- that he shouldn't give up on those haunting rhythms. Eventually, the five most famous girls in the entire country will be performing his songs.

"Reynaaa!" Kristen yells, and the worried woman appears in the dining room. "Take a picture of us," Kristen instructs, immediately softening when she makes her demand. The girls want a picture with Martin; even after the scumbag pap did exactly what they knew he would do- betray them- they're willing to forgive him. This was a group of imperfect girls reminding Martin that his worth as a person is not defined by his mistakes. It's a powerful statement made by powerful individuals, and Martin does not let it go unnoticed. He wants this picture more than anyone. Less than an hour ago, Martin had vowed to never get in front of the camera, and now he's going to do just that. It's become clear that there are no absolutes in this world. Martin will be in the picture because he knows it's right, not because he's taking orders.

After showing Reyna how to use the camera, Martin puts his arm around a sitting London, then flashes a toothy grin. On this dark night in LA, the pap gets his picture taken.

Reyna hands the camera back to Martin so a professional can review the frozen frame that has instantly become important. Martin looks at the screen and laughs, "One of these things is not like the other."

"Because you're fat?" Sienna asks.

Chloe puts her fork down. This conversation regarding who looks fat has frozen her appetite.

"I guess the cat's out of the bag," Martin says, still looking at the picture.

"Please don't eat the cat," Sienna requests.

London puts her fork down. This talk of eating a cat has caused her to lose her appetite. She would never eat a cat. She won't even eat at that Chinese food restaurant on North Beverly as a precaution.

"Why don't they want pictures of us eating?" Dakota asks, going back to her meal and to an offhand comment Martin made before the photo op started.

"Because it's hard to write a story around someone successfully using a fork," Martin says, sitting down at the head of the table, across from Sienna.

Chloe feels uncomfortable with this whole line of questioning, so she tries her usual avoidance trick, "But they want pictures of me walking to my car?"

"Yeah, especially if you get a ticket."

"Oh! I get lots of tickets. They must be happy!" London squeals.

"Actually, you get so many tickets that they don't really care about those photos," Martin tells London, then he shoves a large piece of steak in his mouth.

"What's worth the most?" Sienna asks, her cat eyes becoming slits. Martin finally has a useful purpose- if Sienna can find out what type of picture is in the highest demand, she'll know what to steal when she goes through her friends' phones.

"Upskirts, nipple slips, caught-in-the-act cheating, mental breakdowns, drug use, and missing wedding rings," Martin effortlessly rambles out. "One time I photographed a girl and hit all those targets in a single night."

Everyone at the table begins to go through their mental archives of when their tit popped out, then they cross reference it with any married men they might have been caught kissing that night. All of the girls deduce that they weren't responsible for Martin's prized night.

"What happens if there's something that you don't want to come out? How do you hide it?" Chloe asks.

"Well…" Martin begins, then pauses, "…you have to know that nothing stays a secret now so it's a matter of taking control. For example, let's just say, as a hypothetical, you get in a huge fight with your boyfriend, which ends with him punching you in the eye. The story breaks, maybe his fist breaks on your nose, and you have a black eye and bruises from it. You're looking rough, but you also have to take your kids to school and-"

"-okay, first off, we don't have boyfriends that would do that and second-"

"-Dakota, hypothetical means, like, a made up situation," Chloe advises.

"Right, Chloe. Or it means the statement is conjectural," Martin says, glancing at Sienna with the implication that he wasn't referencing any of her past relationships.

Sienna perceives this as a slight and spits back, "You're fucking conjectural."

Martin slowly nods to acknowledge Sienna. Given the circumstance, it was the most polite reaction available. The girls remain interested despite being mildly confused, so Martin continues his lesson, "You have these bruises, but you still need to pick your kid up from school. Instead-"

"-wait, why do *I* need to pick up my conjectural son?" Kristen asks, baffled, "I'd just send the nanny or the babysitter or something."

"Okay," Martin says, remembering Joel's rules, "You're all too responsible, so let's use an imaginary celebrity. 'Jenny' let's call her. Jenny has bruises, and she needs to go get her kid, but she doesn't want a firestorm of attention."

All of the girls listen closely, thinking that they might know which Jenny is being referenced with this place filler.

Continuing his explanation, Martin says, "What Jenny-"

"-Jenny Preston!" London guesses aloud, interpreting his start of a sentence as a question. She looks around eagerly to see if she's right.

"We just created this Jenny out of thin air. I chose the name arbitrarily," Martin says, frustrated.

"So you're confirming Jenny Preston isn't in an abusive relationship?" Dakota asks.

Martin rubs his fingers on his forehead, then presses on, "To answer your original question, what Jenny would do is get someone to take pictures of her bruises the day before she has to leave the house. That way, Jenny can look at the pictures, she can pick the ones she likes, then when she's ready to release them, she can actually profit off the photograph. If it's a picture worth twenty grand, the photographer will sell it, then give some of the proceeds from the sale to Jenny. This way, the bruises are old news, the hype is muted, and the victim gets to keep most of the money from the picture. You all know the other option... I take up residence in Jenny's bushes so I can snap the picture for my agency. In option two, Jenny gets nothing for the photograph, *and* she needs to issue a couple more public statements through her people."

"Keeping control is good idea," Dakota says, considering the technique for possible use in her war against her abusive father.

"Sure, except you'll get all the paparazzi mad at you for staging, and we'll make your life hell. It's like when people do work without union guys," Martin adds, showing them both sides.

"Well, whatever," Dakota says, brushing it off, "I'm sure my conjectural future husband won't bruise me like Jenny's hubby did."

"How *is* Jake?" Chloe asks Dakota while they're on the topic of future husbands. Based on the nightly conversations Chloe has been having over the phone with Dakota, things were getting pretty serious between "JAKOTA." Chloe hopes that Dakota is right and her future husband wouldn't turn her into a Jenny. Jake could get R&B star level dangerous if he has that anger inside him.

"He's scarily unshakable," Dakota admits, and London's eyes flare as she fears that Jake has upgraded his fabricated human being software and downloaded a love patch into her friend's body.

"Maybe that's a good thing?" Kristen asks, thinking about the fact that her boyfriend has kept her from drowning both literally and figuratively.

"I need an exit strategy. I need that one sentence that I know will destroy everything. There's no self-destruct button right now. I'm afraid that there's a high probability I could end up in love with Jake forever."

Today, Sienna explained the rules of how to keep her quiet.

Tonight, Martin explained the rules of dealing with a paparazzi baiting crisis.

Just now, Dakota explained the rules of dating a powerful man.

In a room full of people who only to answer to themselves, there certainly are a lot of regulations being noted.

"Don't you want to be together with someone forever, though?" Sienna asks, hoping that Dakota will agree so she won't feel so lonely and pathetic.

"Of course, in theory, but what if I love someone that much, then I can't figure out how to escape? I'll probably end up getting hurt," says the girl who has been taken advantage of since birth. Dakota arrived in this world a pawn.

"That's a dangerous way to live," Chloe warns, fearing a future flee.

"You do the same thing," Dakota says, her eyes narrowing.

"Do not," Chloe responds. She's confident this conversation won't happen. Then it does.

"Yeah, you do. You and Stanley keep out of each other's lives so you never end up talking about the serious shit," Dakota says.

"How do you know what we talk about?" Chloe asks, defensively. "And even if you were right, that's what couples do sometimes. When Woody Allen was married to Mia Farrow, they lived in completely separate buildings."

"Right, but who the fuck would willingly agree to live with Mia Farrow?" Dakota asks.

Chloe sighs, "Okay, bad example. She really is the worst."

London nods her head emphatically. Marrying your daughter is creepy, but not as creepy as marrying a redhead.

"So has any one talked to Lindy lately?" Chloe asks, staying on the topic of fucked up marriages that should have never happened.

"Oh!" Sienna pops out of her chair a little bit, "I have! I have!" she says, waving her hand in the air, "Want to know why?"

"Because you're not a lazy whore who refuses to her leave house?" Kristen responds, hoping to keep Sienna away from an encore performance.

"That's correct, Kristen." Sienna says, pointing her knife. "Lindy's good, she doesn't hate you all for totally flaking out. She said it's fine. She was at Rolendo with Emerson Crandle."

"Ew," London says, chewing. Chloe gets excited. Was London's, "Ew," because her food tastes bad? Did she bite into something weird? Chloe is preparing to selflessly give her plate away, when London finishes her thought, "Emerson looks like the type of girl you'd see in party pictures with exposed piping in the background."

"She's only famous because she's black and in that computer movie," Sienna says, a safe distance from Emerson. At Rolendo, Sienna kissed Emerson's ass and suggested, "Maybe, like, the black girl in the computer needs to call tech support to get her out and I show up all hot and in glasses. I even already own glasses. I'm perfect for the part. Think about it."

Dakota's eyes pass by Chloe's plate. The salmon side is diced so finely from the faux activity that it looks like Chloe is eating baby food. "Was that not good, Chlo?" Dakota asks, daringly.

The entire table looks at Chloe's plate.

"Stanley made omelets before I left," Chloe tells them. It wasn't a lie- he really did make omelets.

"Oh, you mean seven hours ago?" Dakota asks.

"No, it was like..." Chloe trails off and all the girls hit their phones which light up with the time. A thick, yucky, off-putting silence lingers, like Sienna had gagged everyone.

It's clear that dinner is over, and Sienna's plan has fractured, so she releases her friends back into the wild. Even after their emancipation, the girls feel distinctly less-free than they did this morning.

46- Meet the Parent.

Jake reaches across to the passenger seat of his Range Rover. An unexpected, brake-screeching stop caused his bag of goodies to explode onto his dashboard like a pinata, then settle on the floorboards next to a box of various juice cleanses he's considering.

For the past four weeks, Jake has maintained a perfect track record of fulfilling the texted lists Dakota would send him. If Jake was to believe in omens, he would take the dashboard explosion as a sign that tonight will be different. Even if he didn't get the 144 text messages from Dakota today about a kidnapping, this mess would still lead him to believe that trouble is on the midnight horizon.

One by one, Jake drops the items back into the bag. A package of coffee, a box of peanut butter Cap'N Crunch, the current issue of *Elle*, a pack of Pall Malls, a plastic container of strawberries, and a box of tampons all return to the paper bag.

Sometimes, instead of an *Elle*, it's a *Vogue*. Sometimes, instead of tampons, it's toilet paper. Sometimes, instead of strawberries, Jake would find a Blu-ray of a cheesy road trip comedy and pop it in the bag as a surprise.

Different items for different days, and like the unique contents of his one night luggage, staying with Dakota is always a surprise and a gift.

With his groceries re-bagged, Jake eases the Range Rover back onto the road, then guns the engine. He can't shake the weird feeling that he'd recently collided with, and despite having his night neatly placed back in the bag, something feels ominous.

Like any other normal person who barely just escaped a car accident, Jake takes out his phone to text his girlfriend about it, while driving to her house.

Dakota calms his fears about the night with texts like, "Hurry, i miss u," and, "U better not have forgotten the peanut butter capt crunch."

As the Range Rover pulls up to Dakota's gate, a flurry of frantic movement in Jake's periphery distracts him from buzzing in on the intercom. Looking to his right, Jake sees a man trying to scale the wrought iron bars of the gate. When he lays on the horn to get this unskilled climber's attention, the possible intruder looks toward the SUV like a deer in the headlights. The shadowy figure's increasingly prominent forehead shines in the moonlight and it ignites something dangerous inside the imposing Jake Wesley. Jake understands that he's staring at Paul Dabney. It's incredibly clear that Dakota's father is trying to get back onto her property because he's ran out of information to sell to the blogs.

Donald Wesley, Jake's father, devoted his entire life to his work with CARDIN. As a defense contractor, CARDIN's business was making the world a safer place. Well, at least that's what it says on their website. The real life dealings of the company may differ a bit from the information in their "About Us" tab (for national security purposes, of course).

Donald Wesley's goal in forming CARDIN was to eliminate bad people. He's told Jake many times that there's more than one way to get rid of someone. The first step is finding out what your enemy's most basic motivation for evil is, then you either negotiate with them on this issue, or you locate the motivation, then you send a sniper round tearing through it, until every ounce of that motivation leaks out in a stream of syrupy red.

Unwilling to attempt the latter, Jake decides on the former.

Leaving his bag in the car so he won't be accused of trafficking "mountains of cocaine" into the house, Jake hops out of the Range Rover and approaches Paul Dabney.

Paul makes his way to a slightly damaged portion of Dakota's gate, then snakes his arm through the bars. It's clear that Paul wants this heavily fortified gate between himself and Jake.

"Can I help you?" Jake's deep voice asks Mr. Dabney's bald spot.

Quickly yanking his arm out of the gate, then turning around, Paul finds himself face-to-chest with a hulk of a man. It was easy for Paul to tell the rags that Jake Wesley, a man he'd never met, was killing his daughter, but when Jake stood before him with clenched fists, it became clear to Paul that his daughter isn't the Dabney that Jake is going to kill.

Backing up, Paul assumes that from 15 feet out he should be able to agitate Jake enough that the neighbors will call the cops, then the paps will hear it on the scanner and they'll show up just in time for Paul to rush Jake.

Paul Dabney scans the street for someone walking their dog or a paparazzi staked out on a whim. Finding neither, Mr. Dabney decides to act batshit crazy, his specialty. "You! I don't want you anywhere near my daughter! You're ruining her-"

"-here," Jake says, interrupting Paul's words by holding out a folded wad of money.

Mr. Dabney recovers from the flinch he involuntarily made in response to Jake's arm moving toward him, then he takes two steps forward and cautiously grabs the bills.

This is what it's come to. Paul Dabney used to have more money than he could count.

Then *everything* happened.

Jake looks at this excuse for a man, knowing that he could twist his bald little head off, and he says, "That's what you're looking for in the end, isn't it?"

Paul counts the bills and realizes there's over $300 in his hand.

"I'll give you that much, every week, if you stay away. It's an allowance. Every week that I don't see you near this gate, or on the blogs, or in the magazines, or chatting with the paps, you get that money. All you have to do is *stay away*. From what Dakota has told me, you excelled at doing just that for the first fifteen years of her life, for free, so I'm sure you'll have no issue with this agreement."

Mr. Dabney looks at the money, counts it again, then asks, "How do I know you'll..."

"I'll mail the cash to you every week."

Paul takes out his wallet and slides the money inside, then removes a business card and cautiously gives it to Jake.

"Send the money here," Mr. Dabney says. Jake looks down at the bright orange rectangle. He sees a name, an address, and a phone number. There's no business on the business card because Paul's way of making money is so ugly that only a fool would advertise it.

Jake pockets the card, then reaches his hand out to seal the deal with Mr. Dabney.

Paul Dabney looks at the giant paw that extends out to him, then he backs away. He's still not totally sure that this discussion will end with him retaining all of his teeth. "It's a deal," Paul says, then turns around and lurches into the shadows.

As Jake watches Paul Dabney abandon his daughter again, he feels very close to his own father.

Paul Dabney walks back to the car that Dakota bought him, and he chooses to get inside and drive away. He leaves feeling better than the last time he gave up an important woman in his life. Paul will never see Dakota again, just like his wife. Both women are dead to him now, but at least he could still visit his wife's grave, if he wanted to.

47- Post Dramatic Mess Syndrome.

The glow of Stanley's laptop lights up an otherwise dark balcony. Chloe grabs an abandoned, half-consumed cup of cold coffee off the kitchen counter, then heads out to explain what happened.

Alerted by Chloe's barefoot shuffle, Stanley glances over at his girlfriend and asks, "How's Ms. Wolfe doing?"

Chloe laughs a tired laugh as she walks over to her boyfriend. "Good," she says pushing Stanley's laptop shut, then she moves both the laptop and her coffee cup to the side table, with the mischievous fantasy of the cup "accidentally" getting kicked over onto the very sensitive computer.

"Did you escape unscathed?" Stanley asks, then fills her in, "They were speculating that Sienna was disassembling you girls, then sewing your parts together to build a single, highly obedient super friend."

"You read the blogs?" Chloe asks, fearing that the constantly open laptop was polluting her house with half-truths.

"I wanted to know where my girlfriend went today," Stanley tells Chloe.

See, they aren't distant. Stanley hates the blogs, but he cares enough about Chloe to go on them and get the information she didn't provide.

"Are you hungry? I can make you something," Stanley offers, eying his laptop. Chloe reviews this question. There's a chance that Stanley wanted to continue his work in the kitchen while making an elaborate meal. There's also the chance that this was another pathetic attempt to confront Chloe about the food issue.

"No, I ate at Kristen's."

"Was the food good?" Stanley asks hopefully.

"It was great, we got it from Jackyl."

"You get the salmon?" Stanley asks, proving even further how much he pays attention.

Chloe nods.

"They didn't really get any pictures of you," Stanley tells her.

"Yeah, gotta love hoodies, they make the perfect cover-up in those situations."

"We're probably the only people that ever actually use the hoods on them," Stanley theorizes.

Tired of concealing herself, Chloe mumbles, "I have... an idea... will you listen while I practice out here?"

"Sure," Stanley says. She gave him the day; he'll give her the night.

"Yay!" Chloe squeaks, popping up, then moving inside to grab her lyrics. She wants to rush, but she finds her body incapable. The house is too big, the walk is too long. The trip allows time for reflection, and Chloe hates every reflection she sees, yet she can't stop looking. She begins to realize that she feels threatened by Sienna's display today. That non-practicing bitch was able to crank out those songs, one after another, and even though her piano playing sounded seizure inspired, her singing wasn't that bad. To make sure her lead singer position is solid, Chloe grabs her "social!heavy" labeled folder and Stanley's acoustic guitar, then anxiously heads back out to her boyfriend.

When she returns to the balcony, she finds that Stanley has reclaimed his laptop and he's typing away, as though ten hours of singularity wasn't enough for him.

Chloe leaves the guitar balanced on the edge of the door frame, then walks over and sulks in a chair opposite Stanley. She hugs her folder and acts weepy.

Alerted by three extra-long, extra-loud sighs, Stanley looks up from his laptop, then asks, "What's the matter?"

"You aren't paying attention," Chloe whines, pushing out her bottom lip.

"I can listen while I'm on my laptop."

"No, you don't care about my band," Chloe declares, now in full girlfriend mode.

"I do care. I want to hear your progress and it's natural to listen while I type."

"I don't do this to you. I don't text the entire time I'm with you, doing stuff you like. I take an interest in the things you enjoy. I watch your team do sports so you should show me the same respect."

"You... watch my team... do sports?" Stanley repeats the statement slowly because it disproves her point.

"Yup, I even wore a baseball cap in public once. I make sacrifices for you."

"You were wearing it because you didn't have time to put on makeup," Stanley says. Upon seeing Chloe's well made-up death stare, Stanley says, "Sing away."

"I want you to play guitar," Chloe tells him, almost in baby talk, a lesson she had learned from her best friend.

"Okay, get my guitar," Stanley says, making an effort to show the same interest in the band that Chloe had shown during the Dodgers game, when she cheered, "Go Dodgers! Those blue uniforms really give your eyes a 'wow factor' that the other team doesn't have!"

Chloe pops up, grabs the guitar, then presents it to Stanley, all in one fluid motion. "Here ya go," she says with a little giggle.

"How do I know what to play?" Stanley asks.

Chloe sits down very straight in her chair, only moving to grab a clipped sip of the stale coffee. She puts the cup back on the table, opens her folder, then yanks out a packet, and says, "Tabs."

Taking the pile of papers, Stanley opens to the first page of tabs, then balances the sheet on his keyboard so the glowing laptop screen functions as a light. He begins to strum out a sloppy interpretation of the first song, and Chloe's fears dissipate when she realizes that Stanley *does* care. When it's her time to come in, Chloe quietly sings what she's been practicing in a guest room upstairs with her voice coach for the past month. As Stanley's fingers begin to move naturally, Chloe's voice floats with an organic assurance. By the second song, they're a duo. Stanley will even lean over and join Chloe in singing lyrics when the chorus comes around.

Living in the same house, singing the same song; Stanley and Chloe.

48- Addressing Room.

Chloe wakes up feeling free.

Stanley helped her become confident about being the lead singer of the band, and now that she's received this assurance, it becomes crucial that all of the members of social!heavy come together to work as one.

A text from London, reading, "SHOPPING," buzzes on Chloe's phone. It's time for a little reward after all this restraint.

An apple, 20 minutes in front of the mirror, a semi-distracted listen to a recording Chloe made on her phone of some demos- it begins as a good morning.

A reasonably traffic-free drive, 15 minutes in line for coffee, half a photoshoot with London on Santa Monica Blvd- it continues to be a good morning.

"I will buy things and it will make me forget about Sienna," Chloe explains to London, as she shuts the door of the Fred Segal dressing room. This is her plan to continue her good morning.

London looks at herself in long mirror on the wall, then fixes the stubby ponytails on either side of her head. Chloe had noticed that there's something wrong with London today- something off- besides just her extensions.

"I don't understand Sienna. Why'd she think we'd fire Martin?" London asks, noting, "He could, like, destroy our lives. Or, you know, at least fuck them up for a couple of sad days."

Chloe ignores London's truth and focuses on the shopping. She slides off her dress then picks up one of the tiny bras she needs now that her old bras are too big. Chloe has boxed up her loose intimates so she can make a donation to Marcos the next time he brings food for Stanley.

London notices that under Chloe's boobs, her ribs are showing. Chloe is disappearing.

Catching London's gawk, Chloe asks, "Do you think I'm pretty?"

"Of course, that's one of your best qualities," London says, because it's true, not because it's the right thing to say. London couldn't help but notice that when Chloe put on all that weight, she became less interesting. It was almost as though Chloe wasn't nearly as alive when she was eating.

"Aw. You're my best friend," the slim socialite says as she puts her arm around London's high waist.

"You're pretty enough to be my best friend too," London says, putting her arm across Chloe's shoulder.

"So did Tobe get scared when you were kidnapped yesterday?" Chloe asks. London's smile flickers away, "Oh, I have to actually go call him," she says, sliding out Chloe's grasp, then disappearing from the dressing room.

Chloe stands in her potential new underwear and wonders why it was necessary for London to leave this private space to make a call. Maybe London knew that if she cocked her elbow to bring her phone to her face, while Chloe tried to hop into a pair of skin tight pants, all it would take is an off-balance trip to set in motion a very blogworthy afternoon. Just because Chloe knows how to deal with a black eye it doesn't mean she can pull the plan off in public. Martin's hypothetical situation had the injury happening at home, but Chloe knows that, sometimes, embarrassing moments happen in the center of a party.

If Stanley was to get a domestic violence reputation, he'd need at least two really good auditions- maybe even one with the lead actress- before he landed the part. Chloe doesn't want to be a Jenny. Being a Jenny seems hard. Chloe is having enough trouble handling being Chloe.

Outside the dressing room, London scrolls through her texts. She has no new messages from Tobe. To block her frown, she lifts her phone up to her face, but she doesn't select anyone to call- this gesture is just to hide her sadness from other customers and their casual cell phone snaps.

Maybe Tobe isn't texting because he saw London snooping around this morning? At this point, that hypothetical situation might be better than having to confront him about what she found. If London can't even talk to Chloe about her discovery, she'd never be able to bring it up to her boyfriend. At least she can still say that Tobe is her boyfriend. She leans on this fact.

Chloe walks out of the fitting room wearing a smile. Of course she's happy, how could anything be too small on her slight frame? "I'm going to get the underwear and the pants," she says.

"Okay, bye," London says loudly into her phone, pretending to end the call she was too cowardly to make.

"How'd it go?" Chloe asks, as London follows her over to the register.

"Fine. Oh, actually, that was Joel, he wants us to go to the studio."

London wasn't completely lying. She did get a text from Joel this morning, but she didn't remember about it until she started scrolling through her phone. It seems that the surprise she received at the foot of Tobe's bed kicked any memory of the text out of her mind.

Chloe gets close to London, and quietly, through her teeth, she asks, "How does he expect us to get Martin into the studio with a mob of secret vampires following us?"

London turns away from the register girl, then whispers, "Martin's already there, and it's not what you think, go along with it." London has no idea why Joel wants her to go to the studio, but she doesn't want to be alone with her thoughts, so she'll trick Chloe into thinking something fantastic is about to happen.

49- Be Careful What You Bitch For.

Riding a strobe of flashes, Chloe and London slide through a side
entrance to get safely inside the studio. They walk through the courtyard, into
the building, down a dark cranberry hallway, then for the first time, they enter
a large recording room. No one told them to go there; certain doors were
closed and certain doors were open, so they walked through the open doors
until they reached the room they're destined to be in.

A warm, insulated space greets them. To their left is a giant glass wall that
reminds Chloe of one of her most frequented restaurants, Dorée. On the other
side of the glass, Martin is sitting in front of a massive knob and dial covered
board. London thinks Martin looks like the captain of a spaceship. She
imagines he's watching those gauges purposefully so the girls can progress
safely into uncharted territory. There was no question, Martin belongs behind
the board. The band absolutely made the right decision by inviting him to
explain himself, then inviting him to stay for dinner. This morning, Martin
had e-mailed out the picture Reyna took, and now it's the background on each
girls' phone... even Sienna's. The photograph has been elevated in importance
because, beyond just capturing a moment, it serves as evidence that the girls
are capable of moderating their reactions, and it's proof that they don't believe
Martin is the enemy. Sienna was wrong to assume that Martin wants to take
over the band; he's just doing all the shit that the girls lack the technical
knowledge or attention spans to take care of. Just because the maid does all
the laundry and washes the dishes, it doesn't mean she's going to take over
the mansion- she may want the mansion- but as strong as that desire is, she
knows that there are a million things that will keep her from moving into the
master bedroom. Even if she was gifted the mansion, the property taxes would
destroy her. She'd have no choice but to put the house on the market, then go
back to her old apartment.

"Martin!" Chloe yells loudly at the glass, but he doesn't respond.

London starts dancing seductively, watching her reflection in the glass,
hypnotizing herself with her own movements. When her pointy frame finally
catches Martin's attention, he smiles and pushes up a knob so he can hear in
the girls, then he presses down a button.

"Perfect timing," Martin tells them over the intercom.

"Can you hear us?" Chloe screams, and Martin's eyes bug out, answering
her question.

He presses the button down again and says, "Walk over to the piano."

The recording space is wide open, but the walls are covered in acoustic
tiles so it looks like a Kubrick set. In the corner of the rectangular recording
area is a piano.

London moves swiftly to collect the "presents" that Martin has left atop the piano. She finds five carefully hand labeled folders, each of them identical to the one Martin had at their meeting with Joel. One of the folders is noticeably skinnier than the others- it's labeled "Sienna."

Instinctively, Chloe is jealous of Sienna's folder- it's just how she's programmed.

"Go on, take a look," Martin says over the intercom, knowing that he'll redeem himself with these presents. He worked hard on these gifts because sharing his re-invigorated passion makes him feel like he's taking advantage of his time, instead of taking advantage of the girls. Damn all those hours wasted waiting in front of some empty house, praying for a troubled woman in a divorce scandal to walk outside. Martin's life has gained an energy that renders inactivity poison. He didn't sleep last night, maybe from insomnia or maybe from adrenaline, but he realized what the next step would be toward building this band, then he took it. To create a highly successful version of social!heavy, the girls had to be provided with confidence, guidance, and autonomy. This mix is the recipe for them to believe in Martin again; for them to believe in each other again. They've have had so many advantages, but what they haven't had is some old dopey guy who wants nothing from them besides their talent. Martin is willing to provide that piece of himself, and he's confident that it will serve them well.

There's a uniform basic problem for the men in these girls' lives. Stanley, Tobe, Jake, and Johnny have it all, but they have no clue when it comes to one of life's greatest questions... what do you get the girl who has everything? Martin feels like these folders successfully answer that question.

Chloe and London each open their folder. They find:

- *A picture of Martin and the other guy that was in Bright Feathers.*

Martin, still behind the glass, points between himself and the old picture. London looks over as he continues this gesture while grinning. She gives him an uncomfortable smile back.

- *A revised copy of the tabs to all 9 songs.*

"I sang while Stanley played the guitar last night," Chloe yells toward the glass.

Martin asks, "How'd you sound?"

"Stanley said I sounded amazing, but he might have just been saying that because I once wore a baseball cap."

Another uncomfortable smile is exchanged- this time it's from Martin to Chloe.

- *DVD-R labeled, "Performances."*

"Ew, Martin, what's this?" Chloe asks as she holds the DVD by the edge, just in case it has DNA on it.

Martin makes a gesture that might be a beckoning motion. Neither girl moves. He presses the button and says, "Come on."

Chloe looks at London, and asks, "Was that a 'Come on, follow me' or a 'Come on, how could you puke on my son, he's only a toddler' type statement?"

The girls look back to the booth, both hoping that they won't have to explain about the time London puked on a small child, and they see that Martin's no longer behind the glass. They both begin to fear that London puked on Martin's Godson and he just put it all together.

A buzzing noise cuts through the quiet space, and Martin enters the recording room, then holds door open. The girls see by his reaction that his, "Come on," was the first type so they collect the folders and follow their producer.

Martin leads them next door, to the other side of the glass, then he takes the DVD from Chloe and pops it into one of the seemingly endless number of disc slots on the left side of the console.

"Look," Martin says, pointing up at the flat screen hanging in the left corner of the giant soundproof glass window.

"This is terrible, change the channel," London says, peering up at a man wearing a white, billowy, pirate shirt and leather pants. He's prancing around a foggy stage, while an emotionless pale guy in a pirate shirt plays a giant synthesizer, near another guy, in yet another pirate shirt, who wails away on a guitar.

"This is shit," Chloe says.

"This is Robin LaManche's band," Martin says.

This means nothing to either of the girls.

London starts looking for the remote to change the channel to CTV or maybe to a show that counts down "Hollywood's Worst Baby Names." London had already watched the show once and she liked it so much that she decided that if she ever had a child, she would name him Adolph, just so she could top the list. It's really an unstoppable name, that is, until Sienna gets in vitro, then names her kid "Clitty" just to best London and poor little Adolph.

"This should mean something to you because Robin LaManche was your first producer, remember?" Martin re-informs the girls. They stare back at him blankly, and he sighs, "The old guy that Rod brought in."

"We're such a good judge of character," Chloe says. With a hand on her bony hip, she shakes her head back and forth, and tells London, "We knew that guy sucked even before we found out he was a fog pirate."

"We were in the same room as a fog pirate?" London asks in her baby voice.

Martin sighs a chorus of sighs, then tries again, "This is what a New Wave band looks like when they perform. I made this DVD so that you could get some ideas. It's an example."

"Ew. We have to run around the stage like a bunch of douchebags?" London asks, unhappy. "I'm getting flashbacks from when I did runway for the GUESS F/W show and now I need a shower."

"Oh, yeah. That's was bad. I was front row. You did look like a douchebag," Chloe recalls.

"Don't be jealous you didn't book it," London says arching her pointy nose in the air.

Martin herds the conversation back on track, "I'm not saying you have to perform like this, but it's good to get some ideas. You can ignore the clothes, it was just a fad."

"Like neon?" Chloe asks.

"Or adopting black kids?" London tags on.

Martin looks at London as she ejects the disk. "Yes girls," he says, like a tired father.

"We'll be fine on stage, Martin. We've been dancing on tables since we were fifteen," London assures him with another troubling statement

"Will you watch the DVD just for me then?" Martin asks.

"Again?" London responds, taken aback, "We just watched it."

Chloe puts her disc back and looks at what else Martin gave her.

- *A packet of lyrics.*

"Martin, I already have these, what do you think I've been doing all this time?"

"I just made you an extra copy with some slight alterations to make them a little more current."

"The lyrics are fine the way they are," London says, protective of work she inherited- how socialite.

Martin clarifies, "At one point I made a reference to Elizabeth Taylor and the whole image of Liz has a different meaning now."

"No, it doesn't. Dakota was Cleopatra for Halloween last year. Elizabeth is still Elizabeth. Here or gone."

London shakes her head in agreement with Chloe. Martin didn't realize what he was doing by removing Elizabeth. To replace someone because they got old, and fat, and dead was exactly what every socialite fears. They never want to think about the possibility that they'll no longer be on the guest list or that they'll be asked kindly to step down off the table. The last thing they want to dwell on is the fact that someday they'll be replaced by a girl who's younger and more "now."

Chloe looks at the final item in the folder.

- *A CD labeled 'social!heavy.'*

"Is this?" Chloe asks, doe eyes consuming the disc.

"Yup, it's the instrumentation I recorded. Those are the tracks. It's not what is going to be on the CD, it's just something to play along with," Martin carefully explains.

Chloe holds CD. This is every part of their songs except her own. Chloe doesn't have a female singer to follow along with, all she has is Martin's old tinny vocals.

Since she isn't given a shadow, Chloe finds herself chained to nothing except herself, and that anchor is getting lighter by the day.

50- Tobe or Not Tobe?

"I need some company," London says to Chloe and Martin after they exchange hugs goodbye in the studio's enclosed courtyard.

"Aw, Hun, are your animals alright?" Chloe asks.

London nods her head in a confused range of emotions.

"Do you want me to come over to your place?" Chloe offers, unable to combat London's sad eyes.

London squeaks, "Yes," then turns and stares at Martin. She makes very direct eye contact with him, her heavy eyelids almost shivering with over-the-top sadness.

"Okayyy," Martin gives in, throwing his hands up. Joel would rip his arms off and make his bones into drumsticks if this rendezvous at the Francis mansion is caught on camera, but Martin agrees to go because it's the right thing to do. This is not Joel's band, it's London's band.

"I'll leave a half hour after you, then I'll park at Petsville, LA and walk up," Martin tells London. He's been in London's neighborhood so often that he has the entire layout memorized.

The girls make sure they have all the folders, then leave for London's house.

All the paps immediately clear out with the girls, but Martin waits until 4 PM to leave, a full 40 minutes after his old peers sped away behind his new peers. Graciously, social!heavy has given him a second chance, and the thought of going back to only knowing them from behind the camera lens again worries Martin. This makes him careful, in the very same way the girls have become careful.

Leaving a territory where he's king, Martin takes to the road, only to enter the foreign, air conditioned planet the girls rule.

During the drive over, Martin receives:

A text from Chloe, "She keeps asking for u."

A text from his boss, "Need those Francis pics. NOW. Stop flaking."

A text from Joel, "So they can really play the instruments? What the fuck? Kinda impressed."

And a text from the phone company, "Your automatic bill payment of $74.75 will be withdrawn from your account on 7/2."

Martin arrives at Petsville, LA, then begins a calm walk up to London's house. Approaching the mansion, the pap looks for his buddies, but there are no secret vampires to be found. Knowing that this unlikely peace could be disrupted at any moment, Martin texts Chloe, who sends Alonja out to the gate.

The door of the gate cracks open, and Alonja sticks her head out, then she screeches, "Ms. Francis no here." Alonja was sent out to let the visitor in, but she instantly recognized Martin as one of the people that used to go through the trash when she would bring it to the curb, and he was not going to gain access to the trashcans inside the house.

"No! I'm not here to-"

"-shoo. Shoo," Alonja says, flicking her hand at Martin.

"No shoo! No shoo! I'm the person that just texted Chloe. Here. Look," Martin says nervously, holding out his crappy phone to Alonja. The maid cautiously reviews the text, then looks at Martin's stupid I'm-no-threat-to-you-or-your-respective-employer smile. Convinced of Martin's innocence, she pushes the gate fully open and lets him inside.

Walking up to the house, Martin attempts small talk, "This place was always weird to me- it's pretty much built into a jungle that didn't exist until the house did."

"You wait here," Alonja says, pointing at a spot about ten feet from the door, "I get Ms. Francis."

"You know London, she loves animals, so I guess why not live in the jungle?" Martin replies weakly at his own observation.

Alonja quickly goes inside and locks the door behind her.

"Locked out," Martin texts to Chloe, then, moments later, the lock clicks and the door opens. Martin doesn't wait for someone to peak their head out, he rushes inside before Alonja returns.

The door shuts and Chloe gives Martin a hug out of nowhere. "Sorry about that," she says, "London's upstairs talking to Heath Ledger and giving him his medicine."

"Pardon?" Martin asks in a high pitched voice.

"Heath is one of her dogs. She talks to him. I think it's like some sort of therapy for her, in addition to that court ordered therapy she has to do for her probation. She can telepathically communicate with her pets- it's sort of like she's Tarzan," Chloe says, then leads Martin through the dining room.

"You mean Aquaman?" Martin asks, as his eyes first admire the long, pristine dining room table, then bounce to a spotless, stainless steel kitchen that's roughly the same square footage as his apartment.

"No. London had no siblings to talk to growing up so she had to talk to her animals. The same thing happened with Tarzan."

"That's kind of sad," Martin says.

Chloe opens the fridge. Martin gets excited that she's grabbing a snack, but she only grabs a Red Bull. "I don't know. Maybe it's not sad. London Francis wouldn't be London Francis if she had parents that cared about her. All she had to do was make it to sixteen, then her life became awesome. She's as famous as she is because she was raised by kittens, not adults," Chloe says, then cracks open the can.

This is the type of house London chose to live in- you could talk openly about her, even knowing she's in the same place you are, and she'll never be the wiser- her house is just that big.

"But it'll never stop. She'll always need more attention because her parents will never give it to her," Martin theorizes.

Chloe smiles at him- what a cute, fat, common person thought.

"Good. Craving attention is the only way you stay relevant. And the only way you stay *good enough*. We don't want to be reality TV whores. You see how quickly their stars fall. London will never fall because she'll never do anything that would cause people to get sick of her face."

Martin considers this as London bounds into the room like a fawn. "Martin!" she screeches, decidedly happier than when they were in the studio courtyard. Martin gives London an I-acknowledge-that-I'm-a-fat-guy-and-you're-a-beautiful-woman-so-you-don't-want-to-be-hugging-me hug where his butt sticks out and his jaw is careful not to hook on her shoulder.

"Come on," London says, grabbing Martin's sweaty palm. Hand-in-hand the duo proceeds through a series of ornate rooms that are filled exclusively with pictures of London. During the tour, she provides a running commentary on her possessions. This one-sided dialog merely consists of her pointing to different items, then saying, "Cute," or, "Super cute."

Behind London, Martin undertakes a wheezing climb up a seemingly never ending staircase, then they both drift down a London-portrait adorned hallway. It's obvious that London likes pictures of herself, a lot, but she rarely requests Martin to photograph her. Either she doesn't respect him as a photographer or she respects him as a musician. Martin abandons this train of thought in the door frame of London's bedroom. Dozens of eyes are on him, like he was a celebrity leaving The Ivy. Tiny dogs, furry kitties, colorful birds, and a pig in a diaper stare at Martin with varying degrees of intrigue. London makes a kissy noise with her mouth and half the animals start licking themselves, while the other half shift their gaze to her as she clasps her giant hands together and announces, "Everyone. Gregory... Greg! Pay attention."

A gray cockatoo looks at Martin.

"That's better. Okay babies, this is Martin. He wrote songs for Mommy, then gave Mommy the credit for them because Aunt Sienna is a reckless psychopath who cannot be trusted."

Martin doesn't know what to do, so he nervously nods at the animal kingdom, then waves hello. Pointing at a little chihuahua that's been dyed pink, he says, "That color looks really good on you." The dog yawns at him, then falls over and goes to sleep instantly.

"What a bitch," Martin says.

London looks horrified.

"Kidding! I meant in the female dog way," Martin clarifies, his mouth dry.

"Rock Hudson is not a girl."

"That little pink dog, I meant," Martin says, pointing at the cotton candy looking puff.

"I know. Say you're sorry to Rock Hudson," London demands, through clenched teeth.

"I'm sorry..." Martin mumbles.

"I'm sorry..." London repeats while spinning her hand in the air, beckoning Martin to give a full apology.

Martin looks around, annoyed, then says, "I'm sorry, Rock Hudson."

Rock Hudson does not acknowledge the apology, as he is asleep.

"He forgives you," London says, her bubbly disposition back again, then she shoos Martin out of the room, and continues the tour of the upstairs.

As he makes his way through room after room, Martin realizes that Rock Hudson didn't deserve to be called a bitch. He's a perfect reflection of London. In the same way the real Rock hid his sexuality, London hides her intelligence. Both Rock and London arrived so good looking that it would be of no benefit to them to change the system that announced them as royalty. To show the real person behind a very public persona would be to volunteer their life fully to the court of public opinion. London and Rock both prove it's better to play up to whatever *they* think of you, then, in private, share your special gifts with the people who deserve them.

In the end, people might not exert the energy to learn who you really are, but the people that love you, those Elizabeth Taylor's, they'll pay for a bronze plaque to memorialize the person they knew and loved.

celebUtard
"The Band That Plays Together."

It looks like even **Sienna Wolfe**'s kidnapping spree couldn't keep **social! heavy** together. We knew the group was too good to be true. Not good enough that it would require a **Yoko** for the breakup, but, you know, still good.

This afternoon, **Chloe Warren** and **London Francis** were out shopping at **Fred Segal** (pics after the jump), then they were seen entering their regular studio in Burbank (pics after the jump), while Sienna Wolfe was pulling into **Kristen Paxton**'s driveway (if you can't find the location of the pics on our site, then maybe you shouldn't be on the internet).

Dakota Dabney, meanwhile, was nowhere to be found. Either she didn't want to take sides, or she's passed out in her own vomit. The world may never know... unless you have pictures (send them to us).

Lines have been drawn / sides have been taken. What we want to know is why Dakota Dabney is staying neutral, despite the fact that she used to be Sienna's best friend.

Also, why would Sienna and Kristen unite? The only thing these two girls have in common is that their names have been used as a synonym for something shitty.

The biggest question of all is why does all the hiding, and cute outfits, and warring, and kidnapping make us so damn excited for this New Wave album?

We'll take our meds and call you in the morning.

Until next time, stay tardy, celebUverse.

51- A Name That Will Stick With You.

Martin reclines in his chair by London's pool, inhaling the chlorine drenched air. He smiles, realizing that this is so much better than the last time he was invited into a socialite's back yard. "So what does Tobe think of your drumming?" he asks, then he takes the pitcher from Alonja and fills up his glass with more lemonade.

London lays with her long limbs stretched out, sucking up every last ray of LA sunshine until the sun falls, and she dodges the question by asking, "Did you know Sienna was at Kristen's house today?"

"I know, I sent her there," Martin responds simply.

"Do you know how it went?" Chloe asks, running by, out of breath.

"I'd assume poorly," Martin says. He continues watching Chloe as she attempts to get the ball back from Rock Hudson during their game of fetch.

"You've been with us for too long," London says.

"Don't forget, I was following you *before* the band," Martin reminds them.

London thinks about this for a second, then says, "Yeah, sorta crazy how it all worked out, ya know? Do you believe everything happens for a reason, Martin?"

"If it doesn't then everything would seem pretty pointless."

"I know, I go back and forth about it too," London says, eyes closed.

"It's different for you though. You have so many people in your life on a day to day basis that I can't imagine the universe can keep up with making sure everything has meaning," Martin tells her.

"I guess," London says. Her bony shoulders are practically crushing from the weight of the universe, but she's still trying to stay casual.

"What's the weirdest fan interaction you've had?" Martin asks after a momentary silence. It was the type of question that a common person would ask a celebrity, and Martin wants to stay common, despite being in the back yard of a bikini clad millionaire.

London goes through her weirdo memories. There were so many strange interactions she's had. The guy who offered to buy her underwear for a thousand dollars... the guy who would email photos where London's face was photoshopped onto his girlfriend's body in all his vacation pictures... that weird pap who hit her on the eyebrow with his camera when she was walking into the Lexington, then tried to give her a bouquet of flowers when she drunkenly left the club.

London recalls, "Hm, there was this- wait. Okay. Well. Yeah, I guess this guy could have been a fan. Or, I don't even know if it was a guy. Whatever, I was out to lunch with Kristen, and when I went back to my car, I saw that I had a piece of paper under my windshield wiper- it wasn't yellow like the parking tickets are so I actually picked it up and read it."

"Was it a fan letter?" Martin asks.

"I couldn't tell."

"What did it say?"

"Fairy Pussy," London says, confused.

"That's it? You got a note on your car that just said 'Fairy Pussy' with no explanation?"

"Yeah. Just 'Fairy Pussy.' I looked around to see if there was someone waiting to film my reaction. Like, I didn't know if they were doing it for one of those shitty reality shows or whatever, but there was no one there. I'm not sure if it was from a fan... or from someone who hates me."

"Maybe they meant 'Hairy Pussy' and their writing was sloppy?" Martin suggests, trying to process this unique phrase.

"No it was definitely a capital 'F.'"

"You're sure?"

"Yup, plus like everyone has seen my pussy and it's always hairless in pictures or videos. I had it lasered, like, right after puberty. There would only be a two month window for them to find me anything but hairless," London explains.

"Did you ask Kristen about the note?" Martin inquires, un-phased because London's pussy has become such a normal topic of conversation.

"No, she was super drunk and it's hard to bring up Fairy Pussy in conversation anyway. The whole way home, while trying not to get pulled over, I was thinking about Fairy Pussy. Did it mean that my pussy was cute like a fairy? Did it mean that I'm a fairy, like I was gay? Was it meant for someone else's car? When I looked around after I got the note, I didn't see any fairies. Plus, they don't need cars, fairies can fly," London coos.

"I believe they can," Martin says, mystified by this entire pointless, yet too-odd-to-be-bad story.

"I know, so it must have been meant for me! What do you think it means?" London asks.

"It sounds like something out of a David Lynch film," Martin says, then he sips his lemonade.

London is silent for a moment as she does a mental run through to recall if she's met David Lynch at a party. She hasn't. "Um, I guess it's a little lynchy," she says.

Martin chokes on his lemonade, then gasps, "Please don't ever describe anything as 'a little Lynchy.' He's a director. He directs films."

London nods at this, then decides maybe this Lynch guy was involved in the last movie she downloaded. "Did he do the movie where it's like puppies

vs. big dogs and both of them are at a severe disadvantage because neither
have opposable thumbs and weapon combat is essentially impossible, except
for when they carry weapons in their mouth, but then they run the risk of
choking?" she asks.

"Let's continue on," Martin says, unsure if he can describe Lynch without
spending the entire night out by the pool.

"But you didn't answer the question."

"I was asking the questions," Martin tells her.

"Right, but then we started talking about my Fairy Pussy and I asked you
one. It's like 10-1 your questions to mine. Don't be selfish Martin. What does
it mean?"

"Okay. I'll answer. I think it was someone being a smart ass. I think that
they did it for a laugh."

"Intended for me, or just someone random?"

"I think it was intended for someone random. They were probably
intrigued by your unique car. If they had known it was you, they definitely
would've written something more specific."

"Oh."

"Did you want it to be given to you on purpose?"

"A little. I think about what it means from time to time and that would be
stinky if it meant nothing."

Chloe and Rock walk back to London and Martin, as the sun finally bows
out.

"What are you guys talking about?" Chloe slurs, still not in possession of
Rock's beloved, slobber-covered ball.

"We have a name for the album," Martin announces.

Chloe looks at them blankly, then her eyes flutter back and she crumbles
to the ground.

52- Shoe Boxed In.

Martin is instructed by a revived Chloe to, "Leave, now."

Realizing that he doesn't know how to assist this sick girl, Martin figures the best way to help is to abide by her request. It's a moment of great conflict for him, because, as a paparazzi, collapses like these- the low points of a socialite's life- actually improve Martin's quality of life due to their photographic market value.

Left alone with Chloe, London is unknowledgeable about how to handle this crisis, yet she's intensely focused on providing comfort for her troubled friend. This isn't the first time London has had to spring into action at a moment's notice and attend to a medical emergency. Two years ago, London's dog, Anna Nicole, ate a full bottle of London's Valtrex after chewing off the child proof cap.

This time, dealing with a person who's capable of differentiating between a Valtrex bottle and a toy, London tells herself that she can take ownership of this tragedy without locking herself in her shoe closet and crying until the maid cleans up the body.

Texting is the answer. Again. Always. Forever.

London leads with the most succinct text she can assemble, "Chloe fainted."

"They get a pic?" Dakota sends types back, knowing that the fainting issue was... well, an issue, but if it occurred in public, it would be a *scandal*. At Lindy's divorce gala they were insulated by crazy fathers, and CIA operatives, and Mexicans. There was enough crossfire, and it was a closed party. If Chloe faints in a restaurant, it'll be everywhere.

"No. Happened @ my house," London texts.

"Y didn't u stop 2 eat after the studio?" Dakota texts back.

"Dunno. Wasnt thinking. Wut do I do?"

"Get her to eat something?" the common sense text reads.

London carries her phone into kitchen, then places it on the counter. She swings the fridge open to find an abundance of champagne and Redbull, but not much else. Spotting a bag of three apples sitting lonely in the crisper, she decides they'll have to do. After spending some time figuring out how to open the crisper, London grabs the apple bag.

Next, she opens her snack cupboard and locates a jar of peanut butter.

She now has the ingredients for the cure that will save Chloe's life.

After looking through multiple drawers in her kitchen, London realizes that she keeps her knives in a block of wood on the counter. She archives this fact for when some insane fan breaks into the house, ties her to chair, and forces her to eat dinner with him like they're husband and wife. She definitely could use the knives to fend him off. If that failed, then she'd at least be a prepared hostess and he wouldn't have to eat his steak with a butter knife.

Playing a memory game and going back through the cabinets for a plate, London finds one on the fourth try.

After centering an apple on the plate, London places the knife on the tough red skin of her target. When she puts pressure on the apple, it rocks back and forth, and despite not making any progress, London remains determined not to call Alonja. She *will* figure out how to cut an apple.

Lifting the knife, London is about to deliver a vertical chop, when Chloe shuffles into the kitchen.

The disoriented girl backs up for a second as she sees London Bates with her weapon raised.

"Were you going to kill me in my sleep?" Chloe asks, both hands on her bony chest.

London looks at Chloe, then at the phone on the counter. If Chloe sees a text vibrate on the phone, she'll assume London was leaking news of this evening's very embarrassing moment. This perceived betrayal would ruin their friendship, and London would have to kill Chloe with the knife to put an end to the madness.

"I was making apple slices as a surprise," London says, confident she could overpower Chloe in her current state. After acknowledging this, she reminds herself she's supposed to be playing nurse, not grim reaper.

Right when Chloe should begin protesting the snack, she instead makes her way toward London, then starts opening drawers. Chloe takes out an apple slicer from the drawer under the microwave. "Use this," she says, holding the spoked structure out. London is unsure if her knife could overpower the apple slicer so she disarms Chloe.

London is so confused. How did Chloe even know she even had one of these slicers, much-less where to find it? Is there some sort of kitchen starter kit that everyone gets when they purchase an oven? "Stuff in the kitchen is scary," London says, sliding a finger across the sharp spokes of the slicer.

"I know what you mean," Chloe says, filling a coffee cup with tap water, then she drags her feet in the direction of the TV room.

Once Chloe is out of sight, London runs to her phone and texts Dakota, "Call Stanley?"

"No. I will," Dakota sends back. London knows that it's better that way. Dakota is the only one with a last name that matters to Stanley.

London slices the apples, then glops some spoonfuls of peanut butter in the center of the plate. After carefully arranging the slices so they look pretty, London admires her culinary prowess. She wishes that she could upload a picture of this triumph, but she decides, no, nurses don't do that. This is a cure, not a chance to get more followers. If only apple slices could have saved Anna Nicole from a Valtrex induced coma.

London walks into the TV room, then sets down the plate of apple slices on the table. Chloe has her head buried in a pillow at the end of the sofa.

Without the assistance of her boyfriend, London turns on the TV. She knew she couldn't call Tobe and ask for help. He wouldn't care.

London has DVR'd reruns of *Tristan's Landing* for moments like this, so she cues up an episode where Tristan and Jenny are almost torn apart by two extremely serendipitous group pairings for an English project. Each character finds themselves tasked with studying and working closely alongside a smart, popular, attractive one-off character that merely exists to stir the pot, then exit stage left after 44 minutes. The episode's climax deals with Tristan confronting Jenny about her group partner, and Jenny yells, "Sometimes a Freud study session is just a Freud study session!"

Comforted by Stanley's distant presence and scared by what happened earlier, Chloe manages to lean over and take an apple slice. She dips the apple in the peanut butter.

Sinking back into the couch, Chloe watches the boy next door as he articulately conveys his deepest innermost feelings.

Suddenly, London's phone vibrates and it sends her into a panic. It's commonplace for London to receive texts, but since she's talking about Chloe behind her back, she feels extremely guilty for every improper lowercase that's been typed. Looking down at the screen of her phone, London sees it's not a text from Dakota, but instead a call from Tobe. She wants to answer the phone. She wants to talk to her boyfriend, but she doesn't know what to say.

The phone eventually stops convulsing. Unable to speak to a boy with a secret problem, London turns to the one person who knows best what it's like to hide something ugly, "Chlo?"

"Yeah," Chloe responds absently, her eyes never leaving the past shadow of her soul mate.

"I found something," London says, her arms twisting over each other when she admits this.

Chloe stops chewing the apple and looks over at London, "Like a lump?"

"Huh? What? No. I meant I found something at Tobe's house."

"Oh no! Like a girl?" Chloe asks, her eyes drifting back to the TV.

"Yeah, I found Sienna."

Chloe puts her hand up her mouth. London wonders if she should run and get a bucket so that Chloe doesn't purge apple chunks on her semi-new, probably expensive furniture. London isn't sure what the sofa cost because she just sent her boyfriend at the time, some probably-gay Michael Lorrie model, to buy it.

Almost in disbelief Chloe says, "That bitch. That evil bitch. She reall-"

"-no. It's not her fault," London says.

"I can't believe you're sticking up for her," Chloe responds, as her alien eyes implicate London.

"I found her in a shoebox. I found pictures of Sienna in a shoebox."

"Wait. I'm so confused now," Chloe says, retreating to the apple slices to keep her already dizzy head from spinning. In her fractured state, Chloe somehow finds herself jealous that it could even be rumored Sienna was petite enough to hide in a shoebox.

"I noticed these cut up magazines in Tobe's trash, and I thought maybe he was cutting out pictures of me. Remember when Sienna's sister made her that collage? I thought it would be like that, so... I went looking around."

"London, you never go looking around!"

"I know, but it was a good looking around, like an Easter egg hunt. It wasn't the Johnny Foster type of digging-for-corpses type look around," London says, trying to make her paranoid hunt seem like an innocent trip over a dead body.

"And you found that he was cutting out pictures of Sienna, instead of you?"

"Yup," London's little voice says, then she swallows hard.

"How many?"

"Two full shoe boxes of pictures."

"That's like three months of pictures!"

"Some were of him," London says.

"Sienna is photographed 2-1 compared to Tobe," Chloe points out.

"Unjustly," London says, still fighting for a boy she didn't want to fight with.

"I'm sorry, London," Chloe says warmly, then gets up and gives London a loose hug.

"What do I do?" London asks.

"I'll think of something."

"Do I talk to him about it?"

"Not until I think of something," Chloe instructs.

A tiny part of London wants to tell Tobe what she found so that he could inform her that it was all some sort of preparation for a Wiccan curse on Sienna. She'd be able to get past something small, like the fact that Tobe's a crazy person practicing black magic to destroy one of her friends. The relationship could handle the dark arts and bitter destruction of her bandmate. What London couldn't move past is the fact that Tobe is using London to get close to Sienna.

Chloe abruptly and definitively makes the decision that she will destroy Tobe Price.

How do you destroy someone who's perceived as being perfect? You find out what they're hiding, then you use it as leverage.

In this case, all the field work has been completed.

Today, London spent the day taking care of Chloe after her situation.

Tomorrow, Chloe will spend the day taking care of London's situation.

53- No One's Business is Just Their Own.

The morning sun creeps into the living room as Stanley sits in front of his laptop and checks the blogs just to make sure that Chloe actually spent the night at London's, recovering.

Stanley's phone begins vibrating across the coffee table, so he grabs it, then answers the call without even looking at the screen.

"Stanley," Dakota says, before he can say hello.

"Hey, Dakota. Can I call you back in a bit? I'm... buying t-shirts," Stanley says, struggling to form a lie, as lying is not Stanley's forte.

"No you aren't," Dakota counters quickly. She's been around Stanley long enough to know him. This is why she believed that Stanley and Lindy did actually have a history when Chloe mentioned it.

Stanley moves his laptop off his lap, then takes a sip of his coffee, preparing for this conversation. "Okay, I bought my shirts, what's up?"

"Did Chloe text you about what happened yesterday?"

"Yup," Stanley says, knowing this is why Dakota called. Chloe's quick, "I fainted. Gonna sleep at London's ilu," text, would, of course, be followed with numerous other texts and phone calls. Stanley was worried, but felt oddly at ease that London was taking care of his girlfriend.

"Stanley. Chloe has an eating disorder," Dakota says, as a direct and unwavering statement. The phantom conversation finally takes form. Suddenly, the phone becomes slick in Stanley's hand, as his entire body breaks out in a sweat. He knew this moment would come, but he put it off, indefinitely. If he discussed this with Chloe, he might lose her. It was easier watching the pounds disappear while Chloe stayed, instead of the other way around.

"She has a bad stomach. Not a lot agrees with her," Stanley's says, his mouth dry because all the moisture in his body is draining out of his pores.

"When she said she had a bad stomach, she meant that she had a fat stomach," Dakota points out.

"No, that weight was because of all the issues. That's when her stomach was at its worst. But she's better now. She can eat a meal and keep it down."

"Yeah, when there aren't fingers reaching into it, Stanley! Have you been paying attention at all?" Dakota yells.

After a crackle of silence, Stanley goes on the hard defensive, "Listen, Dakota. Do you think it's easy overseeing every moment around here? I'm turning on TVs, and paying bills, and making sure that there aren't three different guys showing up here, each looking for the laundry. I'm sorry I can't scrutinize every detail as intensely as someone with as many life pressures as a hermit crab."

Dakota is used to this belittling, it's the easiest way to cut her down, so she responds, "I hope you don't say that to Chloe."

"Of course I don't."

"Then why is it okay to say it to me?"

"Because you're making these... these allegations."

"They aren't allegations, Stanley. This is one of Chloe's best friends telling you something about her, and you're too stubborn or delusional to listen. I'm sorry if this isn't a conversation that you want to have with Chloe, but every question you're asked can't always be about TV-"

"-enough Dakota. This isn't your business. You need to stay out of it."

"I have been staying out of it, Stanley. I have been staying out of it! I have no choice but to get involved now. Chloe's not going to be on the front page because of this band, she's going to be on all the covers of those magazines because-"

"-this conversation is over."

"Convenient. You certainly had no problem talking to me when you were auditioning for my mom's show," Dakota says, knowing it will keep the conversation from being over.

"You're going to hold that over my head forever?" Stanley asks.

"If it wasn't for my mom, you would just be Stanley, not Tristan."

"Your mother was a saint. I know I owe her everything."

"Okay... so are you going to talk to Chloe about this?"

"No."

"Why?"

"What can I say that she already doesn't know herself?"

"You can tell her that it hurts you."

"You're always saying that people assume you girls are dumb. Well, she'd have to be stupid to not know that. If you still believe that everyone else is wrong, then there's nothing that I can say to her."

There's a long silence and Stanley wonders if he finally convinced Dakota to just let it go.

The sound of a lighter being flicked clicks over the line, then a deep inhale proceeds it.

"You know, you shouldn't smoke," Stanley says, "I'm not sure if you're aware, but it's really bad for you."

WORTHLESS HUMAN REPORT:

Sienna Wolfe

Sienna Wolfe, commercial modeling heiress, has recently added "rock star" to her list of "accomplishments." The list now reads as follows: modeling heiress, rock star, probation violator, bigot, and, get this, Mitchell Haughton's best friend.

Please refer to our previous report where we provided a mugshot and witness testimony related to Sienna's latest arrest. That arrest occurred at a party celebrating Lindy's divorce from Mitchell. Since then, we've photographed Mitchell and Sienna at a very public event- a party held by fellow worthless human, Diego Mestizo, that he uncreatively deemed "Third Episode Premiere Party"- as well as during a private meeting, away from the spotlight, in Mitchell's car.

Our sources are now saying that the Wolfe/Haughton duo will be stepping out again tonight.

Without information on what happened at Kristen Paxton's house earlier in the week, we can't speculate on if Sienna is social!heavy's keyboardist, but we can confirm that if she wanted to ensure that there was no chance Lindy Porter could ever take her spot, Mitchell would be a *key* player.

53.5- The Mistress of Bait.

The sound of someone trying to buzz into the gate makes Stanley's stomach turn. It's entirely possible that Dakota could have called in transit, knowing that Stanley would dodge the one conversation he'd been putting up glass walls to isolate himself from.

Stanley walks over to the intercom, then looks at the security camera.

He sees that it's a FedEx delivery.

There's still a chance that Dakota stole a FedEx truck, so Stanley remains on edge. He buzzes the driver in, then watches the screen carefully as a black delivery man hops out of the truck, in this man's hands is a fat white envelope.

Even before the delivery guy reaches the walkway, the excited actor swings the door front door open and flashes a welcoming smile.

The FedEx driver smiles back as he finds himself face-to-face with a man he watched get murdered by a sadistic clown two nights ago on basic cable. Despite being totally sure who this envelope is being left with, an autograph is requested, not so this guy can show his friends, but so he can keep his job. Stanley quickly signs his name, a brutally familiar action. Men on eBay copy this signature onto glossy pictures of Stanley and support their families by selling the forgeries to Midwestern housewives. This is the power and importance of a signature in the Hills. The delivery guy hands over the white envelope, then jogs back to his truck.

Stanley closes the front door, locks the deadbolt, then buzzes open the gate so the delivery guy to leave. After he's sure the gate is shut and Dakota can't get in, Stanley makes his way toward the kitchen. That blunt call is all he can think about. Dakota's mother, Lynn Dabney, created Stanley's career, and even though she's gone, on occasion, Dakota will sound just like her mother, and every time it happens, it shakes Stanley to the core.

Lynn Dabney was a crucial part of so many young stars' lives- when the cameras were rolling *and* when they stopped rolling. A producer who looked after the kids on *Tristan's Landing* like they were her own, Lynn was one of those special people who could usher a teenager into a position of fame, then teach them what the appropriate reaction is to this gift. Stanley almost feels as though Lynn might have been talking through Dakota today. If only that was the case. Lynn would know what to do about Chloe. For a moment, Stanley considers calling Chloe's mother, but if he isn't going to respect Dakota's wishes, he should at least respect Chloe's, and leave her mother alone. It wouldn't be fair to discuss a rapid deterioration like this with Linda Warren.

Stanley finds a distraction in the form of the white envelope that arrived.

The size and shape of this envelope is familiar to Stanley; there's only one thing this gift could be.

The horror studios generally go through Stanley's agent so this *must* be an unsolicited script. It's likely that the script had to be sent via FedEx because a passion filled director wanted to put the project directly in Stanley's hands, and was afraid that Stanley's agent would assume he doesn't have the range to pull the character off.

Stanley selects a knife out of the block on the counter, then carefully slices the package. Before he looks inside, he puts the knife back in the block, shedding a weapon he brandished in far too many horror films. No more protecting the virginal girl only to die at the start of the third act.

Mystery project in hand, Stanley walks out onto the balcony.

"Come home. I want to know ur ok," Stanley texts to Chloe, as he sits down.

It's easy to lose track of how much someone means to you until you have something that you want to share with them.

A song.

A restaurant

A screenplay.

This is a screenplay, right?

"Back in 30," appears on the screen of Stanley's buzzing phone.

Not wanting to go back to work on the computer, Stanley decides that he should peek inside the package.

Tearing open the previously sliced envelope, Stanley grimaces as the unbound pages almost take flight in the wind. Acting fast, he prevents a wind whipped disaster and the script remains in order.

Stanley looks down at the page and reads, "Dear Ms. Warren."

His heart sinks.

Stanley walks to the edge of the balcony and considers throwing the script in anger, spreading the pages across the side of the Hills, but he doesn't go through with it because someone would have to pick the pieces up. Cleaning up after Stanley is a maid's job, but Stanley refused to give in to the trend so, in the end, the mess would just land back on his shoulders.

The wounded actor takes a deep breath, then begins to review this bundle of papers. Maybe there's also a part for him in the script? According to the cover letter, Chloe is up for the part of "Julie." The letter mentions that Chloe's agent keeps trashing every script that's sent to him so it was essential this screenplay be sent directly to actress born to play the part.

Stanley figures that he'll give the project a read-through and if it's any good, he'll suggest it to Chloe. If it's trash, then he'll make like Chloe's agent and dispose of it properly before she gets home. Stanley is the perfect judge to decide if Chloe's agent is blocking all her scripts because he doesn't perceive her to be an actress, or if he's just protecting his client.

At the bottom of the cover letter, Stanley looks at the signature of who sent the script. He laughs, then turns the page. All of the jealousy in Stanley's body floats into the warm air, then gets blown away like loose script pages.

As soon as Stanley reads the title of the screenplay, he's hooked. He can't pull himself away. Page, after page, after page, Stanley immerses himself in the world of this unmade movie. An old cup of coffee from yesterday sits on the side table next to him. Unwilling to leave the screenplay even for a moment, Stanley drinks the stale black liquid.

Gulping down the last of the coffee, and possibly an insect, Stanley reads a particularly funny part of the script and the coffee collides with a laugh.

Chloe walks in the front door and immediately takes note of an echoing, distressed choke. She follows the noise to the balcony, then runs to Stanley's aid with unsure footing. "Are you choking? Do you need me to Heimlich you?" she asks, wishing she had London's medical expertise.

As the choke subsides, Stanley's laughter remains. Chloe looks at him like he's a really well groomed homeless person.

Finally gaining composure, Stanley smiles at his girlfriend with that special glow that's only reserved for only the most important people life has offered up. He lifts the script to show the in-demand actress.

"Aw, babe! You finally got a comedy script? See! Things are turning around for you," Chloe says, basking in Stanley's warmth like it was a tanning bed.

Stanley wipes his eyes. He was almost crying about the status of his career, then this script showed up and made the tears finally flow. Tears of laughter, not tears of defeat.

"It's another horror script," Stanley says, then smiles.

"Oh... a horror comedy? Those can be good," Chloe says, feeling refreshed today.

Admiring how supportive his girlfriend is, Stanley demands, "Come here," then pulls Chloe onto his lap with his free hand. Pointing down at the page, he reveals, "It's actually for you, not me."

"They sent me a script?" Chloe's doe eyes flutter with a mix of confusion, excitement, and worry about how this would make Stanley feel.

"Well, they sent you a pile of papers under the guise of a screenplay," Stanley says with a residual giggle.

Chloe rubs her cheek on Stanley's five o'clock shadow. It feels good to sit in the sun with her love as he fights back pure laughter.

Stanley puts the script in front of Chloe, then says, "You're Julie, I'm Kane."

Chloe looks down at the dialog on the page. Did Stanley really want her to do a read-through? She's only been an actress for roughly a minute. Isn't this rushing things a bit?

"Come on," Stanley says, coaxing her.

Chloe reads Julie's first line on the page aloud;

> JULIE
> What was that?

Stanley picks up as Kane;

> KANE
> I don't know, but it's
> madder than a baby
> pissing nails.

Chloe looks at Stanley, then she smiles a smile as wide as her eyes and she continues;

> JULIE
> I wish we had a baby that
> pissed nails so we could
> board up these windows.

> KANE
> It's no use, the Ghorbies
> have claw-hammer-like
> claws.

"Ghorbies!" Chloe says, her butt rolling on Stanley lap as she laughs, "The bad guys in this are Ghorbies?"

"Don't break character," Stanley says, sporting a mock serious face.

"Right," Chloe responds, straightening her posture, sitting stoically;

> JULIE
> Damn. You're right. What
> can stop a claw hammer?

> KANE
> We can.

Stanley looks deep into Chloe's eyes after delivering his line.

Chloe, never breaking eye contact, tells her hero;

```
            JULIE
     If you're right, then
     I'll nail you.
```

Chloe has to close the script. "This is not real. I refuse to believe that this is real," she says, giggling.

"I know, it could single-handedly destroy someone, not only as an actor, but as a human being. You can't unsay those words," Stanley says, still in awe.

Chloe holds the script in her hands, it's *the answer*. Stanley, from a chair on the balcony, managed to do the impossible. In the lap of the boy next door, Chloe finally found a way to defeat a threat far more deadly than a Ghorbie.

For all of Stanley's help, Chloe does what any good Julie would do, and she nails him.

54- Stick to the Script.

Wrapped in a bed sheet, Chloe calls London and informs her, "I'm treating you and Tobe to lunch today."

"Lunch?" London asks, not exactly protesting, but slightly worried that Chloe will crush Tobe before they can even order a London Francis sorbet. Maybe this is Chloe reaching out though? Maybe this is Chloe's version of diced peanut butter apples? London can't help but think about that urban legend where the kids bite into apples with razorblades inside them.

"We're going on a double date," Chloe tells London.

"A double date? Oh. A double date. Hm. What are-"

"-don't worry about the details, just show up at Dorée with your boyfriend. The reservations are for 2 PM."

"I don't know."

"2 PM. At Dorée," Chloe repeats, then ends the call.

"She go for it?" Stanley, Chloe's newly appointed acting coach, asks.

"Of course, she's London, when does she ever pass up a lunch date?"

Before the discussion of passing up meals can become alarming, Chloe makes a second call, "Hi, Martin? Yeah, it's Chloe. Who are you following today? Ew... Ew... Who wants pictures of Emerson Crandle? Alright, well after you're done photographing nothing, be at Dorée, 2 PM. Oh... and Martin, these photos are important. Be as aggressive as possible when you take them... No. No. This isn't a plan, just take lots of photos. It's for band promo."

Chloe ends the call, then looks at Stanley who raises his eyebrows at the misdirection he just witnessed.

"Oh please, of course he knows this is a plan, I just had to tell him it wasn't so he doesn't get nervous. Martin is aggressively average- he's not used to this," Chloe defends her actions.

Stanley shakes his head in agreement, "He doesn't have LA's finest acting coach so he can't be given a lead role."

"There can only be one Kane."

"And one Julie," Stanley says, then kisses Chloe.

"A brunch, there are going to be two Julies," Chloe corrects Stanley.

Since Chloe doesn't play an instrument, today she'll play a scumbag.

55- You Can't Keep Something a Secret if it Never Happened.

"So, Chloe, how've you been?" Tobe asks, totally ignorant as to what's about to happen, like he didn't look both ways when crossing an incredibly busy street.

Chloe purrs, "Things are amazing. I mean, life keeps surprising me."

London can't tolerate Chloe's sly smile, so she averts her eyes and looks out the signature floor-to-ceiling window that Chloe demanded they sit next to. Dorée's massive window shows everyone exactly what IMG, and CCA, and Harper LLC want the public to see. Chloe obviously chose this table for a reason, and if Tobe Price wasn't so self-absorbed, this seating arrangement would have set off alarms in his head. Instead, Tobe just looks at this highly visible lunch as a way to show Sienna just how many friends they have in common.

On cue, Martin appears at the window and begins snapping shot after shot in that skeevy invasion-of-privacy way that all paps exude.

"Hey, hey, hey," Chloe says, flagging the attention of a passing waiter who's focused on carrying a tray of bruschetta to the table behind them. The waiter carefully serves the tray, then arrives at Chloe's side.

"That guy's gotta go," Chloe says, pointing at Martin.

The waiter, a tall, pale, German-looking guy with a ponytail, clasps his hands together, then says, "Unfortunately we can't-"

"-chase him away like the pesky fat pigeon he is," Chloe demands, then she shoots a pointed glance directly at London to make sure she holds in her smile.

London finds the whole situation funny- the idea of an unsuspecting Martin being chased away. It reminds her of last July, when she got to visit a farm that breeds teacup piggies and the owners let her chase one around for a couple minutes.

The waiter looks at Martin, then back at Chloe, more precisely to her hand, to the $50 bill between her fingers. He takes the cash, then disappears, while everyone at the table stares into Martin's lens as though they're posing for perfect pictures.

The German looking waiter reappears on the other side of the glass and yells something aggressive. Martin lowers his camera so that it hangs from his neck strap, then he puts his hands up in a universal expression of passive cowardice.

Backing up, Martin disappears from view, as does the waiter who chases after him.

Stanley looks at London, London looks at Chloe, Chloe looks at Tobe, and Tobe looks at the waiter who reappears, forehead glistening. Once he catches his breath, the waiter advises the table, "That man will not be an issue for the duration of your meal. I can also have someone pull your cars around when you're finished, if you like."

"Thank you, you're good at what you do," Chloe says, and the compliment is almost worth as much to the waiter as the cash in his shirt pocket. All he hears all day long are complaints from rich assholes. It was nice to be recognized for his hard work for once.

"Okay," Chloe begins, leaning across the table, then with a sexy whisper, she explains, "Now that we have some privacy, I wanna tell you a little secret. Will you keep it?" Chloe's eyes move across the faces at the table, then her gaze settles on Tobe, who looks back at her with genuine interest. This isn't his usual dead eyed near-squint that makes Chloe feel like Tobe is either imagining fucking her or trying to figure out who exactly she is. This is real, legitimate engagement coming from Tobe.

Everyone shakes their head in agreement that the secret will stay just that.

"You have to promise. Verbally," Chloe issues a hushed demand.

"I promise," everyone drones out.

"Alright. Good. Well... the other day, Stanley and I ran into Larry Mendelheim- you know- that fat, super Jewish producer guy? He said that he has this movie that's going to start shooting in around two weeks, and he saw that we were hanging out with Sienna again, so he gave me a script in hopes that I would pass it on to the lovely Ms. Wolfe. I was going to give it to her, but on the ride home, Stanley read some of it and he said that it was-"

"-like nothing I've ever read. I mean, it left me breathless," Stanley says, pitch perfect. There was a little extra enthusiasm in Stanley's voice because, for once, he's running lines with someone who can actually pronounce the word "embodiment" correctly.

"Right, sooo, I got to thinking, and I'm going to tell Larry that Sienna isn't interested... then I'm going to take the role!" Chloe whispers in an excited hiss across the table.

Stanley looks at Tobe, and he could've sworn that Tobe was so surprised by this revelation that his hair moved.

"What? You can't just leave the band!" London says, outraged. Maybe she's the born actress out of the social!heavy girls? If she's caught on to the scheme, then she's the female De Niro. Well, a hotter, better smelling, less Italian De Niro. If she hasn't caught on, then she's as stupid as the blogs make her out to be.

Chloe casually provides some additional misinformation to sweeten the pot, "We aren't planning on putting an album out for a while, and they start filming in two weeks, which means I'll be done before we ever even work on the project."

Everyone at the table is silent for a moment.

"So," Chloe says with a devilish grin, "should I do it?"

"Know what? Do it. You always run lines with Stanley on his scripts, and he nails his roles. You're either a really good reader or an amazing actress," London votes.

"You should definitely do it," Tobe agrees, too aggressively.

Stanley rubs Chloe's back, focusing on her flawless plan and disregarding her untouched meal.

56- Label Us.

Another meeting. All four members of social!heavy stand in Joel's office. Sienna is there too. Joel sits at his desk, while the girls form a half circle across from him. "You're going to have to pick one," he says, and the girls look down at the desk covered in papers which are each emblemized with a logo. These logos represent the different labels that put in a bid to sign social! heavy. Joel had K.Kay print the logos in different sizes, each size corresponding to the amount of money the respective label was willing to offer. If there's one thing Joel has learned watching these girls and their sex tapes, it's that they view bigger as better.

"We have a demand to make," London says.

Joel exhales. He remembers his demands back in his tour days. Since these girls don't want raven haired virgins, the demand is probably going to be something that's even more difficult to acquire, like blonde virgins.

"We want complete creative control," Kristen says.

Joel takes away one of the bigger logos and also one of the medium sized logos. He wishes they just wanted blonde virgins.

"All these labels will give us that?" Chloe asks.

"Yup."

"You're sure?" Kristen asks skeptically.

"Sure," Joel says, relaxed. "It shouldn't be that much of an issue. All these companies are screwed because of the internet, and you five make up over sixty percent of the content on the internet so they're falling all over themselves to get to you."

"Sixty percent," Chloe repeats, a little disappointed, like she wanted to negotiate this figure.

"What are your other demands?" Joel asks. He can't help himself. Part of it was business. Part of it was the fact that he picks up a couple magazines a month just to read about these girls that he sees at least once a week in person.

"We have an album title, it's *the* album title," London says.

Joel arches his eyebrows and opens his hands, waiting. Kristen slams her heel down, angry about being left out of the decision. She can't remember discussing the album title, ever. Did the alcohol really wash away all those brain cells like the rehab people claimed?

"Fairy Pussy," London and Chloe say at the same time.

"You know about that?" Kristen asks, her hand flying up to her mouth.

"What?" London asks. An awkward moment hangs, then London explains, "Someone left 'Fairy Pussy' in a note on my windshield."

"Oh. Right," Kristen says burying the topic, happy to move away from it. The fact that they'd picked this title proves that the girls didn't know the "Fairy Pussy" note was a code that Kristen had with Mitchell Haughton.

Back when Kristen was off the rails, Mitchell would secretly pick her up, and they'd go on benders together. Exclusive orgies and not so exclusive (but still discreet) orgies were common. Kristen rationalized that it's not against the law to be bender buddies with someone. Okay, maybe the stuff Kristen did with Mitchell *was* against the law, and maybe it sort of broke a couple of his marriage vows, but Mitchell was one of the few people that never questioned what they were doing, and the old Kristen liked that. Since drugs and alcohol were in the equation each time, like that X in the girls' unopened high school math books, Mitchell and Kristen became intimate on numerous occasions. Mitchell would use the word, "pussy," during drunken, half flaccid threesomes with his PA and Kristen. Kristen hated it. Not the threesomes- she hated the word. When Mitchell pushed Kristen for a better option, she said that pussies should be referred to as something nicer and more magical. Thus "Fairy Pussy" was created, originally in jest. At this point, Mitchell had stopped using his phone because Lindy would go through it nightly, so to communicate, he'd leave notes for Kristen. Each time Mitchell found a new boy, he'd send Kristen the "Fairy Pussy" note. Even if someone found their secret message, they'd be temporarily confused, somewhat intrigued, and ultimately left out of a really good orgy.

"You can't have the word 'Pussy' in an album name," Joel says.

"There was a group called 'The Pussycat Dolls,'" Kristen mentions, now agreeing that "Fairy Pussy" needs to be the name of the album. Their music aims to be as pretty as a fairy, but as dirty as a pussy. The name is an allusion to the way the girls used to cut each other down behind each other's backs. It's a code, a very uncreative code, but that's okay. This opportunity is not about denying the past- it's about taking all the dirty things that were done in the past, then making them shine.

"The Pussycat Dolls situation is different," Joel flounders.

"Why?" Kristen asks.

Joel brings his fingers up to his temples, "Because they don't mean pussy like, you know. A pussy."

"They definitely do," London says.

"Well..."

"See, Joel," London taunts, pointing her perfectly manicured finger at him.

"You don't want to be associated with another female group though, you might as well name the album Spicy Pussy if you're going to do that," Joel tells them.

"Ew, Joel," London says, making a disgusted face.

New rule- all meetings have to include Martin. Martin is the voice of reason and the girls listen to him because he's also the voice on that tape.

Sighing, Joel picks out the biggest logo, "These guys will give into your demands. However... if I give you Fairy Pussy, then you're going to have to let me pick the cover of the album."

"What do you want on the cover?" Chloe asks, suspicious that Joel might have been working for this angle the entire time.

As a platinum artist, Joel knows that what will sell this album is pretty close to the album title. He explains, "I want the cover to be a picture of you girls, no drawings of fairies all spread eagle or any of that shit."

The girls look at each other, then London agrees, "Okay, if we can have Fairy Pussy, you get final approval on the cover."

"You girls give me a headache."

"Sorry we're so much trouble," Dakota says in a London-like voice.

"No, I mean your five different perfumes are mixing into one toxic cloud and it's burning my brain," Joel says, his eyes bloodshot.

No less than two of the girls freeze after hearing this, wondering if their brains were being burnt as well.

Maybe their scars are so deep, they can't even feel the damage anymore?

57- Places Everyone.

"That literally took two hours. No decisions related to New Wave music could possibly take that much deliberation," Stanley says, after a "quick stop at Joel's office" had unexpectedly turned into a test of boyfriend commitment.

Chloe gets into the front passenger seat of the car and immediately checks her eyes to make sure they aren't red from that perfume cloud Joel was bitching about.

Finally with someone to talk to, Stanley bursts with information, "I was stranded in this damn electric car, and I'm not sure how this thing works. I had no idea if the radio burns fuel because the fuel is electricity so I literally just sat here on my phone because I didn't want to have to rub a balloon on the side of the car to get us down the freeway. From what I read, those blogs are getting worse... but I have to admit that, for a bunch of strangers who've never even had dinner with Sienna Wolfe, I'm surprised with how well they know her."

Chloe lets the rant happen while she rolls down her window, getting comfortable, relaxing after a long day of acting. Bored with playing pretend, she tells the simple truth, "It took a while in there because we were picking labels. Joel wanted us to sign with this one label who offered him a boatload of cash. I could tell. He printed out all the logos in various sizes and it was way too purposeful. One label's logo actually had a cat photoshopped next to it."

Stanley laughs as he pulls away from Harper LLC HQ without a photog in sight. It seems almost eerie.

"Do you like who you signed with?" Stanley asks.

"Sure, I mean, we'll sell ourselves."

Stanley raises an eyebrow.

"Not like that, pervert!" Chloe eeks, slapping Stanley's arm as he shifts up a gear. "I just meant that there will be such a big demand for our album, it really won't matter who puts it out."

Stanley merges, unafraid, onto the freeway in Los Angeles. He goes from being parked near Joel's office, to being parked in traffic. Looking to his left, Stanley sees a middle aged woman staring back at him. Once he makes eye contact with the woman, he rolls up the tinted window quickly, leaving her wondering if she just caught a momentary glimpse of Tristan or if the traffic is driving her insane.

Chloe decides that she'll focus on her own game while they wait for the traffic to move. Quickly selecting a contact that only existed in her phone due to a polite gesture at a party, Chloe puts the call on speaker. A bored sounding secretary answers the call with a flat, "Mendelheim Company," and Chloe's voice pitches up an octave when she says, "Hi, could I speak with Mr. Mendelheim?"

"Who's calling, please?" the secretary asks.

"Chloe Warren."

"Oh," the secretary gasps. Mendelheim must have really wanted Chloe for this role if even the secretary knew the significance of her calling. "Ms. Warren, he's in a meeting, but I'm sure that he'll want to speak with you. One moment please."

Chloe waits as the mellow guitar hold music plays on speaker phone. The hold music begins to feel like a victory tune that was composed to celebrate Chloe's greatness, like when a general comes home from battle and they play bagpipes- or something to that effect. The longer she waits on hold, the more Chloe realizes that the bagpipe spectacle she's imagining might be something that happens during a funeral procession.

Now Chloe is nervous.

"Ms. Warren! Did you look at that script I sent over?" Larry Mendelheim's hyper-nasal voice screeches from the phone so loudly that Chloe turns the speakerphone off.

"I did," Chloe responds.

"What did you think?"

"It's... it's shit, Mr. Mendelheim," Chloe says, throwing all her cards on the table.

"Of course it is, Chloe," Mendelheim responds.

"And-I-can't-do-it-but-" Chloe says in one breath so she can quickly arrive at her second statement, "-what do you think about Sienna Wolfe for my role?"

"That's-a-shame-you-don't-want-to-do-it-but-" Mendelheim says, out of common courtesy, quick enough so he doesn't squander the chance to cast a super socialite in his movie, "-you think you can get Sienna Wolfe to do this film?"

"I know I can. This band thing isn't her gig, her real passion is film. Know what? I'll help you out here, expect a call from Sienna's agent later this week."

"Later this week, but-"

"-Mr. Mendelheim, you have my word. If she doesn't take the role, I will."

Chloe had to up the stakes. A socialite always has options, except for when it comes to contract negotiation. Now she *has* to make this plan a reality.

58- Divide-Ends.

London puts her head back on the pillow and announces, "We named our album..."

Tobe doesn't respond. He kisses London's ear.

"...it's called Fairy Pussy..."

Tobe kisses London's cheek, then asks, "Why does that sound familiar?"

"...which is rock and roll, but also a little camp," London continues.

Tobe kisses London's neck, then mumbles, "For some reason your album name is making me *very* horny."

"...and I taught myself how to program my drum machine..."

Tobe slides London's bra cup out of the way and kisses her left breast.

"...I actually bought these DVDs that I watch while..."

Tobe kisses London's stomach.

"...I practice and that's why I asked you to set up the TV in my workroom..."

Tobe kisses London's inner thigh.

"...and it's okay you didn't do it. Alonja figured it out..."

Tobe wants to thank London, but if he does, she'll become a person; a real, living person that would demand some sort of basic emotional recognition.

All he has to do is release the poison, then he can drift off to sleep next to London. She can stay the night- as nothing more than a warm, breathing, body pillow. London has given Tobe a way to speak with his dream-girl, so he's able to forgive her for the gray hairs that have sprouted since he met this praying mantis of a cancer.

London tells herself that everything will be okay. Tobe will pass Chloe's test. Even if he doesn't pass the test, is it really *that* bad? Maybe the test is like the SATs and it's just a dumb reality that attractive people don't have to face because all they have to do is go to the job interview and people are like, "Stand in my business and I'll give you this box filled with money."

This is a test that can't be put off, so there's no choice but to find out the truth. Better now than two years, five years, ten years from now. London remembers what happened at Lindy's divorce party and she doesn't want that stress on her name.

Letting everything melt away, London lays there and lets Tobe do all the work. It doesn't feel right. When Rock Hudson licks London's face, she feels the love; when Tobe licks her, it's like he's trying to finish a lollipop.

59- What's My Motivation?

During the traffic jam, Stanley started feeling guilty about having Martin chased away like the obedient pap was a beach bird who was annoying fat tourists. Stanley's experiences with Martin have been universally positive, however one night stands out among all of their shared interactions. On this particular night, maybe being careless, maybe wanting to get caught, Stanley was snapped in a trio of frames that would be worth a significant amount of money. He's sure the pictures were taken, but Stanley has never seen those three snapshots. No one has. This doesn't fit in with Stanley's understanding of the world he lives in. The pictures were of America's boy next door with a literal girl next door, Lindy Porter. Stanley wasn't lying to Chloe- he does have a history with Lindy. Stanley and Lindy tried for a normal relationship so their courtship remained a secret- that's how Stanley rationalized it. The real reason why Stanley hid this girlfriend was because Lindy was underage. Martin had snapped pictures of Stanley and Lindy together, kissing. A photo that would be worth a substantial amount of money never surfaced. This does not happen in LA, yet it did.

Arriving at home, still seeped in guilt, Stanley asks Chloe to invite Martin over for a nightcap, in order to make up for earlier.

After a quick call, everything comes together, and Chloe is so pleased that it was Stanley's idea, not something she had to force him to agree to.

An hour and a half later, Martin arrives wearing his standard issue uniform- camera bag, dad jeans, a black t-shirt, and a toothy grin. This is the first time he's ever been invited into Chloe's house. He appreciates the moment greatly. Martin understands that paparazzi are never invited into mansions. Music producers, however, have an open invitation to drop by whenever. This is why Martin made the trip, it was proof of the transformative possibilities of social!heavy.

Stanley meets Martin at the door, then leads him through the house, out onto the balcony- Stanley's favorite place in the world.

Martin takes in the view, his awe on display, then the fatigue from running away from the waiter gets the better of him, and he plops down in a chair. After slinging the strap of his camera bag across the back of the chair, he looks to his hosts, unsure if a single event caused this moment to happen.

"Do you drink scotch, Martin?" Stanley asks.

"Actually, I don't. Do you have any coffee?"

"I'll go put a fresh pot on," Stanley says. Chloe half believes this means he's going to drive to Starbucks, then sit there on his laptop, while Chloe has an awkward conversation with Martin.

Chloe pulls a chair over next to the off-duty music producer. She studies his fat face as he looks out at the bright lights of the big city. He seems to have a different type of appreciation for the view. It's not just pretty to him, it's a shining melting pot of his art.

"Look at that," Martin says, almost to himself, "thousands of pictures that aren't being taken, but should be."

"You can't capture everything," Chloe says, painfully aware of this after watching her best friend's constant losses.

"You can try."

"But then you'll never end up in the pictures," Chloe responds.

"Not true. I'm in every picture I take."

Stanley returns to the porch as the coffee brews.

"Not bad, huh?" Stanley points out to the city.

"If I had known I could get this view by annoying you guys at dinner, I would have taken up residence outside of Dorée a long time ago."

Chloe giggles, "The look on your face when the waiter came out."

"They never do that! We have an agreement! They don't chase me away!"

"When you tip them $50 they do," Chloe says, then smiles innocently.

"You! What! Where's my $50?" Martin asks.

"You get to use those pictures, they should be worth something. You can even say you saw the money exchanged."

"What a job!" Martin says, then his eyes fix on the railing of the balcony.

"Do you like what you do?" Stanley asks Martin.

"I don't like prying into your lives-"

"-no," Stanley rethinks his question, "I didn't mean it like that, I just wanted the honest answer."

"Why did you want the honest answer?" Martin asks.

Stanley furrows his eyebrows and it makes his forehead look even bigger.

"I do like it," Martin says, giving Stanley a chance, then bailing him out.

"Why?" Chloe asks.

"Can't say."

"Because you don't know?" Stanley asks, his brow relaxed.

"No. I know."

The actor who craves his old status and new roles shakes his head, understanding, yet not. He likes Martin. It was nice to have a guy around the house to talk to, even if the guy worked a day job for the enemy. Martin is the type of enemy you could sit down for coffee with. Stanley likes to sit. He likes to have coffee. This is what he needs.

Everyone has become a slave to a screen. Chloe has her phone, Martin has his camera, Stanley has his laptop. Tonight, those items have been set aside, and this imperfect trio simply has each other.

As the actor goes back inside to grab a coffee for the paparazzi, Martin takes his camera bag off the back of the chair. Chloe watches as he unzips the bag, then removes, not a camera, but instead two circular pieces of Tupperware. After grabbing a pair of plastic forks out of the side of the bag, he opens one of the containers, stakes a fork in the contents- a piece of cheesecake- then hands it to Chloe. He carries out all of these pre-planned actions without a word. Chloe reluctantly holds onto the plastic dish gifted from her guest.

Martin opens the second container. He forks the cheesecake, then takes a bite. He waits for Chloe to do the same, and when she doesn't, Martin quietly tells her, "My Mom used to make cheesecake. The best cheesecake. It was my favorite thing in the world, and that's what she'd make for me on my birthday instead of a regular cake."

Chloe's hand moves to her fork as Martin continues, "After she passed, little stuff turned big. It's weird which memories start to balloon when that distance of death arrives. With her gone, I'd never eat cheesecake because, when I did, it never tasted as good as hers. I started to hate my birthday, all because of this one sensory memory."

Chloe looks down at the perfect triangle that seems to hold a diverse significance.

Martin continues, "One day, I get a call from my sister, Mary, and she tells me that she found this bakery that *must* have Mom's recipe. I was skeptical, but when you're given a chance to reach out and grab a memory that is purely good, you take it. So I made a trip out to the bakery that weekend and I tried a slice. It tasted absolutely identical to my mother's cheesecake. That bakery was on the way to your house, so I picked us up two slices. I hope that you'll try it. You won't regret it."

Chloe looks at Martin, then she breaks off a piece of the cheesecake with her fork, ready to accept the challenge, and reward herself for her scheming. She understands what it's like to hold on aggressively to the memories of moments spent between child and mother. When half of this privileged union is compromised, the memories become as much a responsibility as they are a blanket. There's a need to share these memories with others, to keep them fresh, to keep them alive, to remember why they're so important. Each story told feels like inviting Mom to sit at the table, one more time.

Stanley freezes in the doorway when he sees his girlfriend bringing the cheesecake up to her mouth. Chloe takes the bite, savoring the moment.

"I wasn't lying, was I?" Martin asks.

He wasn't. Martin was the one person in the Hills not lying.

Chloe and Stanley feel honored to have such an important guest tonight.

60- I Organized an Apology Dinner So I Can Forgive You.

Sienna smiles fondly at the girls as though they had just named her homecoming queen.

Dakota, Chloe, Kristen, and London each frantically shake a Nintendo controller in a different direction.

On the TV next to Sienna, Dakota's character is jumping on Chloe's character's head. Chloe's character falls over, gets back up, then meets the same fate. Kristen's character is running from one side of the screen to the other. London's character is slowly walking in tight circles, far away from the commotion, except for when Kristen stops by momentarily.

"Thank you all for coming," Sienna says, her hands clasped together. Sienna's eyes drift to the TV screen for a moment since no one is looking at her. "The fact that you arrived this morning, on your own terms, without force, makes this day even more special."

Sienna's pageant smile fades as the girls seem to be getting more and more into the game, and less and less aware that Sienna exists.

"Hey! Retards. What the fuck are you doing?" Sienna barks, standing in front of the TV.

Dakota yells, "Sienna! I was just about to-"

"-what, jump on Chloe's head and make her fall down?"

Chloe smiles at Sienna for sticking up for her.

"Yeah," Dakota says timidly, "I was winning."

"The point of the game is to collect all those coins on the screen, you had no coins," Sienna says, gesturing angrily at the screen behind her.

"Ohhh," the girls say in unison, suddenly understanding the objective of the game they were enthralled with for the last half hour.

"I was avoiding the coins!" Kristen admits with a laugh.

"I know, I thought they were trolls!" London adds.

"When I touched the coins, it looked like my character got a disease," Chloe notes sadly.

Sienna's face contorts, like she was trying to get a toddler to paint the Mona Lisa, but all she's being handed are paintings of multicolored, disproportionate, nightmarish dogs.

"Enough games," Sienna says turning the TV off, then she immediately clarifies, "Enough video games, I meant. I'm still going to participate in sadistic mind games and vaguely blackmailish tactics. Which brings me to my heartfelt moment. I just wanted to say I'm sorry about kidnapping you before."

"It's fine," all the girls say, unwilling to have a heart-to-heart about this. They know that Sienna is just lonely because she doesn't have anyone else in her life.

"And I've been thinking about some ideas," Sienna says, backing away from the TV, then sitting on a crimson therapist-style lounge next to the sofa.

"About anything in particular?" Kristen asks.

"Yes," Sienna answers, her mouth hanging open for an awkward moment, "I've been thinking about social!heavy."

"Me too!" Kristen says, as though this has gone from a video game competition where the rules are vague, to socialite a competition where the rules are tattooed on each girls' brain. "I think we should get stickers with our band's name on them! Like the ones you see all over The Pit," Kristen suggests with excitement.

Sienna immediately waives this off, "No, we don't need stickers."

"Did you already order them?" Kristen asks, worried she was upstaged with her suggestion.

"No. We don't want stickers! People stick them near potties," Sienna says with disgust.

"I know! Like at The Pit!" Kristen responds with an enthusiasm that she hopes will be AIDS contagious.

"I like it," Chloe says supportively.

"Do you really want someone staring right at your band name while they're pissing out of their butt from all the laxatives they're taking to stay skinny?" Sienna asks, eying Chloe.

This certainly was a point to consider.

Sienna sees that she's painted a picture that most of the girls aren't comfortable with. This means she's winning, so she continues, "We might as well release social!heavy toilet paper."

"Would they be able to make that?" London asks.

"Of course they could," Sienna huffs, staring down the manicure on her raised right hand. She hates her stupid hands and this increases her frustration, "We're us. They'll do anything for us. But you aren't seeing my point, there will never be social!heavy toilet paper."

"But," Kristen says, fiddling with the Nintendo controller, "it just seems like, you know, you were talking about the butt pee or whatever, so a roll of TP might be a life saver for the person in that stall, then we'd get a lifelong fan. It would be super soft 6 ply social!heavy-flow butt pi-"

"-no!" Sienna barks, shooting down a possibly genius idea. She tries to get them on track, "We need to be as far away from assholes as we can be."

All four girls on the sofa arch their bodies away from Sienna.

"Not assholes like me. I meant the shitting type, you assholes."

"What do you suggest, then?" Kristen asks.

"Condoms," Sienna says with a faux confidence she's perfected.

"You don't use condoms," London points out, referencing Sienna's sex tape and her previous gripes about condoms being, "The most unfun thing since Kristen Paxton."

"Right," Sienna confirms, "But other people do... like gays and poor people who can't afford birth control pills."

"I thought you wanted to avoid assholes," Kristen says, finding the hypocrisy in what Sienna thought was a can't-lose proposition, "Won't condoms be just as close to assholes as the toilet paper?"

"Fine," Sienna says, giving up because she has nowhere to go, "But the stickers will be pink."

"Obviously," the girls respond.

61- If It's Not a Kidnapping, Then It's an Ambush.

"It's delicious, isn't it, Chloe?" Sienna asks.

"Top notch," Chloe says, cutting her meal into fine pieces.

"Doesn't look like you've eaten very much," Sienna says, then points her knife at Chloe's full plate.

"Not everyone has as big of an appetite as you, Sienna," Kristen hops in to play defense.

"Or they do, and that's the problem," Sienna spits back.

"What were you doing with Mitchell Haughton?" Kristen asks, referencing a blog post she'd been sent.

"Six months ago I should have asked you the same question!" Sienna says. Her guests are immediately quiet. No one wants to know what Sienna was doing with Mitchell, nor do they want to know why Sienna responded like that to Kristen. The sounds of knives and forks on plates provide an ugly soundtrack in Sienna's massive dining room. The girls eat the dinner Sienna's chef had been working all day on. They don't speak. Their words can and will be used against them on some blog written by an angry gay guy.

A much needed reprieve, in the form of a clanging doorbell, prompts Sienna to get up and prance out of the room.

The girls look at each other, horrified by the fact that Sienna is answering her front door. They know that the day is going to take a bitter turn for the worse if Sienna is performing tasks that are in her maid's job description.

Popping back into the dining room, Sienna says, "Everyone, I'd like to introduce... Tyler Peterson."

A kid, no more than 20 years old, stands before them with a camera in his hands. His spiky black hair makes him look like he should be hanging out in a Taco Bell.

"He's going to take pictures of us," Sienna says cheerfully, then holds her smile as she watches London's face mutate into a grimace.

"No, he isn't," London says, then she goes back to eating her roast beef.

"Yes. He is," Sienna says with an edge in her voice.

"Oh," Tyler gulps, realizing that he stepped into the Wolfe's den. "I, can, er-" he stammers out, turning around. Sienna grabs him by the shoulders and prevents his escape. "You can take our fucking picture," she hisses.

Another kidnap for Sienna Wolfe.

"I'm calling Joel," Dakota announces, taking charge. Chloe is the lead singer, but she's too physically weak to rally the troops. Kristen is the musically inclined member of the group, but she's more comfortable behind the keyboard than at the podium. Sienna has no interest in the music, and it seems, no interest in proving to America she's more than just a hot coke whore. She just wants power. She wants to be ahead of everyone else. Dakota used to be "Bonnie and Bonnie" with Sienna because they could spend the entire night together, and they'd have a better time making fun of the people dancing than Kristen had getting totally drunk. Dakota never has a good time with Sienna now- their friendship has fizzled.

Dakota calls Joel's office phone- no answer. She tries Joel's cell and after two rings, he picks up and accepts the verbal attack. "Call Sienna and tell her to stop. Tell her to behave," Dakota demands.

"Oh no," Joel says, exasperated, "Did she ruin the shoot?"

"Yeah. She did. She brought some kid in here to take pictures of us instead."

"Fuck. Okay, I'll call Tyler and have him-"

"-wait. Tyler. Tyler Peterson? You knew about this? Is he some lovechild that one of your whore fans shat out in the 90's?"

"No. None of my love children are talented like Tyler," Joel responds regretfully.

"Okay, but why is Tyler not-your-talentless-bastard-child here?" Dakota asks.

"He's a good guy, the label works with him."

"The label? Ugh. You're a douchebag, Joel."

"Dakot-"

"-douchebag, Joel. You. Are. A. Douchebag," Dakota says, then ends the call.

"Well! Now that that's settled..." Sienna says, clasping her hands together, "Where do you want to start, Tyler?"

"I. Uh. Could. I, uh. Have a glass of water?" Tyler asks, as he white knuckle grips his camera.

"Rodriga!" Sienna screams, "Aquaaaaa!"

"I think it's 'agua' in Spanish," Dakota says bitchily at Sienna.

Sienna turns to her ex-best friend and says, "Oh. Alright. Do me a favor and please stop telling me things I don't give a shit about, por favor."

62- Sometimes a Picture Isn't Worth 1,000 Words.

Inside Dakota's Benz, London calls Martin and puts him on speaker so all of the girls can complain.

"Hello?" Martin answers meekly.

"Hiii," Kristen and Chloe caw from the back seat.

"We had to call you," Dakota says.

"Oh no. Why are all of you on the phone at once? This can't be good news," Martin huffs, already sounding stressed.

"You'reee correcttt!" Dakota says in that too loud voice she always puts on when she uses the speakerphone feature. This expression of overblown emotion is why Dakota isn't allowed to attend her friends' wakes when they OD.

"Oh great," Martin says.

"It's not super horrible, just shitty horrible," Dakota tells him. The girls look at Dakota, then Chloe moves her head closer, "Sienna and the label brought in a photographer to shoot us at her house."

There's a momentary silence, then Martin audibly hoists himself out of a relaxed position and asks, "Does he need my lenses? Okay. Fine. No, it's okay, I'll be up."

"Um," Kristen mumbles, "No, Martin. There's another photographer that wants to take our picture. He has all the lenses and everything."

"Oh. Very good," Martin says agreeably, then another silence screams out in the car.

"Will you be mad if we do it?" Kristen asks.

Martin laughs his cackle of a laugh, then says, "For fuck's sake girls, you're famous. Do you know how many pictures are taken of you on any given day?"

The girls think about it.

"Not enough," Dakota decides, then adds, "This one's different though, we asked this guy to take the pictures."

"Well, not us," London clarifies, "Sienna."

"What's his name?" Martin asks.

"Tyler Peterson," Chloe says.

"I've seen his work. He's a good young photographer," Martin assures them. "The pictures will come out great."

The girls sit in the car and no one really knows what to say. They expected that this whole disaster would require an apology and at least a promise that the other photographer meant nothing to them. They'd have to say cute things like, "It'll be impossible to smile for a camera without you behind it, Martin."

Instead, Martin handled the situation gracefully. He handled it in a rational, sensible way. The girls say goodbye to Martin and they feel disappointed.

The shoot goes fine. It's 80's themed. The band wears clothes that Sienna had in her closet- everything looks modern with a tinge of futuristic minimalism. It's fun, it's cool, it's only vaguely British, it's not Martin, so it's work.

It was all "To the right." / "Just go crazy."/ "There you go." / "Love that." / "Hold that." / "Right there."/ "One more."

It was sex talk without the tingle.

The pictures come out pretty.

Of course they do.

63- I Scream, You Scream. This Neighborhood is Low Income.

Kristen and Chloe drive aimlessly to lose the paps they had acquired as they left Sienna's house.

It'll be dark in an hour, and the girls wonder if they might be able to book a late night quickie at the studio. They know there's only one person who can put this practice together. The band needs Martin to function, it's a fact.

"Do you think Martin's mad?" Kristen asks, her attention shifting between the road and the instrumental soundtrack of their drive.

Chloe rests her head on the passenger side window, and responds, "No. He told us he wasn't... right?"

"Right, but what happens when *you* say you're not mad?"

"I'm usually mad," Chloe responds, suddenly agreeing with Kristen.

As the vocal-less CD from the folder plays over the stereo, the girls become consumed by Martin's absence.

"We should visit him," Kristen suggests, worried about an imagined betrayal.

"Okay. Do you know where he lives?"

"Yeah, hold on, I have his card," Kristen says, turning toward the back seat.

Chloe leans over and grabs the wheel, steadying their path so they don't drive through a sidewalk sale. "He puts his real address on his card?" she asks, not alerting Kristen to the red light they blow through.

"Um, yeah, Chlo. He's just a normal little fat guy to everyone else, so it's not going to be chaos if people know where he lives. It'll just be easier to narrow down the places to look if a kid goes missing."

"Kristen!" Chloe scolds.

"Fine. If a wedding cake goes missing," she corrects her slander.

Kristen pulls her purse onto her lap, then turns the car away from the worried looking oncoming traffic. She reaches inside her bag and looks for the card. When she finds it, she hands it to Chloe, who copies the address into her phone's GPS. This card is different than the one Martin gave London. The XV3 card only had a phone number, this card has all of Martin's information. Chloe avoids the Batemanesque impulse to start asking questions about the card.

Less than 20 minutes later, the Benz pulls into the parking lot of what looks like a two floor Best Western.

Kristen reaches into her purse for her phone. She quickly picks Martin out of her contacts, then waits until he answers. "Hi, Martin? Yeah, it's Kristen. We're outside your apartment... Yeah, your apartment... Oh, don't worry, we won't come up. We don't want to get Hep-C. Do you want to go somewhere around here and... Ice cream? Okay, perfect."

"Ice cream?" Chloe asks, now unwilling to go along with this plan. "Hasn't Joel given Martin marching orders to remain anonymous, otherwise we have to deal with the whole pap and celeb taboo that Brit-Brit started?"

"He said he knows a secret ice cream place."

"He would," Chloe responds, angry that Kristen agreed to a fat person plan like "getting ice cream." Martin convinced her to eat that cheesecake, but she won't eat this ice cream. Especially not at a secret place. If Chloe's going to eat food, she'll make damn sure that she's photographed doing it.

Martin makes his way carefully down the stairs, then speed walks toward the car. He's wearing a white t-shirt and a pair of jeans that are just tight enough to make his torso look like a double decker hard serve ice cream cone.

As soon as Martin gets in the back of the car, he says, "Driver, take me to the Beverly Hills Hotel."

Neither of the girls laugh, but both welcome him with a, "Hiii Martinnn."

"Hi girls," Martin says, "Did you girls behave yourselves at the shoot today?"

"Yes, Martin," they both say, together.

"You kept your undies on right?"

"Of course!" both girls caw, taking mock offense.

"Good girls."

"So. Where are we going?" Kristen asks, looking at Martin in the rear view mirror.

Martin leans into the front seat and grabs Chloe's phone out of her hand. He punches the address into the GPS on the phone, then hands it back up toward the girls. Kristen looks down at the still lit screen and merely says, "No."

"What!" Martin complains, "You wanted to hang out, this is where no one will take our picture."

"The police will, and I don't look good in chalk outline," Kristen says.

"Oh, live a little, Kristen."

Never one to resist peer pressure, Kristen takes temporary ownership of Chloe's phone and begins the driving.

"Use that hoodie in the back seat," Kristen demands.

Martin looks to his left and finds a pink hoodie. He reluctantly picks it up, then shrugs and puts his arm through the left sleeve.

Kristen spots a jutting pink arm in the mirror, then says, "No, on your head, you ass."

"Oh. Right," Martin responds, draping the hoodie over his businessman haircut.

Chloe doesn't protest their dangerous destination because it gives her an excuse to stay in the car with the defense of not wanting to become a casualty of inner city gun violence.

The girls sink low in their seats as the houses start getting closer and closer together. The windows of the houses start growing bars. Kristen has to slow the vehicle every 25 feet so someone can cross the street in an inappropriate place. Instead of people trying to see who's driving the luxury automobile, it's almost as though they don't even acknowledge the car is on the road.

The phone announces that they've reached their destination as they drive over a gutter filled with trash, and Chloe makes an announcement of her own, "I'm going to stay in the car."

"You're missing out," Martin says, then he pops the door open and spills out like an excited child. Before shutting the door, he asks, "Kristen, you aren't afraid of an ice cream stand too, are you?"

Kristen surveys the area, then opens her door.

"Gimme the keys, if I hear gunshots, I'm driving away without either of you idiots," Chloe warns.

Kristen tosses her an excessively accessorized key chain to Chloe, then shuts the door. Chloe immediately activates the power locks, then crouches down in her seat.

Kristen feels confident that she's made the right choice by getting ice cream with Martin. She's been in neighborhoods like this before, and she was looking for a lot worse stuff than ice cream.

Martin notices that Kristen has shed the makeup from the shoot. Maybe she doesn't have any makeup on at all? She looks beautiful, healthy, and well rested- almost as though her lifestyle change is being reflected in her appearance.

Martin isn't jealous that another photographer worked with the girls today, but he *is* jealous that the photographer had such beautiful subjects. He wasn't at the shoot, but he could be sure Bright Feathers was.

The band, and Martin, seemed to have arrived at a crucial unity, and because of this progression, tomorrow will be social!heavy's first formal practice. Martin has caught bits and pieces of each girl's talent and they seem ready. The girls will arrive together, play together, and become social!heavy, together.

Kristen double-times it across the lot in her heels, Martin at her side. They head toward a thin, heavily graffitied ice cream stand that looks like one of the bathroom stalls at The Pit, except this graffiti wasn't done by an artist with a trust fund.

"Great, now there'll be two members of social!heavy gone by the end of this week," Kristen says, looking around.

"What do you mean *two*?" Martin asks, his pace slowing.

"Oh... just that someone here will probably murder me."

Martin nods at this, "Right, of course, but who's the other member?"

Kristen brings her arm up and rubs her neck, "I was just counting myself as two people. Because of my importance and all."

"Bullshit," Martin says, keeping up with Kristen, "Who's the other girl that will be out of the group?"

"Use your head, Martin."

"Alright, my head says it's Sienna."

"That's a bingo. We're taking care of the Sienna problem, don't worry about it."

"Oh no. You aren't going to kill her, are you?"

"What? No. Do you really think we're a bunch of hot Charlie's Angels assassins?" Kristen asks. If Martin confirms this is really what he thinks, Kristen won't hold it against him.

"No, I figured you'd pay someone else to do the killing. I guess I just look at you girls as young adults who are rich enough to write a check for just about anything."

"Accurate. We are, but that doesn't mean we'd do it though."

"So, how are you getting rid of her?" Martin asks, his concern mixing with intrigue.

"By making her an offer she can't refuse."

"Kristen, that's a line from *The Godfather*!"

"I never claimed I made it up," Kristen responds.

Martin nods, "Okay, but the point of the line is that either the person accepts the deal... or they're dead."

Kristen puts her nose in the air- an expression she had learned from London, and she says, "Guess Sienna better accept the deal then."

Realizing that they now need to order, Martin asks for two cones of lemon drop. The black guy in his early 20's working the stand looks at Kristen cockeyed. It wasn't the typical look that a guy like him usually gives Kristen. It was a curious look. "Don't I know you?" he asks, before he considers fulfilling the order.

"I'm in a toothpaste commercial," Kristen brags, smiling at the man with her believably toothpaste-commercial-white teeth.

"Yeah! Yeah you are! Your teeth look good as hell," the guy says with the appropriate amount of excitement for meeting a pretty commercial girl.

As soon as the ice cream man goes to work making the cones, Martin asks, "Toothpaste girl?"

"It's a safe bet," Kristen says, then lowers her voice, "I've noticed that if you can't watch someone prepare your food, never tell them you're a socialite because you don't want any secret ingredients added to your order."

"So you choose to be the toothpaste girl?"

"Remember that chick that did the commercials who said, 'Yum! Like a tidal wave in my mouth'? Well, she vaguely looks like me so I chose her to be my Clark Kent."

Martin finds it amusing that even Kristen's mild mannered alter ego is someone that appears on TV at least four times a day.

"Hey, lady!" a voice from behind Martin and Kristen yells. They both turn away from the stand and face a little kid on a BMX bike. He's wearing shiny gym shorts and a wife beater.

"You fine as hell. You know who you look like?" the kid says with a snarl.

"The girl from that toothpaste commercial?" Martin asks, then finishes it off with that damn smile.

"You look like that Kristen Paxton lady that goes to all them nice parties and shit."

"Oh, that's very nice of you," Kristen says, moving closer to Martin.

"I know you ain't her though," the kid says, his demeanor not brightening, "cuz' I seen you was drivin' your own car. Ain't no way someone rich like Kristen Paxton drives her own car."

Kristen smirks, then asks the boy, "Oh yeah? Then how do you think she got all those DWIs?"

64- Fantragic.

Tobe ignores another call from London.

He has to keep his phone fully charged for the trip.

No, this isn't trip. It's an adventure.

This is storming the castle to save the princess.

Tobe will carry out this heroic act the same way every action hero rescues the girl- with a screenplay.

Going through his closet, Tobe finds a Tom Ford suit he's been saving for a special occasion. He puts the suit on the bed, but before he can even reach for a tie, he decides, no, no suit. As he's carefully putting everything back on the hanger, Tobe gets an idea. The $21 white American Apparel V-neck t-shirt. The $500 black Rick Owens jeans. The $1,500 Band of Outsiders leather jacket. It's classic and more importantly it doesn't make him look like an FBI agent who wants to question Sienna about her ties to Diego Mestizo. It makes him look like Tobe Price, a guy who Sienna Wolfe should be pressed up against a million times over.

Tobe has researched, worked out, and waxed in preparation for this moment. He was patient- he didn't rush it- but the entire time he was waiting, his nerves were getting worse, his obsession more extreme. Although the introduction tonight might be a little rough to get through, Tobe possesses a bombshell secret and that's better than bringing Sienna flowers and a poem.

Once he puts himself together and takes some selfies with a digital camera to make sure he looks as good as he thinks he looks, Tobe rides the elevator down to the parking garage, then pulls out the Audi R8 V10 plus for a nighttime race.

Tobe's blood cannons through his veins as he blurs fast to his destination. He needs to evenly distribute the blood so it doesn't congregate in his groin when Sienna answers the door. The night passes, reflected across the sides of his house-priced automobile, and he shifts into a higher gear, the R8 growling. Tobe is driving tonight, not because he couldn't get a driver, but because if things go as planned, he'll have a couple of glasses of wine with Sienna, then he'll pull the classic, "Oh, I'm too drunk to drive, and you know how young Hollywood is a target now. They're hunting us down for DWIs."

There's no way Sienna could effectively argue this point. She certainly didn't in that *Vogue* interview when she said, "I'm one of the biggest police targets- right after the NBA players, rappers, and other fringe elements."

The R8 continues to slice the corners of the winding road until the GPS has Tobe make a sharp turn onto Sienna's street. The elevation and the proximity to Sienna become too much and Tobe pulls to the side of the road when he spots a familiar mansion. That two page spread he tore out of a

Home and Garden Magazine in his doctor's waiting room proved to be invaluable. All he had to do was scan the magazine clipping, reverse google image search the house and, like that, he had an address. He sits, idling, wondering if he should do this- if he *can* do this. Deciding that tonight's the night, he puts his phone in his jacket pocket and he's about to turn the car off, when he sees the perfect setup. Down the street is a fire hydrant. Tobe immediately drives to the hydrant and parks in front of it. On the unlikely chance that he can't get Sienna to drink, all he'll have to do is distract her until his car is towed. There's a chance that Tobe might have to excuse himself to go to the bathroom, then quickly sneak out and Molotov cocktail the house adjacent to the fire hydrant, but one way or another, he *will* stay the night at Sienna's. The R8 is collateral in a high stakes bet. Tobe can afford to lose it for Sienna. He has many cars, there's only one Wolfe. Well, technically there are two, but Sienna's sister lives in one of those countries that survives off fundraisers, and Tobe won't give up his penthouse for an endangered Wolfe.

Tobe slides a stick of green gum into his mouth, then gets out of the car and looks up at Sienna's neighbor's house to see if there's an open window that he can lob a flaming bottle of gasoline through. A large furnished balcony juts out on the second floor of the house, and Tobe figures that he'll just have to make do with what he's been given. You know the old saying, everything burns.

Tobe crosses the street, then stops for a moment and ties his new Gucci patent leather oxfords. He inhales the brisk air and it feels like this is the one place in LA that isn't suffocating. It's like all the pure air from London's forest surroundings is emanating out of the Wolfe residence.

Walking to the gate of the castle Sienna is trapped in, Tobe pauses.

No. It can't be. That voice...

Was he being haunted? This is worse than any heartbeat under the floorboards. At least when you're being haunted by the heart, you can just leave the room or sell the house. With the haunting that Tobe is experiencing, he can't avoid persecution. This spirit has her own car-service available 24-7. This spirit has access to a private jet. London Francis is the physical embodiment of the internet, and the internet is everywhere now.

As the gate swings open, Tobe backs into the branches of Sienna's view-obstructing bushes. Focusing on the click-clack of the heels on the concrete, Tobe's sinks deeper into the shadows.

The perfume, the voice, the pumps. Tobe is absolutely certain that London Francis just walked out of Sienna's house. All of this information is too much for him to process and, almost instinctively he slides off his jacket, then stuffs it in the closing gate, taking advantage of the troubling moment.

To conceal himself, Tobe backs deeper into the bushes, then he tries to imagine that his entire body is covered by his concrete hair, even though almost every inch of his body is waxed, just in case.

London steps into view and Tobe watches as she walks in the direction of her car. How did he not notice her car? To be fair, in this neighborhood a Bentley at the curb isn't likely to trigger a second look. Tobe begins to worry that London will notice that the gate never shut with a clang. He watches, watches, watches; this is the first time he's actually interested in what's going through London's mind.

London stops walking right before she reaches her car. She stands frozen for ten seconds, then turns around quickly. Tobe closes his eyes and tries to fight his brutal anger at London's mere existence.

His fears are pacified when he hears London's heels click on the pavement again. He listens as she opens her car door, closes the door, then speeds off. He can't tell if it sounded like an angry speed off or a drunken speed off. He's going to assume the latter.

Tobe moves out of the bush, then looks down the street at his R8 parked in front of the hydrant. He sees at his vanity plate that reads "VAN1TY" and he knows that London caught him like a leather jacket in the gate of the prettiest girl in the world.

Tobe slides inside the gate, then carefully extracts his jacket. He slowly lets the metal connect and lock him inside. The magnets take hold to keep intruders out. Tobe is not an intruder; he's inside the gate.

It's now or never, or, if Sienna doesn't have cameras, it's time to look in a window and at least jerk off a bit so the trip isn't a waste. Tobe tells himself that he can't spend his entire life masturbating to Sienna Wolfe because, if he gives up again, he'll never be able to use Sienna Wolfe's vagina to masturbate his dick. Tobe is glad he has the screenplay information as a gift for Sienna because the poetry is not flowing tonight.

Making the long walk to the front door of Sienna's mansion, Tobe puts his jacket back on and spits his gum at a spiny plant next to the stairs.

Finally reaching the porch, Tobe rings the doorbell, then circles through casual poses until the door opens.

Light pours out of the house, framing Sienna as she stands in a tight gray t-shirt that has the number 29 on it. She's wearing heavily sliced, super short jean shorts with purely cosmetic pockets. If Tobe had to guess, he'd presume that the shorts were designed by Rag & Bone. They could also be Ksubi, but Tobe hopes they aren't. Shaken by the fact that he can't ID the designer of Sienna's shorts, Tobe manages to blurt out, "Hi. I'm Tobe Price." He stands his ground and this sets off a little celebration in his mind.

Sienna cocks her head to the side, and says, "Oh, really? I had no idea."

"I just wanted to make sure..." Tobe trails off, as he peeks past Sienna into the house.

"What? That I'm not just squatting this house?"

Tobe tells her cheerfully, "It's a nice house."

"Are you going to buy it from me in a hostile takeover? Is that why you're here?" Sienna asks. Reviewing things, she adds, "How'd you even get rich?"

"Oh. No. No. I won't be buying... your house. I would. But. You live in it. So. I won't," Tobe says. He runs his hands across his hair. Focus, Price.

"Good. My cat thanks you," Sienna says, then she looks at Tobe with cat eyes, realizing that she could steal something beautiful from London. Sienna bites her lip, then cutely mentions, "When we moved here, it took kitty like two weeks to find the litter box. He doesn't adapt well. The crazy part is he held it for those two weeks. Or the maid cleaned up his shit. Is that why you're here? Did The Box escape?"

"The box?"

"My cat."

"Your cat's name is 'The Box?'" Tobe asks, personally horrified that he didn't know this.

"Yes, that's his name," Sienna says furrowing her brow, "It's what London brought him over in. He was a housewarming gift. Kitty was scared at first, so he'd live in the beer box and everyone would be like, 'Where's the box?' and, 'Let's bring the box downstairs,' so we just called him, 'The Box' even though he got tired of the box. Or the maid threw it way..."

"Could I come inside?" Tobe asks, while taking mental snapshots of anything he can see in the house.

"You haven't told me why you're here," Sienna says, her arm barring Tobe's entrance into the house.

"It's sort of a long story."

"Does the long story also contain the answer as to why you're covered in dirt?" Sienna asks, eying him.

Tobe looks down at his coat and sees dirty lines running across his chest from the smog painted gate.

"And does this long story end in you killing me?" Sienna asks, pouting about her possible death.

"No," Tobe responds with a trustworthy smile.

Sienna figures that if she isn't going to be murdered, what's the harm? "Okay. Come in."

It's a good thing that London came over and acted like such a "Kristen" tonight. Without London asserting herself like such a bossy bitch, Sienna might not have had the inspiration to fuck London's boyfriend.

FAMEDIET

River White- "I Love social!heavy!"

Celebrities are just like us sometimes! We caught up with actor, producer, father, humanitarian, greatest human being alive- **River White**, as he was leaving the set of his top secret new movie. He gave us the inside scoop about what's on his playlist and which new band he can't get enough of! Here's our full transcript of the interview.(Click after the jump for the video.)

FameDiet: River, everyone at Fame Diet wants to know... What's. On. Your. Playlist?"

River White: Ah, I have the **Stones, Bryan Metro, Punchc*nt Love**, a little-

FD: -**social!heavy**?

River White: *(laughs)* Is that frozen yogurt?

FD: No, it's a New Wave band with **Chloe, Sienna, Krist**-"

River White: -they have a song out?

FD: Not a song, but they have a lot of press releases out and-

River White: -not a fan of press releases.

FD: So you're saying you're not a fan of social!heavy?

River White: I just said that I thought social!heavy was a yogurt stand. Are they a group that releases press releases?

FD: No, they release music."

River White: You just said they haven't released any songs. *(pause)*

FD: I love you... and **Mariana**.

River White: *(laughs)* Thank you.

FD: Could you look into that camera and say you love social!heavy?

River White: If I do, will you stop taking pictures of my kid at the park?

FD: We'll try.

River White: I love social!heavy.

FD: Thank you, River. I love you.

River White: I love you, too.

There you have it, a FameDiet exclusive- River White loves FameDiet and social!heavy!

64.5- Wolfe's Den.

"And this is a collage that my sister made for me. It's just a bunch of family photos," Sienna says, gesturing toward a poster sized mix of pictures hanging on the wall in her living room. Tobe's eyes frantically bounce across each photograph of Sienna. There's a red carpet photo from the premiere of a movie about robotic insects, at least ten pictures from *People,* and a photo from a *TeenRave! Magazine* that Tobe remembers buying like it was illegal contraband. In exchange for the magazine, he provided a six pack of Mike's Hard Lemonade to a 13 year old who had a pierced lip and bangs that were dyed like a raccoon's tail. Tobe chose her because she seemed to be no stranger to irrational decisions so she couldn't judge him.

"These are great... family photos," Tobe says, gritting his teeth when he sees two pictures that aren't in his shoebox. He desperately wants to yank the collage off the wall like it's a Crabner, then take it apart and steal the photographs, but he can't. There will be more pictures in the future. "That's the best collage I've ever seen," Tobe remarks sincerely.

"Whatever. I once made one of just dicks. I cut out all the dicks in a porn mag and made a huge collage of them, then when it was my sister's birthday, the same year she gave me this collage, I gave her the collage of dicks. Do you know what it costs to send a dick pic collage to that Africa place?" Sienna remarks, annoyed, "The shipping costs probably could have fed a tribe there for a year. It's so fucked up. They need to get their postal service in order." Sienna straightens her posture, "But... I'm sure you didn't come here for African dick collages. Or maybe you did?" Sienna says, then her eyes narrow, "Why are you here, did you read all those bad things I said about you?"

"You said bad things about me?" Tobe asks, his eyes lighting up with glee.

"No. Actually, you're one of the few people that doesn't work on. I don't think I've ever spun anything horrible about you before. You must be a good guy, Tobe Price."

"I am," Tobe says, without modesty or irony. Wasting no time in the double crossing of his pawn-girlfriend, Tobe leads Sienna to the topic he's burning to discuss, "So this band thing..."

"Ugh, that damn band," Sienna huffs, "It's like, yeah, awesome, let's waste our time doing nerd shit like practicing skills and collaborating."

"Collaborating is shit," Tobe responds sincerely. He pauses for a moment, carefully, then returns to the topic, "However, I think we could form our own collaboration of sorts. I have some... information."

Sienna now *notices* Tobe Price, and Tobe feeds off this diabolical energy. He's convinced that the look Sienna just gave him immediately turned his hair even more blond. Not wasting the intrigue, Tobe slowly walks toward the girl who's even more beautiful without photoshop. "I was at lunch with Chloe and Stanley," he says.

"I know, I saw the pictures," Sienna responds, with a hint of boredom.

"Oh. Yeah. The pictures. The seating arrangement wasn't my idea. I was invited by London Fr-"

"-yeah, I know London, your girlfriend," Sienna says as her patience grows thinner by the second.

"She's not my girlfriend," Tobe snaps. "She's not my girlfriend," he quietly repeats. Finally, he was able to verbally confirm what he always felt, London Francis is not his girlfriend. Tobe was able to ride London to the top, then ditch her, like a chairlift. He knew it would be fine, and London would just head back down and collect someone new for the same exact trip.

Sienna cocks her head to the side and gives Tobe a look as to say, *I'm calling you out on your bullshit.*

"London is confused," Tobe states plainly.

"Wouldn't be the first time," Sienna says, and Tobe grins widely at this.

Sienna drifts across the room, then relaxes onto the sofa, leaving room for her guest. Tobe has to compose himself before he can approach this invitation to intimacy. Once he's mentally sure his hair looks great, he moves to the couch, then sits down, but leaves a gap of space between himself and Sienna's curled legs. Almost shaking, he continues his story, "We were at Dorée, and, I guess to distract us from the fact that she wasn't eating, Chloe started yammering, but something strange happened, and she actually mentioned something worth discussing. In a hushed tone she told us she was given a screenplay and-"

"-a screenplay? Like for a movie? A movie-screenplay? Someone sent Chloe a movie? I don't believe it! A couple months ago the girl was damn near a size six and now she's going to be in a movie?" Sienna asks, instantly enraged and engaged.

"Not if we stop her," Tobe says, delivering a line he'd been practicing on the ride over. He didn't deliver it as intensely as he wanted to; he would not make for a good costar.

"Keep going," Sienna says, her eyes flickering with glee. Tobe had fantasized about hearing those words come out of Sienna's mouth. The night is turning out perfectly and he owes it all to London. She got him to Sienna. London Francis is a good friend, while Tobe is nothing of the sort, so he unleashes the information he promised not to divulge, "Chloe talked about some producer guy. Shit. His name was Mendel-something."

"Oh. Okay. Awesome, a producer with a Jewish name in LA? That shouldn't be too hard to figure out. Did she also say that the co-producer was a Tyrone-something from Compton?"

Tobe laughs, then slaps his knee, angry that he didn't commit this crucial piece to memory, "Mendelheim. Harvey. No. Not Harvey..."

"Larry Mendelheim?" Sienna asks, a little less excited.

"Yeah! You know him?"

"Yup," Sienna says, popping her lips.

"That makes sense that he'd send you the script then."

"I never got a script from him," Sienna responds with rushed concern, as she realizes she's being fleeced.

Tobe's heart races, this is going perfectly. He calms himself, then purrs, "Exactly. He gave it to Chloe, to give to you."

"That bitch! She hasn't mentioned anything to me."

"She's planning on telling Mendelheim that you aren't interested, then she's going to take the role."

"This is insane. This is insane, Tobe. I came back to those whores to do them a favor because they were gonna be the shittiest New Wave band since... well, all other New Wave bands."

Tobe wants to harness this reaction so he segues straight into revenge mode- Sienna's favorite. "I was thinking, what if we call Mendelheim and tell him that you'll do the movie? We already know you're who he really wants. We'll cut Chloe off before she can strike up a deal."

"Has Chloe accepted the role yet?"

"No, she's going to accept it later this week," Tobe responds.

"I'll call tomorrow," Sienna says, worked up.

"Don't you even want to know what the movie's about?" Tobe asks, feeling protective of Sienna.

"I don't give a shit what this movie involves, I'm not letting Chloe Warren star in it. I can't wait to finally get out of this 'New Wave' band. I'm so done with those girls."

Tobe notices that Sienna used "New Wave" as a synonym for shitty.

"I don't blame you," Tobe says, encouraging her alienation so that she has to start anew, with him.

"At last I'll be free of this awful band and their diarrhea stickers."

"Dia-" Tobe begins, but then looks at the beautiful rare flower in front of him, and he remarks, "You're exactly right."

"You know what, Tobe Price?" Sienna asks, slowly moving across the sofa toward him.

Tobe stares into Sienna's bedroom eyes, as she tells him, "It turns out you aren't a huge douche after all."

It was a start.

OXYGEN WASTER
The Price is Right For Sienna Wolfe.

This morning, we received these <u>pictures</u> of **Tobe Price** doing the world's most put together walk of shame. Not news, right? Take another look at the background in picture <u>above</u>. That doesn't look like **London Francis'** house, does it? That doesn't look like the lobby of Tobe's penthouse pad, does it?

That's Tobe Price leaving **Sienna Wolfe**'s house at noon today. Please keep in mind that noon to a socialite is like 6 AM for everyone else. It's the hour of the morning when you'd leave after a yummy sleepover. There were no signs of any pillow fight wounds and it doesn't appear that Tobe got a facial, but then again, our guy should be looking at Sienna's face for evidence of that, right?

<u>After the jump</u> we have pictures of Tobe collecting a ticket off his car, which is parked directly in front of a fire hydrant. He probably wanted to be close to a water supply just in case London caught him, and brought down the fire and brimstone everyone knows she's capable of causing.

Hell hath no fury like a socialite scorned.

65- This Means War-ren.

The recording room is silent. The band waits for their harshest critic before they start playing.

"You're sure you reminded her last night?" Martin asks London, his face buried in his hands.

"Yeah. I went to her house and repeatedly told her how important today is," London says in her baby voice.

"Oh, for fuck's sake, what's the matter London?" Martin asks, his temper getting short. He has to balance all these delicate flowers in one vase and they seem to all be flopping out and ruining the beauty that they're capable of when bunched together.

"Nothing's wrong," the little voice says, diminutive, "I guess I'm just nervous about playing the drums."

"Don't be nervous, this is our first run through. Just have fun," Martin says, his edge disappearing as he provides the type of advice that would be dispensed by a JV basketball coach.

Dakota, Chloe, and Kristen look back to London. They all know that she's not nervous about her drumming. Out of all of the members of the band, London has probably made the biggest life change for this moment. She devoted herself to playing the drums, to the point that the neighbors even noticed. You would've thought that London was throwing Molotov cocktails in their windows the way they complained to the blogs and police about the noise.

Sending a jolt through the entire band, the silent failure of their first practice is shattered as the soundproof door buzzes open, and Sienna Wolfe walks in.

"Thank you, Jesus," Martin says, looking up at the ceiling.

Sienna takes center stage in front of social!heavy, and announces, "I'm quitting."

Thank you, Jesus, Dakota, Kristen, London, and Chloe all think to themselves.

"You can't quit," Chloe says from the front of the band, as the frontwoman. Behind Chloe's back, her red nails cross themselves. The girls notice this and adjust their attitudes accordingly.

"I can. My agent said it's in our contract."

"Well, this is more than just a contractual thing," Martin jumps in. He can't see Chloe's fingers.

"Don't be a bitch," Sienna snarls.

"I'm not being a bitch!" Martin protests in a high pitch yelp.

"Don't yell at Martin," Dakota screeches at her ex-best friend.

"Well, he called me a bitch," Sienna says, bitchily.

"I didn't, you called me a bitch!" Martin pleads his case.

"How silly of us, you aren't being a bitch, Sienna," London says jumping in.

"It's clear that you're just being 'Sienna,'" Chloe says, completing the statement.

Sienna stands high in her heels, but she feels like she was knocked on her ass. She just took Kristen's spot for good, and that's bad. To counterbalance this shift, Kristen will accept extra duties, and things will carry on. Was this movie role really worth it? Did Sienna even want to be in this dumb band? She decides this movie will be a stepping stone, while this band will sink like one.

"I'm gone, girls," Sienna announces, moving away from her old band, metaphorically and physically, "...and I get custody of London's boyfriend."

Right before Sienna reaches the door, London begins laying down the drum beat to the first song. Slowly, one by one, the girls smirk at each other and begin to assemble into *something*.

social!heavy is born in the most perfect of circumstances- as a *fuck you* to everyone who claimed they were less than.

celebUtard
"social!heavy Gets Social - Lighter."

In the same way we watch our grandmother smoke those cigarettes, knowing that they'll eventually kill her, we watched as **Sienna Wolfe** pretended to actually be part of **social!heavy**, knowing that she would someday destroy the band. We remained very aware that Sienna was the one thing standing between us and a social!heavy album. To stop her, we wanted to set up a faux interview, then **Michael Corleone** her in a restaurant.

That probably sounds extreme, but we're really excited to hear this band, and if we have to trade in our scalped tickets for gas money to the **Sunny Palms Lodge** to interview all the girls in rehab in a month, we're going to be really pissed. We'll probably do the old "We're not mad, we're just disappointed" guilt trip, before groveling for a social!heavy unplugged set in the activities room.

We were sure that Sienna would ruin this band, but then she just stepped away. Things are fine now.

How did social!heavy get rid of Sienna, you ask?

She left!

Doesn't that seem impossible? Cockroaches don't just pack up and go; trust us, we know, our apartments are testament to that. Herpes doesn't magically disappear, just ask **London Francis**. Apparently, Sienna was offered a part in the new **Larry Mendelheim** horror flick, which if it's anything like his last shlockfest, **The Toxic Perrier**, it'll be awesome- if you're drunk/spins-drunk/legally dead- but if you're sober, you'll want to commit suicide because you can't live in a world where this movie was allowed to be made.

Somehow, possibly under the influence of a real life Toxic Perrier, Sienna Wolfe dropped out of the buzziest band in the industry to star in a movie you need a buzz to enjoy. No news on what the flick is about, but they start shooting next week. Luckily, Mendelheim is shooting Sienna Wolfe so we don't have to.

Until next time, stay tardy, celebUverse.

66- No Comforting, Just Confronting.

After social!heavy's successful practice, London didn't go to the club, she didn't open a bottle of champagne, she didn't even listen to the secret demos she recorded on her phone. She just enjoyed the company of her babies, then went to bed.

London endured a normal night because she had to be like a normal person who wakes up early for work, and it was essential that she appeared refreshed in the morning.

London's phone alarm literally barks her out of bed at 11 AM.

She slowly and carefully, with great purpose and care, gets ready for the day.

It's time to confront Tobe Price.

London calls the paparazzi on herself, then leaves.

Driving alongside the aggressive camera flashes, the primped rock star carefully signals every turn so she doesn't lose the secret vampires. She knows she looks good, and she tries not to look sad.

Retaining every last pap, London arrives at her destination, and illegally parks in front of Tobe Price's building because, without question, she wanted everyone to know that she drove to Tobe's place after those hurtful photos showed up. She frames the pink Bentley directly in front of the entrance to the building, and Martin appreciates London's consideration for photographic composition as he snaps pictures from his double parked van.

Even the doormen in Tobe's building appear to know what's about to happen, and they barely look at London as her heels clack through the lobby.

On the long elevator ride up to Tobe's penthouse, London doesn't practice what she's going to say. She's not an actress. None of the girls are.

Stepping out of the elevator, London makes her way to Tobe's never locked door. There's one layer of security to get into Tobe's life. Beyond the front desk, it's possible to walk right inside his home, and he'll leave the door open as a reminder that it'll be just as easy to get shown out.

"I know everything," London says, appearing in the door frame of Tobe Price's bedroom, looking purposefully hot.

Tobe rolls over and sees London dressed in a short pink DSquared dress and matching pumps. What a funny thing for London Francis to say, "I know everything." She's too nice, coming here to have this conversation. Tobe didn't even have to put on pants to put an end to what they had. It was wreckshit in bed.

"Well, you caught me," Tobe says, lifting his hands in the air.

"You aren't even going to defend yourself?" London asks, not moving from the door frame.

"How can I? You've cracked the case. Well done."

"You lied," London says, hurt.

Tobe sits up abruptly and his entire demeanor changes, "So what London? In our world, everything is a lie."

"It's not fair."

Tobe looks at London disdainfully, and says, "Lots of things aren't fair. And sometimes the shit that isn't fair causes people to lose a hand, or lose their house, or lose a mother. Real people have to deal with real problems. Things may seem dramatic in our fairy tale world, but don't misinterpret people's interest as them giving a shit."

"I'm losing you though. That sucks."

"It's not that big of a loss. You'll get over it."

"How could you say that?"

"Because I'm like the puppies, and birds, and that absolutely insane looking pink dog you have. If any of them run away, you can replace them by just walking down the street."

London thinks about this for a moment, then says, "Maybe you're right, losing you isn't that big of a loss because it's clear that you don't understand me."

"What's there to understand, London?" Tobe responds coldly.

"Maybe if you investigated that question, you'd regret what you're doing."

"I don't need to investigate it. There are thirteen guys that follow you around daily who do that for me. I'm not sure if you've read their findings, but they aren't exactly gushing about you."

London leans heavy on the door frame. Tobe is wrong. Those guys don't hate her. It's their editors. It's the bloggers. It's the trolls. It's the fat girls. It's the jealous people who take a grainy photo just to send to a website for a check not even big enough to pay their rent for a month.

London has Martin as proof that some people do see something important about her under the makeup and headlines. He took a moment to reach out to her, and he realized that there's a worthwhile person behind the cloud of the London Francis branded perfume. London considers that maybe she just needs to reach out to Tobe in the same way. It's true that her love is fractured between all her babies, and that can be difficult for someone who's very used to massive amounts of attention. Maybe Tobe will take a little more work than she originally anticipated, but the new London is willing to put in the extra amount of work. All Tobe has to do is make the tiniest of efforts.

This all could be fixed if Tobe told her that it wasn't his car she saw after leaving Sienna's. She wanted him to say that the contents of his shoebox was assembled so he can masturbate to pictures of Sienna with no emotional attachment. She needed him to say that it wasn't him walking out of Sienna's house in those pictures. She wanted to be lied to, because he's right, everyone in her world does lie.

Maybe, in a way, those lies are easier to digest than the truth.

Tobe lays back in bed, tired, worried that London is about to forgive him. To prevent this, he addresses her very clearly, "Let me put this in terms you'll understand. All kittens are cute, but just because something's cute doesn't mean you can take it home."

London stares blankly at Tobe.

"You're not following what I'm saying at all, are you?" Tobe asks.

"Um. I think I am. You want to go to Petsville to look at kitties!?" London says, feeling pathetic for this statement. This is Tobe Price's second chance, no matter how unearned it is. If he isn't going to say the words, London will, and all he has to do is agree with them.

"I... Wha... You...?" Tobe spatters out, touching his smooth forehead.

"I picked my house because it's within walking distance to the pet store," London tells him, trying to move past their fight since Tobe isn't showing any signs of remorse.

"What's considered walking distance for you, like four or five yards?" Tobe remarks sarcastically.

"No, I pass like 20 yards, one of the yards always has a cute dog in it. The dog looks like the one in those *Beethoven* movies. I bring him a treat most times. I have to walk in a big L and it takes like ten minutes. Well, double with paps."

Tobe knows that he has no choice but to be horribly mean to London. As it stands right now, she'll easily forgive him, and that's a huge problem.

London has served her purpose and now Tobe needs her out of his life. There's only one sentence that could work as the eject button on this relationship, so through an evil grin, Tobe asks London, "Don't you feel stupid?"

"Wait. Why would I feel stupid?" London asks, worried.

Tobe shakes his head and laughs a tiny laugh, "Wow. You don't feel stupid because you're too dumb to know you're stupid."

"You're the self-centered... isolated... delusional.. jerk," London says, angry, hurt, almost leaving, but unable to turn her heels. She didn't want to walk out on yet another guy.

"Oh congrats. You read *Oxygen Waster*," Tobe says, bored.

"Has all of this been fake?" London asks, not crying. She won't cry until she gets to her car, she promised herself that. Since no one seems to be telling her the truth, London needs to stick to her promises.

"All of this... has been a lie," Tobe says, feeling both relief and regret.

"I can't believe you!"

"What? Should I have started a fake band to deal with my problems instead?"

"Now we're a real band," London says, hoping that since Tobe is paralleling their relationship to the band, they could follow the same path.

"No, you're not, and you know that. Just like you knew this was a fake relationship."

"I didn't know," London says in her baby voice.

"That's. Because. You. Are. Stupid," Tobe responds, hammering each word into London's empty head.

67- Practicing Being Real.

Martin sits behind the giant soundproof window. He figures this clear barrier is the best way to handle the second practice. It wouldn't be right for him to stand in front of the girls, picking apart every time they don't hit a note exactly the way he did when he played the songs so many decades ago. Martin has to distance himself from his music so it can become social!heavy's.

The girls take their places- Sienna is nowhere to be found- and with a classic 1-2-1-2-3 count, they begin. Martin leans over and mutes the sound from beyond the glass. He sits in silence and watches as the band slowly realizes how to move together, yet shine separately.

It's a choppy process for London, whose long arms seem exceedingly gangly as she slams her kit.

With Kristen, a shy artist becomes an exhibitionist on the keys.

Dakota moves with her guitar, proving it's more than an accessory.

Chloe, as a frontwoman, is like a pot of water that's being brought to a boil. She doesn't move for the entire first song. She's frozen, holding the mic like a monkey holds an orange. During the second song, she realizes that the mic stand moves. She picks it up during the chorus and carries it across the room, graceful and natural. By the third song, the mic is out of the stand, and Chloe is visiting her bandmates during the performance- a lean toward Kristen, a slow creep to Dakota that's seductive to the point that Dakota stops watching her fingers and looks at Chloe's mouth.

With a quick turn, Chloe makes eye contact with Martin through the glass and shoots him a look that wordlessly informs the wannabe frontman that his songs now belong to the girls. Instantly, Martin relents, signing over the rights to the music without lifting a pen. These girls are good enough to take possession of the songs without the usual mess of lawyers.

Martin leans back in his chair, watching these beautiful women bring his dream to life.

After 50 sweaty minutes, social!heavy comes to a stop– the last song is over. Martin wants to immediately inform them of just how good they are, but he finds his eyes blurring and his cheeks sucking into his face. He wishes that he had his embarrassing sunglasses to hide his reaction. After sweeping his thumbs across his eyes, he takes a deep breath, then forfeits the glass wall of safety and makes his way into the recording room.

The girls are all frozen in their places, waiting to hear if they do, in fact, have talent. That's all they want, one single non-inherited skill that can be utilized outside of the bedroom.

When they practiced yesterday, Martin said that they shouldn't talk about the music, they should just play through it. Being the impatient girls they are, this means today is the day they find out if they're good.

Time slows down.

In a room that was engineered to be totally silent, the girls wait to hear if they're worth listening to.

Of all the photographs Martin has ever taken, none of them will outlive this freeze frame that was never captured.

Kristen stands at her synthesizer as it sections her perfect frame in half. Below the synthesizer, her extra tan legs move back and forth with nervous anticipation. Her little navy colored Acne short-shorts match her Pedro Garcia sandals in the careful way that Kristen now coordinates all facets of her life. Above the synthesizer, Kristen's bare arms cross over her gray Alexander Wang racer-back tank top. She looks confident, as though any bad review could not be attributed to her; Kristen is the only experienced musician in the room, besides Martin. Her blonde hair stays neatly behind her ears, far away from her frozen eyes that are directed not at Martin's reaction, but instead at his stomach. In the end, she needed to be able to tell herself, if she's in a failure of a band, at least she isn't Martin. At least she isn't fat. She can find a new band, Martin is stuck with his man boobs.

Next to Kristen, Chloe stands in a white Diane von Fürstenberg sundress that's dotted with blue flowers. She holds the mic by its cord, unwilling to put it back in its stand. If Martin says they don't have what it takes, Chloe will take another stand to prove that she's the natural frontwoman of social!heavy. No one is taking this mic away from her.

London sits behind a drum kit that isn't even hers. Her eyes are smoked with makeup, her cheeks are flushed a cherry-red. For what may be the first time ever, London's brow shows a glimmer of sweat, not from the sun on a private beach or the afterglow of sex, but due to hard work. As London waits for Martin's approval, her strangled drumsticks extend her stick thin arms even longer.

Dakota impatiently stands in her ripped stockings and her clingy Fornarina dress that bares the dark picture of a wolf. That wolf is tight against her heart. Dakota's guitar is on the ground. She put it there just in case Martin tells them they don't have "it." If Martin says that social!heavy sounds terrible, Dakota will walk right out of the studio forever, like her ex-best friend did during the first practice. Dakota is tired of being a circus sideshow, but she'll take that life over being someone *they* don't want to see. At least kids feel like it's worth it to buy a ticket to gawk at the snake-lady.

Martin can't hide his pride as he runs his hand across his chin. "That was brilliant. Absolutely brilliant," he says, finally figuring out a way to describe what he just witnessed.

social!heavy becomes light when he says this. Their wide smiles seem to turn them into different people. They wear a look of joy and accomplishment that also simmers with the type of nervous anticipation that accompanies the first day of private school.

Martin's camera is in the van. So it goes. Even if he did take this picture, everyone would just claim it's photoshopped because the girls seem too happy, too proud, too together. The photograph would look like a hoax. It would seem like a Mendelheim movie, populated with higher class actresses.

"We sounded good?" London asks, desperate to be told she didn't waste her time learning to drum.

"About that," Martin says, then he immediately realizes why producers sit behind that giant pane of protective glass. The girls sense his hesitation and their smiles drop. They felt like they sounded good, but maybe music is like the phone and they sound different to themselves than they do to everyone else

"Joel asked me to record you, that's why we're practicing in the studio again," Martin admits.

Chloe looks at London, London looks at Kristen, Kristen looks at Dakota, and Dakota picks up her guitar, then walks toward the door. Just before she makes her exit, Dakota turns and asks, "Don't you bitches want to hear our band?" Above all the girls, Dakota is ready to address the matter head on. The last time she felt this mentality was when some random girl's amateur sex tape was erroneously labeled as being hers. The only thing the tape aroused in Dakota was a feeling of righteous indignation, especially the part where the look-alike removed her mouth from an okay-looking male model, then leaned over and spat into an old t-shirt.

It's the 21st century, who spits?

FAMEDIET
Francis/Price Split Confirmed.

Both **London Francis** and **Tobe Price** have been silent today on the subject of their relationship, but as you can see from our pictures, London has been sending smoke signals all day long. These brand new images confirm what everyone already knows, Tobe has gone the way of **Sienna Wolfe** (in more ways than one).

London started her day high in the lair of love that Tobe Price calls home. Our photographer places her at the scene for a half hour, then, get this, Tobe and London *didn't* go have brunch. Anyone who knows London, knows brunch is her essence, and the fact that she left the penthouse without Tobe, stopped at **Starbucks** without Tobe, then arrived at the studio with no one but the paparazzi by her side, all seems to indicate that the conversation she had in that penthouse was a goodbye.

Looking visibly happier after her studio session, London hopped in her car and headed down Melrose to the extra close **John Frieda Salon**. As you can see from the before and after pics, it looks like Ms. Francis did what every good girl does after a breakup- she got a sexy, bedheaded, wavy curled haircut to remind Tobe of what she looked like coming out of the water in that bikini.

A new look for a new London.

Starting the day frowning and ending it with a smile, London Francis seems like the embodiment of happiness. Unfortunately for Tobe, you can't put a Price on happiness.

68- About To Set the World On Fire.

They've finally done it, but the damage from not doing *anything* for so long is still there.

These are the scars on the arms that control the keys.

"This was supposed to fix things," Kristen says, her face flowing from golden to dark as the fire flickers in the pit in front of her.

Johnny feels Kristen crumble into him, and he knows exactly why she's cracking again. "You're going in the right direction," he says, holding his girlfriend close. The night had started with such positivity. Kristen ran into Johnny's back yard, ecstatic that her band was, "Rough, but the good rough. The perfect rough." Then things got rough when text messages from Sienna started vibrating over and over and over on Kirsten's phone. Sienna had acquired information from Mitchell, and she seems eager to discuss it with Kristen, and maybe additional parties.

Kristen holds onto Johnny to steady herself as the mini earthquakes continue to vibrate out as fast as Sienna can send them. Talking to Johnny's chest, Kristen asks, "Why do I feel like things are falling apart, when everything is coming together?"

Johnny's soothing voice purrs out, "You have to wait until you play that first show. When you're on that stage, and you see the same people who questioned your fame now admiring you as someone who's not only rich, or beautiful, or skinny- but also as someone who has this amazing talent that she's sharing with the people most important to her, then you'll understand your impact. People need you, Kristen."

"Why? What do I have that they need?"

"Because you- us- the models- the socialites, we've become a necessary part of society."

"Only if you're a handbag designer, horny C-list actor, or a club owner," Kristen spits back.

Johnny knows that Kristen will relapse without a reminder of her worth, so he grabs her hands, demanding eye contact, as he tells her, "You're important for everyone. You're that crucial piece. Think about it, all day long people are bombarded with subway ads about debt consolidation, about going back to college for a degree to get the 'job they deserve,' about getting tested for STDs- then they glance down at the news on their phone and read about some CEO getting a golden parachute for running a company into the ground. Once they get to work, to that job they don't deserve, they deal with customers who don't even treat them like they're a human being. They escape to lunch, only to come back to a scolding from their boss because their break lasted three minutes too long. After all that, when they've had enough, they sneak away to the bathroom, and they go on their phone to look at pictures of you, or Chloe, or London driving the wrong way down a one-way street. It's a little mindless break from everything."

"I don't want to be mindless anymore."

"That's the thing, you're not, the stories they write about you are. We're the comic relief in the really depressing, shitty, soul crushing movie of life. People take breaks out of their day to look in on your day, just so they don't plant a ball point pen into their boss' neck. You have to let people laugh at you or there are going to be a lot of bloodstained Van Heusen dress shirts."

"People hate us, Johnny."

"Because it's safe to hate us. They can hate us because we drive nice cars or because we have too much money. They can hate us because they know they'll never have to apologize for it. People can talk shit about us from behind that screen and write a mean comment about my hair or your dress and that's a little tiny bit of therapy. The fact is, most of the time, the villains these people hate are the same idiots they see every day, and they can't say these hurtful things to someone they know personally."

"They can if they're Sienna Wolfe."

celebUtard
"social!heavy live."

"Spend a night with **Chloe Warren**, **Dakota Dabney**, **London Francis**, and **Kristen Paxton**," read the update that was posted on **social!heavy**'s website tonight at 5:34 PM PST.

By 5:47 PM PST, the first ever social!heavy concert had sold out. Even those shitty seats where you're in the stands, but you're technically sitting behind the stage, were sold. Although, those bad seats were probably bought by a bunch of pretentious assholes who just wanted to say that they had "backstage passes" to the concert.

Normally, a band releases a single, then a video, then an album, then a second video, then they go on tour.

social!heavy has decided to do whatever they want, again.

"They may only release live records," was a quote their manager, **Joel Harper**, gave us when we called him after the announcement. "There's something about how they sound without the autotune bullshit as a barrier. That much beauty on stage at once, it's one of those you-have-to-see-it-to-believe it moments," Joel told us, and part of us believed him when he said it. The other part, the bigger part, the private part, tells us that because of all the articles we've run about these girls being a bunch of waste of life, over-privileged coke-heads, we've forced them into this situation. They have to prove they're *more*. They don't need more money and they don't need more fame. All they want is for us to believe that they deserve what they already have.

We wish we had tickets to give away in a cool contest or something, but we don't. Another party that these girls get to go to, while you stay home and google them.

Until next time, stay tardy, celebUverse.

69- Playing Games, While Playing Games.

Tobe finishes four games of Madden, back to back to back, to avoid the fact that his cell phone remains silent. Sienna has stayed distant, even after they connected so perfectly.

Riding high off his fourth win, Tobe's confidence is bolstered enough to make a call that doesn't involve a square, triangle, circle, or X.

The lock screen picture of Sienna at the Santa Monica Pier is swiped away to reveal the wallpaper on his phone, a picture of Sienna relaxing across a sofa lounge during a Sundance after-party, then that picture disappears as well and Tobe's contacts appear. He presses down on Sienna's name, then puts the call on speaker. No one talks on the phone anymore- it's gone the way of writing letters- and this makes it special. The call timer on the phone begins to climb and each ring seems to reverberate for eternity in Tobe's high ceilinged penthouse.

Four eternities later, Sienna's voice materializes on the line, "Tobe Priceee."

"Sienna!" Tobe says, his voice metering up too high, then he tries to correct it, "Sienna."

"Is someone chasing you or something?"

"Paparazzi," Tobe says, then laughs good naturally. "Anyway, I was just calling to see if you wanted to have dinner."

"It's 3:30 in the afternoon. I just woke up like an hour ago," Sienna says.

"Okay, right, I meant lunch. Breakfast? I can... eat any version of a meal..."

"Sure," Sienna says nonchalantly.

Tobe waits a moment, off-put by the casualness of her response, and he suddenly feels unsure where to make reservations due to the meal ambiguities. He clears his throat, yet still mumbles, "If you're busy..."

"Nope, I don't have anything to do, I've made a positive decision that I won't waste my day on a group of girls with 'Kristeny' haircuts, as they pathetically try to play instruments."

"Oh, yeah, you saw London's haircut?" Tobe asks, making sure it's clear he's apathetic about his ex.

"Oh no. Oh no," Sienna panics, her entire demeanor changing. Tobe instantly regrets mentioning the haircut. He thought that Sienna had already seen London's new look. *Everyone* has seen the new haircut. Tobe was ecstatic when he saw it. The blogs viewed it as a wavy new chop, while Tobe felt like it was a nail in the coffin. It's clear that this haircut has ruined the date, like Sienna's meal was covered in the hair London got chopped off, so Tobe needs to turn the tables, fast.

Almost hyperventilating, Sienna says, "Please tell me you're joking. Please say that was a joke. That's a joke, right? London didn't get a haircut, did she?"

"It's just a-"

"-it's not," Sienna says, in pain.

"Check the blogs," Tobe responds grimly, deciding that since he was dumb enough to let this slip, he might as well utilize the "partner in crime" position.

"I'm putting you on speaker," Sienna says, then she brings up *ThisSpoiledBitch*. Sienna huffs big breaths as she stares at a picture of London, looking fresh. Her hair now has a wave. A brand. New. Wave.

Sienna takes Tobe off speaker and brings the phone back up to her face. Her stubby fingers tighten around the little piece of metal and glass. *Don't throw the phone, don't throw the phone, not again,* she tells herself and, in a rare moment of self-control, she manages to maintain a grip on the near-projectile. Sienna couldn't throw her phone, she has an important call to make.

It's time to get London off the front page.

70- Un-Sienna-ing Sienna Because Sienna is Too Sienna to Still Be Sienna.

"Oh no, the blogs have Sienna out and about today," London says, a drop of sweat falling onto the screen of her phone. The workout Martin organized for the girls has proven to be less rock and roll, and more boot camp. Luckily, taking another cue from Joel, Stanley helped Martin find a dance studio that's so heavily mirrored the place looks like a funhouse. The girls can't pull themselves away from the reflective wall- they're like a group of moths around a porch light, or London Francis around a vodka filled porch candle jar.

Stanley has accompanied the girls today because Chloe shouldn't be working out. He couldn't tell her not to go, however he *could* wait with a full tank of gas, ready to rush her to emergency services before 911 is ever called.

So far, Chloe seems okay.

All of the girls seem better than okay.

"Sienna is over," Kristen declares, closing the case so London will put her phone away.

"Obviously," London says, wiping the sweat off her forehead with her white Karl Lagerfeld jersey tank.

Until this point, Stanley had only occasionally glanced up from his computer- once to look at Chloe to make sure her heart wasn't giving out, and again to suggest that the girls try some classic rock and roll moves. The latter was met with Dakota saying, "No, Stanley. I think we all got a taste of your dancing during the prom episode," then she made excessive and choppy hand movements, miming Tristan.

Stanley pulls his eyes away from the laptop again because *finally* what's happening past the screen is more interesting than what's on it.

"That's a good idea. We shouldn't use it anymore," Dakota says, either misunderstanding or twisting the statement.

"No. Dakota. I meant that *she* is over," Kristen explains.

"Oh. Okay," Dakota meekly says, checking her face in the reflection of the giant mirror. Luckily, she isn't breaking out from the stress, yet.

"It's her fault," Kristen says with a tinge of a smile, "It's like she tripped over her own shoelaces."

"I don't think she owns shoes that tie," London scoffs, then she tries to twirl a drumstick in her right hand. London is right- in Sienna's shoe closet, everything is a pump, a sandal, or a flat. There isn't a shoelace to be found. If she was going to hang herself, she'd have to do it with a designer belt.

"Can 'Sienna' be over since Sienna is over?" Dakota asks.

The girls slowly, one by one, nod in agreement. They realize that this tabloid-like persecution was "Sienna" so it can no longer be *a thing*.

At Dakota's insistence, "Sienna" is over.

Sometimes, when your best friend can't help stitch your wounds, she can at least protect you from the sharks who smell your dripping blood.

celebUtard
"The Leaking An Rx Won't Fix."

With rumors of **Sienna Wolfe** dating **London Francis'** ex-flame, **Tobe Price**, she'll soon be photographed at **Walgreen's** getting a prescription to ex the flame burning in her nether-regions.

It's a quick and simple fix.

Maybe, possibly, we might have been in a Walgreen's attending to a related issue recently, so we know.

What? Don't judge us. It happens to everyone at least once/twice/once a year.

Whatever, we feel we've strayed from our point.

Our point actually arrived in an anonymous envelope at our office yesterday.

The **celebUtard Sexy Intern Boy** (and possible reason why the hypothetical Walgreen's trip occurred) dropped a package on our desk and, of course, when a big package falls into our hands we have to give it some attention (also possibly why the hypothetical Walgreen's trip occurred).

As it turns out, we had been sent the script to the new Sienna Wolfe movie, *Ghorbies.* We immediately read the script- well, the first 20 pages, but we didn't need to read any more. Getting the script for *Ghorbies* in the mail was like receiving a letter filled with anthrax. No. It was worse. At least with a letter full of anthrax, we would've had fun powder to sniff. With this script all we could sniff was the bullshit filling each page.

This is a work that arrives so humorless it becomes funny, but then it gets so funny that it gives you a headache and makes you feel like you have to take a shower.

We can't post the script, but we can post an opinion.

Our opinion?

These Ghorbies aren't going to scare theatergoers because they're only a threat to socialites with fragile social standings.

Until next time, stay tardy, celebUverse.

71- I'm so Not Sienna, but I'm so Like Sienna, Soon I'll be Sienna.

"I'm next," Dakota says, nervously looking around the red-themed restaurant.

"For what?" Jake asks, as he spoons up some of the peach sorbet that London had been constantly telling him he *must* try, despite his fruit allergies.

"I'm the next girl to be kicked to the curb," Dakota says in a wobbly voice.

"You girls didn't oust Sienna, she took a movie role and left," Jake points out, then shovels a huge glop of peach sorbet into his mouth in hopes that it will close up his throat so he won't have to spend another night wrestling with Dakota's inability to let toxic people go.

Paying off Dakota father was the best money Jake had ever spent. If he was going to help Dakota move past Sienna, at least he didn't have to bargain with another asshole dad. Sienna's dad has already disappeared... for free.

"I found out it was a setup," Dakota says to Jake, giving him highly classified information.

"A setup? A setup? Are you listening to yourself? You're telling me that London Francis wrote and produced a movie just to get Sienna Wolfe out of social!heavy? That's madness," Jake says. "I can't believe that. Sienna was thrown out because she's Sienna."

"We don't use that term anymore."

"I wasn't using a term. I was just saying that it's her own fault. Sienna is abrasive, and she's selfish, and she's manipulative," Jake lists, just getting started. He's an author, he has a thousand ways to describe Sienna and none of them are nice.

"Exactly! And we're like twins, we're practically the same person."

"No. You aren't," Jake responds, sure that there's a large chasm between where Dakota Dabney ends and Sienna Wolfe begins.

"She's always been my best friend," Dakota sheepishly admits.

Responding like a lion, Jake says, "That's not true, she's gone behind your back and she's given your personal secrets to complete strangers. She would feed information about you to your father."

"Because she knows that I probably should talk to him. After Mom passed, I became Paul's only family. She was helping me with that issue."

"She was helping you? Please. You just called your father 'Paul.' Don't let Sienna warp your perception. Paul is selfish and if he includes you in his life, it's only to benefit himself. Same goes for Sienna. You think that she gave all that valuable information to your father so that he could swoop in and save you? Save you from what? Your new work ethic that's helping you develop a real, actual talent? All you've really done for the past few months is practice, excluding the moments you spent kidnapped by your so-called best friend. You're a better person for leaving Sienna to deal with herself."

"You don't get it. You weren't there before."

"Maybe so, but I'm here now, and Sienna Wolfe is not your best friend. She's not your friend at all," Jake says, delivering the hard news- another skill his father taught him. The lessons were not easy.

"I know, it's terrible," Dakota says, opening her purse. She takes out a Pall Mall, then lights it with the flame of a trembling Bic.

"That's a good thing."

"No. It's not. How are you comfortable with that track record, Jake? Everyone who's ever loved me, I've left along the way when they got too heavy," Dakota says, a string of smoke snaking up her freckled face.

"If I ever become like your father or Sienna, I hope you have the strength to leave me, too." Jake says bluntly.

"That's just it, it doesn't take any strength to leave someone- it takes strength to stay."

"That type of logic proves I'm right," Jake responds.

"I'm just so confused," Dakota sighs.

Almost as though a silent alarm was sounding, Dakota suddenly stands up, bolt straight, then looks at Jake. She thinks something over, something that only passes as a whisper in her mind, then she makes her exit.

Jake has to act quickly. He takes out his wallet and looks inside it for cash to settle the bill. He only finds three crisp hundreds- the $300 he was going to send to Paul Dabney, and since he had already earmarked the money to go toward helping Dakota, he drops it on the table without a second thought.

Bursting out of the front door of the restaurant, Jake looks for the pap cameras. He sees flashing strobes near his Range Rover in valet and he hears the vampires call out his girlfriend's name. Jake sprints toward the photographers, his shoes beating the asphalt like a drum. The paps notice the aggressive approach, and when they realize it's a hulking Jake Wesley moving toward them like a freight train, they lower their cameras and walk away. They can get the rest of their shots with a distance lens.

Reaching the Range Rover, Jake yanks the car door open and finds a panicking Dakota in the passenger seat.

The moment Jake gets in the driver's seat, Dakota latches onto him and pulls herself over so that she's sitting on his lap. This is new. Dakota Dabney has never had a man to confide in; she reveals herself only in pictures. She can't show the delicate side of herself to anyone without the fear that more tears would follow because of her fragile crumble. On their first date, Jake didn't bat an eye at period-face so Dakota knows he can handle the only thing in the entire world that's worse than that... sad-girl teary-face.

72- No Laying Down, Just Standing Up.

"Fuck. Oh Fuck, Tobe," Sienna gasps.

Tobe had been waiting a very long time to hear those words.

Unfortunately, they arrived over the phone, delivered with a yelp, instead of orgasmic glee.

"Are you okay?" Tobe asks.

"No. I'm very fucking un-okay. Okay? I'm un-okay."

"Okay? Tell me what happened."

"*celebUtard* has the script," Sienna huffs out.

"The script to your new movie?"

"*Ghorbies*... or whatever those things are called. They posted about the movie."

Tobe considers this, then asks, "Like about early Oscar buzz or...?"

"How the fuck did they get the script?"

"Chloe," Tobe says quietly, realizing that he's now enlisted in the Wolfe's pack, and the links in the food chain have been reorganized. Instead of having an "in" with four deadly girls, Tobe's on the outs with them. He's confident that Sienna will protect him, if he protects her, and this keeps him from panicking. Sienna Wolfe is the one woman in Hollywood you do not go up against. Her confidence is unshakable.

"I'm fucked. I'm so fucked. I have to get back into social!heavy," Sienna hyperventilates, "They deleted me."

"Wait, Sienna, you can't-"

"-thanks for the talk, Tobe. Bye."

73- Perfect Makes Practice.

The benefit of having famous friends is that Sienna can locate them, even if they don't tell her where they're going. All it took was a little blog hopping, until one of the photo agencies uploaded pictures of social!heavy in Burbank.

After an aggressive war with LA traffic, Sienna arrives at the scene of her next battle. With her sociopathic charm, she's able to convince the security guard at the studio that the blogs, and the girls, and Martin were all lying about her no longer being in social!heavy. Sienna's famous friends are notoriously unreliable and oft-incorrectly reported about. These inaccurate stories allow her to use the excuse that she's been on a Saint-Tropez vacation and it's more believable than the true story.

Sienna travels down the familiar hallway, then throws the door open to the recording room. She imagines the moment of her grand re-entrance like the part in a movie trailer when the dopey bumbling actor does something wacky and the needle is lifted from the record, immediately stopping the awful pop song that was playing under the footage. In Sienna's mind, her actions are neither bumbling nor dopey, but instead shrewd and cunning. She also anticipates that the music she'll be interrupting will be far worse than any romcom trailer song.

Sienna stands in front of social!heavy, but for some reason, the music doesn't stop- it gets louder and it gets better, like the needle, instead of being raised, was being *sharpened* by her presence.

This is the first time that Sienna has the accidental privilege of watching the girls unite as a band. During the last practice she attended, social!heavy played to Sienna's back. This time, she's staring straight at four individuals who are so pretty that they could have stayed famous for doing nothing at all, yet they chose to find and foster their talents... and they succeeded.

In this moment, Sienna is exposed as a doubter, like the rest. She's become no different from the people she so aggressively loathes.

Sometimes, it's good that these girls are hated by the world, because it means they're doing something right. They'll inspire people to pick up a pen, or type on a keyboard, or click a button down on their camera- all with the intention of making someone who looks great, look terrible. Unintentionally, these hate filled losers confirm their own jealousy by reacting. The pretty look pretty in .jpegs; the ugly look uglier in the faceless comments at the bottom of the page. Sienna is now ready to talk about what big whores the girls are. She's prepared to type out all their secrets and e-mail them everywhere. She's ready to find old pictures and leak them to the media. But, before it comes to that, Sienna is ready to beg her way back into this band so she doesn't feel so alone.

73.5- The Baseball Hat Was a One Time Thing.

Martin looks through the glass at Sienna; as she looks through her green eyes at the girls; as they look New Wave in the mouth and literally fuck it until New Wave loves them.

Martin unlocked the studio door when he saw Sienna on the security camera. He knew that this confrontation wasn't going to end badly, but he never had any idea just how un-badly it would go.

social!heavy has never played together with this level of polished intensity before. It's not like they've ever held anything back, but today, when Sienna tried to snake into their lives, social!heavy went to a new place that no one else knew existed. They hid safely from Sienna by standing their ground and singing their victory chant in her face. They reached out to Sienna, not to lend a hand, but to wave goodbye. These girls are moving on, and their new residence is a location far more breathtaking than the view from any mansion in the Hills.

Watching the band play every song better than he did is impressive to Martin. Watching them do it in front of a girl who never believed in them, never respected them, and never thought this would happen, was absolutely invigorating.

A moment in a day, a note in a song, and now, a picture in Martin's camera.

With a flash, social!heavy ends their set, then stands in humid perfection, looking like New Wave stars. They stare out at the little girl in front of them.

"Not bad..." Sienna says, her teeth barely parting to let the words out. The girls don't say anything. They remain united, as a group, together.

"Sounded like you could use a..." Sienna mumbles out, "Um, use a... whatever the instrument was that I was supposed to play."

"Nope. I'm playing it," Kristen says.

"I could play-"

"-no. You can't," Chloe says with a slow head shake.

"I've changed my mind," Sienna yelps, her voice wavering.

"We haven't changed ours. Goodbye, Sienna," London says, her voice flat.

"I'll work harder, I promise, I'll take the band more seriously from now on," Sienna says.

"You'll take the band more seriously? What are you going to do, start a fan club?" Dakota asks.

"I don't need to, I'm in the band. I'm the..." Sienna points at Kristen's synthesizer, "...I play that," Sienna desperately tells them.

Chloe shakes her head, and informs Sienna, "You don't."

"Check our website," London says.

Sienna knew she was no longer on the site. She checked it today, and the only time she saw herself on the page was when her laptop screen reflected her image. This deletion was what caused her to hang up on Tobe. She didn't want him to hear her cry.

"I changed my mind. Come on. I can't be erased totally, I'm in the group shots that Tyler did. You can't just take me out of those shots," Sienna tells them.

"You're right, we can't," Dakota says.

"So it's settled," Sienna declares, trying to smile.

"I'm glad you see it our way," London says, smiling genuinely.

Sienna looks at the band, then slowly responds, "No, I mean it's settled that I'm back in."

"Tyler's coming tomorrow to take new pictures." London says.

Sienna's hands shake. She holds her stupid ugly thumbs up to her face, and she realizes that she'd already used up her second chance. No amount of begging, or pleading, or kidnapping could change the fact that Sienna is Sienna. Sienna will *always* be Sienna.

The girls, after screaming out their talent and dancing on graves, are now silent. It's not a worried silence, or a stumped silence. It's more of an annoyed quiet, mixed with the minor anticipation of what Sienna will do next.

Sienna remains electric, but social!heavy is wet with sweat so they don't dare touch her.

"I can't get out of the contract. I lied about that part earlier," Sienna mumbles.

The girls don't say a word.

"I didn't even talk to my agent. I mean, I pretty much *just* got the part."

The girls wait for the studio space to be cleared. Sienna won't look at them, but she can feel them. A master of presentation, Sienna's now going against every rule she lives by. She knows she has to make eye contact with the pap lenses, and with the actor she meets in the club, and with The Box because he can't smile or laugh so it's the only way Sienna can find out if he's having a good time while on vacation with her in Belize. Right now, Sienna can't look anywhere but the floor. The rest of the girls want her to look up because a picture is worth a thousand words, and they know Sienna can't handle that pile of words- she's already suffocating because of this conversation.

"Of course, I said yes to the movie role, and that complicates things... but I can fly between Vancouver and LA for practice," Sienna's lips manage to throw out.

The girls sigh in an annoyed unison.

"Or we can do an online video thingy for the rehearsal. I'll set up the xylophone in my trailer. We start shooting at like seven in the morning and none of you are even up by then so..."

As the girls begin to lose their patience, Sienna loses herself. The tear that was holding onto her fake eyelash finally makes a suicidal jump and plows through her heavy eyeliner.

"Dakota, don't do this," Sienna sniffles.

Dakota has heard this plea before, from her father. She looks at Sienna, and she feels sort of bad for her ex-accomplice. Bonnie and Clyde stayed together until the end... right before they were ambushed and killed. Dakota is tired of being ambushed. Dakota has too much to live for now.

"Don't throw me out like I'm disposable," Sienna begs.

"Stop begging, you made this choice," Dakota says, removing herself from any family she once claimed. Dakota has a new life, finally free of her father. Things are getting better; Dakota is getting better, with help from her friends. She knows what must be done. "This is goodbye for good," Dakota says.

Sienna Wolfe doesn't stay around after she's told this. She walks out of the studio, rejected, like an eliminated reality show contestant- the lowest form of celebrity.

celebUtard
"Exclusive Sienna Wolfe Interview."

This is going to sound like a lie. We know that. We freely admit that. This sounds like such a lie that we had to triple fact check just to make sure that we weren't posting anything that could get us sued (again). To our surprise and pleasure, it all checked out. Thank you, **celebUtard Sexy Intern Boy**, who had his father review the legalities of this this whole mess.

Speaking of legal action, please remember a couple months ago when we totally called that **Lindy Porter** thing. It sounds like we're lying sometimes, but we're really telling the truth.

Yesterday, at 5:14 PM PST, our editor received a call from a girl claiming to be **Sienna Wolfe**. The voice was very Sienna-esque, and the complaint about our sweet young secretary sounding "pre-tarded, like the type of retarded they could still catch early and reverse it with medication," definitely seemed like a Sienna comment, so after a quick third partying in of Sienna's agent, **Max Corby**, we were able to verify the caller's identity and get permission to record the call.

Click after the jump to listen to the audio, or continue on for the transcript. If you're at work and you need to pretend that you're working on a spreadsheet instead reading America's greatest blog, paste the interview into the spreadsheet... we formatted it real nice for you.

Without further, paranoid, "Please believe us," editorializing, here's the interview:

Sienna Wolfe: So is it recording?
celebUtard: Yeah... wait. Okay, yeah now it is.
SW: Oh no, I better not say anything that could be used against me.
cUt: We'll run a transcript so that people can read everything.
SW: Do I get to choose the picture that appears at the top of the post?
cUt: Sure, which one do you want up there?
SW: Oh! Speaking of photographs and individuals that take them, want to hear a secret?
cUt: You're going to tell us a secret?
SW: Are you as retarded as your secretary? Is there only one of you? What's with all the "us" and "we" on your sad little blog?

cUt: Originally we posted our real names at the end of the posts, but then we realized that we all have the same personality so we grouped ourselves together as "we."

SW: You should just talk this entire interview. That's what people want to read.

cUt: I can tell that you don't think so.

SW: Okay, what the fuck, aren't you a celebrity blog? I just offered you a secret and you didn't even follow up on it like a nosy prick.

cUt: Sorry (*Clears throat*). Tell me a secret or I'm ending this call.

SW: Okayyy, since you forced me- you know that mystery producer that social!heavy is working with? (*Pause*) Well, do you know him or not?

cUt: Oh, sorry, I thought that was a rhetorical setup.

SW: I think you're the one that's being rhetorical here. I'm going to hang up and call a blog that will appreciate this gold. Have fun blogging about some bullshit that a pop star's baby put in their mouth.

cUt: Sienna! No, Sienna, we do want to hear! Please, tell us who the super-producer is!

SW: Well, since you forced it out of me, social!heavy's producer is Martin Turner. The paparazzi.

cUt: So... ah. Um, just so we have this straight... a paparazzi is producing the biggest album of the year?

SW: No, he's not working on the Brit-Brit album, he's working on the social!heavy album.

cUt: I guess I'm just having a little trouble believing that the record company and agents involved would allow this to happen.

SW: They're behind the idea.

cUt: London's agent is Joel Harper. He used to be a rock star, obviously he knows producers...

SW: He's probably more worried about his impotence than he is about making this a good album.

cUt: Ew. Uh. So how does the music sound?

SW: Not good.

cUt: Can the girls play their instruments?

SW: One of London's favorite videos on the internet, that she doesn't star in, features a cat playing the piano. I liken it to the cat video.

cUt: That video is so cute!

SW: ...

cUt: So. How many songs do they have?

SW: Like nine.

cUt: Will there be any more songs on the album?

SW: Yeah, but, like, who buys albums? Okay, gotta go. Bye.

cUt: Wait. What about Chloe's mom?

SW: Chloe's mom?

cUt: Yeah, you mentioned her before and said that you had some information about why she's in hiding. Was it a facelift gone bad?

SW: (Purrs with... pleasure?) Look at you, acting like a real blog. About time. So, Chloe's mom. Well. She. Okay, this is a scoop and a half. Are you ready?

cUt: Yup.

SW: You're sure you're ready?

cUt: Sienna, please!

SW: Okay. Well, since you twisted my arm. You know how Chloe's mom hasn't been seen in like forever and a month?

cUt: She's been missing for while.

SW: That'll happen when you have a secret baby that you adopted.

cUt: Are you saying that Chloe Warren has a secret sibling?

SW: Sorry dear, I already stayed on past my time limit, and I just ran like forty red lights so I have to go and check my grill for pedestrians.

Sienna Wolfe hangs up

So there you have it, the queen of backstabbing, Sienna Wolfe, tells us that the biggest album of the year has been placed in the hands of an overweight **XV3** photographer, and **Linda Warren** has a secret child.

Yay, us! Best blog ever! Getting scoops and rubbing elbows with girls who have sharp elbows. More to come later in the week!

Until next time, stay tardy, celebUverse.

74- Child-like Mentality.

Scarlett Porter stands at the door of her best friend's home. In the crook of her right arm is a bottle of 2005 Château Palmer, and two wine glasses are wedged between the fingers of her left hand.

A new maid, who introduced herself as "Patricia," had greeted Mrs. Porter and asked her to wait outside. The antique mission door was left slightly ajar, and from where she stands, Scarlett can hear, but not see, the conversation playing out deeper inside the house.

"Scarlett Porter? She's at the door?" a fragile, but familiar voice asks.

"Si. En la puerta," Patricia responds, seemingly unsure if this visitor should be shooed away like all the rest.

For a moment, there's only silence, and Scarlett briefly considers inviting herself inside, but immediately thinks better of it. She waits, because no one else would. In a way, Scarlett had gotten used to waiting for this invitation.

Eventually, this patience pays off and the door creaks open, revealing Linda Warren- a much older, slightly puffy, slightly gray, slightly artificial looking version of Chloe Warren.

Scarlett smiles, then lifts the bottle of wine, suggesting, "Palmer?"

"Come inside. Come inside," Linda says warmly.

Scarlett enters the house, then makes her way toward Linda's slightly tribal living room where they usually have their drinks. It was good to be back in a home that had become mysterious in the recent months. Scarlett surveys her surroundings and notices that all the African masks Linda used to have hanging are now missing.

Seating herself on the sofa, Scarlett reclines comfortably, and says, "I knew it."

"Knew what?" Linda asks, avoiding eye contact.

"You can close the door on me, but Ms. Palmer is another story. If you saw this bottle, then turned me away, I was going to get the LAPD to come here and take you away on a 5150."

"Oh, please. You're always welcome here. But the Palmer is a nice touch... and the glasses?"

"I thought you might need them."

"Scarlett, I'm not a savage, I have stemware."

"I know, but remember that time I didn't see you for a month because you were convinced they were going to elect that sad looking Democrat and you smashed everything breakable in your kitchen? I wasn't sure if we were seeing a repeat."

"That was a one-time thing, all of my glasses were..." Linda's voice fades as she moves to another part of the house- hopefully only temporarily.

Scarlett has to make a decision- stay and wait for Linda to come back with the decanter, or get off the sofa and make a direct sprint for the back door to thwart a possible escape attempt. Just as Linda begins adjusting the buckles on her Bettye Mullers, she hears footsteps heading in her direction.

Patricia walks into the room with a small decanter and a corkscrew. Scarlett refuses to doubt her friend any longer. She removes her shoes; Linda will return. Patricia takes the wine bottle and removes the cork with ease. The new maid already seems to have lots of experience with opening wine bottles.

As the red wine glops into the decanter, Scarlett fully abandons her chase idea. She's in a tranquil living room, relaxing with a bottle of Palmer, as some lullaby-like music plays from another room in the house. She understands how Linda could stay here instead of heading to a crowded, stuffy restaurant. It's relaxing, like opening the cover of a *Vogue* magazine, then sitting inside one of the ornate editorials. Since she has the time, Scarlett takes note of everything. The dark mahogany, the sleek fireplace, those old cranberry curtains- it was a home that she hadn't visited in a while, but occasionally mentally retreated to.

"What are you most proud of?" Linda asks, reentering the room, startling Scarlett so much that she jumps up from a relaxed slump to perfect posture.

The soft lullaby music is the only sound in the house for a cold moment.

"My marriage," Scarlett responds to the possibly empty room. "I'm most proud of my marriage," Scarlett says, a little louder, this time with conviction. Her decisiveness allows her to slouch back on the sofa, her feet turning away from the floor. The ease of the moment crackles when she hears the smile in Linda's understanding voice, "As you should be."

There's a peacefulness in the room; The type of delicious vanilla that can only be achieved in perfect surroundings, with the people who have been around since back when the surroundings were less than perfection.

Scarlett looks to her friend and her smile freezes as Linda sits down.

Cradled in Linda's right arm is a small, blanketed bundle. "He's my son," Linda says, sensing Scarlett's look. "I adopted him. Charlie helped. Every step of the way."

Scarlett had heard about Sienna Wolfe's revelation, but she was never one to throw meat to the wolves.

"The whole trip brought me closer to Charlie and s-s-s," Linda says, making a bizarre hissing noise instead of finishing the statement.

Scarlett wants to say that this will not repair Linda's marriage, but she remains silent.

The evening begins to bend and warp. Suddenly needing the Palmer in the decanter, Scarlett leans over and pours a glass. She places the glass in Linda's free hand, but not without hesitation. Once her friend takes the Palmer, Scarlett pours a glass for herself.

Linda Warren feels an unexpected ease as she sips her favorite wine, while she sits with her favorite friend, and holds her new reason to smile.

Scarlett wants to say a baby is not a glass of Palmer. It's not something that you can reach for, while ignoring the rest of your problems, but she remains silent.

"Charlie and I decided on a name, Shane. Shane Warren," Linda says.

Scarlett wants to say that embracing a last name that you share with your distant husband will not perpetuate the illusion of life in a fairy tale, but she remains silent.

"You have your marriage. You have that person by your side every night... for a while, I had that with Charlie, but then he got so successful, so busy. He's always traveling... he has his own schedule. There's only so many times I can remodel this place before everything is as it should be. Then, what's left?"

Scarlett doesn't want to answer this question; she wants to ask when this trip with Charlie took place.

Linda, both distant and present, says, "I sat down and I thought about what I'd like to change about my life, and I decided that I could no longer live alone. I don't have a job. Charlie is always away on business or in late meetings, and I'm just... here."

"You have us," Scarlett says, "You have Chloe."

Linda passes by this comment, "Then when Charlie and I went on that trip, we saw Shane and things finally made sense. Life became exciting, and real, and..." Linda loses her words, yet tries to continue, "So Charlie and I made an agreement. We have a verbal contract that's clear about everything; me, him, our marriage, his properties, his money. We were careful, and quiet, and together we decided we'd adopt Shane. It's been good. It's been very good for me. It wasn't as much of a fight as I thought it would be. Now I have him, and he's going to be here for at least for another 16 years. And that's more than... well... after that, I'll be able to feel together, and important, and necessary, and permanent again. We'll all be able to sit at the table, and we'll look like one of the families you see in commercials. We'll be a *family*, not just people in the same place. That's why I'm going to keep Shane from the vultures as long as I can. I've avoided our dinners as an investment toward my dream dinners in the future. Someday, they'll catch me out on a walk, and they'll put the pieces together. The story will break, then I'll be back."

There are a million things that Scarlett wants to say to Linda, but after speaking with her friend, the only appropriate thing to say is, "Thank you for letting me in."

celebUtard
"Pap-roducer?"

Sienna Wolfe used us like we were **Tobe Price** and we have to admit, we kinda liked it.

As soon as the "lone Wolfe" hung up on us, we broke her story.

After the post went live and we were deemed champions of the internet blogosphere, we called **Joel Harper**, **London Francis**' agent and **social! heavy** mastermind. Point blank, we asked if **XV3** photog, **Martin Turner**, is social!heavy's producer. Joel asked us who we heard that from, and we said that Sienna Wolfe had told us during a very exclusive interview which he could read on our blog.

Joel confirmed the information provided to us by Sienna. He was just like, "Oh, yeah," and not like, "Nooo, why God! I'm ruined!" The whole thing felt anticlimactic. Joel also mentioned that some of the songs are co-written by the doorman at **F-Clipse**, and the backup vocals for the live show will be performed by **Walt Dornstein** from **CTV**. Then Joel asked if we wanted to be the lighting tech for the stage show. Needless to say, we felt a little silly by the end of the conversation.

I mean... there you have it folks, the first ever social!heavy album is produced by... **The City of Los Angeles**? What a genius marketing scheme, having the "little people" work right alongside the big names, but the question is, why is Sienna going along with it?

Was the second ousting of Sienna all a plot to take the social!heavy buzz from bumblebee to African killer bee status?

One thing's for sure, Joel was a musical prodigy, but he's even more of a genius when it comes to his work with these socialites... these rock stars?

So tell us, **LA**, are you excited for *our* concert this week?

Now if you'll excuse us, we have to go read up on submasters and lighting rigs.

Until next time, stay tardy, celebUverse.

74.5- Friends With Secrets.

Scarlett Porter stands with the half consumed bottle of Palmer cradled in her arm like a baby. No matter how many knocks she may echo on Linda Warren's door, no matter how long she stands on Linda Warren's porch, the friend that she has known for so long will never again answer the door. Scarlett is sure of this.

As she sits down on the stairs, alone, tears brim in Scarlett's eyes. She reflects on the fact that her best friend doesn't have a secret baby or even a devastating flesh eating virus- she's merely started a new life, one of her own creation. A life all to herself.

Two months before Linda's mother's funeral, Scarlett was informed of a genetic downfall that plagues Linda's family. Linda explained that someday she'd be unable to deal with the fast pace Scarlett was so used to. Linda mentioned that when she started to get saggy jowls, she decided to get them fixed. It was effort and pain to correct her imperfection, all the while knowing, in the end, her friends would gossip about the fact she went under the knife. They would make sure that everyone knew her more youthful appearance wasn't good genes, it was the work of a surgeon who has more clients on TV right now than WME. Linda Warren does not have good genes; this is the problem.

Scarlett couldn't deny that they gossiped about Linda behind her back. This resulted in an out of control cycle where Linda got the facelift to stay in the good graces of these judgmental witches, yet she still found herself being sniggered at when they thought she wasn't looking. Linda knew they all had work done too, but somehow that didn't make the cattiness any less painful. This was a tiring life for an old woman to lead. It can be exhausting working every day, trying to keep up with how to look, how to act, how to dress; eventually, it becomes too much. Linda is getting older and falling apart, she doesn't need to be ripped apart too.

There are facts that now cannot be disputed.

Linda Warren was shut out by her daughter.

Linda Warren was ridiculed behind her back for her sagging face and desperate surgery.

Linda Warren was sneered at by mistresses who had splintered her marriage beyond repair.

Linda Warren has early stage dementia.

Scarlett should have known Linda's retreat would eventually happen. It was only logical that, someday, Linda would feel like life was getting too out of control, and her only option would be to scale back, close the doors, and simply disappear. If she couldn't deal with all these aggressive societal pressures when her mind remembered the words necessary to defend herself, she certainly wouldn't be able to handle the passive aggression now.

Chloe cannot count on her mother to save her from the illness that is destroying her because her mother's illness has already vanished any trace of Chloe.

It was easier for Scarlett to believe the blog reports that Linda was hiding a secret child. The thought that Linda didn't call because she was embarrassed about her condition was infinitely more impossible to deal with. Scarlett heard from a friend that Linda had been going to the doctor for some non-cosmetic reasons, but it was impossible for ageless Mrs. Porter to cope with the fact that her best friend was slipping away from reality.

Linda's face looked younger because of the work, but her mind is 62 years old. After taking all of this into consideration, Linda Warren did what any truly powerful woman would do in a position of frailty- she set up a new life, in the home that she'd spent her entire past life building. The delusion of this child was just the beginning. It would get worse as Linda continued to fade.

Scarlett Porter didn't lose her best friend, little by little, day by day. Linda simply picked a day, and, without a goodbye or a warning, she stepped away.

Scarlett fears she will always feel as alone as she does at this moment.

Linda Warren was the only person who could make Scarlett look forward to those dinners. She was the only person would could understand how hard it was to raise a celebrity instead of a daughter. She was the only woman with a mansion that felt like home.

Scarlett Porter leaves the remainder of the Palmer on the steps. If Linda wants someone to drink it with, Scarlett will gladly return and help finish off the bottle.

As Scarlett walks back to her car, a cold thought strikes her. The woman that answered the door isn't the new maid, she's a live-in nurse.

75- Hungry Like The Wolfe.

"Outside seating."

That was the only request Sienna made when Tobe re-asked her out.

Sienna needs to be photographed today. She knows that if she steps out with Tobe, the pictures will show up in every magazine that lines the "Entertainment" section of the two bookstores left in America. Tobe doesn't give a shit why she wants these photos because, no matter what, it will be good for his shoebox.

"social!skeevy," the headline could read above the pictures. "Perfect People Plotting," also sort of works, but Tobe can't think of a fourth P-word to really make it pop.

The caption doesn't matter, it will be cropped out regardless. Finally, Tobe will no longer have to stack pictures of Sienna and himself atop of each other. After today, when Tobe extracts his shoebox selections, he'll be standing next to Sienna in a single, seamless picture.

This new relationship is more than a crush. It's more than a hobby. It's more than an obsession. It's a responsibility.

If Tobe can't make this work with Sienna, if he can't hold onto her, he'll have to go back to the shoebox. If he loses Sienna Wolfe, he'll have ruined not only his fantasy, but also the only relationship he's ever had with a partner that he finds genuinely interesting.

Sienna Wolfe is Tobe's social!heavy.

It's almost time for Tobe to realize his dream, so he prepares.

He does sit-ups.

He showers.

He grooms.

He dresses.

He drinks some scotch.

He calls the paps.

He drives to CARGO.

After all of these essential steps are completed to Tobe's satisfaction, he steps out of his R8, tosses his keys to a guy who he hopes is the valet, then he takes his Ray-Bans off to behold Sienna Wolfe in all three dimension.

On time, for once, Sienna steps out of her car, and she doesn't give her keys to anyone. The wounded Wolfe is hoarding everyone's attention, her low cut black Michael Lorrie tank top and the tiniest pair of Isabel Marant shorts pull all eyes in her direction. She approaches Tobe, and the cameras capture it all.

Tobe hugs Sienna and this unity becomes engrossing. Realizing he's wrapped around her too forcefully, for too long, Tobe loosens his hold, but

Sienna stays pressed tightly to him- almost as though he's the only thing anchoring her to the earth. Sienna Wolfe is notoriously unaffected by gravity. She has no frown lines and her boobs are perkier than a cheerleader drinking a frap, but today it seems like there's a force pulling on her. Or maybe she's just holding the pose for a photo op.

Releasing Tobe from the most necessary grasp of his entire life, Sienna takes his hand and pulls him into the restaurant.

Tobe picked CARGO because he saw some very HQ paparazzi photos of Dakota and Jake in the outside seating area a while back. This means, with the right table, the paps will find their angle and the pictures will number in the hundreds, possibly thousands, considering how good Tobe is feeling about his hair today.

As the "it" couple walks through the restaurant, dozens of camera phone shutter clicks go off, and Tobe has to resist the urge to double back and hand out his personal e-mail address to everyone so he doesn't miss a single snap of his date with Sienna Wolfe.

Out on the patio, Sienna finds a square two person table that gives the paparazzi a clean shot through the gate, and she takes note of this vulnerability. "Ugh, between the real paps and the charity paps that London takes in, I feel like these men are the fathers I never had," she says, referencing the impending swarm. The two identical tables behind Tobe are unattended placed at an angle that would allow for privacy. The fact Sienna chose the most visible table should bother Tobe, but given a hundred chances to choose another table, he'd always select the same chair.

The first paparazzi appears at the gate- a guy that Tobe remembers bumming a condom off of a couple months ago- and he commences snapping pictures. A tapeworm as an appetizer.

Attracted by sound of the flapping wings of a secret vampire bat, more paparazzi rush to the gate and begin to jockey for position.

The strobe slows after only a minute when the photogs begin to feel they've got their coverage of Sienna stealing London's boyfriend. If London hadn't bounced back so fast, these pictures of Sienna and Tobe might be worth more.

Tobe sees Sienna's smile drop for split second, and it's such a telling slip that when the paps catch it, their flashes get a second wind.

Rewinding a collapse that had already done permanent damage, Sienna goes back her standard issue fake-smiling and the paps back off again.

"Are you okay?" Tobe asks, seeing his chance to finally get inside her head, or even better, back into her embrace. He made sure that he didn't wear a gray t-shirt so Sienna could freely cry on his shoulder and the evidence would be undetectable. He was also afraid that he would visibly sweat through the shirt.

"They kicked me out," Sienna says, angling her face away from the cameras. She looks to her right, at a young surfer with his dad as they tolerate a silent meal together.

"I thought you quit?"

"I did, then, right after, they kicked me out of the band."

Tobe clears his throat, hoping that Sienna will look back at him. She doesn't, so he talks to the side of her face, "Well... then, good, you left them. They didn't leave you."

"It's the last word, stupid," Sienna says. Tobe and Sienna's eyes meet and Sienna knows her *I'm going to make you feel like douche* look is so effective that it'll overpower any sign of moisture in her eyes. "That's the only way to win arguments- getting the last word in, as long as it's something coherent and not something idiotic like, 'Rehab actually works,' then you win in our world."

There's a quick beat where both Tobe and Sienna look over to a passing waiter, and demand, "Could I have a gin martini?"

Their eyes meet again. It's one of those moments that requires a relaxed giggle. It was texting a best friend at the exact same time they hit *Send* on their unintentional response. It was an odd little coincidence that seemed like it should stand for something significant, but in reality, both Tobe and Sienna are just functioning alcoholics who feel less than functional at this particular moment.

Sienna's giggle fades and her pout makes its first full appearance after a quick tease earlier. "This whole band thing sucks... for a different reason now. I'll be remembered as the one who left before they made it, like that guy who left The Beatles."

"The difference is, you're already internationally famous," Tobe says, proud of her for this fact.

"Yeah, but I'll be the internationally famous person who dropped out of one of the most successful bands in the world. I'll be John Lennon."

"John Lennon was killed."

"Right, he might as well have been, once you leave a band like that, you're nothing."

"No. You don't understand. John Lennon was assassinated."

"I have been too," Sienna realizes, "They assassinated my image and there's nothing I can do to bring it back to life."

The waiter returns with the drinks, and Sienna begins downing the carefully prepared martini like her throat was on fire and the gin was the only thing that could put it out.

"Your image is fine," Tobe says with a bit of a smile as he watches the flashes capture Sienna's binge.

"I want all the attention," Sienna causally declares, then puts her empty glass down and politely dabs the corner of her lips with a napkin.

"That's impossible."

"Of course it is, now that I left the female version of The Beatles," Sienna laments.

"Trust me, they aren't the female Beatles."

"I know, their music is more dance-able and they have better haircuts," Sienna mopes.

Sienna Wolfe would've been fine with being kicked out of a shitty band like The Beatles, but she was kicked out of social!heavy- the coolest, sluttiest, most kick ass band on earth.

76- Checking Your Reflection in a Wave.

As a photographer for XV3, Martin's job is to go beyond the movie character, or the toothpaste commercial, or the online profiles set up by people whose responsibility it is to make their clients appear like upstanding citizens who live life with robot-like perfection. Martin is tasked with sneaking around the carefully planned lies, then capturing who these celebrities really are. As he performed this task and photographed a particular socialite circle, it became clear to him that Chloe, Dakota, London, and Kristen all yearned to break down the wall that slices between who they *are* and who America *thinks they are*. Sienna Wolfe has achieved this goal, to some degree, but she's headed in the wrong direction. She's lost her head and she's now morphing into her fame template. After she confided in the blogs like they were friends, the girls knew Sienna was doomed. Martin is now sure that London was absolutely right that one afternoon walking back from the pet store when he tailed her like a lost puppy. Martin didn't- and still doesn't- want these girls to fall apart, unless they prove to be four enemies that can't exist as one.

Witnessing these socialites become women, as their hard work is displayed in every note, ranks as one of the purest feelings Martin has ever enjoyed.

He watches the young band play their final rehearsal before their premiere concert.

London's right hand fiddles with the drum machine, while she hammers her kit with the drumstick in her left hand. Dakota spins with wild precision toward Chloe, who has one foot on a speaker, a speaker just high enough that you can see her underwear, unless you're standing where Kristen is, behind the synthesizer, next to the keyboard. Kristen's blonde hair bobs forward and back- moving fluidly with *their song*.

Martin looks away from this scene and surveys the seats of the massive Staples Center.

This was 60 seconds in LA.

One minute.

77- Stage Play and Screenplays.

"How was I?" Chloe asks, bopping up and down in the dressing room.

Obviously interested in the couple by her side, a blonde girl covered in tattoos sets out multicolored palettes of makeup in front of a well-lit mirror and tries to look busy so her eavesdropping isn't too obvious.

"It was. Absolutely. By far. New Wave," Stanley says, pulling Chloe close by her thin waist, then gently kissing her.

"It's believable?" Chloe asks, her wide set eyes studying every nuance of Stanley's reaction.

"It's fantastic. People are going to be blown away by your talent," Stanley says.

"I hope," Chloe responds, sliding her skinny ass into the makeup chair.

Stanley reaches into the man-bag slung over his shoulder and he pulls out a familiar looking envelope.

"Ohhh, you want to role play while I get my makeup done?" Chloe asks, assuming he brought the *Ghorbies* script.

Stanley, with a devious smile, says, "Maybe we could call Julie herself, Sienna Wolfe," then he hands the envelope to Chloe.

Those distinct doe eyes glance down at the unexpected present. Chloe looks up and smiles in the mirror as the makeup artist begins her work.

"Can I?" Chloe asks Stanley, looking at him through the mirror. Stanley nods his big forehead in approval.

Carefully, Chloe opens the envelope, then slides out a stack of paper that's tied with in a string of twine to keep all the pages pressed together, in order.

"Consider this me climbing in your window," the first page reads.

"Is this what you've been up to on that damn computer?" Chloe asks. She doesn't know what the sentence on the cover page means, but she has a feeling that the hundred and thirty pages under it might provide her some insight.

Stanley confirms his project with an almost shy nod. It was such a Tristan move. He must have done that exact motion a thousand times during the show. "Read it and tell me what you think," he says, then gives Chloe a kiss on the top of her head before walking out of the dressing room.

Untying the twine around the pages, then flipping the cover to the back of the stack, Chloe finds herself staring down at a screenplay. The last time she held a script, it contained the answer to her problems. Chloe hopes this screenplay is no different, yet completely different at the same time.

"Can I read while you do your makeup tests?" Chloe asks, and the tattooed girl says, "Absolutely," not caring that it will make her job harder. She's as curious as Chloe is about this mystery script. The tattooed girl has always wanted to do makeup on a movie set. She also used to secretly watch *Tristan's Landing* in her room while she did her homework every Wednesday, but she'd never admit that to anyone.

Chloe finally has Stanley's project. She finally has a glimpse into the mind of a man she still feels a fan-like curiosity about.

When the curiosity surpasses Chloe's fear, she begins reading:

```
EXT. WOODS. NIGHT.

Six FRIENDS sit around a fire, in the woods. The faint
sound of CARS can be heard. We're witnessing a little
suburban camping during a road trip to a music festival.
This is not real camping. This is not a test of survival.
Yet.
```

Chloe is already shocked. The woods? Why would Stanley, a guy who's been trapped in the woods for the past five films, finally get free, then head right back into the forest? Why is he tunneling back into his jail cell?

Maybe he was inspired by the second chances that were thrown around so frequently these past few months? Maybe he thought there was something brave about confronting his fears in these woods?

Chloe reads on. The characters are quickly established in the opening scene. They're indulged adolescents, making inane conversation. One of the girls makes a joke at another girl's expense. Chloe doesn't laugh, not because the joke isn't funny, but because she remembers when a similar comment was made to Dakota. It was met with a drink to the face. Stanley defused the situation that night. Chloe thinks back on the incident, and tries to remember if Stanley rushed home so he could write the quote down on his laptop. No, he stayed and protected the girls. He always protects the girls. Or he tells himself that he's protecting the girls to make his silence okay.

The characters start making fun of the festival they're going to. Chloe notices that a lot of them are using "Dad," when describing members of the bands that are scheduled to play. Stanley must be using Joel's band, Luana, as inspiration. One, or perhaps many, of these characters are supposed to be Joel's poor talentless bastard children. Chloe appreciates this inside joke because what's Joel going to do, sue Stanley?

Chloe goes back to reading Stanley's gift to her, and it gets dark.

The story enters a territory that Stanley despises, or so Chloe thought.

The female characters start to get scared by the noises in the woods that seem to be closing in on them.

The male characters start working up the girls.

Everything shifts in the scene when a man in a black outfit, wearing a mask with a red X on it, is introduced.

He addresses the panicked boys and screaming girls:

```
          MAN IN THE MASK
     You have been chosen.
```

When it's clear the kids in the woods don't want to be chosen, an assurance is made.

```
          MAN IN THE MASK
     Your lives will gain meaning...
     after I'm finished with you.
```

The group ineffectively tries to protect themselves. Suddenly a female character is rushed, grabbed by her hair, and a knife is plunged into her neck.

Chloe closes the script.

This was not in her script of how this read-through would go.

Chloe becomes paranoid. Is this a silent scream crafted out the anger Stanley felt having to listen to Chloe and her friends prattle on with inane conversations about their easily triumphed troubles? Is this why Stanley stayed home so much now? Did he loath Chloe and every person in her life?

After completing a makeup look, the tattooed girl takes a step back and asks, "What do you think?"

Chloe's glance in the mirror for the shortest possible second, then her eyes lower back to the page. "Nice," she tells the makeup artist.

With this alien eyed face as a canvas, the tattooed girl embraces the opportunity to experiment and begins to talk about different makeup options.

Chloe is as agreeable as possible. She has to know if it's Stanley behind the mask. A new look is started, and she finds where she left off, then continues reading.

The characters escape, except that one girl... the victim.

Maybe this was Stanley's escape from the woods?

Or maybe the murder was the extinction of Stanley's big titted, inarticulate co-star?

The next scene takes place in a police station. It split screens between characters in a way that will be thrilling. Stanley explains in a single line of action that this scene will be almost "musical" in the way two instruments-exposition and brutal action- play at the same time, working together, like the layers in a song.

The scenes that run tandem with the police questioning follow the various characters who have already given their statements. The drum beat exposition plays steadily, while the dynamic electric guitar of these scared characters trying to process what happened keeps things moving. One of the witnesses- a guy this time- becomes the next victim. He's murdered while taking a ticket off the windshield of his car. The ticket falls to the ground and the audience is shown what he's cited for, "Being Useless."

In the scene that follows, a TV report reveals that the killer left behind a message on the back of the ticket.

```
              NEWSCASTER
      A note found near the victim
      reads, "I am The TXP and I
      have a gift. I am the new
      guardian of American society.
      Bring me your hungover, your
      pompous, your entitled masses;
      and I will destroy them all.
      Too long these oxygen thieving
      parasites have fed on our
      society. No more."
```

Then a twist– the male victim, the son of a very famous rock musician, is shown to be a DNA match for an unsolved sexual assault.

This is where the story explodes. The public turn The TXP into a vigilante hero who brought to justice a pervert that the cops couldn't touch. They look at The TXP as the one person who recognized the fact that these privileged kids can pay their way out of trouble, then just walk away. They celebrate that he decided to bring turmoil to America's rich and pointless just as aggressively as they wiggled out of each mess. These spoiled brats will not escape this time; this punishment cannot be avoided by cutting check. The public turns The TXP into the same type of pop culture celebrity he actively rebels against.

An obsessed cop (to be played by Stanley?) eventually tracks down The TXP at the end of the second act. The capture is the result of a sting operation involving one of the kids from the campfire. It goes perfectly. The cop takes The TXP into custody, but with the villain handcuffed in a cell and his "costume" placed in an evidence locker, a man in a black mask breaks into the penthouse floor of The Olivian, a luxury condo complex that's also the set for a popular reality TV show. After he carves one of the stars of the show up, he carves the message "Abandon All Hope Ye Who Are Entertained Here" on the headboard of her death bed. Since this is a reality TV set, there are cameras placed in multiple corners to capture everything that happens in the house for the audience's enjoyment. When the cops check the footage, it's all static. These crimes were not carried out for fame, they were executed to lay waste to the waste of life D-listers who waste America's time with their mindless toxic waste TV shows. Chloe wonders if the audience will realize they're disappointed to find the footage shows only static.

There are still 35 pages of script left to read.

Mock ups are left for Chloe, and the makeup artist packs up, then leaves. Chloe mumbles a goodbye, while her phone jitters, then goes unanswered. Someone she's never met comes in the room and asks for something. Not paying attention, Chloe autographs one of the makeup mock ups and gives it to the person so they'll leave.

Chloe must finish the script. It follows many of the normal slasher conventions, but she's drawn to two characters, Ellen and Bruce, who were present at the campfire. As the screenplay progresses, Ellen becomes weaker and more obsessed with the fact that she's a target. She's frail and paranoid, delusional and damaged. She's... familiar.

Chloe continues reading, stepping into a scene where Bruce is turned away by Ellen's sister, banned from their house. Bruce's "hard partying" is blamed for dragging Ellen into this mess. Chloe becomes invested in the characters as Bruce sneaks into the house at night because Ellen can't bear to sleep without him. He leaves every morning, just before breakfast.

The TXP continues his crusade. Multiple famous victims show up. Too many.

The determined cop repeatedly captures suspects who are dressed like The TXP. Some of the suspects are women. The sense of doom builds, and Ellen becomes a prisoner in her own home. Her sister will not let her leave.

A character from the campfire experiences another trial by fire.

INT. CAR TRUNK. NIGHT.
C.U. of SCRATCHES on the inside of the trunk from where a
panicking TROY tries to claw his way out. Suddenly, SMOKE
appears in the trunk, then FLAMES follow.

EXT. CITY STREET. NIGHT.
PAN OUT FROM TRUNK: We see that the car is actually
moving. It's being driven by a figure in that now
familiar mask.

```
THE TXP bails out of the driver's seat, right before the
flaming ball of metal crashes into THE HEDERA, a popular
LA restaurant.


EXT. ACCIDENT SCENE. NIGHT.
A FIREMAN sprays out the last of the flames on the car.
The FIREFIGHTERS stare in disbelief at the side of the
charred wreckage where deep SCRATCHES read, "You were
worried about my hood, then you burnt in the trunk."
```

Chloe has kept track of the body count and she realizes that Bruce and Ellen are the only survivors of the original campfire crew.

Two pages later, Chloe wipes her eyes when Bruce goes searching on Ellen's sister's computer and finds "recipes" that can be prepared to poison someone. Ellen's mental and physical collapse was brought on by her own bitter sibling. Ellen is famous, while her sister is not. Ellen is innocent, her sister is not. Ellen had no idea about the poisoning, and when Bruce tells her about it, she acts like maybe she deserves this punishment. Bruce makes a decision and that night, he climbs in Ellen's window, like he's The TXP, and he pulls Ellen out of the toxic environment.

By the end of the film, it's revealed that many of the characters in the background of earlier scenes also carried out the awful crimes the film profiled. The TXP is not one deranged man, but instead a culture of killers in masks, anonymously judging and condemning with no concern for the facts. The TXP found refuge under a warm, protective hood, and anyone could hide behind that hood, for any reason they wanted.

In the final scene, Bruce and Ellen begin their new life together.

It ends with them preparing themselves for a TXP assault, whoever it's led by.

It ends with them hosting a party.

It ends with a culture of fear being ignored, not because it's too complicated to confront, but because the terror began to poison everything.

Chloe looks down at the final lines of dialog on the final page.

```
INT. CLUB. NIGHT.
The music stops and a CROWD forms around the two
survivors.
BRUCE raises his glass to his friends, ELLEN is under his
arm.
```

```
                    BRUCE
There are a lot of people
who think we don't deserve
to be here... but they're
not here and we are. I
can tell you, I don't
think I'd rather be
anywhere else, with anyone
else. So thank you, not
just for being here now,
but for being there in
the past. For helping us
out. For paying attention-
not to pick us apart, but
to pick us up when we
fell. Everything that goes
on in our life is
documented- the good and
the bad- so we hired some
paparazzi to be here
tonight because what
you've done for us is
good, and we want to
share it. So if you see
a camera tonight- hug a
friend, kiss someone you
love... a smile isn't
enough. If they want to
watch, show them love.
Always show them love.
```

Chloe puts down the screenplay. A screenplay to a horror movie. A really beautiful horror movie.

This script is a result of social!heavy.

It's a companion piece to Chloe's life these past few months. At Lindy's divorce gala, Tobe Price wasn't sure if he was speaking with Chloe or her sister. While reading the screenplay, Chloe realized that she was given two roles. She was Ellen, and she was Ellen's sister. In the end, Ellen survives. She survives and she celebrates, with the boy who saved her still by her side. Chloe decides she will only be Ellen from now on. Sienna is wrong. Chloe has no siblings. Chloe is an only child.

Rejecting reality-TV reality, Chloe now craves the complete truth.

Looking back, the truth is that Stanley and Chloe were unhappy with their perfect lives. Then they changed, and so did their outlook.

Stanley slowly realized he doesn't hate horror movies. He hates shitty movies. Completing this screenplay was about taking risks. It was about believing that everyone has the untapped potential to save others, and to escape. A hopeless situation, with a little tweaking and a lot of hard work, can be turned into a dream. The project was about Stanley's frustration over watching his friends receive the worst side effect of creation- criticism- without snagging any of the good parts. It was about making something out of nothing and not being afraid to feel proud of that accomplishment.

Chloe, one day, said, "I'm the lead singer of a band." She lived with that idea in the back of her head, and now she controls the same microphone she once feared. Tomorrow, she'll be singing to a sold out arena.

Stanley, one day, said, "I'm a writer," and he lived with that idea in his lap, and now he has his screenplay in the hands of an in demand actress.

All this time, Stanley and Chloe were both busy on opposite sides of the house, creating a new world, a world they now share.

Instead of Stanley signing on to star in someone else's dream, he created his own, then he signed it, "I love you, Chloe Warren."

This was the first time in years that Chloe had read anything in its entirety that didn't end with a joke or a vicious string of comments about one of her friends. Stanley took a risk showing his amateur screenplay to a girl with a notoriously short attention span, but Chloe was the one he wanted to give this gift to, even if it turns out he isn't gifted himself.

Chloe's eyes pool again as she thinks about Stanley's quiet dedication. Her boyfriend stayed at home, and he didn't go out with her to Lindy's divorce gala or Diego's premiere bash, not because he felt Chloe's life was *trivial*, but because he was intent on proving to everyone else that it wasn't. He knew Chloe so well that he found a way for her to start getting better by herself, without forcing her. Stanley is the one person that cared enough to find a way to inspire a change in Chloe's habits. He was there, every night, in bed next to his sick girl, and even as Chloe's body began to give up, Stanley did not. He patiently monitored her, and he knew that he should tell Chloe that what she's doing is wrong, but there were a million blogs already doing that. He had to take his time and go beyond a simple intervention to get through to her.

The physical deterioration of Chloe was what everyone focused on, but not Stanley. He knew better than to put so much faith in a bunch of troubling pictures. Chloe has a mental disorder and Stanley had to attack this disorder by detailing how deadly it is, how unfair it is, and how, despite the hopelessness surrounding everything, a happy ending *is* possible. It will take work, and companionship, and support, and friends, and family, and time, and a lot of irrational decisions, but Stanley has never given up hope and that becomes fuel for Chloe to remain hopeful as well. This is not a cure, but it is Stanley stepping in to help become an antidote to the poison that is coursing through his fragile girlfriend.

Chloe gets up from her chair and looks in the mirror; the makeup that had been carefully applied an hour ago is now sliding down her face. Everything finally makes sense.

It's perfect, all of it, even her makeup at this very moment. This is how she'll ask for it to be done tomorrow. social!heavy will finally show Los Angeles who Chloe Warren, Dakota Dabney, Kristen Paxton, and London Francis really are. There's a chance that people will fill the arena tomorrow just to see a car crash- to see the girls fail- to see the girls cry. social!heavy is still very much about the crowd pleasing mentality, so they'll give the vultures the pleasure of seeing them cry the moment the concert starts. They won't play it off as camp. social!heavy will pretend to be having a meltdown in front of everyone, then, slowly, they will find their instruments and they'll put together a show.

Leaving her makeup streaked and affected, Chloe travels through the behind-the-scenes corridors until she finds her boyfriend. With force, Chloe wraps her arms around Stanley and whispers, only to him, "Let's go to dinner."

As one screenplay destroys a life, another screenplay saves a girl in peril. Welcome to Hollywood.

78- The Truth.

London puts her fresh extensions back in a ponytail so she can redo the makeup that had just been completed by the tattooed girl. Looking at her reflection in the mirror, then seeing Martin behind her, London asks, "What are you doing?"

"I'm changing the memory card for my camera. You see this?" Martin asks, as he holds up a little black piece of plastic. London looks at the card through the reflection in her mirror, and Martin says, "This has hundreds of big, big pictures of you girls."

"I don't care, Martin," London says flatly, then she gives her eyes a much more Cleopatra look.

"Sure you do, I said the pictures were of you."

"I don't care."

That card contains pictures that are worth a substantial amount of money. Martin can sell the pictures, put out a coffee table book, then string together enough real photography gigs to never have to work on the street again, unless the shoot called for it. Martin looks at London like she's a stubborn little girl, then he begins to rant, "I know-"

"-why did you do this for us, Martin?" London asks. She's so close to her dream now, and there's only one person who can stop her transformation from happening. There's still a chance- a small chance- that Martin isn't who he says he is. This is the last time London can confront him about it, before everything jolts into unstoppable motion. She knows she shouldn't think this way, and she has no evidence of Martin's betrayal, but she's been trained to never trust something that's too good to be true. London doesn't want to find out, again, that she's too stupid to realize why she's stupid. Everyone has an agenda. She still isn't sure why Martin Turner's 3,000 word exposé hasn't popped up in *The New York Times Magazine* yet. People don't rescue London Francis, unless they want something from her. Everyone walks by when she's hurting and needs help because they figure that she's rich, she can pay someone to fix everything.

This doesn't just happen with London, either. They never take away Kristen's keys because, "It's her dumb fault for not calling a car." They don't force Chloe to eat because, "Remember what happened when Chloe *did* eat? Yikes." They'll never tell Dakota's dad to, "Shut the fuck up and stop ruining your daughter's life!" because, in a way, maybe they think she deserves the torture. No one ever stopped to care, then London met Martin. He's helped the girls so much, and he hasn't ask for anything in return. They *always* ask for something.

Martin begins his final test before he can walk on stage to celebrate his long lusted for success. He pauses for a moment to clear his throat, then he says, "I told you why I did this, I was tired of reading negative article, after negative article about you."

"Then just don't read the magazines. Don't read the blogs. They're easy to avoid," London says.

Martin's legs move apart and his back arches against the unforgiving metal of the chair he's sitting in, "It didn't seem fair that those things were being said."

"Lots of things in life aren't fair," London responds, copping a bitch stare that Sienna used to give her when she tried to make counterpoints in an argument. "And sometimes shit that isn't fair causes people to lose a hand, or lose their house, or lose a mother," London says, as these sharp stolen words finally gain meaning.

Martin sets his camera down on the table and begins to take London seriously. He tells her, "Well, I didn't think I could help any of those people. I felt like I could help you."

"Why give us your music without even signing a contract for residuals?"

"Because lawyers will ruin it. Because lawyers ruin everything. Because I like you girls."

"Why us?" London asks, becoming redundant.

"Because you're four-"

"-we aren't victims," London says, putting words in Martin's mouth.

"I'll tell you why!" Martin yells at London. He had to respond aggressively so that London would listen.

Quietly, he explains, "I have four sisters- Julie, Mary, Cindy, Lori. That's oldest to youngest. And I'm after all that," Martin says, almost in a whisper, like he still isn't ready to admit this, but if he was going to, it was only going to be to London. It's time to let London know him, like he now knows her.

In a hushed tone, Martin explains himself, "My mom was old... older, when she had me. Sort of like Chloe's situation, but by the time I came around, my mother already had four daughters and all the problems that arrive along with them, so she was tired. My sisters took care of me a lot of the time. They would talk to me. Like... *really* talk to me. I was this little man sitting on the edge of his Raiders sheets, and they would tell me about the stuff they needed to figure out. They'd ask me for my opinion because..." Martin pauses, then says, "...I was the only male in the house that would sit there and actually listen to them. Maybe it wasn't the best thing, teenage girls taking advice from a seven year old boy, but they appreciated me."

Pressing the backs of his thumbs on his closed eyes, Martin goes back to his quiet tone, "I mean, I wouldn't even follow my own advice, but they always

asked for it. They told me everything. Every little thing. All of it was
fascinating. They always cared, and they were always kind... but you know
what they did that really changed my life though? They pooled their money
together and got me my first camera when I was eleven. From then on, the
football players came off the wall, and eventually my whole room was covered
in pictures of my sisters. That probably sounds strange, but if we kept the
pictures downstairs, I knew one of the girls would steal the album and destroy
all of my best work. They'd do that because they didn't listen to me when I
assured them they weren't ugly. They did however listen to my father... when
he confirmed all their worst fears. I'll never forgive him for that; they were
just girls, and you don't talk to young girls like that. You just don't. I wanted
to prove my father's words wrong so I'd take pictures of my sisters, then
they'd give me some of their money to get my film developed at the drugstore.
I'd wait around for the one hour it took to develop the pictures, and I'd read
all those magazines- *People, US Weekly*- every rag that my agency sells
pictures to now. After an hour, they'd hand me my envelope of developed film,
and I'd put the gossip magazine back on the shelf. The disposable snapshots
would be instantly forgotten, while I took home the pictures that mattered.
Every single picture, even if it was invaded by a thumb or washed out in an
orange light, it was like doubling my best memories, tripling my fondest
moments. Each time I went back to those pictures, I could relive that time
with my sisters, even if they weren't living in the house anymore. When my
sisters went back to the pictures, they'd pick out what they hated about each
photo. They'd show me their perceived imperfections... the 'flaws' were always
the same things my father would point out to them. These were invisible
defects, they were all imagined. Every part of the picture had its place.
Nothing was ugly. My sisters were beautiful. It's strange, I never really
remember looking at my mother and thinking she was pretty. Her makeup
was always clownish, and her hair was yellow instead of blonde, but my sisters
had cat eyes and strawberry blonde hair. I would sit up at night, with a little
flashlight, and I'd shine the circle at different pictures on my wall. Those little
moments looked perfect, especially if you had the back-story. My dad didn't
pay attention enough to get the back-story. He just looked at his daughters,
and he told them that they were too skinny, too fat, too tall, too short, their
nose was too bulbous, their nose was too piggish. All they ever heard was a
critique on things that they couldn't fix, and if they couldn't fix it at ten,
fourteen, eighteen- then, when they were thirty or forty, they still carried that
perception of imperfection. That's how my sisters live, to this day- unhappy
with things. They're still haunted, even though the bastard has been dead for
decades. It was just a bunch of words. One man's voice. I tried to reverse what
he did by taking even better pictures. I wanted to be such a good

photographer that no one could deny my sisters' beauty. When I got out of my father's house, I tried to express myself through music, feeling like a failed at photography. When I failed at music too, I got a cubicle job, but I guess I was haunted. One day, I threw away all my ties and refused to go back. I quit my job and I signed with XV3, agreeing to take pictures of celebrities. I'd take pictures from the bushes at weddings or from the entrance of a courthouse. I'd memorize when women would pick their kids up from school, and I'd wait for them so I could take their picture. I thought that they might see my photographs someday and they'd be amazed at how beautiful their wedding was. I imagined they'd be reminded of how hard it was to go to court for that DWI, and they'd see my picture in their head every time they got into a car after a long dinner. I thought they'd find joy in my pictures of them picking up their kid from school on a sunny day- a mother and daughter walking down the street, hand in hand. Maybe they'd frame my work, if I got it right. That's what I told myself so I didn't have to accept what was really happening with those pictures. Deep down, I knew that all my work would end up on the blogs or in magazines. Most of the time, there weren't nice things printed above the photos I took. Instead of having those pictures of beautiful people, living a beautiful life, framed on a desk, they were framed with a back-story, an incorrect, mean spirited back-story. It always made the person, and the photograph seem ugly. I knew the people in the picture would read the article, and I knew what those words would do. I mean, someone told me about a quote that River White gave where he agreed to become a fan of our music if the paparazzi stopped taking pictures of his kids. That has to be a sign. I don't want to stop taking pictures, I just want to take different pictures. My father is dead, but before I met you, I was continuing his shameful legacy. When I followed you girls, all I could think about was the fact that one voice ruined my four beautiful sisters, and you have a thousand voices saying awful things about you."

London stands up, then slowly walks over to Martin. She reaches down and holds onto his fat little fingers, as his watery eyes look up at her with that appreciation he talked about moments ago.

A man with a long beard walks in the room and tells London she has a blog interview she's late for. London lets go of Martin's hand, then picks up his camera. "Take one of me," she requests.

Martin accepts the camera, then London steps back while the proud producer frames her up. He waits as London's long body pops into position, then, *click*.

Martin lowers the camera and looks at the little screen.

"Well. How do I look?" London asks.

Martin admires *their* work, then says, "Like a rock star."

78.5- You Can't Scandal The Truth.

No one in social!heavy has ever said, "I really wish I had some privacy," and meant it, unless they were caught doing something wrong. Privacy is something these girls only desire when they're headed down: falling down drunk, fainting from missed meals, bending over to hoover a line, or dropping down to share a quiet moment with someone semi-special.

Martin could always tell if a picture would destroy someone's life for a week or two. That's why he never published the photos of Stanley and Lindy. He would've felt too guilty putting those pictures out into the world. It seems ridiculous to feel sorry for people who are blessed with so much, but it's the old superhero paradigm that they might be able to fly while everyone else walks, they might be able to pick up a town car while everyone else can barely even pick themselves out of bed, but with this exquisite existence, they're forced into an unorthodox lifestyle. Time and time again, these girls dip their fingertips into the radioactive cesspool that is Los Angeles- sometimes, this action will increase their power, other times it will prove to be toxic.

In the end, it's all about evening out the playing field. The average person will see a London Francis, a Chloe Warren, a Dakota Dabney, a Kristen Paxton- and they'll feel slighted.

London can get a new boy by merely entering the room, while *they* spend their lives staring at their crush from across the room.

Chloe lives in a house with the boy next door, while *they* had to move out of their apartment because a boy broke their trust.

Dakota is able drop the perfect off-the-cuff quote in the middle of a chaotic mob, while *they* can only think of the right words five hours later when they're about to fall asleep.

Kristen is able to drop her bad habits, at the drop of a hat, growing and progressing simultaneously, while *they* are sitting in a cubicle that they've inhabited for the past ten years, dreading going home to a person they've grown bored with.

social!heavy is a group of super-girls, who, during their teen years, found great power, yet chose to reject any responsibility. Given all of this, there was always one critique that everyone could resort to.

One insult was their kryptonite.

~London Francis~ ~Chloe Warren~ ~Dakota Dabney~ ~Kristen Paxton~

HAVE NO TALENT.

Tomorrow, those same four talentless girls will skillfully play a sold out concert.

OXYGEN WASTER
Doing Familiar Things, Different.

Oxygen Waster photographer, **Jimmy Pixx,** was on scene as **Kristen Paxton** was carried out of a restaurant tonight.

Normally, a picture of this disaster would be at the top of our post. Not for this update. Most of the time, it's easiest to just let the pictures tell the story, but this time, Pixx's story is far more valuable.

We aren't going to shorten this post and hide most of it after the jump. We're letting a block of text appear on the frontpage today because the text is good, and important, and it needs to be here.

Mere hours ago, Jimmy Pixx was lined up outside of celebrity chef **Milo Richards'** restaurant where Kristen Paxton, **Dakota Dabney**, **Jake Wesley**, and **Johnny Foster** were eating. He didn't get a picture of them going inside, but multiple diners coming out verified, without a doubt, the socialite posse was holding court at a table in the back of the restaurant.

Jimmy Pixx waited, while the crowd grew. There were rumors about the double daters sneaking out the back, but Jimmy still waited. He was captivated with a buzzing curiosity about these socialites on the brink of becoming legitimate.

Eventually, the restaurant door burst open, and all eyes were on an ugly exit. Just as many feared, and even more hoped, everyone was, in Jimmy's words, "visibly pretty fucked up." Dakota walked out first, yelling for the photographers and fans to get out of her way. Behind her, Kristen Paxton, the girl that was so proud and so vocal about her addiction recovery, was now hanging off Jake and Johnny's shoulders for support, and her purse was draped around her neck, like a massive alligator-print noose. While her feet occasionally graced the ground, she never successfully walked.

Making her way through the crowd, Dakota held out a hand, like her tiny, ruby tipped fingers could cover all of the embarrassment that was unfolding behind her. Cameras strobed and Jimmy's **Nikon** captured hundreds of photographs of the debacle.

Kristen was halfway to the car, in the middle of the mob of people, when she retched a guttural heave and everyone stepped back, then continued to photograph. Kristen retched again, and when her head jolted forward from the sickness, the violent movement caused her purse slip off her neck and fall to the ground, exploding her possessions out onto the sidewalk. The open purse threw up hundreds of tiny, shiny, pink slices of... something. The crowd scrambled to grab the glimmering items, desperate to know if Kristen Paxton was **Diego Mestizo**'s mule for some experimental new drug. Jimmy Pixx picked up one of the pieces of shiny contraband, then smiled. The pink paper was a gift from Kristen- to Jimmy, to the eBay autograph guys, to the gawkers, to the fans. It was a signed concert ticket to social!heavy's sold out show.

"Thank you all for your support. I'll see you tomorrow," Kristen said to the mob, completely serious and stone sober. The crowd was confused, but they pushed each other over to get the remaining scattered tickets. This gift wasn't just a way to get into an exclusive concert- it was evidence of a story that could be told the next day to family members or co-workers. The ticket could be sold on the internet for a small fortune. The ticket could be placed in a purse, as a reminder that people can and do change, and unlike we're lead to believe, that change isn't always for the worst. Sometimes, people will surprise you. Good surprises still *do* exist.

Kristen and Dakota got in their hired town car, then watched the mob collect the scattered tickets. As you can see from the pictures, they look like two of best friends in the world, having the time of their life, right before the biggest day of their life. That shot, the one you see below, of the girls peeking out of the car, their boyfriends beside them, *that* is the picture that we decided to run. *That* is the story here.

Tomorrow night, social!heavy will take the stage and our photographer will be there to capture it all, not because he'll be hiding out, like an unwanted pest, but because he was invited.

After the girls sped off, Jimmy Pixx had a chance to give up his ticket for $300 when a tired and sweaty **Paul Dabney** held out three bills and begged Jimmy, "Please sell me that ticket. I have to be there. It's my daughter's big night." Jimmy Pixx had seen Paul Dabney at work too many nights. He used to gleefully watch as Mr. Dabney set up, and set off, a million different highly bloggable disasters in a row... but then Dakota provided Jimmy with a nicer, kinder pleasure.

Looking Paul Dabney in the eyes, Jimmy said, "Yeah... tomorrow is your daughter's big night. And I will do everything in my power to make sure you aren't there."

celebUtard
"Paul Dabney: 'I Will Save Sienna Wolfe.'"

It's like Christmas Eve.

We all got into our jammies and we left out a Mojito and some **Plan B** for **Dakota Dabney**.

After we climbed into bed, visions of **social!heavy** began dancing in our head, and right when **Kristen Paxton** was supposed to shimmy over to us and plant a kiss on our cheek, our phone beeped with a text. When you're a celebrity blogger, you barely get to finish a lesbian wet dream before someone sends you some sort of dumb shit they think is important.

Dakota Dabney danced out of our heads and **Paul Dabney** forced his way in with a crowbar of stupid bullshit.

We were tricked into calling Paul Dabney because of his "bombshell details" that we honestly wished would just detonate in his head.

"**Sienna Wolfe** and I are a lot alike," Paul revealed to us, unprovoked.

Imagine being compared to Paul Dabney. *That* is rock bottom.

We broke up **Lindy Porter**'s marriage, and even then we weren't accused of being like Paul Dabney.

Paul Dabney is famous because of his deceased wife, **Lynn Dabney**, and his daughter, Dakota Dabney.

Sienna is sort of like him because she's famous, in part, because of her ex-best friend Dakota Dabney.

Poor Dakota. The dead-weight around her neck can't be easy to carry.

Neither can her guitar (Dakota. Can we carry your guitar tomorrow, like, can we be a roadie?).

Tomorrow night. Tomorrow night. Tomorrow night.

....

What were we talking about?

Oh well, it was probably *nothing.*

Actually, wait. Don't go yet. Do you hear that? Listen close...

Behind the asinine statements of an irrelevant man-child, we hear the sound of a nail being hammered into a coffin. Is it just us or do those silent screams coming from inside the pine box sound an awful lot like the regret soaked yelps of Sienna Wolfe?

Until next time, stay tardy, celebUverse.

79- The Single Casualty of a Self-Waged War.

Martin wakes up, gasping for air, damp with sweat. He looks around his small, dark bedroom with tired eyes, and he feels a thump in his chest.

It's 3:13 AM, but Martin doesn't want to go back to sleep because it will pull him away from his dream. After waiting decades to bring his songs to an excited audience, everything has fallen into place. He's sure that the experience feels better now than it would have back then. The years and years of failure allowed Martin to lead this project with an assured handling that only time and experience can provide. The artist ran from his art until the distance allowed him to be totally open about alternate avenues of distribution.

Unable sleep, Martin hoists himself out of bed and walks into the pitch black living room. He staggers forward, blind until his finger finds the light switch. With a quick flick, the messy apartment shows itself. Martin doesn't know if he should pack a bag and leave the girls with their music, or if he should force himself to get two more hours of sleep, then grab an early morning Green Mile and head off to the Staples Center to make sure everything is perfect.

Martin Turner's heart hammers against his rib cage like a concrete cracking earthquake.

A thudding drum beat forms in his chest.

No, not a drum beat. A knock.

Martin steps forward. Again. Again. His bare feet sink into a cheap carpet that's filthy with a thousand bootprints from five hundred nights of standing in the rain, waiting for a stranger to appear.

The front door continues to tremor with aggressive thuds.

It was not his heart that woke Martin tonight, it was the rhythmic knocking on his static door- a rhythm he doesn't recognize. It was a beat struck by someone who didn't study Martin's Bright Feathers.

This time, *Martin's* privacy is being invaded by a celebrity. He knows who's behind the door and he knows he should refuse her violent call for help, but he doesn't. Martin will always stop to help. He will always delete photographs and open doors for these girls, because no one else will. He remembers how much it meant to him that his sisters asked for his help with their problems, and as long as there are men saying ugly things to pretty girls, Martin will be there, as a mirror, to show these girls the beautiful truth.

A slide lock is pulled away.

A door is opened.

A victim pushes her way in.

"You," Sienna growls, slamming the door so she can't be thrown away, again. Martin hangs his head in shame, unable to look at this mangy Wolfe.

"You ruined my life," Sienna screams, moving toward the hostage of a host.

Before he can formulate an answer, Sienna grabs Martin by his chubby cheeks.

"Are you happy, you fat, disgusting man? Does this make you feel good? Does this make you feel significant?" Sienna hisses, her smeared mascara inches from Martin's sleep encrusted, bloodshot eyes.

"I didn't..." Mark tries to say, and Sienna lets go of his face, pauses for a moment, then slaps him.

Martin places his fingers over the hand print Sienna left behind, as his seemingly innocent actions are stripped of their camouflage.

Sienna waits for a retaliatory action.

She closes her eyes and begs for the connection of a man throwing away everything, like she did.

The punch never arrives and this drives the imperfect girl mad.

Sienna opens her eyes, and locates her next target.

A camera sits on the cluttered coffee table.

Martin tore away Sienna's base so she'll destroy his.

Sienna's imperfect thumbs grasp the most expensive item in this shabby apartment.

"Please," Martin gasps, as a silent agreement is broken- a food chain is snapped. "Please don't."

"I won't let you exploit anyone else," Sienna says, raising the camera, ready to introduce it to one of Martin's painted cinder block walls.

It's at this moment that Martin remembers what had set him on this path. This memory lowers him to his knees. "Sienna, please, don't."

"Why show restraint, when you... *you people* show none. You take all of my private moments, and not only do you document them, but you sell them. I can't go anywhere without you suffocating me. I! Can't! Breathe! With! You! Here!" Sienna spits out in gasps, her chest heaving between sobs.

Martin wants to tell Sienna that he's not the one who called those blogs, *she is*. He wants to remind Sienna that *she* was the one that quit the band. He wants to say whatever will get Sienna to put the camera down. He wants to, most of all, apologize.

"I'm sorry. I'm guilty," Martin admits, because he has to. Martin didn't "expose" Sienna, but he has sold pictures of her body. These weren't pictures she posed for. These were pictures that happened while a young girl was merely trying to get out of a car. These were pictures that stumbled into existence. How could Martin rationalize capitalizing on a split second of a split? He's strayed from what made him love photography, but the fact is, he still loves the act, just not the dirt. He needs his camera. These moments will slide though Martin's fingers like handfuls of sand if he's robbed of the evidence that the black box with the clear lens provides.

"I just want my friends back," Sienna whimpers, looking down at Martin while holding the camera above her head. The weight of a machine that has made and destroyed her, in equal measure, pushes down on Sienna yet again. It finally becomes too much and gravity brings the once mighty Wolfe to her knees.

She's now level with Martin.

A little fat man and a genetically blessed little girl both fold from the responsibility of their communal world.

Handing Martin the camera, Sienna says, in a tiny voice, "This is dumb, but that camera reminds me... I don't know why I'm telling you this... but when my mom was somewhere across the world shooting an ad campaign behind a camera like that, I'd make Anna, our nanny, take me to the giant billboard they had down on Fairfax. The billboard was of Mom, in a summer dress. My sister wouldn't go. She said it was dumb. She was right, like always. But. Okay. So I'd bring this box of stuff with me to the billboard, and, uh, I'd take the things out, one by one, and... I'd show the hundred foot version of my mother everything she was missing while she was on location. She was off living this amazing existence, and she left me behind. Some guy behind a camera stole years with her that should've been mine. Now you've taken my friends, and I don't want to be abandoned again, Martin. It didn't feel good being that alone. All of this does not feel good."

Without another word, the kneeling pair lean toward each other, and an essential embrace presses two very different hearts together.

No one knows who Sienna's father is, but tonight, he's Martin.

80- social!heavy Live.

Today.

Every decision London has made recently represented a careful turn to navigate her toward this very day.

New Wave took her boyfriend, Tobe Price.

New Wave took her close friend, Sienna Wolfe.

New Wave gave her a better friend, Martin Turner.

New Wave brought her closer to the people who are most important in her life.

There's so much riding on this one night in LA, and if it doesn't turn out perfect, all those positives may no longer so heavily outweigh the negatives.

London's long arms are shaking from the nervous idea of exposing herself to thousands of people. That fear of exposure was something that the girls had discussed with each other. They decided, as a comfort, during the sixth song on the set list tonight, the stage lights will go green and the girls will be wearing reflective contact lenses. It will be the moment everyone was waiting for, all four girls in the glow of night vision, writhing and sweating. The pervy boys will finally get the orgiastic night vision tape they've always wanted.

Tonight, cameras are allowed. Tonight, cell phones are allowed. Tonight, recording devices, and flash photography, and courtroom-style sketches are all allowed. They were never off limits before, so why place restrictions now? Stanley's right, let the secret vampires capture the good since, for so long, they've shown everyone the bad.

London knows that she has to center herself. She needs to affirm exactly what tonight will be. Walking into her room, she looks over her little animal kingdom. This will be her first audience of the day.

Beginning her speech with mommy-like discipline, London addresses her babies, "Marlon Brando, stop chewing on the bed skirt! Christopher Reeve stop running around, you're stressing out Heath Ledger!"

Heath Ledger, a Welsh corgi, curls into a ball, or at least attempts to, but his fat body and tiny legs make a less than perfect sphere. London bought the corgi because it was the exact opposite of her gawky frame.

"Okay guys, tonight is Mommy's big concert! We have all this great stuff planned, like, at one point, I'll start tickling Chloe, and she'll laugh into the mic. Guys get off from stuff like that, you know, Gregory Peck?"

Gregory Peck, London's cockatoo, doesn't say anything, although it does appear he's nodding in silent agreement.

"We're going to show them how hard we've been practicing. You know all that banging downstairs? That was Mommy working on her music. Well, the drum banging downstairs was... anyway, it may not sound like much, but with the rest of Mommy's band it's magic. Trust me, you have to hear and see us all together."

Gregory Peck looks tired so London covers his cage, then caps off her speech to her babies, "Tonight, everyone will see how hard Mommy worked, and they won't say mean things about her anymore. Of course, I don't expect an apology, I just expect..."

London pauses, unsure of what she wants the reaction to be tonight.

"I just want to make people feel good. About life. And about me," London tells her family.

Heath Ledger rights himself, then looks at London with the type of look James Dean used to give her, right before London traded James Dean for a piece of furniture.

To keep her mind off the day's pressure, London decides she'll walk down to Petsville, LA to see if they have a brother for Heath Ledger so he doesn't go all James Dean on her.

After carefully applying her makeup and taking about 30 selfies to make sure she looks her best, London leaves her house.

As she opens her front gate, she expects the flashes to hit her in a flurry, but she's surprised by the silence, by the calm, by the privacy. The paps aren't waiting. This is suspicious. Maybe they assumed she'd already be at the venue? Maybe they're in transit? Maybe they just wanted to give her some breathing room on this insanely important day? Martin must have called in a favor.

London makes her way down the street, and when she passes the big *Beethoven* dog's house, she blows him a kiss because she forgot to grab a treat. "Sorry, Bee! I'll bring you a CD of our concert next week," she calls out. The Beethoven dog calmly watches London until her stick-like frame disappears out of sight.

London walks into Petsville, LA and the bells hanging from the door clang to announce her entrance. Marky told her once that the bells are important because the noise wakes up the puppies and kitties so they look less dead for customers. London wasn't sure what to make of the statement at the time, so she just said, "Cuteee. Baby animalsss."

The first thing London notices in the pet store is the fact that there's a new girl behind the register. The girl is sporting a cockeyed, bitter look, but London is undeterred by this act of passive aggression as she merely assumes this is how acne covered girls in training bras respond when they see their idol.

Approaching the register, London snaps her long fingers down and rings the reception bell sitting next to the "Help This Super Sad Looking Guppy Get

Coral in His Tank" charity collection tray. As soon as the bell tinks, all the animals start going crazy.

The new girl, already standing in front of London, responds dryly, "Ah, yes. That is precisely what the moment needed."

"Hi," London says, waving at the teenage employee. The new girl smiles a tight lipped expression that certainly is not a smile. After a sigh, the girl responds, "Welcome to Petsville, LA. My name is Sarah, how may I help you?'

"Hi, Sarah-Beth-"

"-my name's not-"

"-I'm looking for a corgi," London interrupts.

Sarah looks at London with even more hatred, then says, "We don't serve beverages here, this is a pet store."

London laughs, "Oh, Sarah-Beth!"

"I told you-"

"-and I'm telling you. Corgis are puppies. I guess I'll go look for myself," London says, realizing she's getting nowhere with the new girl.

"Allow me to assist you in your pet selection, I can assure you that none of our puppies are from mills and all of them are very happy in their cramped living quarters. It goes without saying they would be even happier in your house and-or apartment after you purchase them," Sarah says, reading off of a crumpled piece of loose leaf in her hand.

London begins to walk back to the puppy cages, and Sarah follows behind her like a lost puppy.

"Aren't you supposed to, like, be doing a concert or something right now?" Sarah asks.

"Yup," London confirms.

"Why are you shopping for puppies instead of performing?"

"Chloe says that we have to be late."

"Chloe Warren?" Sarah asks.

"Is there another?" London responds, looking back at the curious girl.

When they reach the nursery, Sarah stands between the puppies and London, then watches the socialite's overly makeuped eyes to see if London spots a corgi. London's face expresses pure joy as she looks at *each* of the dogs, so Sarah assumes that either all of the dogs are corgis, or London is just really into captured-against-their-will cute things. She sides with the latter.

"How exactly are you going to pull it off?" Sarah asks.

"The concert or pet ownership?" London asks.

"Let's start with the concert."

"We're going to be the craziest, most kick ass, out of control rock band ever," London promises.

"Aren't you afraid that it's going to be a disaster?"

"Aren't you afraid of that, Sarah-Beth?"

"No," Sarah says, then she steps away from the puppy pen, totally caught off balance because London might have just read her mind.

As soon as London Francis walked into Sarah's life, this boring day at work became a moment that could be recounted a thousand times. "The day I met stupid ass London Francis." Sarah knows that when she tells this story, people will listen to her, *finally*. Anytime social!heavy was on TV or randomly started playing on a friend's laptop, she could tell her friends, "I talked to London right before her first concert."

If the entire gig is a disaster, no one will want to hear about a chance encounter with a girl who leaks videos of herself giving blowjobs to most of the C-list. They wouldn't listen to a story like that from a girl whose job it is to shovel shit out of animal cages.

Sarah slowly confronts the reality that she's having a conversation with this insanely beautiful, insanely rich, insanely popular girl- all the while looking at puppies. The whole thing somehow melts Sarah's heart. She considers telling her friends that she goes by Sarah-Beth now, just so she could tack on, "It's what London Francis calls me."

"I think you're afraid," London says, and Sarah's eyes go wide. "If today is a disaster, you'll lose something amazing," London mentions, in a playful way that makes her words all the more sinister.

"Not really, it wouldn't affect me at all," Sarah tries to convince herself.

"You aren't afraid?" London asks, trying to get closer, but Sarah backs away.

"Well, I am, a little, but I'm mostly afraid of what this band will sound like," Sarah says.

"Afraid for your mind because we might blow it? Don't worry, I'll call my agent and he'll get you tickets, right in the back- so we don't get too close to your mind," London says in her baby talk voice.

"I don't want tickets from your agent. I'll get the tickets with my friends, if they want to go, which they probably don't, because they're smart like me."

London quickly asks Sarah-Beth, "So you've never rubbernecked when you've driven by a car crash?"

Sarah stands still, her hand on her cell phone, but she doesn't take it out of her pocket to snap a photo. As much as she'd like to take a picture and sell it to a blog with a fake story about London buying a cat to sacrifice on stage, all she really wants right now is to continue this conversation with a girl who walked out of a magazine and into her life.

London doesn't find what she's looking for so she decides to go. "Tell Marky if he gets a corgi in, I'll buy it," London says, beginning her exit.

The moment those extra-long legs move past the chameleon tank, Sarah calls out, "Hey, stop!"

London doesn't acknowledge this demand.

"Were you serious about giving me tickets to your show tonight?" Sarah yells across the store.

London rotates on her heels, and Sarah asks her, "Could I have four tickets? I want to take my friends. They love you."

"What about you?"

"The four number includes me."

"No. What I'm asking is... do you love me?" London asks, her baby talk voice absent, her sleepy eyes now piercing.

"I... I'm not sure," Sarah says, crinkling her loose leaf script. Marky never taught her what to say if *this* happened.

London turns around and resumes her exit.

"I don't-" Sarah yells.

London pauses, dispensing a second chance.

"I don't hate you anymore..." Sarah-Beth tells her new friend, "...and I'm sorry if I hurt you when I did."

ACKNOWLEDGEMENTS

God- Thank you for providing me with the talent to write this book. Without you none of this would have been possible.

Mom & Dad - Thank you for supporting all my novels and providing me with such a good upbringing I had to flee to fiction to find drama.

My Editor - My genius only pales in comparison to your son's. Thank you for telling me what should stay in, removing what didn't belong, and not giving me a hard time about the "ew" moments.

Amanda - Thank you for letting me crash at Ora Manor so frequently while I was writing this book. You know I'll always be there for you (sometimes even with the bail money).

Bret Easton Ellis – Thank you for putting a name to the style of fiction I write, and for creating work that helped me shape that style.

I'd also like to thank: PH, SP, LL, MF, GW, KR, JF, NJ, NR, KS, DD, PSB, RG, BS, JVB, JM, ML, Bridge, Alexa, TheSuperficial, TMZ, PerezHilton and any other blog with a comments section full of grumpy douchebags.

BORING LEGAL SHIT

Before you sue me about something in this book, e-mail me. I'll fix any legal issues related to this novel. Don't sue me. I live in Newark. I'm broke. What are you gonna win from me in court? My *Gossip Girl* DVDs?

If you have print, ad, or editorial work in any of the major fashion magazines, my novels will always be free for you. E-mail me a link to your modeling work and I'll e-mail you a free digital copy of my novel. If you write those boring ass articles in between the editorials, you get nothing from me besides a small amount of resentment and some residual jealousy.

Feel free to post excerpts of this book on your blog, tumblr, twitter, facebook, or apartment walls. Please don't get any of this tattooed on your body. I once wanted a Thug Life tattoo. Imagine if I got my way.

If you downloaded this novel illegally... I honestly don't blame you. Paying zero dollars for a thing is way better than paying four dollars for a thing. I get it.

If you want to read more of my celebrity and fashion satire, visit: hbgwhem.tumblr.com or frejarizona.tumblr.com or tjamesreagan.com

If you're an agent and you want to represent my unpublished novels, email me at: tjamesreagan@gmail.com

ABOUT THE AUTHOR.

T/James Reagan currently lives in Newark, New Jersey.
He likes fashion models, and bad pop music, and blonde people, and sad people.
He has ten unpublished manuscripts available for query.

You're

Not

Worthless